ABOVE THE LOWER SKY

ABOVE THE LOWER SKY

TOM DEITZ

An AvoNova Book

William Morrow and Company, Inc.
New York

ABOVE THE LOWER SKY is an original publication of Avon Books. This work has never before appeared in book form. This work is a novel. Any similarity to actual persons or events is purely coincidental.

AVON BOOKS
A division of
The Hearst Corporation
1350 Avenue of the Americas
New York, New York 10019

Copyright © 1994 by Thomas F. Deitz
Published by arrangement with the author
Library of Congress Catalog Card Number: 94-17819
ISBN: 0-688-13716-4

Library of Congress Cataloging in Publication Data:

Deitz, Tom.
Above the lower sky / Tom Deitz.
p.   cm.
''An AvoNova Book.''
I. Title.
PS3554.E425A63   1994   94-17819
813'.54—dc20   CIP

First Morrow/AvoNova Printing: December 1994

AVONOVA TRADEMARK REG. U.S. PAT. OFF. AND IN OTHER COUNTRIES, MARCA REGISTRADA, HECHO EN U.S.A.

Printed in the U.S.A.

ARC   10 9 8 7 6 5 4 3 2 1

No contest!

This book is for Russell Cutts, who, one night over a six-pack of Corona, had the excellent good taste to say "Dolphin magicians."

Thanks a bunch, Russ!

Wado!

ACKNOWLEDGMENTS

thanks are due to

Russell Cutts
Beth Gwinn
Gilbert Head
Greg Keyes
Adele Leone
Reid Locklin
Paul Matthews
Buck Marchinton
Scott McMillan
Chris Miller
Joel Respess
B. J. Steinhaus
Mike Waits

Part One

Chapter I:
A Dark and Stormy Night
(Clononey Castle, County Offaly—United Eire)
(Wednesday, August 31—near midnight)

" 'You're wrong!' Andrew snapped. Whereupon he turned sharp left in the middle of the meadow—and disappeared."

'Yuummbu're wruummbng,' Andrew snapped. Whereupuummbn he turned sharp left in the middle uummbf the meaduummbw—and disappeared.'

"Bullshit," Kevin Mauney groaned in tired-eyed turn—and flung himself back in his chrome-and-black-leather office chair, green eyes fixed accusingly on the computer screen, where the garbled parody of what he'd just enunciated in perfect Georgia-accented American English taunted him, oblivious to the fact that a small fortune in electronic demons had served up anything other than what he'd requested. And it wasn't like he'd asked the MacAm to attempt anything complicated either; no more than transcribe what he told it, while editing out extraneous noise.

Which, for the eighth time in three days, it had blatantly failed to do.

So maybe the wee folk really *were* jealous little

3

isolationists and were jinxing it for spite, as Cameron McMillan, his solicitor, had half-seriously warned while shepherding the unruly tidbit of illegal tech through customs a year gone by. Eirish nationals weren't supposed to have access to even the temptation of Ameritech, after all, duty-free or not. That McMillan had managed to maneuver a dozen Apple MacAmericas through the morass of protectionist legislation anyway was due as much to the economic clout of a thriving community of expatriate American novelists (all of whom swore faithfully not to resell their grey-market toys) as to McMillan's finesse at navigating the labyrinths of import law.

Trouble was, somewhere between Lilburn, Georgia, where Smallfoot, Inc., stamped out the software, and here in the heart of UniEire, something had gone haywire with the junk-noise filter, so that while the antique Steeleye Span CD that had been soothing Kevin's muse was ignored just fine, all the 'Os' in his dictation got confounded with the thunder that was bellowing and booming west of the keep like a whole battalion of fairy drummers on the march. Which resulted in gibberish.

" *'Buhl-shee-ut!'* " the screen displayed helpfully—half a minute late.

Kevin growled at it, felt for the bottle of Guinness on the flagstones at his feet, missed it, and shifted his gaze from the cursed CRT to the slit of darkness a meter to the right, which also happened to be the lone south window in the top level of the tiny sixteenth-century towerhouse-cum-keep in which he was besieged. The thunder promptly roared louder. Lightning struck across the road, bleaching the world bone white. Kevin steeled himself for the ensuing concussion.

It obliged.

It also blew out the phone.

And upset the Guinness.

And *that* did it! Sighing, he told the MacAm "Off," mopped at the mess on the floor with a stray sock, and rose, to flop against the white-plastered wall— which felt reassuringly solid and gremlin-proof. Granted, Clononey wasn't much of a castle, as castles went; but it had been a steal when he'd used the windfall from the movie rights to his second novel to flee the States on his thirtieth birthday three years back. On the other hand, his needs were simple, and if his great hall was only five-by-six meters, and the whole pile held no more floor space across four levels than an American ranch house did on one—well, that was as much castle as he plus old Mrs. Shaughnassy *could* maintain solo. Though if the computer glitches kept up, he might take to leaving cream for the brownies just to hedge his bets.

This might be the first fourth of the twenty-first century, after all, but (love for his adopted land notwithstanding) change progressed faster in some quarters than others, and UniEire was definitely in the latter camp.

Abruptly, the lights flickered, then returned—at half fizz, courtesy of batteries that had apparently not been charging as they ought. Somewhere in the murky chaos, the CD player whirred, clicked, and served up "Cold, Haily, Windy Night."

Which *had* to be an omen—though of what, Kevin had no idea. Bad weather had come to be a given lately, and the fact that the stuff presently clobbering Clononey was the leading edge of a genuine US-style hurricane made little difference in the real world. The place had held up for five hundred years; it could certainly manage the additional sixty Kevin figured he'd be hanging around.

More lightning.

"Go away," he muttered to the embattled sky. "Just go the fuck away!"

Yeah, sure. Like his words actually contained anything like the power his editors claimed hid in his fantasy fiction. Folks *believed* in magic when they read *The Unmarked Road* and *Road of Light*, so reviewers on six continents agreed, and seven-figure sales plus a bag of fan mail a month bore out. He wished *he* believed in it now—at least enough to turn aside this storm and get him back to work on novel number three.

"Go away!" he repeated, louder.

The power promptly slipped again. The pulse of the storm picked up alarmingly. Lightning flared brighter—and more frequently yet. Thunder ceased grumbling and commenced to shout. The hesitant patter of rain against glass turned insistent. And with it came sharper smacks that could only signal hail.

Scowling, Kevin grabbed a Driza-Bone from the brass rack by the foot of the turnpike stair, dragged it on, and trudged barefoot toward the roof. Rain, he could cope with, but the vaunted Hopi solar cells up top that kept his toys humming, his batteries charged even on cloudy days and by moonlight (so he'd believed), and his power bills within reason *weren't* designed to deal with hail. He'd have to cover 'em pronto—if it wasn't too late already. Otherwise—well, he wondered if replacements would reflect the going rate in UniEire, the US, or Hopitu-shinumu. Hopis (the Indians) were funny about such things—witness the sliding scale of cost, third-world-versus-first—and could afford very good lawyers.

He completed exactly one circuit of the tight spiral staircase in the southeast tower before the rain hit him—from a door he'd left cracked and shouldn't have. But even forewarned, Kevin wasn't prepared for the force of the gale when he stepped out of the turret; nor for the fact that hail might strike him hard enough to actually slice his face—which it did, leaving a sting across an angular cheekbone and a stain of blood on the thin fingers he raised to probe it.

He was too late anyway. One cell—one two-meter-square sheet of an obscure gold-tinted plasti-alloy-ceramic—had already been spiderwebbed beyond repair. The other, protected in part by the battlements, but mostly by the angle of the rain, was still intact. Bending nearly horizontal (and wishing he weighed more than sixty-eight kilos), he dragged out the protection kit that had accompanied the cells. A flick of studs opened it, to reveal a red aerosol can. He nudged the nozzle toward the surviving panel and pressed. A thick foam fanned out, mixing instantly with the rain to form a rubbery film across the fragile cells. He sprayed until the good one was covered, then gave the damaged twin a go for good measure. Sunshine—should it ever return—would burn the stuff back into a powder which could be vacuumed up and reused. And get the Hopis (the cells) fired up again in the bargain.

Meanwhile, Kevin resigned himself to candles, of which, per his housekeeper's advice, he had stock-piled a slew.

He had just turned to go back inside when a par-ticularly vicious gust slung him toward the southern parapet. He staggered, slipped, rolled (through pud-dling water), and lodged against the wall, where he caught his breath. Then, cautiously and rather shaken, he dragged himself to his feet. The maneu-ver gave him a view through an embrasure, to where a good chunk of County Offaly lay dark and nervous beneath clouds that would have done Doré proud. Lightning to the west looked like fireworks, which meant that the tenth-century round tower at Clonmacnoise was taking another buffeting—and probably damage.

Which wasn't his problem. Conversely, if the makeshift garage in the forecourt came down on the Beast, *that* would not be good—not with the RX-9 still in the shop. It was when he craned his neck to check that he saw the traveler.

The strip of highway that skirted Clononey was little used at best—since he'd been up top, exactly one set of headlights had slashed across the pavement. And since no one in his right mind would be out on a night like this *sans* vehicle, the lone figure hunching its way along the road a quarter klik away was bound to attract attention. What with the driving rain and the glowering dark, Kevin got no more than a suggestion of a shape—certainly not whether it was male or female. Only that it was wearing a long coat and moving uncertainly—though that last could be a function of the wind. Probably he should go down and invite whoever it was in—do unto others, shelter from the storm, and all that good stuff.

On the other hand . . .

No, he told himself. He'd do the right thing. He *was*, after all, half a Southerner.

A quick jog downstairs took him past the office. Unfortunately, the power slipped *another* notch one level lower, leaving him to grope for candles and matches in an alcove outside his bedroom. A glance out the window while he rustled up a light showed a car accelerating past Clononey at precisely the rate and trajectory to suggest it had rescued the traveler—nor was the poor wretch in sight. Fine! Someone *else* was playing Good Samaritan.

So what should he do now? The time-chip in his earstud told his brain it was two minutes past midnight; and since the power wouldn't revive beyond the minimal level the unreliable batteries provided until the sun returned, he had little choice but to flat out.

With that in mind, he set the candle on the heavy oak stand beside his tartan-draped bed, padded into the bath, and began to strip. Soggy green sweater joined sopping drawstringed black jeans. He was assessing the state of his scarlet skivvies when a particularly virulent bolt turned the world white, numbed his ears—and made him jump about three feet straight up. His eyes still hadn't rediscovered color when the first knock sounded.

He grimaced at his flame-lit reflection, half expecting the narrow, shock-haired face to shake its head and tell him it was his imagination.

Except there it was again. And since, to use one of the clichés he studiously avoided in his fiction, it wasn't a fit night out for man nor beast, he had no choice but to respond.

First, though, he stepped back into his jeans and, just for good measure, slipped a derringer that would have got him deported into his right front pocket. It bagged awkwardly, threatening to drag the garment off his skimpy hips. Still, one couldn't be too careful.

Another twist of stairs brought him past the guest level (a second round of knocks likewise sounded there), and another thrust him out in the vestibule that fronted the great hall. A massive pseudoak door to his left gave onto the storm—and whoever it had driven to his door.

More knocks. The portal shook. "Who is it?" he called cautiously.

Silence.

Then, faintly: "Kevin Mauney?"

That gave him a start. Few of the locals knew who lived in Clononey, and bloody few of *them* would be out on a night like this. Still . . . what was life without adventure? With that in mind (and pistol in pocketed hand), Kevin punched in the security code, and when it flashed green, pulled back the heavy panel.

He was not prepared for what he saw. For not only did he not know the gaping figure on his doorstep, he was not even certain if it was sentient, never mind its age or gender.

A tentative assessment said traumed-out teenage male, with option to reassign all three. All that was clear beyond a dark, duster-style coat, was a smooth, androgynously angled face, vacant brown eyes, and hair—lots and lots of hair. Soaking wet it was; moss green, and long enough to vanish into the collar of the coat slender hands clutched across its chest. He stared at the hair, then shrugged. Jewel tones had been the rage among the trendy set for more than a year, and it wasn't *that* far from an American point of view to either Limerick, Galway, or Dublin. Shoot, a finger-wide blaze of electric blue bisected Kevin's own natural carrot orange—and *he* wasn't even half strange.

"M-may I enter?" the figure stammered through chattering teeth, though it wasn't cold. It—he— looked utterly miserable.

"Uh—yeah—sure," Kevin replied automatically, as he stepped aside for the . . . lad to enter. For his part, the visitor made no move to progress beyond the vestibule, for which Kevin was grateful, as a pool around his feet was expanding by the second. It was while he stood gnawing his lip at the bepuddled flagstones that Kevin realized that the visitor was barefoot, his feet narrow, neat, and pale in the flickering candlelight.

"I am . . . sorry to trouble you," the youth murmured, as he unclenched his hands from his lapels and slowly eased his coat back. It looked exceedingly threadbare. His voice had a threadbare quality, too, as though he were unaccustomed to speaking. Kevin couldn't place his accent, though the lilt of Gaelic wove through it like silk in heavy linen.

Kevin was there to take the garment and hang it on a hook by the door. Beneath it, the visitor wore a plain black T-shirt and loose, drawstringed jeans, both of which were too big for what Kevin now saw was, saving the shoulders, a boy-slight frame.

He also noted that the moss green hair hung to the gathered waistband.

A car whooshed by out on the highway, its lights briefly setting the embattled outer ward into snaggletoothed relief. Thunder exploded again. The youth flinched—though Kevin had the odd suspicion it was more from the car than the storm.

"Are you okay?" Kevin blurted out, as the lad eased toward the inner door.

"I will be—when I conclude my mission."

"Mission?" Kevin echoed, startled, uncertain what to make of this unlikely guest. Scowling, he snapped the bolt and followed the youth into his great hall. Fortunately, there was enough juice left in the batteries to keep the security light there going, which he quickly augmented with candles as the lad made his way toward the fireplace. He was shaking, Kevin realized, and now that he was aware of it, there really was a chill in the room, summer notwithstanding. A button by the mantel drained the batteries enough to set the gas grate there alight, and the room brightened as flame leapt up among real logs. The visitor said nothing—seemed as traumed-out as ever—but his expression softened as he turned his back to the blaze.

Kevin faced him across the plain trestle table that dominated the center of the room. "I, uh, don't mean to be snotty about this," he began, "and . . . well, you obviously know me—but . . . who exactly are *you*?"

The youth blinked at him and plucked nervously at his sodden pants. "Would it trouble you if I removed these?"

Kevin blinked back, vacillating between paranoid American and Irish lord-of-the-hall, with instinctive Southern hospitality tossed in. Oh well, he had the gun, and the guest didn't look like the aggressive type; he'd play it cool for the next little while, then determine a course of action. Probably this was no more than an overardent fan; he'd had them before. "Bath's in the corner," he concluded. "And . . . are you hungry? Can I get you something to eat or drink?"

More blinks, then. "Yes . . . I suppose I am hungry."

"Get out of those clothes," Kevin sighed, pointing toward the southwest tower. "I'll see what I can rustle up—it'll be cold, though. Power's off."

Not waiting for a reply, Kevin zipped to the adjoining kitchen, where the fish chowder Mrs. Shaughnassy had contrived for supper was still faintly warm on the stove. He ladled out a bowlful, grabbed a handful of cut raw vegetables as a side, and added a slab of bread. Given the power situation, he forewent the 'fridge, but retrieved two bottles of Guinness and one of white wine from the pantry, all of which he crammed on a wooden tray.

A moment later, he set the make-do meal on the table, claimed the bench across the boards from the fireplace—and tried neither to watch nor offer commentary about propriety and ignored directions as his now-shirtless visitor fumbled with the drawstring that secured his pants and let them slide squishily to the floor. At which point Kevin noted several things simultaneously.

First, the fellow wore no underwear. Secondly, had there been any doubt before, he was definitely male. He was also shorter than Kevin had thought: no more than one-seventy sims, and slightly, if gracefully, built. He had good shoulders, though, well-defined chest muscles, and a flat belly, which combined into what Kevin tended to think of as a swimmer's body. And it was a good thing he had lots of hair on his head, because, saving a green splatter at his groin, he had none anywhere else.

But the item that caught Kevin's attention most forcefully, as the youth stood steaming before the fire, was the utterly unselfconscious way he wore his body. Kevin was no prude—he'd been to his share of nude beaches, both in UniEire, Europe, and the States; never mind public pools and locker rooms. But something about this fellow's attitude hinted that nudity was a common state for him. Nor did he seem inclined either to dry off or cover his—well, shortcomings was certainly *not* the word. Instead, he simply turned to face the fire, thereby releasing yet more (and surprisingly fishy-smelling) steam into the room; then, when he was evidently warm (but not quite dry), sat, clutched the bowl of soup in both hands, and drank.

Kevin popped a bottle of Guinness and slid it toward him, but the youth shook his head. "Water," he grunted. Kevin shrugged, swigged from the bottle himself, and returned to the kitchen, where he filled a large earthenware mug.

The lad was peering wistfully at the empty bowl when he returned. The vegetables had not been touched; the bread but nibbled on.

"More?" Kevin inquired patiently.

The youth nodded.

Kevin fetched it.

The visitor drank it more slowly. This time he sopped the bowl with the bread.

"Glad you like my cooking—my cook's cooking, that is," Kevin ventured at last. "But . . . well, I hate to be a shit about this—but I'd *really* like to at least know who you are, and . . . uh, what you want with me."

"Fir," the youth said.

"Fir?"

"You can call me Fir."

Kevin masked a frown with another swig of Guinness. "That only means *man*. It's Gaelic."

"It is as much as I need."

Silence. Then: "So . . . where're you from?"

Fir looked up, scowled, then drank deeply from the water mug. "Most recently? Shannon. Before that . . . I . . . suppose you could say . . . Leenane."

Kevin's frown deepened. "That's a fair way to come—though I don't suppose you walked *all* the way."

"I did not."

Silence, while Fir ate bread and drank water. His hair was drying and looked like emerald silk. His bare shoulders gleamed ruddy gold in the firelight, the skin smooth as a child's. Kevin had to remind himself that while he wasn't averse to varying his sexual diet with the odd fellow, this one was a mite

too odd, good looks and sensual litheness notwithstanding. Finally he folded his arms, squared his
shoulders (having checked once again on the derringer), and said, "So what *do* you want?"

Fir did not look up. "I have a message for you."

Kevin gnawed his lip, trying very hard to be polite,
but feeling his determination fading. "So would you,
uh, perhaps like to *deliver* it, then?"

Fir shook his head. "I can only repeat it at Leenane."

"Leenane . . . ?"

A nod.

"You know that's a two-hour drive from here—in
good weather."

Another nod.

"This isn't good weather."

"The sooner we leave, the sooner we will both be
happy. The longer you wait, the worse it will be. But
I cannot force you. You are master of your life, not
I."

Kevin could control himself no longer. "Are you
implying that I ought to head out in the middle of
the night in a friggin' hurricane to lug a total stranger
to a podunk town somewhere past the back of beyond so he can deliver a message? Never mind that
I'm presently down to one car—which I don't drive
in the rain in the *daytime!*"

"You don't trust me."

"Would you?"

"I . . . " Fir's brow wrinkled perplexedly. "I do not
know. I am not in the habit of considering such
things."

More silence as Kevin sipped, Fir nibbled bread,
and the room filled with unresolved tension.

"I can give you a bed for the night," Kevin conceded finally. "We can talk about it tomorrow."

Fir finished the water, then pushed back from the table, wincing as he did. "Perhaps I . . . *should* rest."

Kevin reached to retrieve the nearest candle. "Guest room's one floor up. If you want to hang your clothes by the fire, they'll probably be dry by tomorrow. Sorry, but battery power means no dryer."

Fir did not reply; simply rose from where he'd been sitting. Kevin was already halfway to the door when he heard the noise: a soft thump, followed by a louder one, then a low groan.

When he spun around, it was to see Fir sprawled facedown on the floor. The lad's long hair had slithered sideways across his shoulders, for the first time revealing the small of his back. But instead of smooth firm skin, a sticky crimson darkness gaped there. It took Kevin a full ten seconds of dumb-faced gawking to realize what it was. "My God," he whispered to the suddenly ominous gloom. "You've been shot!"

God's answer, if any, was masked by thunder.

Chapter II:
Night of the Raven Moon

(Sinsynsen, Aztlan Free Zone—Mexico)
(Thursday, September 1—just past midnight)

. . . Dum-dum-*dum*-dum—*Dum*-dum-*dum*-dum . . .
. . . Wamblee gleshka! Wamblee gleshka! . . .
. . . Dum-dum-*dum*-dum—*Dum*-dum-*dum*-dum . . .

Thunderbird Devlin O'Connor was near to achieving nirvana—which, though a condition traditionally identified with those *other* Indians, was the best term he could conjure for that perfect mindless synthesis of sound, sensation, and soul he was presently experiencing. His dancing, which had already been going well that evening, courtesy of a particularly appreciative audience (of which a good third were a visiting *toli* team from Georgia, Paolo Marquez, who owned the 'Wheel, had informed him), had transcended good some time back and was now, as his set wound down, bordering on ecstatic. He did not have to think at all, had no need to work the crowd and exaggerate more than style deemed proper. Did not have to kick higher than art demanded, swish his bustle more vigorously, or shake the deer-hoof ankle-rattles with greater force. He simply let the heavy drumbeats that pounded into his ears from

17

the air, and up into his feet through the hard-sanded floor, merge in his heart and take over. He did not know the song that accompanied them—Maza-Kute was improvising on the spot—but he recognized most of the words: *Wamblee gleshka*, for instance, meant spotted bird or golden eagle in Lakota. The rest—he'd memorized a fair chunk already, and would get the remainder tonight, except that he had to cut out right after his set if he was going to do anybody any good at the embassy *mañana*. The only thing that would have made it better was if the song had been in Cherokee.

. . . *Dum*-dum-*dum*-dum—*Dum*-dum-*dum*-dum . . .
. . . *Wamblee gleshka! Wamblee gleshka!* . . .
. . . *Dum*-dum-*dum*-dum—*Dum*-dum-*dum*-dum . . .

"Hoka!"
Silence.
'Bird froze: crouched but alert; eyes narrowed and predatory, feather-clad arms outstretched like wings balancing on air: the exact pose of a stooping eagle, whose essence he had sought to emulate.
Silence . . .
Then, like thunder rolling in over his native Smoky Mountains: a swelling storm of applause.
'Bird blinked as he gazed past the glare of footlights to where, ranked in six ascending adobe-paved arcs around three sides of the arena, sat the rustic tables and chairs where over a hundred delighted diners were clapping and cheering as energetically as he'd seen in the five months he'd been moonlighting as a traditional dancer here. His consciousness promptly shifted from soul-born reflex to showmanship. True, the sand was warm underfoot: Mother Earth, his oldest, most loyal ally, but beneath it lay

the concrete floor of the Medicine Wheel, one of many ethnic *divertos* along the Sinsynsen Strip, just south of Aztlan: the OAS's "New World Capital."

He bowed his appreciation, then retreated a pair of steps, raised his arms behind him in tribute to his prototype, and dipped his head in final acknowledgment. Two more graceful strides took him to the rear of the arena, where he extended the eagle-wing fan in his right hand in recognition of the five members of the Drum. The men—sturdy Lakota lads in braids, old-style jeans, and plaid shirts—stood as one, bowed solemnly, then sat again, instruments knee-high before them.

"Ladies and gentleman," the PA system boomed, "Thunderbird O'Connor, doing a traditional-style eagle dance. Music by the Maza-Kute Drum from Santee, Nebraska. Our final set for this evening will begin in fifteen minutes." And then the same in Spanish. *"Damas y caballeros . . . "*

'Bird had already tuned out the announcer as he eased around the woven-cane screen that framed the Drum and concealed the arena's exit. A twist through an archway put him in the men's dressing room, where a pair of local fancy dancers were making hasty adjustments to their elaborate outfits. He nodded a greeting, gave them a grin and a high sign, and continued on.

"Good crowd tonight? *Sí*?" one called, cupping his ear, as he pointed toward the arch, through which the applause was only now diminishing.

"Muy bueno!" 'Bird called back, then ducked into the two-meter-square cubical that—since he was a featured regular performer—was his personal space. Long fingers pattered on a keypad set into the wall-tall mirror that concealed his locker, and it clicked open. Only then did he realize that he was still danc-

ing, still bearing the beat of the new song in his head—shoot, he'd even tapped out the unlock code according to its cadence. God, but he hoped Marquez would see fit to use that Drum again!

He was *still* dancing as he shed his garb.

The bustle went first: the taillike semicircle of eagle feathers on his lower back; then the feathered sleeves; then the porcupine-and-deer-hair "roach" that crowned his head like a mohawk, representing raised hackles. His choker necklace and rattles followed, then the pucker-toed moccasins and buckskin leggings, and finally his loincloth, leaving him sweaty, bronze-skinned, and bare: a fine figure of a slim, hard-bodied Cherokee warrior of twenty-seven—masters degree and lucrative day job in the diplomatic corps notwithstanding.

As was common when he'd been immersed in dancing, he started when he glimpsed himself: his body smooth, clean-lined, and unadorned where the regalia had concealed it—and sporting spiritual body paint everywhere else, notably the eagle eyes he'd drawn around his own, the concentric circles on his chest, and the elaborate (though stenciled) tattoos that banded his neck and arms. He grinned at that: a timeless body beneath his clothes, presenting the face of the past to the modern world in a futuristic city on certain nights of the week. By day—well, in a city designed and built mostly by Mexicans and three-fourths populated by Latin Americans, many of whom had Indian blood, Cherokee coloring like his attracted little notice—even if his actual *features* were both sharpened and dulled by a solid taint of Irish ancestry, the latest but two generations back. Indeed, someone had once told him he looked like an Irishman with an Indian paint job. The description was not inapt.

The business at hand was to resurrect that person.

Fortunately, the Medicine Wheel, like all structures in Sinsynsen, was brand-new and had been conceived from the start as an upscale establishment. It had thus been built to the same strict guidelines as had governed the construction of Aztlan, whose official limits began five kliks to the north. Which meant it had large modern kitchens, enormous dressing rooms—and showers designed to accommodate a whole troupe of sweaty dancers *en masse*.

'Bird had the white-tiled space to himself, and chose the centermost of the five stalls along the nearer wall. He punched in his ID code on a prominent red panel chest-high beneath the head, and closed his eyes. Programming promptly took over, providing precisely the force, spread, and temperature he'd coded into it months earlier. It commenced cold and hard to wake him up, then shifted warmer, mixing in soap to dissolve the makeup. 'Bird always felt guilty about enjoying it—typically he hated tech. On the other hand, sometimes it felt good to have little electronic slaves do his bidding.

It did *not* feel good to still be savoring the pound of water against his back when the program ended. That was the downside of tech: because the solar powered desalinization plant also cracked seawater into hydrogen fuel, Aztlan had water restrictions: so much per cleansing per locale per day. He'd just maxed-out his, and couldn't dial up more for six hours, no matter where he was.

At least he'd had time to scrub away the makeup (the red-and-black swirls spiraling down the chromium drain were proof of that), and indeed was dancing again when he ducked into the drying alcove and let hot dry air caress him for a minute more. Once blown almost fluffy dry (saving his scap-ula-length hair, which always took longer), he snared a towel from the stash by the door and pad-ded back to his cubby.

He grinned when he turned the corner, for there on his counter sat a six-pack of Dos Equis. A folded paper place mat was stuffed into it. He opened it curiously. An unfamiliar hand had written, "Enjoyed the show. Thanks for making our trip more fun—hope this'll make *your* night more fun. The Na Hol-los."

'Bird scowled at that. *Na Hollos*? Oh, right! It was a Choctaw word meaning, roughly, "white thing." In this context it referred to the southeastern Indian stickball team that had been so enthusiastic about his dance. Which reminded him that the world championships began tomorrow, up in Aztlan Sta-dium. The Na Hollos were some kind of upstart, dark horse, underdog outfit comprised of white boys. He had tickets, too, for one of the later games. The opening ceremonies would be broadcast in the morning.

Which was one more reason to get changed, get home, and get his ass in bed!

Five minutes later his dance gear was stowed, his hair essentially dry, and he was prancing out the dressing room door. But where before he'd worn buckskin and feathers, now he sported baggy black cotton britches, purple calf-high foam-soled sneaks, and a sleeveless metallic brown Spandex skin-shirt that made him look bare-torsoed. A gold ring in his left ear, atypically, did *not* whisper the time, but a swirl of silver tattoo in the hollow of his right collar-bone *was* (under protest) his body phone—turned off for the nonce. His hair was unbound and long. A backpack preserved the Dos Equis and diverse other items, two of them bladed, and thus not quite legal.

He paused at the staff entrance to collect the receipt for his cut of tonight's take, which had already been credited electronically to his account. He wished, though, that he could find someone to *talk* to. It had been a *great* performance, and he wanted to share it. Unfortunately, Elena Murray, the stage manager, was giving the Drum a final briefing; and this late, on a weeknight, no one else was about. He considered ducking into the kitchen for a taco, but ditched the idea when a glance at his watch showed that it was now 12:30 A.M. Add an hour to get home, half that to decompress, and he'd be lucky to flat out before two-thirty or three. And he had to be back at work as Cultural Attaché to the Kituwah Embassy by nine.

He was just pushing through the outside door, when an oddly accented female voice hailed him— out of breath, as usual. "Slippin' off, eh? Is *that* any way to act after yer best performance ever? You oughta be out there kissin' *las señoras—señoritas*, rather."

'Bird spun around, his grin already half-grown, to see an ample but attractive black-haired woman of mixed Scots-Greek descent bouncing toward him, large arms outstretched for an embrace. To his chagrin, he blushed. Suddenly he *didn't* want to talk.

"Red Man get big head if stay," he grunted in his worst stage Indian speech, not moving. "Red Man gotta earn *real* pay in mornin'."

Elena halted before they collided and dropped her arms, but grinned back anyway. "After a show like that, I can *certainly* stake you to a taxi—AFZoRTA fare, anyway. Or if yer willin' to hang 'round another *hora*, I can give you a ride. It'll take that long anyway, if you walk."

'Bird tried to school his expression into sad neutrality for his reply. Elena was a neat lady and a good . . . boss, he supposed. But, at thirty-five, she was just enough older than he for her subtle amorous intentions to make him uneasy. Five years younger was another matter. Trouble was, she looked like his mother. "Thanks a bunch," he replied smoothly. "But I *need* to walk; it'll keep me from tightenin' up. 'Sides . . . I've gotta try to freeze that last song in my head 'fore I forget it. If I sing it a dozen times on the way, that oughta do."

Elena managed a crestfallen smile. "Yeah, well . . . take care, then. I never have liked that stretch of beach."

"I'll be fine," 'Bird assured her. "Great Drum, tonight—hope the fancy dancers are up to it. And . . . *buenas noches.*"

And with that, he blew her a kiss—and entered the Mexican night.

It was what 'Bird called a raven moon night: the wind soft as feathers and warm as blood, with the waxing moon focusing the black heavens like an enormous yellow eye, while low banks of clouds to east and west shimmered like the layered pinions of folded wings.

God, but he felt good!—as he sidestepped a clutch of late-night revelers along the flagstone walkway that led to the streetside ramp. The 'Wheel itself rose to the right: a square, low-walled structure of tan sandcrete and tabby, with, in alternating panels along the steeply pitched roof, the golden gleam of the Hopi solar cells that had realigned the world's energy cartels—and political structures—fifteen years back, financing, among other things, the Native Peoples Independence Movement, the success of which had given him his job.

'Bird scarcely slowed for the ramp that cut through beveled sandcrete walls to the crowded sidewalk beside Sinsynsen Strip. (The 'Wheel, like the southeastern temple complexes on which it was based—in spite of its Plains-style name—was situated atop a rectangular, head-high mound with sloping walls. That the originals would have been far higher and made of trodden earth did not matter. What mattered was that the 'Wheel—and others like it along the Strip—provided a vehicle by which he could expound the glories of an indigenous American culture that had, until the Native Autonomy Acts of ten years back, been on the brink of disappearing.)

But that was food for history classes and political science texts, not cultural anthropologists such as he. Besides, it smacked too much of work. No, what 'Bird wanted to do, as he found himself becalmed among a pack of probably Brazilian businessmen watching an electric Chevy whir past (only electrics, and hydrogen- or meth-fueled vehicles were allowed within a twenty-klik radius of Aztlan), was get that song fixed in his head before it evaporated.

The coast clear, 'Bird darted across the street, arriving between the northmost of Sinsynsen's *divertos*. The one on the left, the Moon Crow, was an Irish pub, whose frequent *céilís* he often frequented; the one to the right, called *La Roscade Quetzalcoatl*, an expensive Pseudo-Aztec eatery whose prime virtue was that it was the only source of an excellent local beer called, simply, *Buena Cerveza*. Beyond them rose the range of ritzy hotels that fronted the beaches proper.

A short jog to the left took him past the 'Crow,

across an AFZoRTA line, the highway up to Aztlan, and an extensive parking lot—and onto sand. The Gulf roared into his ears: a drowsing water monster a hundred meters to the right. An irregular skyline of darkness to the left was the not-so-virgin jungle of *El País Verde*—the Green Country—a five-klik scythe of greenbelt deliberately left undeveloped, mostly for aesthetics, but also to shield the citizens of Aztlan from the carnal delights inevitable on the fringe of any world-class city, built from scratch or not. No one lived there—officially—but 'Bird's lone buddy on the police force (a Canadian, since the Mounties had the law enforcement contract for the Zone) had told him more than one tale of midnight raids on squatters' huts and unlicensed dealers in exotic wildlife, of which *El País Verde* boasted plenty.

But if 'Bird was not pondering politics, neither was he considering sociology, city planning, law enforcement, or even exotic wildlife, as he bent his path closer to the shore and headed north. Rather, he was trying, very hard, to recall the words to that song. How had it gone? He hummed the beat; then, on impulse, bent over and unsealed his sneaks (footware was required on the streets of both Sinsynsen and Aztlan, which had always galled him), stuffed them into his backpack, and continued barefoot, his feet finding rhythms in his gait that echoed those of the song:

. . . *Dum*-dum-*dum*-dum—*dum*-dum-*dum*-dum . . .
. . . *Step*-step-*step*-step—*step*-step-*step*-step . . .
. . . *Dum*-dum-*dum*-dum—*dum*-dum-*dum*-dum . . .
. . . *Step*-step-*step*-step . . . *step*-step—avoid
stranded jellyfish at high-tide mark—*step*-step . . .

But he couldn't call back the words.

He was still pursuing them when movement farther up the beach caught his eye.

He walked this route frequently, and often around this time of night, because the stretch of sand was usually deserted this late, and he could therefore commune with the wider world in peace. Perhaps once a week would he encounter someone, typically an amorous couple—or trio—or foursome. Or else it was (mostly) young folks from the embassies seeking a more private skinny-dip than was viable in their compounds or at the big hotels that commanded Aztlan's picturesque northeast coast.

He did *not* worry about being mugged, first because guns were illegal in Aztlan save for police and security personnel, and second because *he* was young, strong, quick, and had wrestled in the sixty-five-kilo class back at Oconoluftee High.

This time, however, something seemed amiss.

He was midway between Sinsynsen and the manicured lawns of the park that fringed the beltway, and there was as little light pollution as one got this close to a city. Which would still have shown him almost nothing until he was practically atop whatever it was—except that tonight the moon, though not full, was bright. And since he had very good eyes anyway, it was not that difficult to determine that what most folks might presume to be a pile of driftwood or a fallen palm was in fact a figure: large enough to be male, and hunched over something with which it was vigorously involved.

The dark hump was still at least eighty meters distant, and was kneeling with its back to him, showing a plain cotton tunic-shirt of the sort the local underclass wore. 'Bird's first thought was that it was digging with a spade, possibly for sea turtle eggs—

though hatching season wasn't far off. But as he eased nearer, the odd flash in the right hand resolved into what seemed to be a blade flicking back and forth around a larger *something* that lay before it, as though someone were whittling away at a length of palm trunk.

But then he caught the sounds: a rhythmic grunt and heavy breathing, with, under it, a steady low-pitched moan that sent chills racing up his bare arms to lodge under the long hair at the top of his spine. He froze instinctively and, as quietly as he could, crept closer.

Another fifteen paces brought him a second set of chills—and a lump in his throat. That was no tree being hewn by that hulking figure: It was a man! A naked, white-haired, dark-skinned man! 'Bird could see the angle of a bent knee, the sweep of an out-thrust arm.

Someone was being assaulted!

Probably some fellow late-nighter waylaid by a desperate squatter.

"You there!" he yelled, surprise having preempted sense. And with that he had no choice but to launch himself headlong up the beach.

The hunched figure started, glanced around, staring straight into the moonlight, to give 'Bird a clear glimpse of a round Mexican face in which a dark mustache made a continuous line with sideburns and shoulder-length dark hair. He caught a flash of uneven teeth as the man snarled, made a final swipe with the knife, and leapt to his feet, a sweep of blood-stained fabric trailing from his other hand. 'Bird had but the briefest instant to wonder why someone would go to the trouble of killing a person for his clothes, then get blood all over them, before the assailant uttered another wordless snarl and flung the knife straight at him.

Reflex was all that saved 'Bird from disaster, hurling him to the ground as the blade swished through the same air his chest had occupied instants before. By the time he had scrambled back to his feet, his heart was thumping like a war drum, and his mouth was clogged with a sick-sour taste he had sampled but seldom before: abject primal fear. The assailant was nowhere in sight (the jungle fingered closer here than anywhere along the whole five-klik strand); nevertheless, 'Bird gave chase, and had dashed a dozen meters along the very plain trail that pitted the soft white sand when a piteous groan behind him braked him in his tracks. Logic immediately wrested him from impulse and informed him that, adept at such things as he might be, there was little likelihood he'd be able to follow the big man once he hit undergrowth, but that 'Bird would be an obvious target there; that he had a good description plus the—murder?—weapon anyway; and that Mounties were as competent as they came.

The victim needed help *now*.

Sparing one last distrustful glare at the ominous foliage, 'Bird jogged back to the assaultee. It was only when he knelt beside the sprawling form, however, that he grasped the full horror of what had transpired. For what he had assumed to be some fellow fresh-air-maven collared for his clothes and stripped, proved to be far worse than he could ever have imagined.

True, the man—if that's what it was, since the victim was lying on its face—*had* been stripped. But not merely of his clothes.

He had been skinned!

Alive!

'Bird's gorge rose, even as his gaze took in a white blaze of skull he had taken for an old man's hair, and ropes of red meat he had assumed were simply dark skin, fresh, perhaps, from a swim. Mostly he saw blood—lots and lots of blood: a dark, spreading stain upon the sand, its distinctive metallic stench fighting aside the pervasive ones of sand, seawater, and not-so-distant swamp. The man's body was awash with it too, and glistened stickily in the moonlight, the ruddiness marked only by paler stripes along fingers, feet, and at the base of the spine above the buttocks, where tendons had lain close beneath the skin.   Still, the fellow had groaned; there was, therefore, some chance he might still be alive. Steeling himself, 'Bird knelt beside him, noting that the man was not very large—perhaps even a teen or boy.

But just as he extended a shaky hand to turn him over, to better gauge the rise and fall of the too-visible ribs and check for breathing—or, possibly, get some kind of statement from him—the figure shuddered, vented a liquid gurgle, and lay still, muscles 'Bird had not realized were tense—with agony, or the expectation of death—relaxing at last.

'Bird was sick then: copiously, and for a very long time. But even as he emptied his gut, he noted the knife on the sand. When he had regained reasonable control, he staggered to it and picked it up with a bandanna from his pocket, careful to avoid touching the oddly shaped hilt, where fingerprints would most reasonably be expected.

And almost dropped it again.

Not because it still dripped blood, but because it was not made of metal at all, but of a dark vitreous material that could only be hand-flaked obsidian!

Which was what Aztec priests had used to flay their victims!

He returned to the body then, and made a slow circuit of the area, at which time he discovered the man's clothes in a wad opposite the side by which he had arrived.

It was only then, with a flayed dead man at his feet, murmuring water at his back, and a suddenly *very* dark jungle straight ahead, that he raised a finger to the hollow beneath his collarbone and tapped the tattooed silver swirl of his body phone. A buzz in his ear told him it was activated.

"Emergency 911," he gritted into the raven night. "I need to report a murder."

A pause, then, in his ear: "Please hold."

"Fuckin' great!" 'Bird spat—with no choice but to oblige.

While he did, music whispered in his head: a popular recent cover of an old folksong called "Twa Corbies"—Scots lyrics, Irish melody, but sung in Neo-Spanish. His anthropologist aspect awoke immediately—and presented him with another set of chills. Corbies—crows—were close kin to ravens, and this was a *raven* night, and his people both associated ravens with death (it was a war title, among other things) and feared a kind of witch called *Kalanu Ahyeliski*, the Raven Mocker, that liked to eat human hearts. Never mind that it was an Irish tune, and the Morrigu—the battle goddess of the Irish Celts—was ofttimes called the Crow of Battle, and sometimes, the Eater of the Slain. Or that the Aztecs, whom the Spanish had conquered all those years back, had worshiped a blood-starved god named Xipetotec: Lord of the Flayed Skins!

Skins they had removed with obsidian knives exactly like that in his hand!

Yeah, he might *be* on hold, but he was getting an earful of omens.

And, though he hated to admit it, Thunderbird Devlin O'Connor, Cultural Attaché to the Kituwah Embassy in Aztlan, believed, very strongly, in omens.

Chapter III:
Dawn of the Dead

(Aztlan, Aztlan Free Zone—Mexico)
(Thursday, September 1—before dawn)

"Damn you, Big Brother," Carolyn Mauney-Griffith groaned into the dark. *"God* damn you!"

She sat straight up from her futon and glared across the Eirish linen coverlet a despairing grandmother in Ennistymon had bequeathed her the previous spring, when she'd turned thirty with no sign of being wed.

"God *fucking* damn you!" she amended, to the sliding glass patio doors, beyond which the sky was barely pinkening. "Even a hemisphere away you won't let me rest!"

It just wasn't *fair*, damn it. She and Kevin weren't speaking. Shoot, for the last three years she'd tried to convince herself that she hated his guts. But if that were the case, why had she awakened in the very-wee hours worrying about him?

Why indeed?

He *should* be fine. He'd spent two-thirds of his life in the American South, after all, where hurricanes were as common as drunks in Dublin. And if Georgia, where he'd mostly grown up, didn't suffer the number or intensity of them Florida did, it still got

33

more than UniEire—until four years ago, at any rate. That was when whatever gods worked the world's weather (she suspected a consortium of Tlaloc, Thor, and Zeus, maybe with Shiva thrown in) had suddenly gone psycho and starting sending those little tropical depressions skipping back across the Atlantic to trouble the Old Country as often as the New. UniEire had been blessed with three class-five blows in the last four years, of which Buckley was only the most recent. Though if last night's forecast was reliable, it was going to shift south—which basically meant that Kev's part of the Emerald Isle would get high winds and driving rain, but not the full force of an actual hurricane. On the other hand, the Eirish still didn't have a handle on how to deal with such things. Not like Floridians.

Kevin, having done his BA in lit. at FSU, did. She therefore had no business fretting about his welfare, much less letting her subconscious get into the act. Waking up worried was one of the things she hated most.

Her ear-watch told her it was still well shy of dawn, and she wasn't due to get up until an hour past that. But she bloody well wasn't likely to get back to sleep now! Sighing, she abandoned the futon and padded down the hall. Her bare feet made no sound on the thick russet carpet; the air vent in the floor tickled her legs like gleeful sprites bent on flipping up the oversized Trinity College T-shirt that was her nightwear of choice. She batted it down reflexively and slumped into the living room–cum-kitchen. Coffee, she wondered, or tea? America, or Eire?

That was pretty much the crux of it, too: America, or Eire? Mom was Irish (an adult before unification, she preferred to retain the old spelling): born and bred in Cong, schooled (as was Carolyn, after she'd switched to marine biology) at Trinity. Dad was American.

Well, no, not really. *Kevin's* dad was from the States for real and sure. *Her* father . . . now *that* was a very good question. True, Floyd Mauney's name was on her birth certificate, but his background in genetics had generated doubt about who Carolyn's sire might be—*such* strong doubt, in fact, that he'd simply stared at Mom over breakfast one summer day three years back and asked her. Mom had calmly sipped her tea and told the truth. Carolyn was not his; her father was Eirish (Irish, rather), and no more would she say.

Dad had gently said "divorce." Kevin had taken his side. Carolyn had thrown in with Mom. And the Schism had yawned open.

Trouble was, she couldn't really blame Kev's dad for being suspicious. He, Kev, and Mom were all medium tall, while, at barely 1.6 meters, Carolyn was tiny. They were fair, she was dark. They had seriously red hair; hers (when not sun-bleached, as it was now) was mouse brown with auburn highlights. They freckled and burned; she tanned smoothly. They had noses, jaws, and chins sharp enough to cut bread; hers were sweetly blunt if not actually bland. Their eyes were bottle green; hers were brown as mud. Not much as single items, but enough combined to implicate the milkman (or, more likely, the graduate assistant).

But in spite of all that, Carolyn still loved Kev. Shoot, she *loved* her de facto dad—or had until he'd screwed up Mom. That was one reason she was here in Aztlan: to get as far away from all that as she could. And the irony, of course—one of many she could list—was that Kev, who had chosen Dad's side, was nevertheless living in Mom's native land!

Damn him!

But she was still fretting about him. So perhaps, in his honor, she should begin the day with tea.

She rummaged through the canisters on the counter until she found a fresh tin of Earl Grey. Putting the kettle on—she could have nuked it, but some things just weren't *proper*—she fished a matching black cup and saucer from the dishwasher and set them on the white faux marble bar that split the kitchen from the living room. That accomplished, she fed the toaster, told the TV "On" in hopes of getting an update on Buckley, and wandered back down the hall to heed nature's morning call.

And was reminded of Kevin yet again when she saw the latest issue of *Eireland of the Welcomes* still open atop the clothes hamper. She hadn't realized it when she'd bought the magazine, but it had included a lavishly illustrated article on the young (that was relative; thirty-three no longer rated that honor in her estimation) expatriate American novelist who lived in a restored castle in County Offaly and had written two fantasy novels, the most recent of which had stayed on the *New York Times* bestseller list for nineteen weeks and been optioned for the movies. The article went on to profile Kevin Alistair Mauney, focusing on his dual citizenship, his academician parents' odd transatlantic marriage, which had seen him and his sister brought up in separate households on two continents, and on his skeptical reverence toward his fantastic subject matter. A sidebar went on to observe that Kevin was only the latest of a long line of American fantasy authors who had availed themselves of the favorable tax status granted writers and artists resident in the Emerald Isle. At present, they paid no taxes in Eire at all and little in the USA. Though with the cost of unification still being borne, there was some doubt as to how long that practice would continue.

She had all Kev's books, too: the volume of college poetry that about fifteen people had bought, and the two novels that half the *world* had bought. In fact, she had every printing, of hardback, trade, book club, and paperback editions alike. She also had the British, Eirish, German, French, Swedish, Russian, Chinese, Finnish, Japanese, and Spanish versions.

Yep, if Kev ever *did* come calling (a few years after hell froze over, she supposed), she'd have no cause for guilt.

She wondered how he felt, though, there in his heart and center.

Probably barely awake at the moment, given the time differential.

A pause to run a brush through her cap of short brown/blond hair, and she returned to the kitchen to see how the kettle was coming (still shy of singing, but the toast was done). She had just flopped down on the sofa and told the TV to try CNN, since The Weather Channel was obsessing on Pretoria, when a ring sounded, simultaneous with which the TV boxed a familiar number at the bottom of the screen.

Christ, what could the Ninja Queen want now? "Phone. Answer. No pix: my end," she sighed with a scowl, and deliberately took a bite of toast. The tube promptly produced the round face of a serious-looking Oriental woman in her early forties. Her boss at the Pan-European Oceanic Research Center, Inc.—Cetacean Behavior Branch: Mary Hasegawa. Carolyn could tell by the way Hassie was twirling her pen through her fingers that something was badly amiss.

"Cary here," she yawned pointedly, through a mouthful of toast.

"You sound like you're eating. Were you already up?"

"As of five minutes ago."

"Well that's a relief, I was afraid I'd have to wake you."

"Something's wrong, isn't it?"

Hasegawa nodded grimly. The pen speeded up until she dropped it. "It's happened again," she said tersely.

"You're joking!"

Hasegawa shook her head. "I figured you'd want to come right on down—while the bodies are still fresh."

"Be there in thirty," Carolyn replied, already rising. "I'll call you back from the car."

"Don't. I've got about a million things to check between now and then."

"Oh, well, in that case, see you anon."

"Cary," Hasegawa added, as if an afterthought, "this one really does look bad."

The screen went blank.

Carolyn had to nuke her tea after all, and while it was heating, searched for something to wear.

Unfortunately, today was laundry day—which meant everything she'd normally have worn for an EVA was dirty. Which left the jeans and loose-weave tunic she'd worn yesterday. Shoot, they were even black, which was fitting, given that she was going to view the dead. She wished, though, she'd thought to ask how *many* bodies.

Chapter IV:
Broken Morning

(Clononey Castle, County Offaly, United Eire)
(Thursday, September 1—morning)

The first thing Kevin saw when he awoke was moist brown eyes. The second was moss green hair. There might have been a touch in there too— or words—something that had actually dragged him up from slumber. But now that he *was* conscious, it was bloody unlikely he'd conk out anytime soon.

Not with a naked crazy man looming beside his bed, looking anxious and impatient—and even younger than he had the night before.

"Unnnhhh," Kevin groaned, suppressing an urge to turn away from what little dawn light contrived to slip past the clouds that grimed his sanctum with a lifeless gloom totally out of sync with the gaudy hangings and framed cover paintings that normally brightened his bedroom. The antique Irish clock on the wall showed 9:31 A.M. The modern American alarm on the nightstand had been programmed for seven and hadn't gone off. He hadn't set the one in his ear.

Fir tapped his shoulder.

Abruptly, Kevin sat straight up and stared wide-eyed at his ambulatory wake-up call. "What the hell are *you* doin' here?" he gasped.

Fir blinked at him uncomprehendingly. "I am awake. You should be too."

To cover his confusion, Kevin yawned lavishly, knuckled his eyes, and peered past the sleekly lurking shape to where last night's fringe-of-hurricane showed no sign of abating. Or at least the clouds continued to glower, and scythes of rain still reaped summer from the air. Another yawn, and he let his gaze drift casually down Fir's bare flank, coming to rest on a certain spot just above his left iliac crest, which he'd had the devil's own time bandaging last night. The bandage was gone now, as was the shiny sheath of antiseptic Spraskin he'd applied beneath it. No more than a pink spot now marred Fir's smooth white flesh. A dreadful . . . *something* awoke in him at that. Not fear, but a subtle unease, as if he were racing headlong into a situation nothing in his life had prepared him to resolve, and all the worse because it came packaged so attractively.

Shuddering, he slid his legs over the side and slumped on the edge of the mattress, eyeing his guest uncertainly. "I *did* patch you up last night, didn't I?"

A vacant shrug. "I awoke with strips of fabric around me. I suppose you put them there."

"What *choice* did I have?" Kevin shot back, grogginess and incredulity combining to banish tact. "You had a hole in your back the size of a hurling ball where *something* bang-type came out; never mind the little guy above your hip where the sucker snuck in. I tried to call an ambulance but the friggin' phone was out, and the driveway looked like a bloody *moat*. You weren't bleeding, and the wound was clean. If you were gonna die, you'd have done it already. I—" He broke off in mid-sentence. "Turn around."

Fir did. Hardly daring to breathe, Kevin reached out and eased the long jade-toned hair away from the small of the youth's back. "Jesus," he hissed. For though a wound of sorts did disfigure Fir's pristine skin precisely where he recalled: where the big lower back muscle bulged beside the spine, with the smaller wound a dozen sims to the left, neither was anything like as large or lethal-looking as it had appeared by candlelight. The lesser was barely visible, the larger level with the surrounding skin and neatly scabbed over, with mere traces of pink to suggest fading inflammation.

"I heal fast," Fir supplied absently—surprising Kevin no end by actually volunteering something.

"Evidently!" Kevin managed, letting his hand fall back to the pieced-velvet quilt. "Uh . . . that *was* a bullet wound, wasn't it?"

Fir turned back around but did not reply. Kevin rose wearily and stumbled sky-clad to a pair of carved wooden doors set into the wall by the east window seat. Opening them, he unearthed a wad of purple briefs and a fresh pair of jeans, then paused and added a second of each. When he'd negated his nakedness with the first and tied the second around his waist, he thrust the rest on his bare-assed guest.

Fir accepted only the pants and donned them tentatively. They bagged on him, but little more than on Kevin. The legs were too long.

"Bullet wound," Kevin prompted.

Fir fumbled with the waist tie. "It was loud, it hurt."

Kevin rolled his eyes and prayed for restraint. "Mind tellin' me how you got it?"

Fir scowled at him. "*When* was right before I

reached here. *Where* was . . . near here. I was walking. Something slick and black came up beside me. A . . . man looked out. There was noise. I hurt. I fell. The black thing left. I got up. I came here."

"And didn't think to *mention* you'd just been shot?"

"It did not seem important. The message did. I will heal. The message will not."

"Messages *can't* heal, Fir!"

Fir did not reply.

Kevin snorted under his breath and selected a loose-knit green sweater from another shelf, before once more facing his guest. "Breakfast?" he suggested conversationally. "And then your spiel . . . okay?"

Fir remained silent, but followed dutifully as Kevin led the way down to the ground floor. It was raining when he checked the second-story window. It was raining harder when he poked his nose outdoors on the first. "I ain't goin' out in that for *nobody*," he informed the other flatly, as he steered him toward the great hall.

"It is important," Fir replied, as he claimed his old place between the fireplace and the table. The fire was still lit—Kevin had left it on LO when he'd put Fir to bed on the floor. He checked the lad's clothes, found the jeans and T-shirt dry (the latter as he recalled: blood-crusted and double-holed), and the long coat he'd retrieved from the vestibule similarly damaged and still a trifle damp. He killed the flame before the day got too warm, and padded barefoot to the kitchen.

"I can't use the stove or the nuker," he called. "I'm runnin' on half batteries 'til I can get the Hopis dried." Hearing no reply, he found day-old donuts, granola, soda bread, cartoned milk, and half a box of

Lucky Charms. Remembering Fir's preference of the previous meal, he filled a pitcher with water—and chose a warm Guinness for himself. Lord knew he'd probably need it.

"This'll have to do," he said, as he set the assembled food-plus-crockery on the table. " 'Course I *could* try to rustle up some bacon and eggs on the fire."

Fir regarded the food doubtfully. Nibbled a granola bar. "Is there more soup?"

"You mean the fish stuff we had last night? It's bound to be bad by now."

"Could I have some anyway?"

Kevin stared at him. "Man, you got a death wish or something? Food poisoning'll get you same as bullets will."

"I have to take you to Leenane."

"I have to take *you*, you mean," Kevin growled back. "And not in this weather; not until I find out which way Hurricane Buckley's goin'. Leenane's on the coast, lest you forget."

"I still have to take you—"

"Please don't say that again!" Kevin choked, as he trudged back to the kitchen. The chowder was where he'd left it: covered, but otherwise room-temp. He sniffed it. It smelled of fish—fish on the verge of turning. He wondered if he dared risk it. Fir, though about as strange as people came, didn't seem stupid; if he wanted the stuff, Kevin supposed he should grant his boon. On the other hand, if he *did* get sick . . . Well, today there'd be no choice but to whisk him to Ballinasloe . . .

His lips curved fiendishly. *Which would make him someone* else's *problem!*

And if he just happened to notify a certain chum in the garda, so much the better. Maybe *they* could get something rational out of the kid. Shoot, they could drag out the old sodium pentothal and arrive at the truth that way. Asking politely, it seemed, did no good.

"So," Kevin began with strained civility, two minutes later, as he slid a dubious-smelling tureen before his guest, "what's so special about this message that I have to get it in Leenane?"

"It would be useless except at Leenane," Fir mumbled between gulps of greasy broth. A healthy swig of water punctuated his first bowlful. A second filling followed.

Kevin puffed his cheeks and tried very hard not to pace. It did look marginally lighter outside. And if he only went as far as Ballinasloe, perhaps he could drop Fir off at the cops without stressing out utterly. Yeah, he'd try that. If food poisoning didn't work, that'd be Plan B.

"Okay," he said at last. "You win. I've seen hurricanes before, back in the US, but I've never actually *observed* one since I became a writer. And since the best way to write about something authentically is actually to experience it, and since hurricanes are always worse on the coast, in the interest of book research, I'll take you to Leenane. But you'd better have a damned good tale when we get there."

"It was good soup," Fir observed brightly. "But could I have a little more water?"

"We leave when you finish that," Kevin sighed, whereupon he scooped up the pitcher and returned to the kitchen. Sometime in the next five minutes he managed to wolf down two granola bars and half a donut. He drank cold instant coffee because he was too impatient to crank up the fireplace again. Hopefully he could find something open in town. Most folks, after all, did not rely on

Hopi solar cells for all their power. So much for self-sufficiency.

Leaving the dishes for Mrs. Shaughnassy, should she prove fool enough to brave the storm, Kevin returned to the great hall. Fir was naked again, but only because he was changing into the garb he'd worn when he first arrived—minus the damaged T-shirt. "No shoes?" Kevin wondered aloud.

"Do not like them."

Kevin could only grimace and roll his eyes once more. "I'll just be a sec," he called, and darted up the stairs. Back in his room he swapped his jeans for a pair of charcoal cords complete with zipper and belt, and chose a black T-shirt to augment the sweater he retained, with another for Fir. Scarlet socks and calf-high waterproof boots completed the ensemble, save for the obligatory wallet and keys. The derringer went back in his pocket—and would disappear beneath the seat as soon as they were under way, to emerge only if Fir proved completely intractable.

Maybe. Kevin had never actually shot at anything besides targets.

Fir had donned his duster over bare skin when Kevin returned—so much for the loaner T-shirt. He had also tied his hair into a tail, which was tucked inside. Which was curious. Most kids who dyed their hair *wanted* it to be seen. Just one more mystery to add to the mass knotting in his brain, Kevin supposed. Except that this one might begin to unravel in less than a quarter hour, should he make it to Ballinasloe with Fir none the wiser.

"Ready?" Kevin called, jingling his keys—only then realizing that Fir might not know what they were. Most cars he looked old enough to have ridden in cranked with plastic cards.

"Yes, please," Fir replied politely. The soup bowl, Kevin observed, as he shrugged into his Driza-Bone, was completely clean. Fir looked content and almost happy.

"This much humidity, it may take a minute for the car to crank—so wait 'til I honk, okay? Just pull the door to behind you. It'll lock automatically."

Fir nodded gravely, and Kevin set his mouth, squared his shoulders, opened the outside door—and dived into the storm.

Actually, it was only drizzling just then, and he managed the twenty meters to the garage with no more discomfort than one slip. And confronted the Beast.

It was a triple black 1976 Mercury Grand Marquis sedan, with every option in the book, not to omit the voracious 460 V-8 that drank very-hi-test in two-klik-per-liter gulps. The car had been fifteen years old when Kevin was born, but had amassed only twelve thousand miles when the elderly aunt who'd bought it new had died, conveniently enough, on his sixteenth birthday. It hadn't been quite his ideal of trendy transportation, but free wheels was free wheels, as his redneck cousins observed, and he'd come to savor the novelty of having the largest car in the Cedar Shoals High parking lot. It was also, as best he could tell, now the largest car in UniEire (the U.S. Ambassador's Continental being a meter shorter and five-hundred kilos more svelte). As such it served both to remind Kevin of half his heritage (wretchedly excessive though it might be), and to inject a dram of drama into otherwise prosaic drives in a country half the size of his half-native Georgia.

He did not, however, *desire* drama in his driving just now.

Frowning, he unlocked the driver's side, slid into

the leather seat, slipped the derringer underneath, and turned on the ignition. Unfortunately the Beast cranked, but the windows were fogged, and he let the car idle while they demisted. The radio was playing something bluesy in Finnish, and he spun the knob until he found weather. The hurricane had turned south—not north as the Eirish had feared. It would not make landfall in Eire at all, though the southern coast would feel its wrath, as, to some degree, would the whole country, Eire not being that large. Cornwall, however, was in for grief.

Happily, he was only going a dozen kliks. Leenane, which he had no intention of visiting, was something like ten times that far.

Eventually the windshield cleared—to reveal Fir already in transit. The odd lad was briefly lost to sight as he rounded the corner of the garage, but reappeared abruptly, a dark blur by the passenger window. Kevin popped the power locks; then, when the youth hesitated, stretched over to flip the handle. Likely it was his first encounter with any car this old, much less an American one.

Fir looked uneasy as he climbed stiffly in. His hands had retreated beneath his coat again—which Kevin had begun to assume was typical. The stiffness he attributed to residual pain from the wound.

"Ready?" Kevin sighed.

"Yes. Please." But with a scowl.

Kevin bit his lip, snicked the car into gear, and eased it into the forecourt and thence beyond the curtain walls. A sharp left put him on the driveway facing the road, and thirty meters (ten of them through hub-deep water, which had nevertheless dropped a third of a meter since last night) and a right put him on the highway heading west. The radio had found some old U2 to play—doubtless another forty-year retrospective. Fir continued to sit stiffly. Kevin flipped down the armrest between them, perhaps as a barrier against insanity should it prove contagious.

The rain really had relented, too; but clouds still hung heavy in a sky dark as unwashed wool. The usual velvet greens of the landscape were reduced to camouflage and khaki, while the pavement shone like black silk shot with silver. Kevin tried to relax, to settle himself into the rhythm of the road; hopefully, the storm would keep traffic light. Another sigh, a shift of position, and he glanced into the rearview mirror—and was startled to see a low black shape glide out of the turnoff just west of Clononey and ease onto the tarmac. *Citroën*, he identified automatically. Ten-year-old ZZ. They had always reminded him of basking sharks.

But why had it been sitting by the side of the road like that? If someone had had car trouble that close to Clononey, surely they'd have applied to him for help. Or . . .

Last night. That car that he'd seen pulling away from where he'd glimpsed the traveler who had surely been Fir; that could very well have been a Citroën just like this one.

Something slick and black, the lad had said. A man. A noise. Pain—and then he fell . . .

A chill sped up Kevin's spine, and he spared a glance at his passenger. Fir was looking at him, too, but his earlier spacey stare had shifted to something far more serious. There was something strange about the way he was sitting, too. And then Kevin caught a movement, and a glint of metal as Fir opened his coat just enough to reveal a rusty, but still very competent-looking harpoon gun, with the sharp-arrowed tip pointing straight at Kevin's side.

"Where'd you get *that*?" Kevin blurted.

"I left it near the machine shelter last night," Fir replied. "I did not think you would let me in your house if you saw it."

Kevin could only gape.

"You can conceal a lot beneath a long coat," Fir continued gravely, sounding more adult and confident by the second, as though the previous twelve hours had all been a colossal charade. "But one thing *you* cannot conceal is deceit. You will not take me to the place of healing, for I am not ill, nor to the place where criminals are kept, for I have committed no crime. But you *will* drive, very fast, to where I told you."

The harpoon tip glittered balefully.

The rain returned, harder.

And Kevin could only frown, drive, and nervously check the mirror. And each time, the Citroën had drawn closer.

Chapter V:
Walking Wounded

(Aztlan, Aztlan Free Zone—Mexico)
(Thursday, September 1—dawn)

"Wake up, kid, we're nearly there."

'Bird jerked reflexively and blinked back to groggy awareness, more than a little confused about where he was, what sort of place he was awakening into, and who in the world was fool enough to call him kid, when he was twenty-seven.

His initial impressions were of glassy smoothness and eerie silence, superimposed on subtle movement. And of the light of a rising sun filtering through heavily tinted windows to stain cream leather upholstery and carpet the color of blood.

Blood!

He had seen too much blood lately, far too much!

That brought him bolt upright, dark eyes wide and staring. He was in a car—a limousine: a familiar red one. Up ahead a glass partition closed off a copper-skinned chauffeur sporting an eagle feather in the traditional (save that it was red-dyed buckskin) cap. The building sweeping by on the the right—a block-long step pyramid in which courses of angled silver mirrors alternated with vertical cast aluminum friezes bearing frosted-glass Tlalocs and Quetzalcoatls—was familiar too: the Museum of the Americas.

He also knew the tired-faced man lounging in the backseat beside him.

It was the Honorable Chief William Red Wounds, Kituwah ambassador to Aztlan. A tall, heavy-bodied man in his early fifties, Red Wounds could have been a laborer or a lawyer (and had been both) as easily as a diplomat. His face was typical hawk-nosed, wide-cheeked Cherokee; his hair, pulled back in a tail and bound with gold, could have belonged to any Native American. His white suit—expensively cut Brazilian silk—could not.

'Bird found himself blushing. It was definitely not cool to doze off in the back of your boss's limo— especially when that same boss had de-sacked himself in the middle of the night and spent the next five hours extricating your ass from authorities who seemed bent on proving that you, Thunderbird Devlin O'Connor, were in fact the perpetrator of a certain grisly murder you had yourself reported. This in spite of the fact that there *was* a trail of both footprints *and* blood leading from the beach into the bush; that 'Bird had given a detailed description of the assailant; that they *had* the murder weapon complete with prints; and that the slain man's skin was yet to be located, while there was no blood on 'Bird's body at all.

'Bird nearly gagged when he recalled that image, his impromptu nap having done nothing to dispel the horror. Red Wounds saw him swallowing and grinned lopsidedly. "Take the day off, kid," he rumbled. "I've had the screws put to me a time or two, and it's no fun. I'm just glad I was here to run interference for you. Them Mounties are good men and do good work, but they can be, ah, a little *too* thorough sometimes."

"Like I'd be fool enough to skin somebody, then rat on myself," 'Bird snorted.

Red Wounds punched his shoulder. "I got you off, didn't I?"

"After they took blood, skin, urine, *and* semen samples—like I'm into buggerin' corpses. Shoot, I don't even do guys when they're *breathin'*—least not very often."

"They were just coverin' their asses, kid."

"Yeah, I know," Bird yawned. "I 'preciate you bein' there for me."

"No problem," Red Wounds mumbled through a yawn of his own, " 'specially when you've got an ironclad alibi until ten minutes before that man died. I reckon even the Mounties know you can't skin somebody as carefully as that guy was in *twenty* minutes, much less what you had."

'Bird scowled thoughtfully. "Yeah, well, I got the impression that they really didn't think I did it, but were being unnecessarily thorough about the whole thing—like somebody was makin' 'em go absolutely by the book. And they were *really* picky about details. They asked me stuff it would never have occurred to me to ask."

"Like what?"

"Like had I had any odd dreams lately."

"And?"

"I dreamed I saw Cathy Bigwitch naked—not a pretty sight, either."

Red Wounds guffawed.

"So . . . any idea what's goin' on?"

Red Wounds's face turned grim. "If there was, I couldn't talk about it."

"And if there wasn't?"

"I make it a policy never to lie to my friends.— And, conveniently enough, here's your place. Don't forget to take the day off. List it as emergency leave."

"Thanks," 'Bird sighed, as the limo glided into an AFZoRTA bus stop across Mankiller Boulevard from the slanted head-high wall that marked the southern boundary of the Native Southeastern Confederacy Diplomatic Compound, of which the Kituwah Embassy was part. Meter-wide bas-relief world circles at four-meter intervals relieved the sandcrete facade. The good stuff was inside the block-square complex.

"If you need me, call me at home," Red Wounds replied, while 'Bird found the door button and triggered it. Hydraulics hissed as seals parted. A wave of hot air fanned 'Bird's face as he stepped out into the rosy light. Then, as the door automatically closed, " 'Bird—be careful."

With that, the limo eased away, leaving 'Bird to blink dazedly on an atypically empty sidewalk, dead on his feet by virtue of having had exactly no sleep save the aborted catnap during the last twenty-four hours, yet dreading to sleep lest the awful image return. Even in the heat he shuddered: That poor man dying in a pool of his own blood, while some nameless . . . *loco* ran off with his skin. Murder was bad enough—but to flay someone? To condemn him to the ultimate nakedness? To deny him even the honor of being buried with his own face?

It was all tangled up with other images, too: with the beat of the new song down at the 'Wheel, with ravens, and with Xipetotec, Lord of the Flayed Skins.

And that last, he concluded, as he waited for a convoy of construction vehicles to rumble past, was the worst. For he *had* heard rumors of a revival of the old Aztec religion, though mostly tabloid stuff. Trouble was, his Canadian captors couldn't tell Mexican Indians from Cherokee, and were just edgy enough about the confluence of either with an obsidian knife and a flayed body to give him more than typical grief. Luckily Red Wounds had been in town.

Except that the chief knew more than he was saying.

'Bird had taken exactly two paces into the street—which put him in the middle of the nearer of the nearside lanes—when he heard a squeal of brakes, and, close upon it, a female voice yelling, "You crazy asshole! Damn!"

'Bird jumped back instinctively—just as a flash of electric orange-red resolved into a car: one of those tiny Mazda targa-topped roadsters with the super-charged H_2-powered rotary engines behind the seats. Best power-to-weight ratio in the world, his tech-nophile pal, Stormy, had told him—not that 'Bird cared, not when he could walk.

On the other hand, he'd just glimpsed the driver, who had actually climbed out of her seat to glare at him over the gold glass windshield. She looked fu-rious—and very, very harried, though how he knew the latter, he had no idea. Perhaps it was the un-kemptness of her brownish hair that hinted at its having been upset by more than top-off driving. More likely, though, it was the wrinkles in her dull black tunic and jeans, which suggested they'd been first to hand when she got up—and probably the last things removed the night before—if she hadn't ac-tually slept in them.

She also looked about 'Bird's age—and, eschewing the bland-toned and too-short hair, was remarkably pretty in exactly the way he liked. Or would have been if she hadn't been glaring at him.

"Advance or retreat," she snapped, and 'Bird caught a definite foreign accent, one he could have placed had he been hitting on all cylinders.

"I'll—advance, I reckon," he managed, attempting

a grin, but not quite succeeding. "I kinda didn't get to sleep last night, and I guess it shows."

"I guess it does!"

"Not drunk!" 'Bird protested, wondering even as he said that why he was bothering to explain himself to this obvious bitch. "Sorry. Go ahead."

The woman slid back into her seat but did not move the car. "I'll wait," she growled. "I want to be sure you're nowhere near before I even *breathe*."

Too tired to argue, 'Bird muttered a muffled, "Thanks," checked both directions carefully (bless-edly, it wasn't rush hour yet), then trotted across the street, wishing, even as he touched down on the other side, that he'd thought to get the woman's name. Oh well, he had friends in the DMV, maybe *they* could tell him who drove a fire orange MX-Z. It was only as it whisked away that he noted the white circle of foreign registry on the car's stubby deck lid: *UE*. In an uncial type? United Eire? Who knew?

All he knew, as he made his way up the short ramp toward the Compound gate, was that he wanted, very badly, to forget the last six hours and sleep.

Fortunately, the Kituwah Embassy flanked the gate on the left-hand side. And even more fortu-nately, it took 'Bird but two tries with the voice box to be let in. Three would have brought human guards (Chickasaw, this week, Seminole/Creek the next, Choctaw the following, then Cherokee-ne-Kituwah) and required questions, though he knew every single Compound guard by name.

Security was security, after all, even for a friendly nation in a friendly city in a fairly stable part of the world.

He spared but the briefest of glances at the Com-pound itself—four truncated sandcrete and cast glass pyramids linked by limestone palisades around a central ball court—before making for a discreet STAFF ONLY door recessed behind a hedge of *Ilex vomitoria*.

Another pause for a code call, and he eased inside. A dash down a carpeted corridor brought him to an elevator, which he summoned. *"Nukhi,"* he yawned into a grille, as he pressed his hand onto the recognition plate and stumbled in.

"Four," an electronic voice translated sweetly, in English—whereupon the elevator rose.

'Bird had already peeled his skin-shirt over his head when he stepped out into the fourth-floor hallway of the apartment level a few seconds later. " 'Bird," he mumbled into the speaker beside his door, and squeezed through before it had finished sliding aside.

He entered cool darkness, broken only by the low shapes of his deliberately sparse collection of furniture. His sneaks followed his shirt a stride inside, and he was reaching for the Velcro-edged triangle that served as both belt and fly when a voice sounded from the low-slung sofa behind him. " 'Bout time you got home," it drawled, the accent mixing north-and-southwestern US with Pan-Indian precision. "Sleeping's damned tiring when you're waiting."

Bird froze with his hand on the bedroom door, his heart abruptly thumping like mad. "Shitfire, Stormy!" he spat. "What the fuck are *you* doin' here?"

The only reply was the thump of bare feet across thick carpet. A hand touched 'Bird's bare shoulder. He spun around instantly, knocking it away as he did. "Jesus Christ!" he yipped. "What're you tryin' to *do*?"

"Check your wiredness coefficient."

"And?"

"Fifty percent over safe max."

The lights promptly brightened to campfire red.

'Bird collapsed against the wall, to see propped against the hall door the lanky black-ponytailed figure of his best friend, Stormcloud Nez. He caught the familiar odors—leather, smoke, machine oil—that always accompanied Stormy regardless of what he wore. Stormy's quirkily handsome face (his nose was too short and perky for any proper Indian) showed a mix of weariness, bemusement, and concern, while his sole garment—a paisley silk breechclout—betrayed both a total lack of self-consciousness and a high degree of foolhardiness—or trust, since it looked uncannily like one 'Bird had last seen in *his* closet.

"Been raidin' my wardrobe again, huh?"

A flick of head indicated a pile of beige, tan, and royal blue clothing that might have been a uniform. "I came straight from work—and since I'm not on official business . . . "

"Then what kind of business *are* you on? Besides, mindin' mine?"

Silence. Then: "Coffee oughta be ready. You need some." There was no room in Stormy's tone for refusal.

'Bird didn't move from his place by the door. "Coffee's the *last* thing I need! 'Specially that sicky-sweet motor oil you make."

Stormy merely lifted an eyebrow and stood straighter—incidentally flexing his biceps as he did, as though to remind 'Bird that he *was*, after all, Assistant Deputy Chief of Security at the Dineh Embassy three blocks west—which basically meant he commanded the night shift. 'Bird wondered where his gun was. Legal or not, he always had one about.

"One," 'Bird conceded finally. "Exactly one, and only if you answer my question."

"Which one?" Stormy called, as he sauntered toward a bank of appliances in the right rear corner.

"I don't need this, man," 'Bird growled, sinking down in a sprawling chair loosely upholstered in soft tan leather. His eyes felt like lead panels lubed with sand. He let them slide closed. His breathing was already slowing. If Stormy'd just give him a minute . . .

"Here, you go, kid: Dr. Nez's finest!"

'Bird started, having nodded off just in that short time. Something wonderful-smelling was poking around in his sinuses; something *hot* was pressed against his elbow. "Thanks," he grunted, and took the coffee. He sipped it tentatively, not having to be told how hot it was. It was, as expected, sweet as syrup—the way Dineh liked it.

"Let me guess," 'Bird said wearily. "Being unable to choose to which tribe you would belong today, you chose the worst of both: Dineh coffee, Makah taste in clothes."

Stormy bared his teeth and sat down on the floor, resting his own steaming mug on a low cedar slab table. "I'd be naked if I followed *Makah* tradition,"—he chuckled—"if I was on a seal hunt, anyway. Fortunately, Mom's folks haven't done those in a couple hundred years."

'Bird eyed him warily through the steam. "Which has nothing to do with why you're here—or with how you got in."

"Red Wounds had your security look up your code, then I used my code and patched in an override."

"That's only half an answer."

"He thought you might need somebody after . . . whatever it was."

'Bird looked up, startled. "He didn't elaborate?"

Stormy shook his head. "He just said you'd had a traumatic experience and had caught a lot of misdirected flak for it, but would probably appreciate having somebody around to help you decompress."

"Mighty white of him."

"I can *leave*, if you don't want me, man."

'Bird started to say yeah, that might be a good idea, but something stopped him. Though of a totally different tribe and tradition, Stormy *was* his best friend. They'd arrived in Aztlan on the same day, had shared a cab from the airport, and had been inseparable ever since. They partied together, played *toli* and *anetsa* together, talked music and archaeology and sex together. Covering each other's backs had become natural for them. Stormy deserved better than he was getting now.

"Sorry," 'Bird sighed eventually. "I appreciate your concern; it's just that what I *really* wanta do is sleep for about a week."

"Fine," Stormy replied sweetly. "I'll still be here when you wake up—with more and stronger coffee."

"Don't you gotta work?"

"Your chief called my chief and got me off. Seems like he thinks this is a really big deal."

'Bird rolled his eyes. "You sure you wanta hear all this?"

Stormy nodded. "I really do."

'Bird told him. And though he'd intended to give the sketchiest report possible (he wasn't one of those people who reveled in recalling bad experiences), he found himself pouring out everything— far more than he'd told the Mounties—so that while he'd given them facts, he also told Stormy feelings, hunches—the whole nine yards, including his indignation at being suspected because he was an Indian, and the odd coincidence of the song that, on a raven night, reminded him both of the Celtic eater of the slain, his own tribe's Raven Mockers, and the Aztec Xipetotec.

Stormy held his peace. Mostly he simply sprawled on the floor, with his head propped against the sofa, sipping coffee. Occasionally he'd ask a question when 'Bird's stream of consciousness threatened to meander, or put him back on track when fatigue made him forget what he was relating.

"And that's it?" Stormy asked, when 'Bird signaled the end of his tale by draining his cup.

"Basically," 'Bird yawned. "Red Wounds gave me a lift, I came home, I met you. I did *not* get to sleep," he added pointedly, as he rose. "So if you don't mind—"

"I do mind."

Bird slowly turned to face his friend, who, though still lying on the floor, looked as serious as anyone could. *"Excuse me?"*

"I said I *do* mind."

It was all 'Bird could do to keep from punching Stormy out then and there. "What the hell do you mean by that?" he gritted.

Stormy's face was set. "First of all, 'Bird, remember that you're my best friend, and I absolutely do not want anything bad to happen to you. But as such, I have a responsibility to look out for you even when you won't look out for yourself."

"And not lettin' me sleep when I'm dead on my feet's lookin' out for me? *Sure!"*

"No, listen, man! I know you're not religious—not conventionally. But I also know you've seen some things in your life that have made you . . . let's say, open to nonstandard experiences. Now, I don't think what you just went through tonight's got anything to do with the supernatural, but my folks—my *dad's* folks, the Dineh—believe that a man who's around a dead body can be polluted by the mere presence of the dead person's spirit unless he cleanses himself. And—uh, call it a hunch—but my sense is that any death as awful as that you came across is bound to leave bad . . . *karma*, if nothing else, around. I really think you need to be purified."

"Can I sleep first?"

"Ideally you'd need to stay up to alter your consciousness suitably. So . . . I'd say no."

"You talkin' a sweat, or something? If I sit in an *asi* with you, will you let me sleep?"

Stormy shook his head. "A simple sweat won't do. You need—Well, we'll see . . . "

"But—"

Stormy rose decisively. "No buts, man. I'll give you ten minutes to shower and make yourself lovely, then we hit the trail. If I have to drag you out of here in your drawers, I will."

'Bird stared vacantly, too tired to protest. "Where?"

"Somewhere you've never been nor heard of. But there's someone there you need to know."

Interlude:
"Tag! You're . . . Out?"
(East of Ballinasloe, County Offaly—United Eire)
(Thursday, September 1—midmorning)

"Okay . . . *Fir*," Kevin sighed through well-gnawed lips, "I really do think it's time you leveled with me."

He spared the merest glimpse away from the sheets of rain that were overstressing his nerves and windshield wipers at well-nigh identical rates, to the rearview mirror, where a certain black Citroën filled most of what view the deluge allowed. Its narrow headlights gave it a menacing look—as if its actions weren't enough. Kevin wished he could see the driver, but all he could discern through the torrents of water was a grey-gold blur of privacy glass. As he flicked his gaze back to the highway—a strip of palest silver winding among hedgerows like an unrepentant serpent Saint Paddy had overlooked—he caught a flash of his own face: narrow, nervous, and wild-eyed beneath a shock of spiky orange hair blazed with sapphire blue.

"Please?" he continued. "I mean, it's one thing to head out in the middle of a hurricane to humor somebody. It's something *else* when some loony's breathin' up your *ass*."

Fir shifted edgily, but never let his fingers move

from the trigger of the harpoon gun. He looked both more and less anxious than he had when this bizarre odyssey had begun fifteen minutes earlier. But he did not reply.

Kevin sighed again. A sudden shift from downpour to drizzle let him speed up a tad. The Citroën did not—likely from increased spray in its windscreen. On a straight road, in dry weather, Kevin could outrun that particular car—but this wasn't a straight road, no need even to consider the weather. Besides, the Beast's wheel was on the left, which was a bitch at the best of times.

"I mean correct me if I'm wrong," Kevin went on desperately, "but that *is* the car that pulled up beside you last night, isn't it?"

"I do not know," Fir replied unhappily. "They all look the same to me."

Kevin rolled his eyes, then squinted them to slits, straining to see ahead, where a dark shape was *barely* visible at the opposite end of the straightaway they had just happened on. He drove faster yet. The wipers labored.

"Okay, Fir, I—*Goddamn!*"

For the Mercury had suddenly jolted forward. He felt the rear end twitch and had to fight the wheel to retain control. His speed dropped ten miles an hour. A glance in the mirror showed it full of Citroën. "Jesus Christ, man! What're they tryin' to do? Run us off the friggin' road?"

"Most likely."

"But *why?*"

"To kill us," Fir whispered.

Kevin felt hands of ice clamp around his heart. He swallowed weakly. Reflex made him mash the gas hard enough to draw away again.

"But what've I ever done—Hey, wait a minute!

That *is* the car that came up beside you last night, isn't it? And they're—Jesus shit! They really *are* the ones who shot you!"

Silence, but Fir looked wildly distressed.

"But *why*?"

Fir fidgeted. "They . . . do not want me to deliver my message."

Kevin pounded the armrest between them. "Well *hell*, Fir, why don't you just tell me what it *is*, then?"

"Because you would not believe me."

"Believe, hell! I fuckin' well don't believe *this*! It's—*Oh shit. Brace your—*"

This impact was harder, and Kevin heard metal crumple and glass—or plastic—shatter. The Citroën seemed to be down a highbeam, which was a blessing. Certainly it had fallen back. Kevin thought he could see it fishtailing, but had his hands too full maintaining control himself to make certain. He had to slow anyway, was closing rapidly on the shape ahead, which proved to be a lumbering lorry, its rear tires spitting out roof-high arcs of spray.

Which gave him an idea. It was stupid, maybe, but so was letting himself be bashed in the butt until he crashed. Oh, the Beast was faster than the Cit, granted, but didn't handle near as well—or stop as efficiently. On the other hand, *he* had over a meter of dead space behind his rear wheels, the Cit had lots of complex drive components up front . . .

"Hang on!" he yelled. And stomped the brake. The Mercury nose-dived, and Kevin felt all four tires twitch as they flirted with several kinds of skids. "Shit!" Fir yipped—which would have surprised Kevin, had he time for such things just then. *"Hang on,"* Kevin called again. He did not need to check the mirror to know it was very full indeed. His knuckles turned white but he held the wheel firm,

as a solid impact flung the Beast forward once more.
But he was off the brake now, and accelerating. A
backward glance showed a buckled boot lid—and
the Citroën now doubly blind, with a crumpled bonnet and dragging air dam.

But it was still coming on. There was, however,
one ace in the hole.

Setting his jaw, Kevin floored the accelerator. The
Mercury kicked down a gear and surged forward.
Kevin had no idea what had convinced him to try
cinema-style derring-do on the back roads of the real
world, but there was something about Fir that told
him this wasn't a game, that some sort of weird, *very*
high-stakes conspiracy was unreeling.

Fortunately, the rain remained light and the highway straight, and in a few seconds he had caught up
with the lorry. Now if only . . .

The heavy vehicle's right turn-signal flashed, as
Kevin eased into its contrail of spray and matched
its nerve-racking crawl. "Please God don't be a
joker," he prayed, then jerked the wheel right—and
stood on the gas again. "Shit," Fir repeated quietly.

"I agree," Kevin muttered. But by then they were
across the road. Bushes lashed the passenger side as
the absence of shoulder forced the Merc against a
hedgerow, but the way ahead was clear. A quarter
klik farther on the pavement ducked under an arch
of trees, masking a series of tight curves that rendered passing impossible to the nonsuicidal. He
gasped in relief as he lurched back into the left-hand
lane. One thing he'd never got used to was the way
Eirish lorry drivers signaled safe overtaking on blind
bits of road. The first time he'd had to pull out on
faith he'd nearly had heart failure, especially since
the wheel was on the off side. He'd been doubly
lucky this time; first because he'd actually made it,

secondly because he'd evidently timed it exactly right. He had a clear run into Ballinasloe, now; the Citroën—should it still be functional—was stuck behind the lorry. If he was triple lucky, he'd lost it.

And gained a fortune in bodywork.

"Well, Fir," he sighed, as he slowed for the first curve, grateful that the foliage above cut yet more edge from the storm, "I've fucked up my car for you. I hope you're happy."

"I am not," Fir countered solemnly. "But now you know that it truly is important that we get to Leenane."

Kevin could think of no useful reply.

"I still have the harpoon," Fir reminded him. "Do not even consider taking me anywhere else."

Kevin glared at him. "I wouldn't *think* of it!"

"You already have," Fir replied evenly. "Several times in the last two minutes. I will not kill you because I need your help—*your* help, Kevin Mauney. But I could hurt you very badly. And I think I could probably drive this . . . car."

Kevin's response was to turn on the radio.

Hurricane Buckley was ashore in Cornwall.

Kevin would as soon have been there as where he was.

Chapter VI:
On the Beach

(Aztlan, Aztlan Free Zone—Mexico)
(Thursday, September 1—shortly after dawn)

Carolyn was still fuming about the numb-brained carelessness of a nameless young Native American as she zipped along the northeast arc of Aztlan's beltway at twice the legal limit, turbocharger screaming like her ancestral banshee, and still with four kliks to go before her exit. Not that the delay was *her* fault, she hastened to add. Not hardly!

What the hell had that lad been *on*, anyway? To come prancing into the street like that? Good thing the MX-Z had racer-class brakes, or they'd still be scraping his shiny black scalp off the tarmac and she'd be wasting precious time explaining that even the best brakes *and* reflexes *and* radar couldn't save someone *really* stupid.

Not that the lad had actually been rude, or anything, just sort of . . . disconnected. Not enough sleep, he'd allowed. *Yeah, sure!* She'd seen the blood red limo that had dropped him off—and she knew what sort of folks rode around in blood red limos. Still, he had been quite nice to look at, though mostly she recalled a foolish grin, an impressive mane, and a slim, muscular bod well displayed by

67

a metallic skin-shirt. But if *she'd* noticed him, distracted as she was, no way some rich local sugar mama—or daddy—wouldn't have eyed him too.

Except that she didn't quite think so. True, he'd looked a tad rough around the edges, but his apologies had seemed sincere. And he'd been far more polite than the rank and file in, say, New York—or Dublin—would have been under equivalent circumstances.

But he'd have had to be blind not to see that she was in a hurry! And why did he have to be haunting her *now*? Granted, she hadn't had a date in a month (hanging out with Rudy didn't count). On the other hand, it wasn't as though she'd done commercials to announce her availability.

And lately . . . Between fretting over Kev (she should probably call up some weather), and worrying about the deaths . . . well, she'd been preoccupied too.

And here, at last, was her exit! She braked for the curve, prompting the breezes playing hurley in her hair to take a time-out. The turbo shifted from banshee to Brunhild. To the right, the bay was a slab of blue glass caulked with white sand, beyond which sprawled the low glass pyramids, colonnades, and plazas of downtown Aztlan.

A glance in the mirror, and she stomped the gas again, along a shimmer of two-lane straightaway. Wisps of sand wafted across the pavement in her wake. Up ahead, less than a klik, was her destination. Far less than a minute later, she was slowing for the gate. Beyond it, splattered across the rocky spit at the northern tip of Aztlan Bay like stormwrack, lay the glass and sandcrete shelves of her employer: The Pan-European Oceanic Research Center, Inc.—PEORCI for short. Except that had been Latino-ized to *Por qué?*, then bastardized to *Why?*—which was doubly appropriate—since it also sounded like the Mayan word for *nahual*: "spirit companion" or "animal twin."

"Carolyn Mauney-Griffith," she told the box beside the gate. She spoke slowly because the damned thing had trouble deciphering the light Irish brogue she had never been able—nor desired, after the Schism—to shake.

This time, however, the gate swung wide first try.

Young Rudy Ramirez was loading a white Ford van when she whipped into the nearly deserted parking lot and cut the ignition. A glance at the cloudless sky told her rain was unlikely, so she chose to forego affixing the Mazda's roof panel. God knew Hasegawa thought the car itself was frivolous enough when there was good public transport to be had, courtesy of AFZoRTA. And bikes.

On the other hand, Hassie didn't mind tech when it suited her. Like now, when she was surely holed up in the idling van with the AC on high, while poor Rudy shifted piles of equipment from an electric runabout to the Ford's cargo bay. The morning light flashed off his copper mirrorshades as he slung one last bag aboard and slammed the tailgate. He grinned at her, looking nearly as good as that Indian had, if more innocent—which he was not.

No, damn it, she would *not* think about that lad! Not when she had corpses to investigate! "N.Q. inside?" she asked warily, when she reached confiding range.

"*Sí!* Indeed she be!"

"Mood assessment?"

"Foul, but trying not to show it. Typical inscrutable oriental BS."

"She was raised in Cádiz."

"Blood will talk . . . *señora*," Rudy teased.

"Too *much* blood, today," Carolyn countered grimly, then eased around to the right rear door, flipped the handle, and climbed in. Rudy always drove, so Hasegawa was crouched in the other captain's chair with all the AC registers aimed at her.

"Sorry I took so long," Carolyn yawned, as she buckled her belt and leaned back against the tan velour upholstery. "I was delayed by a . . . crazy man."

Hasegawa's reply was to pass Carolyn a red plastic folder. "This will give you the scoop better than I can. Fisherman found them on his way back in last night. His wife convinced him to notify us—around midnight. Ortiz checked them out as soon as we got word."

Carolyn flipped open the folder but did not look at the neatly printed pages or the fuzzy black-and-white photos. There was neither disc nor videotape. "How many?"

"As of two hours ago, when those were taken, fourteen. Could be more by now."

Rudy's face was grim as he put the van in gear, his initial frivolity having ceased when he opened the door. He turned the radio on. Carolyn recognized the high, quivery voice of Jenny Bender, former lead singer of Placenta Pie. The song was a last-century Judy Collins tune called "Farewell to Tarwathie," about humpback whales. She cocked her head, listening. Rudy caught her movement and made to crank up the volume. The Ninja Queen slapped his hand, and turned Jenny off instead.

An indifferently paved and still-unnumbered new highway followed the curve of PEORCI Point northwest along a rampart of low cliffs that rose higher as the peninsula merged with the mainland, and stayed that way for several kliks. The terrain to the left and ahead was sporadically forested, with a smudge of mountains beyond. To the right lay the glitter of the Gulf. Gulls wheeled in the air there: high above the waves but level with the van. Carolyn scanned the folder and tried to ignore incipient motion sickness. She asked as few questions as she could, which Hasegawa answered in as few words as possible, so as not to preprejudice her about what they were about to encounter. Rudy frowned, drove, and peered now and then at a set of scrawled directions.

Fifteen kliks later, he brought the van to a halt beside the road, thirty meters from the cliffs. Carolyn recognized the yellow Ford Zig up ahead as José Ortiz's.

Ortiz climbed out as soon as the first door opened. He was a tall, lean Venezuelan close to Carolyn's age, dark-skinned, and mustached, with a stubby ponytail; dressed in a loose white tunic above baggy beige jeans. He met them halfway to his car. His face was grim. A pair of expensive Zeiss binoculars weighted a strap around his neck.

"Anything new?" Hasegawa asked promptly.

"As of five minutes ago, two more have washed up. I've also spotted a couple of floaters." His US-style English was textbook perfect, down to the slang and contractions.

Hasegawa frowned. "And it's just past high tide! So who knows how many we'll get before it's over?"

"If it's *ever* over," Ortiz countered. "We thought it was over last time."

"And now it's started again—much closer to Aztlan."

Ortiz nodded solemnly. "Well," he sighed, "it's not gonna get any prettier if we stand up here talking. Or smell better."

Hasegawa nodded in turn. She was already sweating.

"Way down?" Carolyn wondered.

Ortiz pointed past the front of his car. "Trail in the cliffs the locals use. It leads around that northern point to the actual site, 'bout half a klik farther on. You can't get there from land otherwise, unless you follow the beach practically from 'Why?'—or jump."

Hasegawa groaned.

Rudy jogged up to join them, his corporate tunic already stained with sweat. The straps of two heavy black bags made ridges on his well-tanned neck. Another was clipped to his belt.

"Won't get any cooler," Hasegawa informed them.

Ten minutes later, they had navigated what proved to be a *very* narrow and precipitous trail worn into the side of the cliff. ("Should've used the launch," Hasegawa grumbled. "Faster and less dangerous.") Carolyn breathed a sigh of relief as she hopped down onto the beach proper. The high-tide mark showed a meter to their right, with beyond it forty-odd meters of still-damp sand. Cliffs curving eastward to north and south defined the limits of a crescent-shaped cove.

"Next one's just like this," Ortiz offered, as he led them north. They walked just above the tide line, where the sand was squishy-hard, but not powdery enough to invade their shoes. Carolyn was tempted to shed hers, but Hasegawa would have called that unprofessional. Never mind that she could have done her job just as well that way.

A short while later, they had reached the point where the cliffs edged closest to the sea. The beach narrowed there to a thread maybe four meters wide, which looked as though it vanished utterly at high tide—which was worth filing away for later. Ortiz was in the lead as they rounded the promontory, with Carolyn next and Rudy bringing up the rear. Carolyn had to snake her head around the tall man to see.

Even then, all she glimpsed at first was another crescent cove, near twin to the one they'd just traversed: blue water to the right; waves white as lace; sky blue as cathedral glass. A few gulls. Dark cliffs to the left, fifteen or twenty meters high.

But then Ortiz sidestepped along the base of the escarpment—and Carolyn got the full impact.

"No!" she cried automatically, though she'd been prepared both by report and experience for what she saw. "This is . . . *much* worse than I expected! I—" She broke off as tears ambushed her eyes. She brushed them aside with the back of her hand, even as she heard Hasegawa gasp and Rudy utter a strangled "Shit!"

And then she was running, dashing across sand that shifted from dry to wet as she approached.

Running toward the dead.

Toward where, flung like a necklace of cordwood across the breast of this beautiful bay, lay the corpses of nigh on a score of *Tursiops truncatus*: bottle-nosed dolphins.

"No," she groaned again, as she halted by the first: a well-grown female maybe three meters long. It lay on the sand at her feet, slate gray and white, and sleekly gleaming—though dry sand crusted its eyes, mouth, and blowhole, where it faced upslope. Others lay beyond, some jumbled atop each other—fourteen, the report had said—but she could see more half-immersed in the waves that jostled them irreverently, sometimes lifting them partway off the sand before dropping them again with a heartless

thump, which disturbed whole nations of flies. Carolyn did cry then, unashamed and unheeded, as her coworkers clumped around the closest corpse. Hasegawa had gone pale beneath her sweat. Ortiz was trying to remain stoic. Rudy looked like he wanted to toss his tacos. Indeed, he turned away for a moment, hand to mouth. She heard him swallowing.

The wind shifted then, from south to north, and with it came the stench—not as strong as it might have been had the bodies lain there longer, but death in the tropical sun was still death in the tropical sun. Carolyn gagged but fought it down.

Steeling herself, she eased around to the top of the nearest one's head, seeking to confirm what was already rendered obvious by bloody wounds and flopping chunks of raw flesh on every head she'd seen.

Ortiz joined her. His breath hissed as he got a clearer view. "I didn't get a chance to check out these guys in full daylight," he murmured. "It's . . . a lot worse close up and well lit."

"That it is," Hasegawa agreed, from Carolyn's other side.

Carolyn did not reply, but knelt to begin her examination. And had to fight the urge to cry again. For not only was this dolphin dead, it had been—well, *murdered* was a term she resisted applying to nonhumans—but certainly deliberately dispatched. More specifically, it showed an awful pink-red wound in its forehead: right where its melon—the mass of fatty tissue that housed its echolocation receptors—would have been. All that remained was shredded flesh, shards of bone, and white gristle.

"Same as before," Ortiz hissed.

"Yeah," Carolyn gritted. "Something's bitten their sonar clean off."

"Same modus?" Hasegawa inquired automatically.

Carolyn checked the edge of the skull-sized wound, found a too-familiar pattern of puckers and tears. "I'd say so. It's the wrong configuration for sharks, so the only other thing it could be's an orca. Shape of the bite fits too, though it would need to have been a small one."

Rudy had uncapped the first of his cameras. "Photos like last time?" he asked shakily.

Hasegawa nodded. "Overall shots, then specifics: full body, head close-up, fluke close-up; wounds, both side and top. Dupe everything in black-and-white and color. Keep an eye out for particularly representative examples, and double-doc them. We'll also need to get a couple of these guys back to 'Why?'; but the quality of the wound's the most important thing. Get José to help you drag one up past the tide mark.—We'll help too, of course."

"But why would orcas do that?" Rudy wondered, as he fidgeted with exposures and settings. "Kill what they don't eat, I mean."

Carolyn shrugged helplessly. "I don't understand it either. I mean, first of all, orcas rarely attack other dolphins; secondly if they *did* attack for food, they wouldn't go for the head—except perhaps to kill—but there're no other obvious bite marks on any of them, just that one—in that one spot."

"It's too systematic," Hasegawa observed. "*Way* too systematic. If there was any way in the world I could blame this on people, I would. But the samples we've taken before give the lie to that. Orca teeth in some of them—*fresh* orca teeth, next to impossible to duplicate artificially, and certainly not in the numbers *we're* dealing with."

"Orca tissue in some of *their* mouths, too," Ortiz added. "We tend to forget about that."

"They fought back?" From Rudy. "Good for them."

Carolyn ran a hand down the damp, sleek side of a dead bottlenose. It was still warm—not from its own life, but from the sun. She checked a fin, noted an odd angle, an atypical looseness there. Broken probably. She said as much.

Hasegawa looked up from where she was examining the next corpse up the cove: a young male. "Hmmm, yes, I've noticed that too. There do seem to be signs of a struggle. Not bites, but . . . I suppose you could call them bruises."

"But why?" Carolyn asked, mostly rhetorically.

"Self-defense, I'd assume. Wouldn't you?"

Carolyn scowled. "Which brings us back to why orcas would attack dolphins in these numbers, why they'd kill them all in precisely the same way. And why *that* way and not some other."

"That," Dr. Mary Hasegawa replied, "is exactly what I want *you* to tell *me*."

"It gives *me* the willies," Ortiz said. "It just flat out isn't normal."

"Except that we've now seen four cases, which means it *is* normal—or at least is a significant local aberration," Carolyn countered. "But you're right. This is all but impossible by established precedent."

"It gives me the willies," Ortiz repeated. "I'm sorry, but it just flat out does."

Chapter VII:
Road Trip

(County Galway—United Eire)
(Thursday, September 1—late morning)

I: Ballinasloe

Kevin hated roundabouts—those nerve-racking alternatives to traffic lights and right-angle intersections so popular in the British-and-attendant Isles. Back in the States you stopped, you waited, you moved on. Here—Well, you girded your loins, fortified your intestines, and dived hoodlong into a maelstrom of careening metal that, were you lucky, might spit you out again where you intended. *If* you goosed the gas just right, steered with preternatural precision—and found your fellow travelers inclined to forfeit the right-of-way. It was scary as hell at the best of times, and three years in the Emerald Isle had still made him no master.

Never mind that these were hardly the best of times, what with Fir sitting there silent as a clam, but with the harpoon gun still aimed straight at Kevin's kidneys. Never mind the rain, which made vision anywhere but directly ahead an exercise in supposition. And *absolutely* never mind that there wasn't supposed to *be* a roundabout on the western edge of Ballinasloe anyway.

"Shit!" Kevin gritted under his breath, as he eased one lane over—barely in time to avoid a bite-sized Japanese electric of indeterminate make that whisked in front of him. A horn blew immediately, over his shoulder. He braced himself, expecting to feel a jolt and hear, for the second time in fifteen minutes, the shriek of shredding sheet metal.

But the gods were apparently still with him, for not only had he lost sight of the pursuing Citroën after he'd overtaken that lorry east of town, but he now seemed likely to navigate *this* worrisome whirlpool intact as well.

And there it was now: the sign for the N6 to Loughrea, and thence to Galway . . .

Biting his lip, he checked his mirror, found it clear, and twitched the Merc one lane to the outside. A stronger tug, and the highway clarified, between a row of nondescript new houses.

Fir chose that moment to peer over his shoulder, but Kevin was in no position to avail himself of that distraction—for the view between sweeps of wiper showed flashing blue lights ahead. An explosion of foliage farther down the tarmac looked suspiciously like a fallen tree.

"I have to stop," Kevin said. "Something's wrong up there."

"Not your fault," Fir murmured. "But hurry."

Kevin grimaced as he eased to a halt—his was apparently the only car on this road at the moment. A stocky garda in a fluorescent yellow slicker slogged his way forward, but not until he tapped on the window did Kevin power the glass down.

"Where ye headin', lad?" the man asked wearily.

Kevin didn't know what to say. Good sense suggested he expose his erstwhile kidnapper—if the cop didn't notice the harpoon gun on his own. Which he probably wouldn't. The man, anachronistically, wore glasses, and they were awash with rain. Kevin swallowed hard. "Leenane by way of Galway," he replied at last.

"You'll not be takin' the N6, then," the man rumbled back. "Not for a couple o' hours yet. We've got seven trees down 'twixt here and Loughrea. Best you turn 'round and go home."

Kevin nodded sagely. *Hear that, Fir?*

Except, dammit, there was still the matter of whatever homicidal maniac(s) drove a black Citroën. And, he suddenly realized, there was no way in hell he was taking Fir back now. Clononey, though clearly a castle, was not set up to weather a twenty-first-century siege. In Mercury vs. Citroën, he had some advantage.

"I—uh—really need to get through," he found himself saying. "How're the roads north?"

The man puffed ruddy cheeks. "Fine, far as I know. There's a lane back a bit'll take you to Tuam—if you don't get that big boat stuck 'twixt the hedgerows."

"No trees down?"

"Not that I've heard of."

"Thanks—have a good day."

"Not while I'm out here!" the man snorted, and sloshed away.

Kevin ran the window up. "Well," he began, then noted the tension in Fir's face. "What is it?"

"Go where that man told you," he whispered, "and perhaps we will be lucky."

Kevin scowled, even as he executed a perfect three-pointer in the middle of the highway. "Lucky? What do you mean?"

Fir pointed past what looked like a driveway between hedges, but was in fact a connector to the R348 to Kilconnell. But only after Kevin was a hundred meters down the narrow lane did he realize that a car had zipped past his back bumper and continued on down the N6—a low, black car with broken headlight lenses.

II: Moylough

Fir maintained ruthless silence for the next hour— which was just as well. Kevin had his hands full driving, what with a rebirth of rain coupling with roads that were narrow even for Eire. Never mind downed limbs (but thankfully no trees—reversing three or four kliks was not an appealing notion), and stretches of standing water of unknown but traversable depth. The only reliable radio station was the Gaelic one in Galway. Unfortunately, his Erse, though passable, was nothing to write epics about; and, in view of the weather, they were playing no music whatever. The Merc's cassette player, alas, was on the fritz.

Inevitably, however, the combination of silence, fraying nerves, browbeating himself, and curiosity got the better of him. "So, Fir," he ventured, "what—"

"If I tell you what you wish to know, it will only make you unhappy," his captor replied in precise response to his unanswered queries.

"I'm *already* unhappy!" Kevin exploded, giving vent to his pent-up tension. "And this is *my* car, so I'm gonna ask questions. If you don't like it, *shoot* me. There's at least some chance it won't kill me, but *you'll* be stuck in the middle of nowhere with a car you probably can't drive in spite of that BS you hit me with earlier, and somebody who's got it in for you still on your ass!"

Fir considered this—but not angrily, Kevin was relieved to note. Indeed, he had the distinct impression—as he'd had for some time—that Fir, for all his quirkiness and unshakable determination, was no happier with the situation than he. That under different circumstances, they'd even have liked each other. Shoot, Kevin *did* like him, in a manner of speaking. Or at least was sufficiently intrigued not to despise him outright—as he supposed ought to be the case with one's kidnapper.

"So what is it, exactly, that you do?" Kevin dared anyway. "—When you're not being shot at, or chased by Citroëns, that is?"

Fir blinked at him. "What do you mean?"

"Your . . . job. School. What you do for fun . . . "

A long pause, then: "I . . . fish. I swim."

"A-ha!" Kevin crowed. "I *thought* so! I mean, that's how you're built, and all. But were those jobs, or hobbies, or—"

"—It would only make you unhappy," Fir repeated.

Kevin hissed through his teeth and fell silent. Outside, the tires hissed too, on pavement drowned in rain.

III: Tuam

An hour later the rain slackened enough to show ragged patches of blue sky, though more and darker clouds to the west were not promising—especially as that was the direction in which Leenane lay. They had traversed tiny Tuam with no more incident than lunch at a drive-through McDonald's (Fir had fish), and were now heading west on the R333, bound for Cross—and Cong, where Kevin's troublesome sister had been born. More narrow roads, but though there had been no sign of pursuit for nearly two hours, Kevin was still uneasy, possibly a function of Fir's relentless wariness. As Kevin flicked the wipers off for the first time since they'd started out, he noted a low ridge to the left, crowned with storm clouds, as though it deliberately held them there.

"That's the hill of Knockma," he observed offhand. "They say the king of the fairies lives there."

"Not many people *believe* in the fairies," Fir responded with a vehemence that made Kevin glance sideways at him.

"Not that admit it," Kevin corrected.

"Do you?"

Kevin frowned and repositioned himself in his seat, the highway, while not wide, being relatively straight and not so encumbered with hedgerows as heretofore. "Personally?" he began at last. "No . . . I don't. Basically I don't believe in anything that can't be measured quantitatively—which is not to say I don't *want* to believe. It's just that I grew up rational. My mom was a marine biologist—from right up the way, as a matter of fact. My dad—he was from the States. Taught genetics. They lived apart, 'cept for summers; and each raised their same-sex kid, which was pretty weird—not that it has anything to do with anything.

"But anyway," he went on, "what this meant in the real world was that most of what I had around when I was a kid was science books—journals, and all that. Oh, sure, we did the Easter Bunny thing, and Santa Claus, and such. Trouble was, I was smart enough to figure out the holes in their logic pretty fast. Like, I knew the population of the world when I was five, and it didn't make sense that *anything* physical could visit every household in one night, never mind the sheer mass they'd need to tote around—eggs or presents, either. Unfortunately, according to my more conservative kin—most of whom were Mom's—I also couldn't tell the difference between climbing down eight billion chimneys and turning water into wine or rising from the dead, and apparently I was supposed to."

"But your books . . . ? You write about magic as though it were real . . . "

Kevin wondered how Fir, who apparently knew little else, had picked up *that* little tidbit. *The Unmarked Road* had sold fine, *Road of Light* even better, but he couldn't assume that *everyone* had read them—especially as he was beginning to suspect, from an earlier altercation with the map, that the lad was illiterate. "Yeah, well, I'm a hypocrite, I guess," he continued. "See, the problem is that while I don't see how the supernatural could exist, a lot of people I consider reliable *do* believe in it—and can cite what are to them good reasons. And maybe *I'd* even believe if I actually saw something. I mean, I acknowledge the need for wonder in the world, whether or not there's magic. And I can't help but think it would be great if there was magic—if there really *was* an immortal demigod named Finvarra living under that hill we just passed. Or if the Tuatha de Danaan really did fight the Fir Bolg for the possession of mythic Ireland at Maeg Tuireadh fifteen minutes up this very road. It's just that I don't see how it could happen—and if it did, I'd have to throw a bloody lot of things I *do* put faith in out the window—which would be very inconvenient. Does that make any sense?"

"What about the tracks?"

"Tracks?"

"In your books. The ways between the worlds."

"Oh, *ley lines*! Yeah, well they were just something neat I stumbled on. I just liked the idea of lines of cosmic force connecting places, and all. But they're *almost* science—maybe."

"Maybe."

Kevin shrugged. "I'd sure like to find one *now*—if it'd warp us through to Leenane quicker."

Fir's brows lowered. "Yes," he agreed softly. "That would be useful—because that . . . car is behind us again."

A glance in the mirror, which Kevin had been neglecting, given they were on little-traveled roads, proved the truth of Fir's assertion. "Shit," he groaned, and floored the accelerator. The Citroën shrank—but not as fast as it might; and then he had to brake for a blind curve, cursing the return of the hedgerows that made it unwise to cut the corner as wide as he would have otherwise.

And cursed again, as he found the highway ahead well-nigh occluded with sheep: the vanguard of a large herd meandering down from a field to the left. Having no choice, he jerked the wheel right, then left, and felt the rear end skip sideways as he skidded around a startled ewe. He heard an indignant bleat, but felt no impact as he righted the big car fifty meters farther on. The mirror showed a dirty froth of wooly bodies sweeping across the tarmac like a grimy tidal wave.

The Citroën was not so fortunate—nor were the beasts. Kevin heard several pitiful bleats, even as he saw a pair of animals sail through the air. A dark shape accompanying them might have been more of the car. "What's goin' on back there?" he asked shakily.

Fir twisted around but did not relax his grip on the harpoon gun—or alter his aim. "The sheep are blocking the way," he replied. "The car is surrounded and does not look as though it can proceed."

"But can the *driver* proceed? That's the critical question."

Fir's brow furrowed farther, though his eyes went oddly blank. "I do not think so. The car stopped when it hit the sheep. One of those inside has got out and is looking at the damage—or would be if the sheep would let him."

Kevin chuckled grimly. "Lucky for us! A lap full of lamb chops is *all* we need—which is exactly what we'd have got if we'd hit something that size. Fortunately, we just caught the leading edge."

"Fortunately," Fir echoed speculatively—and surprised Kevin with a grin.

Relief made Kevin grin back. "Luckily, too."

"Luck," Fir echoed again. "Or perhaps it was the king of the fairies."

Kevin stared at him.

Fir stared back solemnly. "They are right about him, you know."

"Sure."

"But they are wrong about Maeg Tuireadh. It was farther north."

Kevin's eyes narrowed, even as a chill went trickling down his spine. "H-how do you know?" The question had begun as an attempt at humoring his captor; but even as he spoke it, as he glimpsed Fir's reaction, he was not so certain.

"Someone told me," Fir replied simply. "Someone very old. Someone who was there."

Chapter VIII:
Lox without Bagels

(West of Aztlan—Mexico)
(Thursday, September 1—midmorning)

"Jesus Christ, man—slow down!"

"Faster you say?" Stormy countered wickedly as he shoved his Jeep Juneau's accelerator even closer to the carpet than heretofore. Which was, and had been for a not-so-good while, already far too close for 'Bird, who sat stoically in the right-hand bucket with both feet pressed firmly against the floor and every restraint in sight snugged tourniquet-tight. He reached up anyway, to brace himself against the B-pillar/rollbar, then grabbed for the coffee thermos when it threatened to jolt free of the holder between the seats.

Gravel spat like bobcats brawling, and something smacked loudly against the kevlar bellypan. Both doors and the rear hatch of the bubble-canopy creaked in sympathy. The Jeep listed alarmingly. 'Bird got a too-clear glimpse of knee-deep ruts on a forty-degree slope, of golden stones the size of his skull—and of a thirty-meter drop straight down six sims from the vehicle's right front tire. He closed his eyes, trying *not* to gasp. Stormy was just jinking with him, he knew. Shoot, most times he enjoyed stuff like this. But this wasn't most times. For, in spite of the coffee he'd been chain-drinking since fleeing Aztlan two hours earlier, he was still four-fifths asleep—or his eyes were. Contrariwise, his nerves were wired into some real hot lasers indeed, and his temper was on a perilously short fuse. The combination . . . Well, Stormy *had* said he needed to purge himself of the pollution his recent encounter with death had engendered, part of which meant altering his consciousness via some sort of ceremony he refused to describe any further. In which case 'Bird was well on his way already.

If they ever got wherever it was.

He dared a glance back up the way they had come: the steepest, most rutted mountain pig-trail he'd ever seen, including in his native North Carolina. Half an hour to the town they'd stopped in for meth, and since then . . . nothing but bare rocks, scrubby vegetation—and lizards. Lots and lots of *big* lizards, of a species that made him wish he'd paid more attention to the biology orientation session he'd slept through before coming here. After all, if Stormy's driving got any wilder, they might well be *eating* lizard until aid arrived. Or lizards might be eating them.

"You're doin' this just to freak me, aren't you?" 'Bird grumbled, as Stormy slowed for a rut even he wasn't fool enough to traverse full tilt. The "road" was worsening rapidly.

His friend smiled fiendishly. "Adrenaline helps you stay awake—and fear generates adrenaline."

"Well, I'm sure on the verge of flight, then," 'Bird gritted. "Though actually I'd prefer to fight, 'cept I don't dare do that while you're drivin'."

"You'd fight *moi*?"

"I *oughta* beat your not-so-furry butt, for puttin' me through this! You're s'posed to be *helpin'* me, man, not scarin' the livin' shit outta me! I mean, I really *did* have a traumatic experience. I really *do* need to sleep!"

Stormy braked the Jeep to a crunching halt just shy of a rockslide that completely blocked what passed for a road. "I *am* doing this for you, man. If I didn't think it was important, I wouldn't be risking my bod—*or* my valuable vehicle." Without further comment, he jerked the Jeep into PARK, set the brake, and climbed out. 'Bird followed. He could hear the engine popping and hissing under the plastic hood. Without benefit of AC, the heat slapped at him, from above in the form of a sun that was searing the zenith, and from stones that were flinging it back from the barren ground.

Scowling, 'Bird joined his friend, who, like himself, was dressed in sturdy boots, worn jeans, and a sleeveless white cotton tunic, unbelted. Gold mirrorshades and Atlanta Tauruses baseball caps completed both ensembles. Viewed from the rear, they could have been brothers, save that 'Bird's jeans were faded blue, where Stormy's were black; and Stormy had added a light, rust-toned serape.

"You're not supposed to know about this," Stormy muttered in a low voice. "You don't see it when you get there, and you won't remember it when you're gone."

'Bird did not reply.

"I need a verbal on that, man. Sorry."

"Promise," 'Bird yawned, and followed his friend over the obstacle, and downward.

They had hiked for nearly ten minutes before 'Bird saw anything more promising than skeletal manzanitas and steep rocky shelves jumbling up to the left and down to the right. Once a pygmy rattler oozed out of his shadow, and twice he spied tarantulas. The former, he could tolerate; the latter . . . Well, there were definitely advantages to living in Carolina, not the least of them being spiders that didn't splay out from under your boots when you squashed 'em. He was a mountain boy, sure; but he liked his mountains with *trees* on 'em, not things that bit back—hard, fierce, and often.

Abruptly, Stormy stumbled. 'Bird snatched at him, missed, lost his own balance, and staggered past a house-sized boulder, beyond which the trail kinked sharp right. And there, for the first time, he glimpsed their presumed destination.

It was a tiny valley, no more than half a klik in diameter, with a slash of green midway along that might mark a watercourse. And as he stood staring, he got the uncanny sense that he wasn't in Mexico at all, but in Utah or Arizona. Or, more properly, in Dinetah, the Navajo nation, which was larger than many of the fifty-four states, from whose company it had, after two years of bitter debate in the UN, seceded, along with most of the rest of the Native Peoples.

Especially as he'd just noticed, at least another klik distant, a small octagonal structure centered in a dusty yard, its conical roof and low log walls still mostly in shadow. "Is that what I think it is?" he wheezed, while Stormy paused to swig from the water canteen—which, besides coffee, was all he was permitting either himself or 'Bird.

Stormy passed the canteen and nodded. "It's a hogan, if that's what you mean. Built by traditional methods, from traditional materials."

"Inhabited by traditional Dineh, too?"

"Absolutely!"

'Bird froze. *That hadn't been Stormy's voice.*

At which point Stormy uttered an undignified yip and jumped at least a meter straight up.

This struck the already punchy 'Bird as hilarious, so that instead of going on guard, he gasped out a strangled guffaw. The mountains laughed back—which he thought funnier still, until he realized that other laughter was weaving with his. He broke off abruptly.

Stormy, it seemed, couldn't decide whom to glare at first: 'Bird, or the short stocky man who had just stepped calmly from the shadows beyond the next outcrop and was ambling up the trail toward them. 'Bird got a sense of a heavy, smooth face and gray hair; but it was hard to be sure beneath the wide-brimmed black felt hat banded with silver conchas. As for the man's age—that was impossible to guess. He moved well, but something about the way he was dressed—old-fashioned tight Levi's and a faded plaid shirt—hinted of a birth midway through the last century. More silver—and turquoise—showed at his belt, on his fingers, and at his ears.

"Ya-tah," the man said, when he had hiked to within two paces. "Mornin'."

"Ya-tah-heh!" Stormy gave back cheerfully.

Uncertain of the protocols of the situation, 'Bird held his tongue.

"Stormcloud Nez," the man went on. "Born to the Makah, wasn't it? And born for the Goes To College Clan?"

"Hosteen John Lox," Stormy replied, with a grin, "whose lineage it would be impolite to reveal in front of strangers. This is my friend, Thunderbird O'Connor."

Lox studied 'Bird for a long moment, then reached up and removed 'Bird's shades and stared at him skeptically—which didn't fit with what 'Bird knew of traditional Navajo courtesy at all, both the stare and the contact being considered rude. "Not Dineh," Lox observed eventually. "Something from the South. Cherokee? Or is it Ani-Yunwiya this week? Or Kituwah?"

'Bird grinned. "Good guess. And all three."

Lox shook his head. "Smart guess. They're the biggest one; you look mixed; and most of you eastern guys've got *belagana* blood—white blood. You've got a lot."

"My grandmother was Irish."

"Good singers, the Irish."

"So I've heard."

Stormy cleared his throat. "I—uh—that is, Hosteen Lox, it seems to me we could talk better off our feet and out of the heat."

"And with something in your bellies?"

"That . . . remains to be seen." And no more was said until the old man motioned them to a rough-sawn bench on the shady side of the hogan.

"Coffee?" Lox offered hopefully.

"Sure," 'Bird yawned. Then, after a glance at Stormy: "That is, if it's still kosher."

"If Hosteen Lox says so."

Lox merely ambled inside. 'Bird could hear the rattle of utensils and the hiss of a Sterno fire. No electricity, he noted (unless the cables were underground), not even Hopi cells. "So what *is* this place?" he asked finally. "And who's that guy?"

Stormy reached down to fondle a skinny black-and-white tomcat that had sauntered by. "Lox is a *hataalii*," he explained. "A Singer. You've heard me talk about 'em—probably read about 'em too. They preserve the Ways, preside over rituals, and so on. Lox went to Yale, then joined the navy and saw the world, then lived the rest of his life near Window Rock, Ex-Arizona—Hillerman country, if you've read those old mysteries—or did until a few years ago. Seems he had this dream about being needed down here, so he hopped in his son's car and drove south and east until the car gave out. Coincidentally, the Dineh were just setting up their Aztlan embassy, trying to be slick and modern, and all that. But what few Traditionals had come down felt . . . uneasy. They felt like Aztlan was too much *belagana*, in spite of the pre-Columbian architecture, and having been designed by an Indian, and all. So a bunch of 'em got together and decided they needed a spiritual retreat nearby, where they could be reminded of home. Well guess what? Just as they were shopping around, along comes Hosteen Lox. And guess what again? He says he knows the right place, says he *dreamed* it. All they've gotta do is help him find it. 'You're a Revisionist,' they allow. 'That don't affect what I can do for *you*,' he tells 'em back. So they drag out the aerial photos of this area, and Lox— he's also a hand trembler—Lox points to the place on the map that he says is the one—*this* place."

"You're kiddin'!"

Stormy shook his head. "Anyway, the problem was the land belonged to some of the local Indians. So Lox looked up one of their elders, and they drank a little and smoked a little, and a day later he had the deed to this valley. Seems Aztlan rests on land the *belaganas* stole from these folks, so it wasn't suitable for a sacred precinct like Lox wanted. But this they've owned unbrokenly. And while it's not Dineh land and therefore not strictly appropriate for some traditional rituals, neither is it polluted by ever having been owned by *belaganas*—which is important."

"Very important," Lox chuckled, ambling out with a pair of enameled steel cups full of an even stronger-smelling brew than Stormy's thermos had contained.

"Local beans," Lox confided. "Man brings 'em to me once a month."

'Bird took a cup but did not drink from it. He gazed around curiously. "What do you live on?"

A shrug. "I got a little garden and a couple of sheep. Catch some stuff. Folks bring me stuff from town once in a while."

'Bird could think of nothing else to say that couldn't be construed as rude or nosy. Instead, he flopped back against the hogan's wall. The raw logs felt good: not cool, but cooler than anything else about. His feet were hot and sore. He wondered if it would be impolite to take off his shoes. His eyes drifted closed.

"Your friend here must think a lot of you," Lox observed.

'Bird started, glanced sideways, to see Stormy scowling at him. "Sorry. What'd you say?"

"Your friend thinks a lot of you."

'Bird shrugged. "He thinks I'm a fool a lot of the time."

"You agree with him?"

Another shrug. "Sometimes. I try not to be. But . . . I guess I try to be myself first of all, listen to my heart, and all that. And if it tells me to do stuff most folks think is foolish, then—yeah, I'm a fool."

"You're a long way from home."

"So's Stormy . . . so're you."

"If you wanted to tell how that happened, I would listen."

'Bird rolled his eyes. He *didn't* want to, as a matter of fact. But Stormy had gone to a lot of trouble and

some risk to bring him here. He'd said Lox was someone he ought to meet. And 'Bird wasn't an asshole
unless forced to be. Scowling, he took a deep breath,
and chased it with as much coffee as he could manage without scalding his mouth, but even so, his
tongue went numb. "Well," he began, "like you
guessed, I'm from a place in western North Carolina
called Qualla Boundary—*Cherokee* by the white—
the *belaganas*. Basically it's where the few . . . Cherokee who eluded the Trail of Tears wound up. It's
not a true reservation, but it's still the seat of the
Eastern Band. I was born before we all got our independence—my dad was a big advocate of that. He
was an anthropologist too, like I am. Went to the
University of Georgia and got active in Native
causes. It was his idea to petition the Hopis for
money for endangered species research—repatria-
tion of wolves and panthers, and all that, plus genetic
engineering. Once that got approved and we could
show we could make a contribution to the world at
large *and* support ourselves without help from the
Feds, they had to grant us our sovereignty, per the
Resolution. He's retired now, and workin' on a
book—when he's not restorin' cars."

"Thunderbirds?"

A nod. "Thus my name—his too. Actually, *his* dad
was into 'em, but couldn't afford one."

"Your mother?"

"She's from the Western Branch. Dad met her at
a powwow. She's a wildlife artist."

"Brothers and sisters?"

"Mom had me, then had uterine cancer. She survived, but I'm a solo."

Stormy smirked at that. "No joke!"

"I am also curious to know what you hope to
achieve down here."

'Bird considered this. "To serve my people as best I can," he replied finally. "I'm Cultural Attaché to our embassy, which means I arrange exhibits, procure speakers, do presentations at schools, other embassies, you name it. I consult at the museum some."

"Not bad for a young man."

"I do okay."

"Wife?"

"Too many choices, and I can only have one. Suppose I chose wrong?"

"So you try out a lot of 'em."

"I do my part."

Silence. Then: "Do you know what *chindi* are?"

'Bird shifted uneasily and took another sip of coffee, then glanced at Stormy askance. It was, he realized, the first direct question Lox had asked him. "They're . . . ghosts, aren't they? Evil ghosts? I think they're the bad part that's left when somebody dies."

"Do you believe in them?"

A long pause. Then, slowly: "I'm . . . not sure. I have some reason to think what the . . . *belagana* call *magic* works—not so much from things that've happened to me, but via people I trust, who have no vested interest in being thought strange or special, who've encountered . . . peculiar things. My dad's seen a *bunch* of things. But . . . *chindi*, as strictly defined? I'd have to say . . . no."

"What has your father seen?"

"Witches. Skinchangers . . . "

"He is a person you trust?"

"He wouldn't lie to me."

"And you? What do you believe?"

"I . . . I don't want to talk about it. What's *that stuff* got to do with anything?"

Lox's eyes flashed fire. "Your friend brought you

here 'cause he thought you needed what we call a Way—I suspect you've heard of 'em, if you're an anthropologist. And some folks say Ways are . . . magic, though I don't like that word. You don't believe in things like that, a Way won't do you any good."

"He believes," Stormy inserted. "He just won't admit it."

Lox glared at 'Bird accusingly. "Oh, I see: you respect your culture, but you're also afraid of it, 'cause to be *truly* part of it, you have to believe in . . . *that stuff*. Only you've been to the *belagana's* schools and they've told you there's no such thing. So instead of stayin' home, where *that stuff* is, and where folks believe in it, you came down here to Aztlan where there's steel and glass and concrete over everything that's real. You came down here to hide from *that stuff*."

"Now wait a minute!"

"Look in your heart and tell me I'm wrong!"

Silence.

"Now tell me what's got your friend so riled up he'd bring somebody like you to see me."

'Bird sighed wearily. And for the second time that morning, laid out the whole disturbing tale.

Lox listened quietly, then nodded. "You did right to bring him here," he told Stormy. "He *does* need a Way—'specially if he's attracted a *chindi*. Probably a Ghost Way or an Enemy Way—or maybe one of them new preventative ones."

"I thought those were only for sick folks," 'Bird broke in. "Sick *Dineh*, as a matter of fact."

"Some would say our whole world's sick."

"I'm still not Dineh."

"No, but you respect Dineh customs or Stormy

wouldn't hang out with you. That's enough for a Revisionist like me."

"But don't they take *days*?"

"This one will. First of all, I need to find out what *kind* of Way to do. Then I need time to collect stuff, time to get things ready."

"So when can you do it?" Stormy sighed, before 'Bird could protest.

"Next week, maybe. Monday or Tuesday, if I push it."

"Anything we can do in the meantime?"

"He can sweat. He can wring out the water that was in him when he saw . . . *that*, and maybe the *chindi* won't recognize him 'cause we're mostly water, and it won't be the *same* him. And he can ease right on out of himself in that lodge, so the *chindi* can't recognize how he thinks. But it's gonna make him sick—sick in the head, anyway. And when *that* happens, he'll need a Way."

"But you think a sweat'll suffice for now?" Stormy persisted dubiously.

"It's all I can *do* for now. Depending on how he comes out of it—how his attitude is, maybe I can do him a Way next week. That's the best I can promise."

'Bird did not reply, did not contribute at all to the discussion. If they'd let him sleep, he'd do anything. He wondered idly if he could sleep in a sweat lodge.

"You keep him awake," Lox told Stormy finally. "I'll build the fire."

"Fire," 'Bird yawned groggily, vaguely aware he was starting to free-associate. "Fire's the same color as blood."

"C'mon," Stormy grunted, rising. "Let's go jogging."

Chapter IX:
In Deep

(Research Vessel Midgarden—
the Gulf of Mexico)
(Thursday, September 1—noonish)

"Screw this!" Carolyn sighed decisively. "I hate remotes. I'm going in."

And with that she pushed back from the bank of computer-enhanced CRTs she'd been squinting at for the last hour and corralled a cup of tepid coffee from the shelf to her right. The screens took no offense from her snub, but continued broadcasting obliviously, bathing her face with flickering blue-green light: the waters of the Gulf of Mexico observed, in rotation, by three dozen remote cameras, half of them umbilicaled to motorized buoys presently defining a square two kilometers on a side in the cove where the dolphins had beached, the others, free-swimming jobs operated from a pair of mice. At present they showed nothing larger than a single half-grown Mako shark and a trio of groupers. No dolphins, living or dead, and definitely no orcas.

"My eyes hurt," she told Rudy with a smile as she slid both mice his way and rose so he could claim her chair. He grinned at her uncertainly.

"My *head* hurts," he shot back, his handsome,

wide-cheeked face all suntan, dark eyes, and white teeth beneath thick black hair. "Comes of pulling the late shift *and* the morning shift."

"Have some of that coffee," Carolyn yawned. "It'll put hair on your chest."

"I don't *want* hair on my chest. Maggie likes 'em smooth. So does Roger."

A black eyebrow lifted delicately.

"First come, first served," Rudy smirked.

Carolyn's reply was to empty the dregs of the pot into his cup and snare a breakfast biscuit from the stash by the console. An unusually strong wave slapped the *Midgarden* as she did, forcing her to brace momentarily as the vessel rocked. It also reminded her of the hurricane in Eire, of which she'd heard little in the three hours since they'd left the site of the massacre—Anomalous Beaching, Number IV, as it was officially, if soullessly, tagged.

"Guess I'd better change," Carolyn yawned.

"N.Q. won't like it."

"She never likes *anything* that's not by the book. But if I show up ready to run, she'll be less inclined to try to talk me out of it. Better yet, I'll just go, and *you* can break the news."

"Easier to get forgiveness than permission," Rudy agreed. "I mean, we *are* marine biologists, for Christ's sakes—"

"Most of the local species of which don't want to get their feet wet," Carolyn snorted, as she ducked into the adjoining companionway to retrieve the requisite gear from the lockers there. "Present company excepted, of course," she added with a comradely wink. Rudy was the newest member of the team, only a year out of grad school at the University of Florida at Miami, with a major in marine biology and a minor in electronics. He knew volumes of theory, most of it newer than what Carolyn had picked up in Monaco three years prior, but had precious little hands-on. He was also the least stuffy person she knew, and while she tended to stuffiness herself, Rudy's easygoing teasing coupled with the fact that as junior man in Cetacean Behavior he got all the trash jobs, made them good foils for each other.

"Where *is* the N.Q., anyway?" Rudy said, as he called up a second set of images from an alternate bank of remotes.

"Down below poring over those photos. She's trying to correlate the fin patterns against those we've got on file. Ortiz is helping, since he did the photography in the initial census."

"I see . . ."

"Well *I* don't—not very clearly. Which is why I'm going down. If there *are* orcas in the area—or dolphins—I can tell a lot more up close and personal than I can staring at a bunch of pixels."

"Sonar says you're wasting your time; says there might be a couple of tame dolphins and that's it. Certainly nothing as big as an orca."

"And you told me last week that the system's badly in need of replacement and not to trust it—and you haven't fixed it in the interim, have you?"

Rudy shook his head. *"Nyet."*

Carolyn rolled her eyes. "I wish you'd settle on a nationality."

"Ah, but this is an international facility in an international city—*señorita.*"

"Hmmmph!"

"You gonna change, or you gonna give me grief?"

Rudy punctuated his question with the inevitable grin, whereupon Carolyn ducked into the tiny head to the left of the companionway. The black tunic and jeans hit the deck, along with the fluorescent orange panties, to be replaced by a sleek bodysuit, blue-gray on the back, buff white on the front, the better to gain the confidence of dolphins. She didn't raise the hood, however, nor slip on the streamlined goggles, nor the cumbersome fins. Scooping her clothes into a duffel bag, she stepped back into the monitor room.

"You gonna carry eyes?" Rudy called.

"I suppose I ought to—but only a skull-mount. Better yet, see if you can bribe one of your trained remotes to tag along. If I wanted to deal with tech, I'd stay on board."

"Good point," Rudy yawned, rubbing the back of his neck.

Carolyn noticed the gesture. "You okay?"

"You mean beyond lack of sleep? Sure."

"Just wondered. You heard Ralston had a blackout last week, didn't you?"

"*Supposedly* had a blackout. *He* says he fell asleep."

"Yeah, but computers don't black out, and— Well, I'm not supposed to know this, but you know the ones they've got monitoring the ring remotes? The ones that run all the time on automatic and only chime in if they see something interesting? Well, there've been a number—I'm not sure how many— of instances in the last month or so of discs being erased, both computer and video."

Rudy spun his chair around and gaped at her. "You're kidding!"

" 'Fraid not. And you want to know the really disturbing thing? They correlate to within one day with the dates of the other dolphin beachings. And given that we don't know when or where the actual mutilations occurred . . . "

"Sounds like you subscribe to the human interference theory—scant hours old though it is."

Carolyn shrugged helplessly. "I don't know, Rudy. I can't imagine how humans could inflict wounds that look exactly like orca bites. But I can't see why orcas would bite the melons out of four dozen dolphins across two months' time—nor, to add the absurd for the sake of completeness, how they could possibly affect the computers."

"Humans with trained orcas?"

"Most logical guess, given the evidence, but not one I like."

"You like any of the others?"

Another shrug.

"You might oughta be careful, you know."

"Why?"

" 'Cause while there aren't enough documented cases of orcas attacking humans to matter, and not many more of 'em attacking dolphins, the fact that suddenly that *is* happening might make you more vulnerable than you think."

"Ah, it's a comfort *you* are, lad," she laughed, lapsing into her brogue.

"Cary?" Rudy asked suddenly. "Has anyone tried to correlate the holes in the disc record versus the mutilations versus those cameras we've been losing lately?"

Carolyn's eyes went wide. "Not unless Hassie has, and she tends to see what she expects."

"Hmmm, and I wonder what would happen if we threw in the date of Ralston's blackout . . ."

"Seckinger said he got nauseous the last time he did a night shift."

"Hmmm again," Rudy echoed. "I, uh, haven't told anybody this, but . . . I got pretty muddle-headed on screen duty last night—had to go sit in front of the

AC with my head down, and all. Figured it was re-
mote-control bends, or some such, all that flickering
light and stuff."

"Well, it's a thing to think about," Carolyn sighed.
"And to run by Hassie, assuming we can assemble
the data without her catching us. But in the meantime, think you could plug me in?"

Rudy rose to join her. "Sure thing."

Carolyn reached into a hard plastic clamshell
holder and removed a pair of thin red hoses with gold
fixtures on either end, rather like coaxial cables.

"Playin' by the rules, is it we are?"

Carolyn nodded. "With as much going wrong as
has been lately, I'd better. And the *rules* say to get
a buddy to plug you in; they're less likely to take it
for granted, since they'd be responsible if anything
went wrong."

"Thanks a lot! You want a wake or a simple me-
morial service?"

"The former, please, with *mucho* beer."

"Maybe I *oughta* screw up then," Rudy laughed.
But his face was all seriousness as he set to installing
Carolyn's gills. One end of each tube plugged into
the suit at the base of her neck, to either side of her
spine. A twist, and they locked in place. The other
ends screwed into gold-plated receptacles above her
carotid arteries. They'd always reminded Carolyn of
those knobs on the Frankenstein monster's neck in
the old movies, though hers were less obtrusive—
and rendered even more discreet by being included
in an elaborate tattoo of interlaced gold spirals that
circled her throat like a permanent choker necklace.
Hasegawa hadn't liked that either, but it came with
the package.

When Rudy reached that step, she raised her chin
to afford him better access, felt the reassuring pres-

sure of his fingers against her throat, felt as much as heard the gentle click as the needle-probe pressed through the valve and into her bloodstream. A knob twisted, and one-sim tubes shot out to either side of the end, inside the artery, fail-safing the seal.

It certainly beat tanks, at least for shallower dives such as she'd be executing. The suit had a micro-porous surface that took in water; a permeable inner membrane separated the oxygen, which was then pumped by the action of her legs and arms into pads along her sides, whence it was mainlined into her carotid. The trick lay in remembering to pump—and in manipulating your breath until the system kicked in. Fortunately, sensors implanted in her carotids monitored the oxygen level in the blood, and, when it reached a satisfactory level, broadcast an override to more sensors in her lungs and medulla oblongata, suppressing the breathing reflex. In effect, she was exchanging internal lungs for external ones. Little could go wrong.

Although if anything were *to happen, it would be today,* she conceded sourly, as a slap on the back from Rudy signed her off.

"Thanks," she told him, her voice already sound-ing odd, as the suit began siphoning oxygen from the air, rendering that in her lungs redundant. A beep in her ear signaled that the system was up and work-ing; a second would be the all clear. She held her breath, waiting. The pressure in her lungs built to the point where she had to release the load of air. She exhaled. And did not inhale again.

Giving Rudy a mute thumbs-up, she made her way down the companionway to the deck. One of the crew looked up, mildly surprised, but Rudy stuck his head out. "She's gone fish, guys. But don't worry, she knows what she's doing, and I'm sending a remote with her to keep an eye on her. It's keyed to her beeper."

"Never dive alone," the crewman, who looked old enough to be Carolyn's father, shot back automatically. "I don't care what they say about remotes."

Carolyn simply shrugged and gave Rudy a salute, then tugged on her goggles and fins.

He slapped a finger against his body phone. "I'll give the Ninja Queen a call," he said. "And I'll be talking to you, too."

Carolyn nodded, spared a glance landward to where the cliffs loomed dark a klik away, put one foot on the gunwale, and flipped forward into the sea.

Water closed over her, embracing her in a cloud of transparent blue. Her ears popped, as the little air remaining in her lungs equalized the pressure. She exhaled slowly until both organs felt comfortable. A vague numbness crept over her lungs as she pumped her arms vigorously, focusing on that motion to quell the inevitable reflexive alarm. And then she was swimming—without breath.

"I show you all clear," Rudy's voice rasped into her ear. "Beep twice if you can hear me."

Carolyn tapped a red spot on her left wrist—one . . . two.

"I read you," Rudy replied. "You should see remote number three to your right, moving toward you. I'll set it to flank at four meters."

Another pair of taps.

"Okay, gal; you're on your own—'cept that I'm definitely watching."

Carolyn couldn't resist a grin, as she found a current and let it waft her deeper—five . . . ten meters—almost too easy, so that she didn't have to use her legs enough to fill the pads. She scissored them forcefully, enjoying the speed that generated. Before she knew it, she had shot headlong into a school of killifish. They scattered around her: flickering darts of life—alarmed now, thinking, perhaps, that she was a predatory dolphin. A larger red-and-blue parrot fish swished by heading the opposite way. She reached out to it, forgetting, for the nonce, her concerns: the mutilations, Kevin—that good-looking Indian she'd nearly squashed. And for that moment, she was simply a fish.

The red-and-blue lad eluded her, however, and she swam onward, dropping another three meters, the remote an arm-long silver shadow four meters to the right. She could see the bottom now, another forty meters below, but a section of it thrust upward to her left, bearing an impressive crown of staghorn coral and anemones. She wondered how the coral had survived so long, given the buffeting this area took in hurricane season—which reminded her of *that* again. She quickly banished the thought. *That* was stress; *this* was the most relaxing thing she could imagine: to drift along with the currents, or contend against them; to be utterly free to choose her direction; and to use her entire body to execute that choice. She felt complete when she dived: wholly at one with herself, and, therefore, with the universe.

If only she had someone to share it with. Not just another diver; there were plenty of them at "Why?," Rudy not the least. But someone who understood instinctively that water was life's ancient home and could simply enjoy it for its own sake.

Unfortunately none were available, and she'd have to justify *this* dive soon enough—and her reasons were tenuous at best. Swimming relaxed her; therefore, it was easier to think; therefore, she could more easily contrive a solution to the mysterious mutilations. "To understand fish," her mother had told her, "you must think like a fish. Our people anciently believed in the Salmon of Wisdom; and to be wise, you must remember that the whole world is around you, and you can never be free of it; therefore, you must enjoy it, and to do that you must remember that everything has its own kind of beauty, even bad things, if you look at them correctly. But you must also remember that fish exist for two reasons: to eat other fish, and to be eaten by other fish. The bigger fish you are, the less likely you are to be eaten. Therefore, you should become the biggest fish you can."

That had been a bit much for a ten-year-old to digest the night before her first scuba lesson. But Mom had been right: it had opened a whole new world—and even Carolyn had been surprised at how well she'd taken to it. Oh, she'd always been a good swimmer—had been at it since before she could walk. But even so, she couldn't believe how *natural* diving felt. The only real problem was with the cumbersome apparatus, which diluted the purity of the experience. The invention of the gills (badly named, they were more like whole-body lungs) had changed much of that. But even they relied on a layer of material between skin and sea. To eliminate that, to have nothing between one's self and the ocean, and to be free to breathe water like fish, or to hold one's breath for minutes on end like cetaceans—that would be ideal!

But only if she had someone to share it with. Someone *human*, she amended—since two nonhuman friends were even now arrowing her way.

She recognized them instantly, the way one recognizes a face, yet cannot describe it: Katana, and Bokken, a pair of white-beaked dolphins Hasegawa had rescued from a bankrupt sea park in northwest

England. Though predominantly a northern species, they'd acclimated well, and seemed perfectly at home in the warmer waters of the Gulf. Oh, Katana had been forced to learn which species of sharks to avoid, and had a notch in his flukes to prove it. But otherwise . . . Well, she sometimes wished *she'd* acclimated as easily.

Nor could she resist a grin as Katana swung in beside her. Bokken arched across her back and flanked her on the other side. She reached out to tickle her, saw her roll over in pleasure, her face displaying the perpetual smile Carolyn found so endearing.

Katana poked her in the butt with his beak, a little too roughly. She slapped him away, then slid her hand down his side to show he shouldn't take it personally. He nodded vigorously and flicked up ahead, to disappear around another eruption of coral. Carolyn saw him and steered that way, swimming strongly to keep up with Bokken, who had likewise raced ahead. By the time she'd reached the outcrop, Katana was lurking around the other side: seven meters away, and spiraling deeper—deeper than her gills were designed to function. She followed until the warning buzz sounded in her ear.

Lucky lad, she thought sourly. *To experience such freedom all day every day, world without end, amen.* And more to the point, to be intelligent enough to enjoy it. Yeah, to be free, intelligent—and completely remote from tech: that was the way to live.

Katana drifted up to taunt her again, where she floated suspended, one hand on a branch of coral. This time it was Bokken who prodded her (more gently than her mate) in the small of her back, indicating that it was time *she* got some attention. Carolyn obliged, and thrust off in pursuit of her. Her target

proved elusive, however, and seemed bent on leading her in a slow spiral up the spike of coral. There
were at least another five meters to go, too, before it
ended and she'd have more advantage.

But maybe if she nipped in closer, she could spend
more energy on speed and less on distance. A flick
of a flipper sent her that way. The remote flashed
along to the right, its path erratic, perhaps confused
by the proximity of the coral and two bodies near
Carolyn's size. She slowed, to give it time to sort
things out—but her shift of pace put Katana, who'd
been following a bit too closely, on a collision course
with her. He twisted away reflexively—which sent
him straight into the remote. It rebounded off his
tail, doing him no obvious damage. But the impact
evidently jammed one of the machine's stabilizers,
because it suddenly shot straight toward the bottom
of the coral mass, straight to where the tangle of
branches was densest. It caromed off one out-thrust
arm, chipping a hand-sized segment free—which
only crippled it further. The last Carolyn saw of it,
it was spiraling toward the sea floor, shards of the
glass that had shielded the camera sifting down with
it.

That's one less remote for "Why?", she thought
wearily. *One perplexed Rudy Ramirez, and one
pissed-off Mary Hasegawa.*

She was still drifting along, gazing at the blue-
green haze that veiled the bottom, when something
nudged her back. She started, spun around to face
it—and found herself nose to nose with a mouthful
of very sharp teeth. Even as she gaped her startle-
ment and tried to push away, her head struck something—or something struck her head. And then
those teeth were flashing even closer to her face.
Something tugged at her neck—No! At the tubes

that connected the suit to her carotids! A terrible tearing pain wrenched at her throat; then another, on the other side. Abruptly, she could not breathe. Fingers clawed at the release on her weight belt. *Up!* She had to get *up*! Had to find air!

But all she found was another impact on the head that filled the world with blackness and shooting stars. The last thing she saw before that darkness enfolded her, was blood clouding the water from either side of her face, and the tubes of her gills drifting toward the ocean floor.

Chapter X:
The Land Where He Dwells In

(Leenane, County Galway—United Eire)
(Thursday, September 1—early afternoon)

Leenane had always reminded Kevin of Vikings—
nor was it hard to understand why, if one troubled
to actually *look* at the place. Poised as it was at
the point of the narrow finger of ocean that was
called Killary Harbour, but which looked so much
like a fjord it might as well have been one, the
town—what there was of it—was scarcely touched
by time. True, the splatter of stone-walled shops
lining the N59 west into northern Connemara, with
a few more flanking the route up into the Sheffry
Hills and thence to Croagh Patrick, sported the
taint of modernity in the form of satellite dishes
and liquid crystal shop signs. But spirit those
away—change asphalt tile to slate or thatch, road
signs to runestones, tarmac to well-trodden mud,
and Ford Maverick four-wheel-drives to sturdy Nor-
wegian ponies—and you might well have slipped
back a thousand years. Even the locals' clothing—
faddishly baggy jeans and belted sweater-tunics—
aided the illusion. Red hair and ruddy complexions
needed no updating.

Kevin, however, had just that moment realized

that he had made yet another mistake. When Fir had told him they needed to go to Leenane, he'd assumed the lad meant the town. Town meant restaurants, pubs, whatever—or friends. More to the point, it meant inside. But Fir wouldn't hear of it. "Only a little farther," he murmured. "I will show you the turn when we get there, so go slow; it is easy to miss."

Kevin could only scowl and gnaw his lip. At least it wasn't raining—they'd left *that* a couple of valleys back—which wasn't a minute too soon. If he never saw rain again, he'd be just as happy. When he got back home—*if* he got back home—he'd give the Beast a new set of wiper blades. Maybe even douse 'em with a pint of Guinness apiece, just to placate the fairies.

If.

For Fir was becoming more wired by the moment; would stare at Kevin fiercely one instant, then glance out the rear screen apprehensively—and, when he twisted back around, wear an expression between resignation and anticipation. He was fidgeting constantly too, and could not seem to hold one position for more than a few seconds.

And somewhere around the time they'd entered the valley that backed Leenane, he'd shifted the harpoon gun's point toward the floor.

At least there was no lurking Citroën. Nor was there, very soon, any *other* sign of civilization. The road was narrow, rough, and crooked; but one truly could not fault the scenery, especially not the line of water stretching away to the right, with, across it, the low grassy humps of the Sheffrys. All it needed was a dragonship slipping silently up the harbor.

Normally that's all it needed. Today, however, the Northmen had best don slickers and run in terror of their lives, for though the whole mass of Eire lay between here and the eye of Hurricane Buckley, there were still sufficient forces disturbing air and water to whip the harbor into a grey-white froth. If it looked unstuck in time at best, now it seemed set to unravel in space as well. If this were a bad science fiction film, Kevin thought sourly, now was the point when the doughty hero stumbled through the time warp.

A movement from Fir recalled him to the present. The youth was hunched forward eagerly, his whole body tense and strained. "There!" he cried. "Past that wall: turn right."

Kevin held his breath at the narrowness of the steep rutted lane onto which Fir had urged him. The car barely fit between a waist-high jumble of piled stones on Fir's side and a tangle of hedge on Kevin's. A sharp curve a hundred meters on doubled the road back, screening the highway completely and bringing them halfway to the shore. The lane ended a quarter klik beyond, in a space just wide enough to turn around in. To the south and west scrubby vegetation covered steep-sided hillocks twice Kevin's height. East was flatter terrain and a complexity of ruined walls that gave onto a brief stretch of sheer granite cliffs.

And north: a jumble of stone edged the pavement and hid the water's edge, which Kevin guessed lay another ten meters lower and twice that farther out. It was as wild and desolate a place as he had ever seen, to be less than two kliks from a town. He stared at it dubiously. Without asking permission, he turned the car around so that it was pointing back up the lane, stuffed it into Park, and cut the engine.

"I can't go on," he said flatly, only then realizing how tired he was. The constant need to keep his reflexes on red alert, plus the strain on his eyes caused by hours of squinting, had definitely got the best of him. "I don't care what you do to me," he continued. "But I have just flat *had* it."

Fir peered at him perplexedly, but made no move to leave the car.

Kevin paused with his fingers on the door handle. "I thought you had a message," he reminded his passenger wearily.

"I do," came the lad's prompt reply. "But if you are to believe it, I have to show you one more thing."

"Why am I not surprised?" Kevin muttered—and opened the door.

Wind hit him—and cold—more of both than he'd anticipated. That was one advantage of a big old American sedan: it took a tornado to upset one, so that you rarely knew how much wind *was* blowing. And even fifty-year-old ones were so quiet you heard no more than a whisper.

Swearing softly, he flipped the Driza-Bone's collar up and jog-stumbled toward the nearest clump of gorse, intent on relieving himself. But before he'd gone five paces, Fir was beside him, gripping him by the biceps and steering him seaward. Kevin exhaled loudly. "Can we hurry, then? *Please?*"

Fir's reply, if any, was whipped away by the wind. And for a moment Kevin's prime concern was keeping his feet, as the strongest gust yet slammed into them, bringing with it a sting of water that definitely tasted of salt.

"This way," Fir yelled into his ear. "There is a way down."

Kevin grimaced, had no choice but to let Fir drag him toward the piled stones that marked the summit of the seaward cliffs. There he discovered that what he had taken for a fragment of wall was in fact the natural terminus of a narrow defile that angled down between larger slabs of granite to the shore. The youth stepped back to allow him to go first. Gritting his teeth, Kevin did—though he was reduced to scooting along on his butt on two occasions. At least the wind was less violent here, and the spray somewhat screened—what with raw, fractured stone quickly rising above his head. He thought once of turning back, but Fir was behind him, blocking the way, so that he had no option but to blunder on.

The last four meters were the worst, because they were the steepest, and he had to use his hands to keep from slipping along faster than he could control. What this place would be like when awash with rain, he didn't want to ponder.

But he *was* pondering that, and how hard it would be to get back up, and how high the tide came, when his feet touched level ground. He staggered, heard rather than saw Fir join him. A glance to his left showed a twenty-meter strand strewn with rounded boulders, with the wild waves frothing and fighting at its edge. To his right the cliffs rose steep—too steep to climb at all in weather such as this, and difficult at best, save for the defile they had just descended.

Fir bit his lip as Kevin caught his eye. He had discarded the long coat along the way, but still held the harpoon. "Promise not to try to escape," he said, almost wistfully. His eyes looked childishly hopeful.

"I . . . promise," Kevin sighed.

"I have to leave you for a moment."

"Good," Kevin grunted, " 'cause I have to piss for about five times that long."

Fir shrugged absently and trotted off to the west. As Kevin turned toward the cliff and unzipped his fly, he saw the lad duck into a patch of darkness that might have been the mouth of a cave. And then, for a while, he gave himself over to comfort.

When he turned back around, it was to face a sudden increase of rain, as a new squall began to roll in—and Fir staring at him uneasily. He had abandoned the harpoon gun, but his hands were far from empty. A grey *something* gleamed there: sopping wet and irregularly shaped—clothing, perhaps. As Kevin stood scowling, Fir shook it out. It unfolded to his feet, and Kevin realized that it was not fabric at all. In fact, the roughly cruciform shape and leathery gleam at certain extremities could only mean . . .

"Do you know what this is?" Fir inquired, his voice grim, his dark eyes deadly serious.

For some reason a lump formed in Kevin's throat. "A . . . sealskin?" he ventured finally. The spray pricked his face. Salt made his eyes burn.

The lad nodded. "And do you know what can be done with sealskins?"

A dozen answers danced through Kevin's brain—including one quite preposterous one. "I . . . think I'll let you tell me," he managed at last.

"You will have to join me at the water's edge, then," Fir said—whereupon he freed one hand and gently but firmly drew Kevin toward the wildness pounding the shore. Water lapped Kevin's boots when Fir released him. "Hold this, please," he murmured, passing the skin to Kevin. Kevin took it dumbly—and flinched, for the inside was sticky. "My God, it's *fresh*," he exclaimed—and almost dropped it.

"It has to be," Fir told him, and while Kevin simply stood staring, quickly stripped. The youth shivered slightly, as the spray sheened his skin and slicked his hair close to his skull, neck, and shoulders. But he did not look uncomfortable; rather, it was a shiver of pleasure, as of a lover's embrace. He looked at home there, Kevin realized. A beautiful naked boy-man pink-white and wild-haired beside a grey-white sea.

"You know, don't you?" Fir whispered gravely, as he retrieved the skin. Kevin did not reply, could only stand in mute amazement as his erstwhile kidnapper found what had been the skin's right flipper and slipped his corresponding hand inside.

"Oh . . . Jesus!" Kevin gasped, taking a step backward—which put him ankle-deep in water. "Oh, *Jesus!*"

For as he watched Fir slowly ease his arm into the skin like someone donning a jacket, there was no mistaking the fact that the sleek grey fur of the sealskin was adhering to the pale human flesh within—and that as it did, those human muscles and bones were reshaping themselves to suit.

Kevin gaped foolishly, too stunned to speak. "You're a . . . *selkie*," he gulped finally, and sat down on the nearest boulder.

Fir nodded again, but made no move to continue the transformation. "I knew I would have to reveal myself for you to believe what I must tell you," he said. "But I could not bring my skin inland, for it cannot abide fresh water. Instead, I put on man's shape here, then swam the loughs and rivers until I reached the Shannon at Clonmacnoise. There, amidst the storm, I took to land. I stole clothes. And there . . . those who pursued us became . . . aware of me."

Kevin took a deep breath. "But who *are* they?" he asked.

"I will tell you anon," Fir answered. "First I must deliver the message I have been promising for so long."

But the selkie had no more than opened his mouth when a sharp report barked into the roaring air, followed by a much closer sound like a grapefruit exploding. Fir grunted but did not fall, though he staggered backward, even as he gazed down at the dime-sized hole that centered his sternum, from which his heart's blood was already flowing. "*This* . . . will kill me," he choked, desperate-eyed.

Kevin could only gape numbly, as though he too were wounded unto death.

A second bark, a second gasp, coupled this time with a sound like glass breaking, and Fir spun completely around—and fell, to sprawl half-in, half-out of the waves. Kevin glimpsed his face, then looked quickly away, for the boyishly pretty features had been destroyed—by the bullet that had shattered the left side of Fir's jaw, and by the grimace of pain that contorted what remained. Kevin was beside him instantly, kneeling knee-deep in the rising waters, oblivious to the way the currents yanked at him. A glance over his shoulder—back the way from which the shots had come—showed nothing. But then his gaze returned to his companion.

In spite of the ghastly wound that marred his face and filled his mouth with blood, splintered bone, and shattered teeth—and a fair bit of pulpy flesh as well—Fir was still trying to speak. "Your sister," he gasped, between lips neither human nor pinniped— for even as he spoke, he sought vainly to wrap the skin around him. "Your sister—she can save us. But she is in danger. You are the Word, she is the Way. I don't know who is the Singer. She—"

But he spoke no more, for a third bullet had found its way between the selkie's eyes.

Kevin saw the look of shocked surprise that smoothed the lad's features, eerily at odds with his vacant stare. As he gaped, still unmoving, Fir's body began to shift and stretch, becoming ever more seal-like by the second. But he had no time to spare for the full transformation, for some sixth sense he did not know he possessed warned him, so that he flung himself sideways precisely as a fourth shot pinged off a boulder two meters beyond him—a shot that, had he not moved, would certainly have slain him.

Before he knew it, he had rolled farther into the sea, seeking the shelter of a large boulder that rose there. The water was waist-deep around it, the waves high, the current strong, but Kevin managed to fight his way to its opposite side, though a fifth bullet sent shrapnel slicing into his cheek as he put solid rock between himself and the direction of the shots. From that vantage point, he could make out a mass of crumpled metal, shredded plastic, and shattered glass that could well be the prow of a much-abused Citroën barely visible atop the cliffs to the east— probably beside the main highway.

He could *not* see the marksman, though a movement among the low bushes there looked suspicious. Still if he stayed on the beach, the tide would force him into the defile, and it was better to have choices than none. Gritting his teeth, Kevin spared one final glance at the sad body of his companion—and finally he admitted it, friend. And shuddered, for the youth was fully transformed now. A dappled grey seal floated there, its body already twitching in the grip of the tide that would soon claim it utterly.

"Sorry," Kevin sighed, "I guess we blew it." Where-upon he took a deep breath, heaved himself back onto the rocky shore—and ran, as best the uneven terrain allowed, back to the defile.

He made it—perhaps because of the way the stones and boulders he traversed made his progress hard to predict, or perhaps because of the way the spray was starting to smash into the rocks behind him, raising fans of foam as high as his head.

Still, two more bullets pinged near him as he paused panting at the base of the crevasse, then began to climb. The Driza-Bone encumbered him, but he had no time to shed it, no time for anything save a desperate scramble on all fours up the steepest stretch at the bottom, then to part run, part claw, part climb the rest of the way to the top.

That was the worst part, too, for he remembered halfway up that while the stone walls sheltered him from the unknown marksmen, if they fired from either side, he was utterly vulnerable from the rim, should his assailants reach there first.

That made his frantic scramblings even more desperate. His hands tore, nails ripped on sharp rocks. Twice he slipped, for water was streaming down the defile again, token of a squall that was rapidly shifting back into a full-blown gale.

Somehow he gained the top—and could scarcely see the Beast for the now-driving rain. Fortunately, he hadn't locked his door, and that was the side that faced him—though that stumbling, hunched-over sprint across twenty meters of open ground was the scariest of his life, not the least because he was effectively blind.

And then one hand smacked wet metal, and the other rain-slick glass, and he was flailing for the handle. He found it, flipped it, and hurled himself inside. Pausing only to wipe the worst of the water from his eyes, he stuffed the key into the ignition, and, the instant the engine fired, slammed the car into low gear and stomped the gas. Stones flew and water rooster-tailed, as massive torque thrust the Mercury toward the sharp curve that gave onto this sheltered shelf. As necessity forced him to slow there, another *crack* sounded, loud as lightning. His ears clogged with the concussion. The windscreen went stark white with spiderwebbing. He braked for a hesitant second—long enough for another bullet to rip into the passenger seat—and was for once glad of the fact that he'd never had the Merc converted to right-hand drive. Whoever was taking potshots at him was surely acting on instinct and aiming where the driver ought to be, not where he was.

Which bought Kevin time to fish the derringer from under the seat and use the handle to smash a hole in the windscreen big enough to see through—and let sheets of what was now a downpour slash across the dash, nearly blinding him again. Another shot skidded off metal somewhere—possibly the roof—as he yanked the wheel hard right and rumbled up the last bit of lane before the highway. He heard metal catch against branches on one side, tear against stone on the other, as he lurched and slid toward the N59 and—perhaps—security. Surely whoever had killed Fir wouldn't confront him on public roads. And if he could just get back to Leenane, maybe he'd be safe there, or could at least contact the authorities.

Only what would he tell them?

That a man who was not a man had forced him to drive at harpoon point for hours on the fringe of a hurricane, only to see that man turn into a seal and die ten seconds too soon? But there was no body to support the latter, and the damage to his car could be construed as evidence of leaving the scene of any number of accidents. Or—

But he had no more time for contemplation, for he had reached the top of the lane. The flopping ruins of the right-hand part of the windscreen blocked most of the view, so he held his breath and skidded the car hard left onto the highway.

He made it—blessedly there had been no other vehicles on the road. But even as he sighed his relief and began to consider where he might find shelter—for with the windscreen like it was he couldn't drive far in a rainstorm, much less a hurricane—a movement down the highway made his heart skip a beat before it even registered.

It was the Citroën—what remained of it. Pulling away from the skimpy shoulder, and accelerating toward him—on *his* side! Metal skipped off the belly-pan as something hanging down broke loose, and as Kevin gaped stupidly, more bits ripped free. It was their last-ditch effort, he somehow knew—whoever *they* were. And it was already too late to turn around.

So his choice was simple: be hit or not, and if the latter, be hit moving or standing still. Which basically meant that he could control his life—or possibly his death—or he could let unknown agencies choose for him.

Steeling himself, he took a firm grip on the steering wheel, and floored the accelerator. The Merc surged forward—into a sheet of rain that blinded him once more. When he could see again, the Citroën was practically atop him. The road was wide enough for it to swerve into the other lane, but he doubted that would happen. Already he was assessing escape routes—whether there was anywhere to go besides stone walls, hedges, or—increasingly—trees.

And then that decision was spared him, because a shriek in the windscreen pillar startled him so much that he flinched. A bullet had narrowly missed his head!

Which was enough: self-preservation reflex overrode deliberate killer instinct. Kevin jerked the wheel; the Mercury lurched across the highway into the clear lane. And skidded.

He caught a flash of speeding, twisted black metal, of gleaming alloy engine bits plainly visible beneath a crumpled bonnet, and then saw only rain. A vivid image of the one game of chicken he'd played as a teen back in Georgia darted across his memory, and then a more imminent persona decided it was time he made peace with a God he now had more reason to believe in. His last thought was that the Cit would hit somewhere behind him, which *might* keep the Beast drivable.

But there was no impact. Kevin's vision cleared exactly enough for him to glimpse—through his own rain-sheeted side windows and the open passenger window of the oncoming car—the passenger's hand seize the steering wheel and shove it to the right.

For an instant, time froze, while Kevin stared amazed at the Citroën as it careened into the stone wall on that side, broke through—and arched gracefully into clear air and out of sight.

Kevin was out of the Beast almost before it stopped. Oblivious to the slashing rain, he dashed across the flooded tarmac to the wall and followed it scarcely forty meters to the point where the car had smashed through.

Swallowing hard, he peered over—and breathed simultaneous sighs of relief and dismay. The cliffs swept close to the shore there, and the Citroën had nosed down into the harbor. He barely glimpsed its taillights before the wild waves swallowed them.

Which meant he had no evidence. No way—unless he was very lucky—to explain how he was standing dripping wet and spottily bloody beside a smashed stretch of freestone wall, with a badly battered '76 Mercury Marquis behind him.

But in spite of all that, Fir's words rang in his brain, graven on his memory as sharply as the image of him lying dead beside the sea: *"You are the Word, she is the Way, I don't know who is the Singer."*

He was still staring dumbly when the first beam of sunlight he had felt in five days struck him.

Chapter XI:
Fisherman's Luck

(West of Aztlan—Mexico)
(Thursday, September 1—late afternoon)

'Bird wasn't sure if he was being *purified* or not, but *something* was certainly changing.

Part of it was chemical, of course, given the mondo amounts of coffee he'd begun mainlining since resigning himself to an afternoon's incarceration in Hosteen John Lox's sweat lodge. But there was clearly more in the belligerently foul (and unsweetened) brew than the obvious component: some herb, seed, or potion that, while not conventionally hallucinogenic, nevertheless had mind-mucking qualities. Never mind the assorted leaves, twigs, and probable roots Stormy tossed atop the red-hot rocks every time he forked more in, that filled the cramped dim space with many a pungent fume. A few 'Bird could identify: sage and *Nicotiana rustica*, among others. But the rest— Who knew what mojo the Navajo *hataaliis* had contrived to placate the spirits in their vast lonely neonation?

All he knew was that he felt somewhere between drunk, stoned, and mellowly giddy.

And that reality was rapidly reining down to a round, sand-floored enclosure built like a miniature hogan, complete with east-facing door and smoke hole centering the roof—the latter now blocked by a tattered blanket. 'Bird barely had room to sit upright on the woven mat Lox had lent him. And only the red glow of the superheated rocks provided any focus beyond rough walls. He *felt* like a bowl being fired in Hell, but the humidity (his own evaporated sweat clouding the air) and the ruddy hue likewise evoked the womb—which was surely part of the plan. And curiously, he always *had* recalled his prenatal days in a drifty sort of way, though he had told no one but his father.

Just as he had told no one *at all* about the dream that had convinced him to prance into the tribal office one fine April day two years back to request an application for a staff position in the new embassy a-building down in Aztlan. In that dream, he had found himself flying above a vast coastal city cast in the image of Teotihuacán, the ancient Mexican metropolis—save that *these* causeways and ceremonial avenues glittered with jewel-toned vehicles, and the plazas thronged with folk from every nation; while the pyramids and palaces were wrought of mirrorglass tinted bronze, silver, or gold, with classical friezes faithfully transposed into a thousand cast alloys and glasses and ceramics. It was a vision of the paradise the city's name recalled: a glorious vindication of a classical architecture that rivaled Greek and Roman, but was homegrown—and therefore ideal for a New World capital.

He'd had that dream when he was eleven. *Groundbreaking* at Aztlan hadn't come until two years later. But the first time he saw holos of the incipient city, he knew he had to go.

That the dream might have been born of what Hosteen Lox had flirted with calling magic had not occurred to him until later. To 'Bird, magic meant formulae, rituals, and antique mumbo jumbo too irrational for one immersed in science since birth to understand. Did he believe in magic, Lox had effectively asked? Oh yes, he believed, though he didn't want to, and had never let even Stormy see the depth of that chink in his armor.

But even as 'Bird's coldly rational side sought to analyze his environment, survey his senses, and monitor his reactions like a laboratory rat, that part of his psyche that awoke when his body demanded sleep—that let the spirits bound in rustic tobacco, juniper, sage, and piñon come creeping out when Ancient Red and Ancient White freed them with their scarlet tongues, to confide unto certain receptors in his brain secrets they might otherwise have chosen not to know—was commencing to assert itself.

'Bird could literally *feel* it now: his subconscious—or perhaps it was his aura or his doppelganger or his astral self—stalking through the corridors of his mind, shutting this oft-used door, or opening that seldom-sought one. And before he knew it, he had lost track of the heat that set brushfires on his body, and the sweat that flowed in rivers from the forested heights of his hair down the long slopes of his bare limbs and the plains of his torso. His breathing deepened. His heartbeat slowed. And his eyes rolled back in his head.

He could still see, however, the telescoping squares and spirals that always lurked behind one's eyelids. Only these quickly resolved into the prismatic shapes that dominated the assembly halls and ministries of Aztlan. And then glass gave way to stone, aluminum dulled to mud brick, and Hopi solar panels became palm-thatched roofs. But before 'Bird

could ponder that new vista, the world changed once
more, and the vast pyramids slumped into low
earthen hills drowned with vegetation; while the
wide avenues dwindled to tangled trails threading
through trees as tall as the sky.

Only *El Capote Mundial*—The World Pool: the
enormous marble-lined basin whose pure blue waters marked Aztlan's heart—did not alter. Pyramids
faced it at the quarters: bronze and silver, copper
and gold, reflecting in its glassy surface. But the pool
occupied the center, silent symbolic reminder that
the last great pre-Columbian civilization had
sprawled across a lake in the valley of Mexico, and,
more subtly, as a tribute to the water from which all
life had sprung.

And here it was again, though no longer surrounded by hard-edged monuments, but by soft
steamy jungle born of the earth that supported its
waters beneath the sky.

And on one bank of what had become a small
square lake bracketed by white-sanded beaches, a
naked man knelt with his back to 'Bird. Perhaps he
was an Indian: Aztec or Maya, Olmec, Mixtec, or Tol-
tec—who knew? Perhaps he was even one of those
brave aboriginal hunters who had chanced across
the Siberian landbridge during the last ice age.

What mattered was that he was fishing.

'Bird had no idea how long he watched that man
ply his cane pole, twisted fiber line, and bone hook,
but eventually he jerked erect, yanked hard, and
flipped something vast and silver far up shore: an
enormous fish of an unfamiliar species, man-sized,
and conventionally configured. It *did not* flop about
as fish do when landed, however; rather, it lay still
and complacent as the man calmly freed his hook,

retrieved an obsidian knife from his belt of braided palm, and began the evisceration.

But as the glistening point touched the juncture of spine and gills, the fish smacked its tail into the man's face. He tumbled backward, dropping the blade. And then, to 'Bird's horrified amazement, the fish caught the knife in one of its pectoral fins, slit the man open from chin to crotch, and commenced to skin him alive.

Blood went everywhere, staining both sand and crystal water. Terrified, and desperate to escape, yet utterly enthralled, 'Bird followed the sanguine streams. Behind him, he could hear the man's heart beating ever more slowly.

But *louder*, too—like a drum. A slow, plaintive drum . . .

In spite of what he had witnessed, 'Bird's soul revived at that, and he found himself dancing down the beach, following those too-red runnels to what was no longer a jungle lake, or a pool in the pulse of a city, but the wide empty beach beside a vast blue ocean.

He stared at it, perplexed and amazed, but the drumming continued—up through his feet, into his ears, and thence through his blood to his heart and his soul.

Nor was he all that drumming affected. Every grain of sand was likewise dancing: rising and falling in synchrony, or weaving in and out in complex patterns.

Out into the ocean, too, that pounding carried, so that even the waves broke and crashed to its thundering cadence.

And out there something moved, coalescing from the spray just at the breaker line.

It was a woman: not beautiful, but very pretty

nonetheless. Short and slender, and perfectly pro-portioned, with a pert nose, sun-bleached brownish hair, and eyes dark as leaves in forest water. She was also gloriously, unaffectedly nude. Abruptly 'Bird recognized her. It was the woman he'd met that morning: the one with the accent, the attitude, and the orange MX-Z.

But before 'Bird could ponder what she was doing here, in what was certainly a medicine dream, the woman began to sing. He recognized neither words nor melody, not even the language—but it followed the beat of the drumming that had excited the sand and ordered the waves around her. And as 'Bird watched, more forms erupted from the sea and be-gan to frolic and dive: the sleek gray shapes of dol-phins.

For a while they simply sported at random, while the woman kept on singing—balanced, as she seemed, atop a perpetual breaker, like something from a Botticelli painting. But then the dolphins' dance became more orderly, became a circle of nod-ding, laughing shapes around her. Eventually they too began to sing, mimicking her song with the clicks and squeaks and barks that some thought might be language. And then, commencing directly behind her and continuing to either side, the dolphins leapt into the air, twisted once aloft, then dived into the sea—and disappeared. When the last pair had exe-cuted their odd obeisance, they alone flicked their flukes against the surface. The resulting spray slapped 'Bird in the face—

—and he awoke: wet, shaking, and very very hot in John Lox's sweat lodge forty kliks inland from the Gulf of Mexico. His stomach was tying itself in knots, his breathing slow and labored, his heartbeat re-duced to a drawn-out thudding.

But the drumming still persisted. The beat in the dream, which was also the beat in his heart, segueing as it grew faster, into the beat of a far more physical drum outside.

Without wondering if the sweat were done, if he had been ritually purified, 'Bird hunched toward the blanket that comprised the door, thrust it aside, and staggered out.

The first thing he saw was sky and cliffs awash with the bloody fire of sunset.

The next was Stormy with eyes so wide they looked fit to pop from his skull within a face that was an awful rictus of shock. And then Hosteen John Lox blinked up from where he sat behind a knee-high wooden drum, looking completely at ease.

'Bird stumped across the few yards between them and claimed the towel his buddy clutched in nerveless fingers. "Do I look *that* bad?" he gasped, as he dried himself.

"You look—I dunno how you look. You look like you've—"

"I do not know what you have seen," Hosteen John Lox broke in. "But I do know the face of one who has gazed on . . . magic."

Chapter XII:
Resurrection Day

"Doctor! Doctor!"

. . . *doctor?*

. . . that meant something . . . didn't it? It was a set of vibrations in the air that tickled her ear, then prodded her brain. That conjured an image . . .

. . . *air*, not water . . .

She was *breathing*!

Her lungs hurt . . . her neck hurt . . . her mouth and throat burned, and something was crammed down her esophagus *making* her lungs hurt . . .

"Doctor!"

(Another voice). "Good God!"

"I thought she was—"

"Well she's not! Not anymore!"

"Brain damage? You check for brain damage? There *has* to be brain damage."

"Not by the EEG."

"But oxygen deprivation . . . ?"

"Evidently everything shut down. It's happened before, though not often in *warm* water . . . "

"Doctor!"

Another noise intruded. A steady *blip-blip-blip*. It sounded familiar. So familiar it was almost as though it was part of her.

But of *course* it was, silly; it was her heart! Her heart went *blip-blip-blip* right along! Clever heart: *blip-blip-blip*, just like that.

Red swam into her eyes: red against blue, fading to black . . .

No—that was only memory. She'd spent a long time without memories, a long time hiding, a long time being gone. She was back now . . .

And with that Carolyn Mauney-Griffith opened her eyes.

She saw white.

At first she thought it was the sky, overcast with rain; but there were *angles* in it—and corners, like a room. Like her room at home. Only there *should* be a glass wall opposite; and something yucky was jammed down her throat; and . . . and who were all those people lurking on the fringe of vision? Except that *one* was closer, was shining a light in her eye, while another lifted her hand, feeling at her wrist.

She flinched away from both, tried to sit up.

The world swam away. When it reassembled, she noticed that all those people wore either white or aqua coats.

"Doctor! Get here now!" one yelled, touching a spot just to the left of her larynx.

A . . . a *door*, that's what it was, swung open, admitting a . . . man, she supposed. A woman followed, another, younger, man at her heels. They looked funny: their faces so screwed up, and the bearded man in front with his mouth rounding into an O.

"Oh my God!" he gasped, as his eyes met hers.

"God, *hell*!" the younger man crowed happily, thumping the woman on the back. "Hassie, she's alive!" The woman was crying. So was the young man.

"Doctor, we thought—"

Doctor . . . ? Abruptly something clicked. *Doctor. Sickness. Pain. Not feeling good. Blacking out.* Yeah, that was it: she'd blacked out, and when you blacked out, they put you in the . . . *hospital!*

People were crowding in behind the doctor now. She didn't know any of them—except that black-haired, round-faced woman and the grinning young man beside her. *Mary Hasegawa . . . Rudy Ramirez.* She wanted to call out to them, but something clogged her throat. She coughed. Spasmed. Reached up to tear out whatever it was, but felt hands restraining her.

"Okay to remove life-support?" someone asked. "Looks like she's back."

A pause, while the doctor studied a bank of machines. "I don't believe it, but yeah, take her back to minimum. Keep the monitors on, though, just in case."

"What monitors?" she tried to ask. And again felt her throat clogged, her tongue restricted.

And then cool hands grasped the sides of her head, and the doctor (she ought to know him) cupped her chin with one hand and slowly withdrew a length of yellowish tubing from her mouth.

Something sharp poked her arm. She glanced that way, but already warmth was flooding through her. When it reached her brain it was like wildfire. Connections reawoke, memories lined up and clamored for recognition. And those people kept staring.

"Why are you looking at me that way?" she asked innocently.

"Because," Mary Hasegawa whispered, "you *used* to be dead!"

"D-dead?"

The doctor glared at the Oriental woman. What was his name? *Nesheim?* "I'd as soon you hadn't told her that just yet," he growled. "You could send her into shock."

Hasegawa ignored him. "Cary?"

"M-mary?"

"How do you feel?"

Carolyn reached for more words, found them, as the flame of alertness raged through her mind. "My lungs hurt, so does my neck; my throat and nose burn. I feel . . . like my brain's on fire, but it's a nice feeling, like everything was waking up, like"—she paused, scowling—"like being hyperalert. I feel like I could reach back to every single memory I've got and find it."

"That'll pass," the doctor informed her. "It's the drug I gave you to stimulate nerve responses."

"Dead," Carolyn murmured suddenly, her scowl deepening. "What was that about me being dead?"

"What's the last thing you remember?" From Hasegawa.

"I . . . I was diving. I was playing tag with Kat and Bo—you should have that on disc."

"We do—to a point."

"Oh, right: Kat hit the remote. And then . . . something ripped out my gill tubes, and then hit me, and—"

"—*Something?*"

"It's not on disc?"

Hasegawa shook her head, her round face quickly resuming its accustomed seriousness. "All the disc shows before the remote crashed is Kat and Bo."

"You think *they* did it?"

"Unless you did."

Carolyn gaped incredulously. "You actually think

a pair of tame dolphins tore out my gill tubes, then
bopped me on the head?"

"*Something* did!"

Rudy edged around to grasp her hand. He grinned.
She smiled back. "We can't tell what happened,
Cary—the tubes were popped out of your suit, and
. . . ripped out of you. Fortunately the valves in your
neck weren't damaged much, beyond a trickle; otherwise you'd have bled to death."

"But I thought you said I *was* dead," Carolyn insisted. "What, exactly, did you mean by that?"

Hasegawa looked thoughtful, ignoring her.
"Hmmm," she mused. "Maybe the O$_2$ sensors kicked
in and shut down brain functions, along with the
breathing reflex."

"If they did, it was an accident," Nesheim muttered. "A one-in-a-million."

Carolyn set her jaw and eased farther up in bed.
One by one the onlookers withdrew. "I'm going to
ask this one more time," she gritted. "What's this
about me being *dead*?"

Hasegawa and Rudy exchanged troubled glances.
Nesheim shrugged. "Looks to me like she's up to
handling it."

Hasegawa started to speak, then paused, gnawing
her lip. She looked at Rudy, eyes misting again. "I
think she'd take it better from you, kid."

Rudy grimaced uncertainly but did not let go of
Carolyn's hand. "Well, uh, it's like this," he began.
"As soon as you went overboard, I zipped back to
the screens and got you on remote—you remember
that. I also called the Nin—Dr. Hasegawa—while I
monitored. No big deal at first: typical fish stuff. You
swam, I watched. Looked like you were enjoying
yourself so I didn't bug you on com. Kat and Bo
showed up. More swimming, then you reached the

reef. The remote freaked a little there, and I started to call you to tell you to back off until it straightened out. But before I did, Kat hit it. After that . . . nothing. Your beeper was hooked into your gill circuit, and when that went, we lost touch. We had to use sonar and visuals. It took a while."

"And I was . . . dead?"

"You were floating face down with your eyes and mouth open, your gill-tubes ripped out, and blood trickling from your carotids. You weren't breathing and you had no pulse. We pumped about a gallon of water out of you, and squirted *nearly* that much adrenaline into your ticker—plus standard CPR and all that, of course—but except for a couple of false starts, it did no good. Fortunately, it was only fifteen minutes by copter to here. We had one on search already."

"How long was I out?"

"Seventeen minutes from the time we lost contact to the time we got you in the boat. Another five to get the copter. Another fifteen to get you here."

"Over half an hour, Carolyn," Hasegawa broke in. "Half an hour with no signs of life and minimal life-support. Once we got you here, we put you on the machine just in case those random beats meant something. But we didn't think . . . we didn't dare hope . . . You were totally flatlined."

A helpless grimace from Doctor Nesheim. "And then your heart began to beat spontaneously, and right after that, your lungs kicked in. All at once you had brain activity—*normal* brain activity, when damage typically occurs after seven minutes. I frankly don't understand it—I mean, you were *blue*, girl."

Carolyn blinked at him, feeling suddenly very thirsty. Her fingers itched too—and her toes. "Well,

I seem to be fine now, though obviously something very strange has just happened to me. Something . . . anomalous."

"Spontaneous Resuscitation Anomaly, Number I," Rudy chuckled.

"Good thing, too," Hasegawa sighed ruefully. "I was having a devil of a time locating next of kin. Your mother's off somewhere in the third world where they don't have *regular* phones, much less body jobs. Your father has an unlisted number. And your brother—"

Carolyn sat straight up in bed. "What about Kev?"

Hasegawa gnawed her lip. "The bottom line is we can't get through. The hurricane has evidently bounced off England and back into Eire again. Most of their dishes are down, and we can't even contact the embassy, much less wherever the hell it is your brother lives."

A troubled frown wrinkled Carolyn's brow, which she hoped nobody saw. "Well, I'm okay now, so no need to keep trying."

Hasegawa eyed her seriously. "You really don't want him to know?"

"He'd only worry, and I don't want that. He'd be happier not knowing."

"I wish you two would decide whether you like each other or hate each other," Rudy grumbled.

"So do I," Carolyn replied. "So what now?"

"What do you mean?"

"Well, now that I'm obviously recovered, we've got an investigation to continue, remember? Like eighteen dolphins mutilated fifteen kliks from here."

Nesheim looked stricken. "You're not going anywhere for a while, Carolyn. Not until—"

"Bullshit," Carolyn shot back. "I feel fine. Now, how soon can I dive again?"

Nesheim's raised eyebrows challenged Hasegawa's. "Well, given that we were a little more concerned with trying to revive you than with checking
the status of trinkets," he began, "I don't know. We'll
have to inspect you for damage, then remove the old
plugs—two days there already. Then wait while we
get a new set made, since they have to be custom-
fitted. At least four days for that. And then another
to reimplant, and five more to heal . . ."

"Weeks," Carolyn moaned wretchedly, flopping
back against the pillows. "You're talking about
weeks!"

"We—uh—well, we're also gonna want to run
some tests," Nesheim confessed, not looking at her.

"What for? I'm alive. I feel good—"

"You were also dead half an hour ago. And, against
all logic, you're alive now, and apparently in full
command of your faculties. No matter how you look
at it, that's not normal. No, we need to give you a
complete workup. Check everything we can think of,
try to figure out what kicked in, or turned off, or
whatever."

Hasegawa peered at her curiously. "Cary . . . can
I ask you something a little . . . odd."

"Sure."

"You didn't by any chance have any . . . out-of-
body experiences, or anything? Tunnels of light,
voices . . . "

"No," Carolyn replied. "There was nothing. I don't
think I even dreamed. It wasn't any different from
being asleep."

"Except you weren't breathing and had no heartbeat or EEG."

"So you say."

"What do *you* say?" Rudy asked cautiously.

"I say that with as many electronic glitches as

we've had around here lately, some of the machines you had on me might have been acting up."

Nesheim bristled. "*I,* however, am *not* electronic. I do not act up. I know a dead body when I see one." He paused, eyed Hasegawa speculatively. "As surrogate next of kin, Mary, I suppose we ought to arrange some psychological tests too, just to be sure. Maybe even hypnotism."

"Fine," Carolyn agreed primly, before Hasegawa could reply. "But I'm not staying here while you puzzle it out. I've got too much work to do."

"Bullshit!"

Carolyn stared at her nominal team leader. The woman was many things, two of them being hard and competent. But she almost never swore.

"Bullshit yourself!" Carolyn snapped. "You can have me the rest of the day, to get whatever samples you need. After that, I'm *out* of here. I can give you anything else you think of by phone as easily as in person. And I've got a vital signs monitor at home."

"How 'bout if we get you a room here? With a terminal and a com-link to the *Midgarden.*"

Carolyn shook her head. "I *hate* hospitals. You can get me a terminal and a com-link at home if you want. But I expect to be back on ship, if not underwater, before that happens."

"Two days here," Hasegawa countered wearily, "and we cram in all the tests we can—if you're up to them. The sooner we start, and the closer to—the crucial moment—the better."

"One," Carolyn shot back. "You can have me the rest of today, tonight, and tomorrow morning. I'm back at sea in the P.M. Deal?"

Hasegawa considered this. "Tomorrow *evening*; and you don't set foot in salt water until . . . Monday, at the soonest—assuming the doctor here approves."

Nesheim rolled his eyes helplessly.

"Done," Carolyn cried.

Hasegawa's face reflected one of her rare defeats. She knew not to argue further.

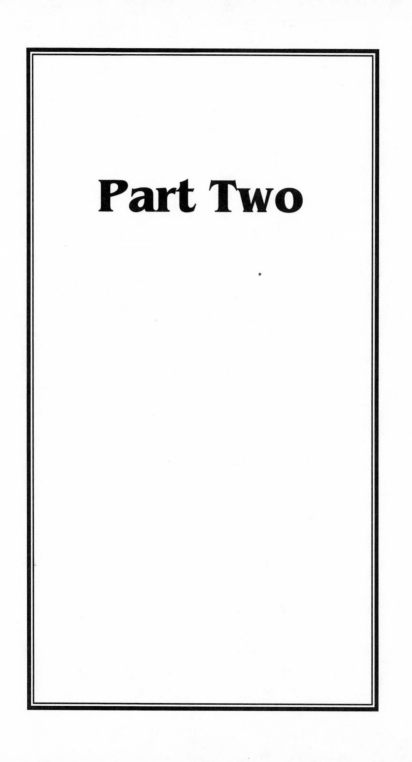

Part Two

Chapter XIII:
Operating

(Galway, County Galway—United Eire)
(Thursday, September 1—late afternoon)

"But this *is* an emergency!" Kevin protested desperately—for the fourth time in fifteen minutes. "I have *got* to talk to my sister in Aztlan!"

"Everyone in *Eire* has an emergency," the female voice on the phone sighed back, as though her electronic persona would fray away to frustrated fury any second.

Kevin held his peace. No sense making someone else's day worse than it already was, just because *he'd* had found himself in crazy shit up to his eyeballs. By his own fatigue-fogged reckoning, exactly two things had gone right in the past eighteen hours: he'd managed to nurse the Beast to civilization, namely his solicitor's town house on the northern fringe of Galway; and the phone there had been working—which the dozen he'd assayed since leaving Leenane had not.

He took a deep breath, slapped a splatter of sodden orange hair out of his eyes, reknotted the fluffy white bathrobe that was his sole garment more snugly around his waist—and waded in once more.

"You're sure?" he persisted, with forced calm.

"There's no way you can patch me through—to the Eirish Embassy, even?"

"There's not a dish standing on the whole west coast, sir. The storm—"

"What about *cables*? Don't you guys still have cables under the Atlantic?"

"We use satellites *exclusively* for international calls, sir. The cables are purely a backup the government uses for diplomatic emergencies. We're not supposed to—"

"How 'bout the US Embassy?"

"The one in Dublin, or the one in Aztlan? There's also a consulate in Galway. Perhaps you could get *them* to—"

"No," Kevin sighed. "I've got a better idea. I'll just *go*!"

"The embassy?" the woman blurted out, off guard.

"Aztlan."

"Will that be all, then? I have other calls."

Kevin scratched his damp bare chest. "Uh . . . one more thing. Can you patch me through to the airport—Shannon, I mean?"

"I'll try. But that's all, sir. *Please*, sir." The woman's voice had gone as chill as the wind outside.

"Fine," Kevin whispered. "Do what you can."

While he listened to static (Muzak, apparently, having been deemed inappropriate for hurricanes), Kevin stared at the oil painting of Fyvie Castle that hung above the phone stand in Cameron McMillan's guest room–crisis decompression chamber. Blue sky showed through the mullioned panes to the left, a holdover from that which had made the drive from Leenane to Galway viable—slowly, albeit, because of the absent windscreen, but without incident, save a pantryful of bugs he was still picking from his teeth.

A long moment later the phone crackled. "This is the best I can do," the operator said flatly—and hung up. Kevin caught a series of pops and snaps, whereupon a recorded message assailed his ears. It was a bad connection, even for Eire. "This is Shannon Airport," it began. "We're sorry to inconvenience you, but all circuits are busy at this time, and we are presently unable to forward telephone reservations or provide information concerning flight schedules. As of noon today, all incoming flights have been canceled or rerouted until further notice. Outgoing flights involving planes presently on the ground will be cleared until nineteen-thirty hours this evening. A few seats are still available. For further information, please contact the airline of your choice."

"The airline of my choice won't answer!" Kevin snapped, and hung up. He was just reaching for the door when a firm tap sounded on the heavy oak. "You decent?" a muffled male voice called. Even through the wood Kevin caught the mix of American and Eirish accents.

"No, but you can come in anyway," he called back, as he hopped aside to admit a tall slim man in his late forties: Cameron McMillan, his solicitor and—at present—savior. To his relief, McMillan held a pile of neatly folded fabric, in very unsubtle colors. He dumped it, with conspicuous ceremony, on the spotless counterpane, then fished in a pocket and slid out a silver hip flask. "You need this," he observed, passing it to Kevin. Kevin unscrewed it and sniffed the contents. "I hate Scotch."

"Then you'll give it a fight going down, which'll warm you faster."

Kevin grimaced, but took a swig, then returned the flask. He eyed the clothing dubiously.

"They're my kid's," McMillan grinned, looking as

though he would have enjoyed the situation enormously, had that which engendered it not been so serious—and had he not been up for over a day. "He's about your size—which I, to the good fortune of my wardrobe, but the likely despair of your sense of esthetics, no longer am."

"His taste is closer to mine, anyway," Kevin chuckled back, as he unearthed a pair of metallic gold briefs. "On the *other* hand—"

"Those were the most conservative ones," McMillan countered. He helped himself to a hit from the flask as Kevin snugged the garment on beneath the robe. "Any luck getting through to Mexico?" he continued, more seriously.

"Aztlan Free Zone, technically," Kevin corrected, covering the briefs with burgundy jeans of last year's cut. "It's an independent state, sort of between Vatican City and the District of Columbia, in case you weren't just being sloppy. Cary's at the Pan-European Oceanic Research Center, Inc., if you want to be really precise. And *no*. Phones appear to be out all over the country. I can't call international because this isn't a diplomatic emergency."

McMillan eyed him warily. "Don't you think it's time you told me what it *is*, then?"

Kevin shook his head and shucked the robe. Lord knew he'd been fortunate to find McMillan home when he'd rumbled up fifteen minutes earlier, to present himself looking a very great deal like the winner of a drowned rat contest. "I need dry clothes and a phone," he'd told his host when he answered the door. "If you don't have at least one of 'em, just shoot me."

"Guns are illegal in Eire," McMillan had answered, and dragged him in.

Now, though . . . where did he begin? "Cam, my

lad," he commenced finally. "I can't— That is, I don't think—I— Goddammit, Cam, I *can't* tell you, except that I just had the weirdest day of my life— which began, believe it or not, with somebody knocking on *my* door craving shelter."

"Whom you then abandoned."

Again Kevin shook his head. "It's too strange. And weird—*and* dangerous. And right now—until I can check on some stuff and sort some things out—I honestly don't think I ought to tell you. It might put you in danger."

"Well, gee, thanks!" McMillan grumbled. "And if you already have, then I've gotta work from a position of ignorance."

"Ha!" Kevin snorted. "That's a good one, only you don't know it. A day ago I'd have said no ignorance was desirable. Today—"

"—You're gonna keep jinking me around."

Kevin slipped a magenta sweater-tunic over his head. "I'll tell you . . . sometime, okay? For now I've gotta get hold of my sis."

"The one you don't speak to?"

"The only one I've got. And we do too speak; we just don't have much nice to say to each other. Not since the folks—"

"That I *do* know about," McMillan broke in. "But what I don't know is what could've happened in Leenane that got your car shot full of holes by something that *has* to be illegal, you soaked to the skin, scraped up like a Belfast brawler, and half out of your mind—and crazy to get hold of someone who last time I heard hates your guts."

"She hates my opinion on *one* topic."

"I speak metaphorically."

Kevin sat on the bed to secure his boots. "I'll tell you in . . . a year, okay? That's what they do in the fairy tales—and I write fairy tales—or thought I did."

McMillan's eyes narrowed. "What's that supposed to mean?"

"I've already said too much."

"Would you say more if I offered to drive you to the airport?"

"You heard that?"

"Only a bit. But if whatever you've got yourself into's made you so desperate to get hold of your sister you're willing to fly in a hurricane, it's gotta be important."

Kevin nodded solemnly. "Maybe the most important thing that ever happened."

"And you won't tell me? Even if I put you out on the street?"

Kevin bared his teeth. "I owe you money."

"Oops. Right. Well, as I meant to pass on before and didn't, the hurricane's bounced off Cornwall, or whatever, and may come back this way. It's—"

"*Shit!*"

It was McMillan's turn to nod. "Right. So there's a state of emergency for the next twelve hours."

"Which means no public transport."

Another nod. "Which means *I* drive you to Shannon, or you sit."

"Or I drive the Beast."

"*Get real!*"

Kevin flopped back on the bed. "I'm still not gonna tell you."

McMillan stared at him. "No . . . I don't think you will."

"You'll probably bill me double for it, too, won't you?"

McMillan cocked his head and began counting on his fingers. "Let's see: three hours there and back, minimum, plus double time for after hours, plus hazard pay for bad weather, plus expenses if I have to get a hotel . . ."

"Plus a full tank in the worst gas guzzler you've got, no doubt."

"Good idea. Dad's been after me to drive the Bentley more."

Kevin rose and studied his reflection in the mirror, probed a shrapnel-scarred cheek. He looked younger than expected, given his experience—mid-twenties perhaps, not thirty-three. The sweater-tunic clashed with his hair. "Uh, I don't suppose you could lend me a couple of days worth of togs, could you? And maybe a shaving kit?"

"Sure," McMillan sighed. "Oh, and did I mention? The Bentley only takes *leaded* hi-test. Shall I put it on your bill, or would you rather pay cash? There's a discount for the latter, of course . . ."

"Whatever," Kevin murmured absently. "Saving money doesn't matter—not when you couldn't save someone's skin."

"Huh?"

"Uh . . . I was just saying how lucky I am to have someone save my skin—and how everyone's not so fortunate." He laughed grimly, pocketed his wallet, and followed his friend into the hall.

Chapter XIV:
Open Wounds

(Kituwah Embassy—Aztlan Free Zone—Mexico)
(Thursday, September 1—early evening)

"I don't *care* if it freaked you!" Stormy grumbled, from where he was checking the Jeep's tires in the waning sunlight of the Kituwah Embassy parking lot. "It was still rude! *Goddamned* rude! Hosteen Lox all but promised to do a frigging *Way* for you—in spite of the fact that you're not even Dineh—and then you just walk out like that!"

'Bird paused at the staff door to glare at his friend. "Cut me some slack, *okay*?"

Stormy's face was as dark as his namesake weather. "What d'you think I've *been* doing, man? I maintained stoic silence all the way here. I figured maybe if I let you catch some Zs—"

"Like I could do that with you drivin' ninety kliks an hour? We had the wheels off the ground more than we had 'em *on*!"

"I thought you wanted to get back! That's what you told Hosteen Lox! *Very* rudely, I might add."

"I *did* have to get back! I've got a job—"

"You had the day off!"

"I've still gotta dance tonight."

"A call fixes that. Say you're sick—which you are.

152

Pollution's an illness, just like pneumonia."

'Bird's glare intensified as Stormy followed him in-side. He didn't need this—not when he was abso-lutely dead on his feet. Shoot, he could barely remember the code that summoned the elevator— and yawned in the middle of it—twice. Stormy leaned past him to say "Four." Clearly. In Cherokee.

"Jesus Christ, Stormy, don't you have a job to do?"

"My job's security," Stormy shot back. "And right now I choose to interpret that as the security of my best friend's peace of mind. Which means I'm gonna follow you into your apartment—*and* stuff you in the shower—*and* put you to bed if necessary. And I'm gonna sleep in front of your goddamn door if I have to—to keep you here!"

"I need to work."

"You *need* to sleep! I'll call 'Wounds and tell him you need another day off."

"He'll have my ass."

"He values your ass too much—or haven't you fig-ured that out yet?"

'Bird shrugged—and lost his balance as the ele-vator halted more roughly than usual. Stormy braced him. "Easy, kid!"

'Bird shook off the grip and stumped sullenly into the hallway, leaving Stormy to make his own way.

Somehow he got the door open. The room beyond was cool, though the sun was slashing beams of golden light across the the bare white wall behind him. Stormy joined him, as he made his way into the kitchen. "Hungry?" he called, from the refrig-erator door.

"I could eat," Stormy answered neutrally, skin-ning out of his serape and borrowed tunic. His boots followed. He flopped down on the sofa and stretched his toes luxuriously in the thick carpet.

"Pizza?"

"What kind?"

"Iguana and mushrooms."

"What kind of 'shrooms?"

"Not the kind Lox probably spiked that coffee with!"

Stormy rose and sauntered over to the wet bar. "Mind if I—?"

"Go for it."

Stormy peered at the selection. "Hmmm. Chambord? Nope, too sweet. Margaritas? Too weak the way you make 'em. That leaves Dos Equis and Dos Equis and—let's see—Dos Equis."

"I think you should have a Dos Equis."

Stormy selected a bottle and popped the cap. "On," he told 'Bird's TV, as he wandered back to the sofa. "Sports." A pause then: "Na Hollos won round one—oh, and you also seem to have a message or six."

'Bird padded out of the kitchen with two paper plates bearing slices of freshly nuked pizza. He set one on Stormy's bare belly. "*Six?* What *is* this shit!"

A startled yip and flurry of movement were Stormy's response. "Body phones don't reach as far as Lox's," he growled. "—Which you well know. 'Sides, you had yours turned off—which *I* well know."

One minute later, beer in one hand, pizza in the other, and both bare feet propped on the ottoman before his favorite leather chair, 'Bird confronted his television.

"Phone: On. Messages."

The screen shifted from the talking head that had commanded it to a vista of autumn mountains. A sequence of numbers superimposed themselves atop it. Two were the Aztlan Free Zone Police, Homicide

Unit. The other four were from Red Wounds, with notes that one came from his home, one from his limo, and two from his office. They'd been following him around like poor relations.

"Replay," 'Bird told it wearily.

A voice promptly spoke from a blank screen. "This is Captain Myllo of the Aztlan District Police. I was one of the officers who interrogated you this morning, and I, uh, hate to trouble you again, but . . . Well, we really need to ask you some more questions. If you haven't responded by eighteen hundred, we'll have to come looking for you."

There was another call, precisely an hour later, with exactly the same wording. Then came the first of Red Wounds's messages: " 'Bird, m'boy, sorry to bother you, but the Mounties have been about to drive me batty tryin' to get hold of you. Gimme a call when you wake up. I'll call 'em and tell 'em you've flatted out and not to bug you anymore. But you call *me* as soon as you can—and *that's* an order!"

The same message repeated two hours later. This time Red Wounds's face appeared, from his office. He looked tired—and irritable.

The third offered the speculation that 'Bird had either turned off both house and body phones or skipped town. Red Wounds had some interesting plans for his ass, should the latter be the case.

The fourth was half an hour old, and from the limo. Red Wounds's expression was exceedingly grim. "I need to talk to you. Call me whenever you can. Time doesn't matter." And that was all.

'Bird took a long swig of beer and lifted an eyebrow at Stormy. "What'd you think?"

"I think you need to call him. Then you need to shower. Then you need to crash—so *I* can shower and crash."

"I was afraid you'd say that."

Stormy tilted his head wryly.

"Phone. Call. Red Wounds." 'Bird told the TV. "No pix, my end."

An instant later a voice rumbled from the speakers. " *'Bird*? 'Bout bloody *time* you called! Where the hell've you been?" 'Bird could hear the metallic clatter of pots and pans being jiggled and surmised he'd caught his boss preparing dinner. He was, after all, a gourmet chef.

"Sorry," 'Bird mumbled, feeling the beer already taking hold. "Stormy took me off to decompress—beyond phone range."

"White of 'im."

Silence. Then: "So what's the deal with the Mounties?"

A pause, the sound of running water. "You alone?"

"Stormy's here."

"Good—since I'm sure you'll tell him this anyway."

"What?"

Another pause. "Well, the good news is that the Mounties found the guy that committed the murder. In fact, they brought him in just a couple of hours after they finished with you. Tracks practically led straight to him. And—"

"Where'd they find him?" Stormy broke in.

"Beach down past Sinsynsen. He had a blood-stained duffel bag with him."

"And let me guess. There was a human skin inside?"

'Bird could imagine Red Wounds shaking his head. " 'Fraid not, though the blood *was* human and matched our bare-boned John Doe. Which brings us to the other news."

"Which is?"

Red Wounds exhaled slowly. "This is gonna be a hard 'un, kid. They got the guy, no doubt about it. Besides the bag, his prints match those on the knife. Fiber evidence, ditto. Shoot, he still had the victim's blood and tissue under his fingernails!"

"Stupid," 'Bird muttered sleepily.

"No!" Red Wounds corrected. "Not stupid at all— but retarded. *Literally* retarded. The guy's got the mind of a child. They won't release his name, but he's well-known in one of those little shantytowns out past the border. Folks there say he's a real sweet guy, wouldn't hurt *anybody*. They say he's strong, but clumsy as an ox. I guess you can see where this is headin' . . . "

'Bird shook his head—a stupid gesture itself, since he had the video off. "I'm too fried to see *anything* just now."

"I bet you are," Red Wounds snorted. "But the point is that while this guy obviously *did* waylay some poor sot—they still haven't identified him, by the way, though they have some ideas—and while he obviously also skinned this guy alive, *there's no way on God's green earth he could've done it!* He's too—excuse me—dumb, to sneak up on somebody, even if he *was* coordinated enough, which report says he isn't. Which also means he's too uncoordinated to have ever flayed anybody as carefully as that man was."

"Hmmm," 'Bird grunted through a swallow. "Very interesting."

"How so?"

" 'Cause he didn't look stupid—retarded—whatever—to me! He had this air of . . . feral intensity, I suppose you could say. Like a cornered carnivore guardin' its kill."

"You tell the Mounties that?"

"More or less."

Silence.

"So, why do they wanta talk to me?"

"To identify the guy, for one thing—though you can do that by vid. But I gather there's a bunch more stuff they want to clarify."

"But it's basically a closed case, right?"

Another pause, during which 'Bird imagined Red Wounds gnawing his lip, which was his primary means of marking time while he pontificated. "Not quite," he sighed finally. Then: " 'Bird, can you keep a secret? Something that'll get my ass in a sling if it gets out?"

"Sure."

"Stormy?"

Stormy—who had been stuffing his face on the sofa—started. "Yeah, sure."

A deep breath. "Okay, 'Bird. I was told not to tell this, and I'm probably taking a risk by tellin' you, even though I know you're a straight shooter, but . . . this wasn't the first skinned body that's been found. The Mounties have done a fine job of hushin' it up, but they've been findin' flayed vagrants—and foreign tourists or construction-types—up and down the coast for the last two years. They won't tell me what the total is, but I gather it's well into double digits."

"Whew!" 'Bird whistled. Stormy strained forward intently. "First *I've* heard of this," he hissed softly.

"Good," Red Wounds retorted. "That means security's better than we'd thought. Unfortunately, that's only part of it."

"Oh?"

"Yeah, well, like I said, most victims have been vagrants or foreign construction personnel—people with nobody to miss 'em if they turn up dead, in other words. And most are still flagged as unsolved."

"And the rest?" Stormy prompted.

"The rest . . . Well, it's real weird, boys. They've all been a lot like this case: clear evidence, enough to convict—but the assailants have all been mentally deficient. Either that, or they've been children under the age of eleven. One was done by a nine-year-old girl! An orphan girl of *nine*! Same kind of obsidian knife and everything. None of the others had families, either."

"The unconnected offing the unconnected," 'Bird mumbled through the last of the pizza.

"Basically, yes," Red Wounds agreed. "But you can see why the Mounties want to keep a lid on it. This is supposed to be the best-policed city on earth. There's not supposed to be any need for crime in the Zone, and yet it keeps happenin'—here and nearby. And not just crime: *sensational* crime—the kind that makes bad international headlines, especially in light of all the talk about the revival of the old Aztec religion—Xipetotec, and all that. Though to be honest, they've seeded some of those rumors themselves, to throw people off the track."

"So who knows?"

"The Mounties, and not all of them. The chiefs of the various embassies, who've been charged with gently enforcing added security. Assorted ministers. The mayor."

"Lots of folks—for a secret."

"Most of 'em are reliable, though. Like I said, this has been goin' on nigh onto two years. And nothing's leaked even as far as Stormy, who's *in* security—so far."

'Bird drained his Dos Equis. "So, what does this mean in the real world?"

"It means that I'll call the Mounties and tell 'em,

very forcefully, that you're extremely stressed-out and fatigued, but will be in touch as soon as you're feelin' like yourself again, but probably not tonight. And it means that I'm tellin' you, right now, friend to friend, to be careful! Cover your ass at all times. And keep Mr. Cloud there with you as much as possible. I'd also avoid late-night strolls on the beach."

"Thanks," 'Bird yawned. "I mean, really. Enjoy your dinner. Sorry I interrupted."

"No problem. Just watch your ass!"

"Good-bye. And *wado*."

"Bye."

And with that, the talking head returned.

Stormy chugged the last of his beer and rose to retrieve another. "So what do you make of that?" he asked, as he sank down on the sofa again.

'Bird rose stiffly and slumped to the kitchen to deposit his plate and bottle. He poured himself a glass of water. But did not answer.

" 'Bird?"

'Bird spun around in place, glaring at his friend. "I don't know *what* it means! *Okay*? I know it's fuckin' weird, and that I'm fuckin' dead on my fuckin' feet, and that right now I don't know anything except that I'm gonna stand in the shower for my allotted five minutes, and wash the grunge of Hosteen John Lox's sweat lodge off. And then I'm goin' to bed and sleep until I wake up—and hope it's in time to make my set tonight."

Stormy looked up, startled. "Hey, man; *I'm* not your enemy!"

'Bird was truly wound up, however. "Yeah, well, I'm not sure about much of bloody anything right now! Shit, man, I wish I could just wash this out of my brain. The body, the sweat, that vision or whatever it was—and all that heavy crap 'Wounds just laid on me, all."

And with that, 'Bird strode from kitchen, through living room, to bedroom door, flinging off clothes as he progressed. Stormy retrieved them on the fly. By the time 'Bird made the bedroom proper, he was naked. "Twilight dim," he told the slanting windows above the futon. They obliged. Stormy studied him as he ducked into the bath, looking very uneasy. " 'Bird—I hate to do this to you now, but . . . we need to talk."

'Bird scowled at him from the door. "While I shower. That'll give you exactly five minutes."

"It may take longer."

"Seven—counting the drying. I've had my weekly shave."

Stormy grimaced, but followed 'Bird into the bath. 'Bird saw him as a collection of angles sprawled across the closed toilet seat. "We need to talk," Stormy repeated. "Specifically, we need to talk about . . . magic."

"We've already talked about magic," 'Bird snapped through the curtain, as a fine spray misted down upon him. It smelled of pines and mountain water.

"Not enough."

"So what d'you want to know?"

"Start with your basic attitude. Like, does it exist or not? Does it work?"

"Jesus Christ, man, I can barely stand up and you're askin' me shit like *that*?"

"Humor me."

"Okay then . . . well basically, it's like I said earlier. I was brought up to believe in it—in some of it, mostly the healing-type things. I've *maybe* seen a couple of things capable of magical interpretation. And I've heard of some stuff from my dad, and all;

mostly a cousin of his he swore was a shapechanger, who had a scale from a giant mythical serpent called an *uktena* that let him shift shape when he wanted. He supposedly knew someone who had an *ulunsuti*, too—that's a prophetic jewel from the head of an *uktena*. He'd had run-ins with a couple of so-called witches. That kinda stuff."

"And you've had medicine dreams, right?"

"Unfortunately."

"Not a thing to be denied."

"Except that as a cultural anthropologist, I'm therefore a scientist—and I'm also a diplomat, of sorts. Which means I've got to run interference between the world that was, and try to understand it, and retain the good things in it, but also try to help drag my people kickin' and screamin' into the twenty-first century."

"They've always been pretty adaptable," Stormy countered.

" 'Cept that it's the Hopis who are more traditional than anyone who turned the world upside down with their bloody *el-cheapo* solar cells."

"Not so *el-cheapo* if you happen to be a big rich western democracy."

"This is no time for idiot lecture, man."

"Fine. So, you were saying. About your people. About magic . . . "

"Uh, well, basically that I just want to do good by 'em—and I don't think it'd be doin' us any good if people thought we were all a bunch of superstitious—"

"You're lying, 'Bird," Stormy interrupted. "You don't know it yourself, but you're lying. The real reason—and look down in your heart and tell me this is wrong. The real reason is that you believe in magic, but you don't want to—'cause then the whole world'll come tumbling down around your ears. You're scared of it, man, both of the thing itself, because of what it *might* be able to do, and by implication."

The water had cycled through hot and was now pounding 'Bird's shoulders with creek-water cold. He could see swirls of sand sweeping around his feet toward the drain. He could think of no response to Stormy's assessment. The guy was right, dammit. He hated to admit it, but he was right.

"So is it a good thing, or a bad thing?" Stormy asked neutrally.

"I don't know," 'Bird yawned, as the shower shut off and warm air reached out to enfold him.

"I don't know," he repeated, to a thoughtfully silent Stormy thirty seconds later, as he flung himself naked across his futon.

Less than a minute later, he was snoring.

He slept for thirteen hours.

Chapter XV:
Resting in Peace

(PEORCI Infirmary—Aztlan,
Aztlan Free Zone—Mexico)
(Friday, September 2—late afternoon)

By 3:00 P.M. on Friday, Carolyn was certain she
had surrendered far more than the pound of flesh
Mr. Shakespeare had deemed expendable four-odd
centuries earlier. In fact, she suspected, it was more
like two or three—and counting. There'd been blood
samples, urine samples, stool samples, and saliva
samples. Her hair had been trimmed, her skin
abraded, and her nails pared. They'd stuck probes
in *down there* and snipped off bits of her bladder,
large and small intestines, ovaries, uterine wall, and
the egg that was preparing to implant itself on that
same organ's lining. They'd prowled in every opening on her head and had souvenirs to prove it, and
had even drilled a tiny hole in her skull to retrieve
a bit of brain, acquiring bone tissue in the bargain.
Liver they'd got through a slit in her side, ditto pancreas, spleen, and gall bladder. A similar incision in
her back had delivered tastes of kidney and adrenal
glands, as well as subcutaneous fat, and tubes down
her throat had produced stomach and lung tissue.
So far they'd spared her heart, for fear of traumatiz-

ing that willful organ whose timely thumping had, apparently, single-handedly summoned her back from whatever demideath she'd experienced the day before. Small comfort *that* was, for sure.

And the verdict was the same: evidence of preliminary necrosis in those areas farthest from the blood supply, but with the dead tissue overgrown by new, living cells that had been thrown up around it in an orgy of mitosis usually seen only in certain cancers. Nesheim had said to think of it as a building weakened to the point of collapse by an earthquake, suddenly shored up by a new and better construction on every side. The building itself was still ruined—but it scarcely mattered with improved replacements ready to hand.

Except that nobody knew what had triggered her body to build all those fine new cells.

Just like nobody knew why her IQ wasn't down there with the pumpkin.

Nesheim's best guess was that the sensors in her gill studs that overrode part of her autonomic nervous system, deadening the breathing instinct, for instance, had somehow (and definitely not by design) also overridden everything else and caused *all* available oxygenated blood to be shunted to her brain, keeping it supplied (perhaps pumped by spontaneous muscle contractions in her neck) until long after her heart had stopped beating.

Mary Hasegawa blamed it on bad equipment and sloppy diagnosis, and claimed Carolyn hadn't been dead at all, merely in very deep coma.

Her nurse, Juana Ornellas, said it was Mictlantecuhtli, god of death, looking out for someone whose time it was not to die.

Rudy fingered that morning's coffee, which, being strong enough to prevent anything from *living* in it, by analogy protected whatever dared ingest it from death.

The Jamaican who swept the floor knew that it was karma—*mon*.

Carolyn had no idea—though Rudy got the gold for cleverness. All she wanted was to conclude these blessed tests and get back into the field. They had more than enough of her to play with for a while (and it wasn't like she was going anywhere). But meanwhile, dolphin mutilations continued unstudied and unavenged, and countless others, maybe even Kat and Bo, were still at risk. Nobody had seen an orca for months, however.

On the other hand, there were gaps in the disc record—lots of them, as the review Rudy had insisted on had determined. Medical records were being checked for the last six months for patterns of reported dizziness, blackouts, nausea, etc. Hasegawa had promised to start interviewing staff with access to records and/or electronic recording equipment, and/or monitor duty (which was practically everyone) as soon as she quit worrying about Carolyn.

Carolyn wished she'd get on with it now. Not because she minded being worried about and fussed over, but because it was so wildly out of character for Ms. Inscrutable of 2024 suddenly to manifest mothering instincts that Carolyn didn't know how to react. It was, to her way of thinking, at least as aberrant as Carolyn's condition—yet nobody was bugging *Hassie* once an hour for blood.

And, by the pattern of footsteps on the corridor outside, here came the vampires now. Carolyn turned her gaze relentlessly toward the bedside TV, which had been broadcasting the Toli World Championships all afternoon. (It was a southeastern Indian game involving two sticks, a leather-covered ball, poles for goals, and a high tolerance for mayhem. It was also similar enough to the hurling played in Eire to hold her attention. Kev had played hurling a time or two, and . . . Well, it *was* an American Indian game, and there *had* been that Indian . . .)

" . . . not *my* fault the slide was ruined," came the voice of a young woman Carolyn didn't recognize. The footsteps halted just upcorridor from her door.

"Good, then *you* can explain why we need to take more samples!"

A snort followed.

It was seen and raised.

The challenger folded.

Dr. Nesheim peered cautiously into the room, like a man fearing sniper fire. Carolyn saw his expression shift from irritation to pleasantly bland interest.

"Hello, Doctor!" Carolyn called with cheery sarcasm, preempting him with his mouth poised on the verge of opening. "It's been a whole hour since you went pickpocketing in my pancreas. So what'll it be this time? Eyelashes? Tooth enamel? *Belly button lint*?"

Nesheim wavered between a frown and a grin. He settled on the latter. "Stomach lining—again. And while we're at it, we'd like to get a tad more lung tissue."

"Two tubes for the price of one, eh?"

"That's about the size of it."

"It's the *size* of it that concerns me!"

Nesheim flicked off the TV just as someone named Lacefield scored. "You know perfectly well it's painless. Just close your eyes, and five minutes from now it'll all be over."

Carolyn's response—to her own surprise—was to bare her teeth and growl.

"Where did *that* come from?" Nesheim laughed

nervously, as he eased around behind her head and pushed the button that stretched her bed flat.

"From my lizard brain, I guess," Carolyn grumbled.

"Gosh, we haven't sampled *that* yet," he sighed. "Now close your eyes and relax. It'll be exactly like before."

Yeah, sure, Carolyn thought grimly. *Just like before.* Just like before was an electrode pressed against a bare patch on her scalp, that deadened sensation in her esophagus and trachea, along with the gag reflex. Make that *was supposed* to deaden them. They hadn't last time, and it had taken all the willpower she could muster not to have a spasm right there on the bed. Nesheim had doubled the power of the inductor (which put it just below maximum safe), and that had done the trick—barely.

Either that, or she'd let herself be distracted by a sudden bout of itching that had nearly driven her mad—as though the annual convention of the virulent local mosquitoes had convened on her skin, concluded she was the banquet, and chowed down. It had faded as soon as Nesheim had withdrawn the inductor, from which she'd divined it was some sort of bizarre electro-neuro side effect. But it had continued, in erratic spurts, right through the night.

And as if by magic, there it was now—not as bad as before, but waiting, as though the mosquitoes hovered but had not yet made landfall. And then she was distracted by gentle hands urging her lips apart while something slid into her throat. She gagged, then felt her tongue and throat go numb. "Doctor, you're over max," she thought she heard someone whisper, but it was hard to be sure, what with the volume of breathing she was suddenly picking up. Funny, how having your own tampered with made you so much more aware of everyone else's. Funnier still how a stick of metal stuck against your skull could trick your brain into playing games with your bod.

And there was the itching, but distant, distant . . . like smoldering embers waiting to erupt once more into flame.

And another whisper. "It's my only choice, if we're going to put her out." Then, louder: "Cary, don't fight it. I'm having to give you too much induct. Just think about something else."

Something else . . .

But *what* else?

What . . . ?

Abruptly, she was floating. Part of her knew she shouldn't be, knew that what was essentially an outpatient operation under light neural de-stimulation shouldn't have put her out like this—not when she'd been wide awake and raring for a fight mere minutes before.

But here she was . . .

Nesheim was nowhere. The nurse was nowhere. *She* was nowhere—or going there fast. For a moment, she feared she was dying again. Only that had been sudden: a blow to the head, then nothing until she'd reawakened to the sound of her own heart in "Why?" 's medical lab.

This wasn't like that, though. It was like floating—or drifting—or maybe like a leaf settling to the bottom of a crystal-clear pool. She kind of liked that image. She wondered, though, what kind of leaf she was. Perhaps hazel, since Col the Hazel was one of the most valued things of mythical Eireland in the tales her mom had told her and Kev. And if she was a hazel leaf drifting down through a pond, then she might encounter some of the others: the Salmon of Wisdom, say, or Grian the Sun.

The sun . . .

She hadn't seen the sun in over a day—her real self hadn't. And with that realization, she ceased settling and began to rise, following the golden beams she sensed lancing through the . . . water, or whatever it was she dwelt in.

Brighter, and brighter, and then . . .

. . . Full light, and blue skies tumbling with spun silver clouds. A beach, the sand coarse and tan. Rocks like the toy blocks of some nameless child of the Fomor, the giants her mother said had once dwelt beneath the seas to the west. And earth: soft earth, rising in low hills covered with grass softer than ancient velvet. Flowers grew in it, blue and purple and white. Hazel trees made a screen around a glade halfway between the crest of the slope and the barren strand. A downward glance showed footprints.

Another woman's, she concluded. Probably *that* woman—as she noted a slender form picking her way toward what was surely a narrow arm of the sea. Almost she recognized that place; almost she could give it a name. But something told her names were not important here, that only seeing was. And . . . *knowing* with the deep wisdom—like that of the salmon.

The woman was beautiful, though, and familiar: slim and middle-tall, with thick red hair to her shoulders and a face all creamy skin and well-cut bones. The eyes, though she could not see them, were as green as the short, sleeveless dress that woman wore as she pranced barefoot across the grass toward the sea.

Mother. Not a name, but a title, and therefore sacred.

Mother . . .

Her mother slowed as she approached a looming grey boulder as tall as she. Carolyn eased closer, only vaguely aware when the sharp grit of the sand shifted to the damp-edged softness of grass. She moved as though weightless, as though she were the leaf she had lately been.

Her mother called out something and laughed. And as that sound rang joyfully off the stone, a young man stepped from behind it. Naked as the day he was born, he was, sleekly wet and gleaming. Short and slight, but with good shoulders and well-cut muscles, and a flag of dark hair plastering his milk white flesh halfway down his back. Sixteen, perhaps, or a year to either side. Young enough to have more curves than angles in his face and no lines she could detect as she drew nearer; old enough to have eyes as grim as his dimpled cheeks and full red lips were merry. Young enough, as well, to display his manhood as though it were a wondrous ornament newly won which he was proud to possess and flaunt; and old enough to wear his body as though he knew exactly what every nerve and bone and sinew could do, for how long, how well, and how often.

He spoke, but Carolyn missed the words, though her mother laughed, and the boy laughed too, and with that his dimples deepened. Silence fell between them, then, yet not silence, for the looks that passed between them as their gazes danced and dazzled were epic as poetry. Slowly, her mother lifted a hand and touched the boy's shining flesh, gently, just above his heart, at the hollow from which the strength of his chest flowed out in broad flat mounds

and soft-edged angles. Fingertips only, she slid it
down . . . pausing at the slit of his navel, then moving on. He murmured something. (Carolyn eased
even closer, yet still could not hear.) Another
laugh—a shy chuckle that could have been either of
them—and the boy took the hand that hovered
above his supple member and raised it to his lips.

The kiss that followed was electric. Carolyn felt it
as her mother felt it (or perhaps she *was* her mother
now, and they felt that soft damp nibble as one). And
then the boy smiled shyly and lowered the hand to
her side—then reached out and undid the top button
on her dress. The second followed, and the third.
With the fourth, the garment slipped to the ground,
leaving her as naked as her partner. Carolyn felt the
brush of cool wind against her bare skin in unexpected places, the tingle of spray from the more persistent breakers, the softness of the grass, the
warmth of the boy's breath as he leaned forward to
touch his lips to the juncture of neck and shoulder.

And then, so subtly she was not sure when contact
was made, his hands cupped around her waist. Very
slowly, oh so very slowly, they slid upward, and she
knew he was going to touch her breasts an ecstati-
cally long time before he did; and that prolonged anticipation was at least equal to the actuality, as his
hands crept ever closer first to the outer curve, then
around their silk-smooth masses, and finally, with
thumbs and forefingers, to her nipples. She shuddered at that, and moaned softly, and before she
knew it, was reaching to clasp his waist (firm and
smooth and barely damp now), and to send her
hands questing, less expertly, across equivalent terrain to that he had lately conquered. He closed his
eyes; tensed and shivered like a luxuriating cat as
her hands stroked his sides and his chest and like-

wise found his nipples. She bent to kiss them, and as she did, something brushed her thigh, something stiff and warm and insistent, that probed and nuzzled and prodded ever higher.

I have a husband, she recalled abruptly. *I have a child.*

I will never love a man as beautiful as this for the rest of my life. He is like one of the sidhe. *He is like—*

"Not the *sidhe*," a voice soft as thought murmured in her ear. And then, with the slow sure force of the sea, he drew her to him.

For a long time they stood there, locked together, as hands found new mysteries and explored them all. He never kissed her again, not on the lips. But eventually he laid her down on a carpet of grass surrounded by hazel, and what followed was the stuff of legends—or of dreams.

I have a husband, she recalled once more, as he entered her with the inevitable surety of a glacier filling a valley.

He would forgive me this, if he could ever know its like. Already I know things about my body I could never have suspected. Things I will remember and show him, and so delight him anew.

And then ecstasy found guilt's hiding place and drowned it with sweet wine, utterly.

The sun had been high in the sky when they joined. When they broke apart at last, it was westering. The breeze had softened, but still bore warmth, and the clouds had cleared. The sun beat down on his white flesh and her ivory. With his breath sweet against her shoulder and her arms tangled in his hair, she slept.

When she awakened, the breath that warmed her flesh and tickled the tiny hairs on her skin was

warmer, and with it came a faint animal musk, min-
gled with the scent of the sea. And the fingers that
had lost themselves in thick dark hair now brushed
something very like plush or . . . fur.

And yet that did not seem curious, though she let
her lids drift open.

And did not find it at all remarkable that the boy
who had lain so long and wonderfully in her arms
was gone, or that precisely in his place sprawled a
sleek grey seal. It was watching her, with black eyes
deep as the caves beneath the sea. She did not move,
was content to lie and remember. Its whiskers
twitched, and its lips curled (—*why was she not
shocked? Why was she not frightened?*—), and,
very softly, very slowly, it spoke, in a voice like dry
sand abrading ancient boulders. *"You are the Road
to the Way."*

Carolyn started—and at once was no longer her
mother, but was looking down at her mother from
her own height. The seal followed her with its gaze,
as though it had watched while she withdrew. And
then, when she was certain she was totally separate
because she could see her feet, there by her mother's
drowsing head, it spoke again, this time to her. *"And
you are the one the dolphins worship."*

And as Carolyn Mauney-Griffith stood gaping, the
seal slipped from within her mother's arms and
made its awkward way to the sea.

Her eyes misted. She looked back down at her
mother, who dozed again, and then she could look
no longer. Her eyes burned—and, somewhere at vast
remove, her skin itched. She tried to knuckle away
the tears, but when she lifted her lids again, it was
upon a square of golden sunlight dancing across the
stuffed seal Rudy had brought her earlier that day,
with apologies for its not being a dolphin.

She smiled at that, and tried to recall that marvelous dream, that had already drifted away like smoke, leaving only a lingering haze of delicate eroticism. She was sweating, she realized, and a warm dampness between her legs spoke well of what she'd dreamed.

Her smile widened, and she scratched absently at a particularly violent itch along her side. But when she moved her hand, her fingers felt odd. Sticky, rather. She raised them curiously—and was shocked to see them crimson with blood, and with shreds of skin hanging from the nails.

That brought her straight up in bed—whereupon she discovered to her horror that she had clawed whole sections of her arms, belly, sides, and thighs raw. Red weals showed across her tan flesh, but the burning—similar to that which had afflicted her so suddenly yesterday—was rapidly subsiding.

Which was all she needed. Probably it was a side effect of the inductor—or of one or the other pills or potions they'd pumped into her. Or maybe it was simply stress. Yeah, that was it: stress rash gone wild, and fertilized to excess with neurochemicals. The problem now was how to keep Nesheim or one of his acolytes from noticing and digging up more esoterica to test her for.

She was still puzzling over that, alternating with trying to reconstruct even the tiniest bits of that wonderful dream, when the door opened and The Man Himself poked his head in. He squinted abruptly, and Carolyn breathed a brief thanks to the Irish sun god, Lugh, or Huitzilopochtli, his Aztec equivalent, that her sometime-tormentor was gazing right into the sun and couldn't see these latest injuries.

The squinting continued for maybe five seconds,

then shifted to an uncertain scowl. *"Cary?* You're not supposed to be conscious."

"Fooled you."

A grim chuckle. "Just like I fooled you."

"How so?"

"We needed to do some brain stuff, and it just seemed easiest to put you under for that while we were numbing you out for the other."

"Asshole."

"Probably. One thing though—seriously. Just an observation."

"What?"

"It took a hell of a lot to get you out. In fact, it's taking a hell of a lot of everything to have any effect on you. Not your fault," he added. "Just curious. You must have a hell of a will to live. Or an endocrine system from Mars."

"Maybe I *do*!" Carolyn snapped. "Or maybe I'm just hot to get the hell out of here."

Nesheim's face clouded. "As to that—I'd really like to keep you at least one more day."

"You wish."

Silence, while she glared at him, and his expression tried a number of alternatives before settling on noncommittal bland. "Oh well," he sighed finally, as he first cocked his head as though listening, then pressed a spot right below his collarbone. "It's just as well, I guess. You seem to have a . . . visitor."

Chapter XVI:
The Great Escape

(PEORCI Infirmary—Aztlan,
Aztlan Free Zone—Mexico)
(Friday, September 2—early evening)

"Jesus Christ, Cary!" Kevin gasped into the phone at the PEORCI Infirmary's reception desk. "What the hell are you doin' in the *hospital*?"

They were the first words he'd said to her in three years.

"Trying to get out," his sister shot back so vehemently he hopped away from the viewer. From what he could see of her room, he didn't blame her: not if the masses of equipment clumped around her bed were any indication. Cary hated hospitals—not because of any fear of pain or needles, but because when you were in one you were no longer in control of yourself. Your time—your very body—was not your own. And to a control freak like Cary, that was anathema.

At least she looked okay—though he wasn't sure he liked her hair that short. Had it really been three years since he'd seen her? Three years since the Schism? Yet except for the haircut and a touch more tan, she looked precisely the same.

She even sported the same expression she'd worn

when they'd parted: scarce-suppressed anger. But this time that barely leashed fury was not focused on him. He hoped.

"Yeah, well, it's what put you *in* that I'm concerned about," he confided. "Nobody out here'll tell me shit!"

"I'd rather tell you in person."

"It serious?"

A wry half smile told him frustration had, for the nonce, bridged the Schism. "Either so serious it's *not* serious, or nothing at all; the jury's still out—as is a fair bit of me at the moment. Snips and bits only, lest you fear the worst," she added, with stinging sarcasm—toward someone out of visual range of the phone, he suspected.

"And they won't let you out?"

"I'm working on that—" whereupon she spared another glare at the nameless Somebody. "Where are you, anyway?"

"In the lobby. They won't let me in to see you. In fact, I had a devil of a time getting *this* far. Fortunately the security guy who came when I threatened that smartass box at your gate reads."

"You came from Eire?"

"You got it."

"When'd you get in?"

"An hour ago, more or less."

"Why?"

"To see you."

"Why?"

" 'Cause I had reason to. More than that . . . well, to use your excellent phrase, I'd rather tell you in person—and in private."

Carolyn gnawed her lip. "We would seem to have a problem."

"I'd say so," Kevin agreed carefully.

"You look frazzled—worse than I do, in fact. What happened to your cheek?"

Kevin touched the shrapnel wound, newly sheened with Spraskin. He chuckled grimly. "It's been a tough couple of days. And I've spent the last one and a bit tryin' to get here. When I left for the airport—which I did *not* do from home—they were lettin' planes out. Then the hurricane shifted, and they *weren't*, and I had to sit in the lobby at Shannon all night. And somewhere in there half the power in Eire went out and I had a devil of a time accessin' my accounts to even *get* a ticket, never mind spendin' money. Shoot, *you* know how it is. Half the country's on fiber optics and photocells, the rest still runs on tubes and wires—and burnin' peat moss."

A sage nod. "It's *well* I know that, lad."

"And that's not even countin' the trouble I had findin' you. You weren't at home, and your house phone didn't know where to connect me. I thought everybody here had one of those implant-tattoo things."

"They've got a limited range. And salt water screws 'em up—or prolonged exposure does. I can't wear one."

"Which isn't gettin' you outta here."

Another nod. "Which isn't getting me out of here."

Silence, while Carolyn snipped at that unseen Someone again.

Kevin massaged his neck. *Lord*, he was tired; transatlantic flights did that to him, and now he had to live the day over. The only obvious advantage was that time and fatigue blurred that awful image that had dogged him since yesterday in Leenane: Fir, his could-be-friend, lying dead by the side of the sea, his face shattered, his body shifting to that of a seal.

Cryptic words leaking from his lips along with his life . . .

"You appear healthy enough," Kevin observed when Cary once more faced him. "Is there a particular reason they want you to hang around?"

"Pound of flesh, Kev. Many, many pounds of flesh. I think they've found a new species of squid that only eats human flesh and are using me as donor."

"You don't have any to spare."

"True. But seriously, they swore they'd let me out this evening, but keep coming up with reasons not to"—she shot a glare at Whoever It Was—"like, just now they put me under without telling me, and when I woke up sooner than I was supposed to, they decided that was grounds for *more* pokes and prods."

Kevin started to reply, then noted a stocky Oriental woman bustling down the corridor. She seemed vaguely familiar. Then he had it: Mary Hasegawa. Cary had worked for her back in Monaco. Before the Schism.

The woman paused, staring at him as though he were a magic creature himself—which, as a novelist, he in a sense was. "Oh," she burst out. "Kevin!"

"And you're Dr. Hasegawa, as I recall."

"I am."

Kevin nodded toward the screen. "So . . . what's wrong with her?"

A narrow-eyed scowl, as composure returned. "She didn't tell you?"

"I—"

"Tell her she *promised*, Kev," Carolyn's image broke in. "Tell her we made a bargain."

Kevin didn't know how to react.

"Tell her you're a frigging poet and will write a satire about her! That used to work even against *kings* back home."

Hasegawa opened her mouth—

"Never mind!" Carolyn snapped abruptly. "Phone off." Whereupon the screen went blank. Kevin flopped against the wall. "Oughta be about a minute," he informed his companion, with a smirk.

"Until what?"

"That was her 'Enough of this shit' tone. Woe betide anyone who gets in her way now."

"You don't mean—"

"Oh yes, I absolutely do! Look, here she comes."

And it was true. For striding down a corridor to his left, with nigh on a dozen frantic medical types in tow, came his sister.

Small she might have been, but so was black plague bacillus, and she was cutting a swath through the assembling bureaucracy like that which had decimated Europe all those years ago. Dressed in a hospital gown, she likewise was, but she was a Celt, and Celts ran naked into battle. Boudicca of the Iceni had been praised for her great white arms; Cary's were thin and tanned, yet none seemed like to stand before her. He grinned as she pressed onward. Only with difficulty did he remember that they were supposed to be pissed at each other.

She had outstripped her detainers now, and the rumble of their protests rode the wave of her fury ahead of her. She was in high dudgeon: the anger he called her warp-spasm, so much did it remind him of Cuchulain's mythical rages.

"You can release me, or you can fire me," she told Hasegawa when she gained the lobby proper. "Either way, I'm not staying here a minute longer. You guys play Frankenstein with what you've got. Recalibrate your machines, and then—*maybe*—I'll come back like the good girl you want me to be. But meanwhile there's a whole ocean full of cetaceans at risk out there, which nobody but me seems concerned about, and I'll go out in a rowboat if necessary to find out what's going on! I feel better than I have in . . . centuries. And my brother, with whom I'm officially incommunicado, has just turned up in the lee of a *hurricane*, for no reason he's yet been allowed privacy to explain!"

"Way to go!" Kevin cheered.

"Way to go!" another male voice echoed. Kevin turned to see a slender Hispanic youth standing behind him. Unlike most of the folks about, he was casually dressed—in pink tank top, white shorts, and gold sneakers. Off duty, perhaps? The fellow smiled as Kevin caught his eye, then did a double take.

"You're Cary's brother! The famous one!"

"So it appears."

The gaze crept upward. "Like the hair!"

Kevin smiled back. He'd wondered how what passed for cutting edge in backwater Eire would play in red-hot Aztlan. The place was supposed to be the tech capital of the western hemisphere, built by the OAS and a consortium of megacorps to put the Fear of God into Nippon, Inc., and Euro, Ltd. But the folks he'd observed in the airport seemed to practice a more conservative aesthetic than he'd expected. Young most of 'em may have been; but baggy comfort instead of flash marked Aztlan's prevailing style. He'd seen exactly one person with jewel-toned locks, and no one with an electric blue blaze.

On the other hand, as this lad had noted, *he* was famous.

"Now see here, Cary!" someone—her doctor, probably, to judge by his lab coat and stethoscope—was protesting. "You can't just—"

"It's a free country, I'm a free person, and if I have

to I'll—I'll claim political asylum and defect!"

"But the tests! We have no idea—"

"You've had time to come up with plenty of ideas," Carolyn shot back, "precious few of which you've deigned to share with me—to whom, let me assure you, it's of more interest than you might imagine. But we've dealt with the death thing, okay? And that's a *maybe* thing, and it's over. I'm alive now, and intend to prove it by example."

The doctor—Nesheim was the name on his badge—glanced imploringly at Hasegawa.

The woman gnawed her lip. "I promised her." Then, to Carolyn: "I promised, and I suppose I'd best hold up my end. But Cary, do *try* to cooperate. How about we strike another compromise?"

Carolyn eyed her suspiciously. "What kind of compromise?"

"You work half a day on the mutilations, and then we work half a day on you."

Carolyn shook her head. "Three days for me, one for you."

"Two and one."

"There's room to negotiate."

Kevin's stomach growled ominously. "Is it possible," he inserted with a facility that surprised him, "that this diplomacy could be conducted over dinner? I've not had a good meal in two days. I'm sick of airports that have no planes, teller machines that have no cash, and phones that connect you to static or stressed-out schoolgirls. Since I seem to be here in Disneyland South, I'd as soon enjoy it. A spoonful of sugar, and all that."

Carolyn lifted an eyebrow delicately. "You've got medicine for me?"

"I've got . . . information for you."

"Well," Hasegawa sighed resignedly. "Since negotiations seem to be derailed, I suppose I'd best make the best of the situation. Very well: Dr. Nesheim, I request that you release Carolyn to either me or her brother here. I swear I'll return her as soon as I can. In the meantime—"

"Food," Kevin and Carolyn chorused as one. "Lots and lots of food!"

"Food," the young man beside him chimed in. "Yeah, that sounds good—and a night on the town. *Con mucha cerveza*," he added—possibly for Kevin's benefit, since his US-style English was excellent.

Carolyn scowled. "I'd hoped to get out to the boat."

Kevin gaped. "But we need to talk—"

"We can talk there. Unlike you, my job allows me to do two things at once—occasionally three."

Hasegawa shook her head. "Sorry, but no. You can quit if you want, but you need to decompress away from all this." She eyed Kevin skeptically. "You too, by the looks of you."

"I know just the place," the youth enthused.

Hasegawa eyed him coldly. "I don't remember that you were party to the negotiations, Rudy."

"It's typical to have a neutral observer."

"You're hardly neutral."

The youth—Rudy?—eyed Carolyn wistfully. "How 'bout if I pay?" Kevin wondered suddenly if the lad was sweet on his sis. He appeared a year or two younger, but with a smile like that, he imagined she'd find him hard to resist. Besides, Dad had been younger than Mom.

"Done deal," Hasegawa conceded, then turned back to Carolyn. "I'm willing to sign you out, but only on the condition that I keep tabs on you until you're safely home. After that—I *suppose* I can rely on your brother."

"I'm very reliable," Kevin agreed instantly.

"You are not!" Carolyn teased.

"What's this place you were talking about?" Hasegawa asked sullenly, glaring at the smirking Rudy.

"It's one of those ethnic clubs down in Sinsynsen."

"Sinsynsen?" From Kevin.

"A fringe district that's part of the Zone, but not part of the City," Carolyn supplied. "It's from synthesis, sensation—and sin, though they keep close tabs on the latter."

"This place have a name?" Hasegawa persisted.

"The Medicine Wheel," Rudy supplied. "Shall I give you a hand with those forms?"

Hasegawa glared at him. Nesheim threw up his hands and stalked away. Carolyn and Kevin exploded in laughter. It had been a long time since they'd done that, Kevin realized, far too long. Abruptly, he reached out to his sister and hugged her. She hugged back. "I need to clean up and change," she whispered, as she pushed away. "Back in a flash."

Kevin could only stare, first at his sister's departing back, then, in bemused resignation, at Hasegawa and Rudy. Hasegawa scowled and followed Carolyn. Rudy gnawed his lip contritely. Kevin raised an eyebrow, and extended a hand. "We haven't met yet—officially—though you seem to know who *I* am."

"Couldn't miss you," the fellow admitted, taking the hand in a friendly grasp. "I'm Rudy Ramirez."

"Mexico?"

"Madrid, by way of Miami."

"You work with my sis?"

"Kind of. Actually, we both work for Hasegawa. Cary does real research; I've got an MS in marine bi. from Miami, but was hired as a photographer. I also troubleshoot electronics—which the environment around here requires more of than you might think. Oh, and I seem to have become official driver; I dive occasionally. And I do monitor duty, like everybody else."

"You seem to be . . . fond of her."

A shrug. "She's real—single-minded, but real."

"You've got *that* right," Kevin acknowledged, peering speculatively down the corridor. "It's none of my business anyway," he continued. "If she likes you, I'm cool."

"Warm, I'd say," Ramirez chuckled.

"Huh?"

"You're not exactly dressed for the climate."

Kevin glanced down at his borrowed traveling togs: dark cords, gray loose-knit sweater worn over a button-down shirt of extremely old-fashioned cut—rejects all, from McMillan-the-Younger's days at boarding school. The gaudier selections were in his duffel bag, also borrowed. "I . . . left in a hurry, in the rain. It's thirty degrees cooler there than here."

Ramirez puffed his cheeks, then eyed Kevin up and down. "You're about my size. Wait here a sec, I think I can help." And with that he darted through the glass outer doors, to return an instant later with a pile of clothing. Earth tones, Kevin noted. Soft fabrics, loose weaves. Oh well, when in Rome . . . or Aztlan . . .

"Just the thing for a night on the town," Ramirez confided. "And if you hurry, you might still beat your sis."

Kevin took the clothing, located a loo, and began to change. Jesus, but things were happening fast. Not what he'd expected at all. He'd spent most of the flight—shoot, most of the last day-and-something trying to decide exactly how to tell Cary about the

selkie and its cryptic message. He'd rehearsed a
dozen conversations, a score of opening lines depending on how he read her mood. In some he got
right to the point, in others he beat around the bush.
In this one he alluded to the Schism, in that one he
ignored it.

What he had *not* counted on was chaos on Cary's
end. He didn't like chaos, was the original linear
thinker, at his best in solitary one-on-ones. Parties
were fine, but not for revelations of the sort he had
to make. And nobody seemed to have noticed that
he *did* have something important to say—which
meant God only knew when he'd get a chance to talk
to Cary solo. Not at dinner—not likely. So hopefully
afterward, either at her place, if she invited him, or
the hotel he'd booked if she didn't. It was nearly
seven now, the watch in his head informed him,
when he thought at it. Revelation seemed unlikely
before ten or eleven—assuming he could make it
that long, tired as he was.

Sighing, he sealed his boots, then peered speculatively at the blue blaze in his hair, which, though
fading, still showed embarrassingly bright. Ramirez
had been right about the clothes, though: the stuff
was comfortable. The baggy off-white pants were no
different from the ones back home, save that they
closed with hand-sized Velcro triangles instead of
drawstrings, though the color would have drawn
mud like flies in most of Eire. And once he got it on,
the tan tunic (basically a pair of inverted trapezoids
with a slitted neck hole in the front half) felt similar
to the sleeved Eirish type as well. Upon consideration, he decided the main difference, stylewise, was
that here folks wore their tunics unbelted, to fall in
soft folds just past the crotch and elbows, screening
the upper arms from a sun he imagined could be

pretty virulent. But the loose weave and open arm-pits and hem allowed maximum access to whatever breezes happened by, thereby providing relief from the heat. With all those reflective glass buildings around, that had to be a major consideration. He wondered what the place would do without air-conditioning.

Hasegawa had rejoined Rudy when he returned to the lobby, having swapped her corporate smock for a tunic similar to his, but in grayed-green instead of tan. She seemed marginally less harried—or more resigned. Even as he started to greet her, he saw Carolyn jogging down the corridor.

She looked much better than before, solely be-cause of the combination of shower and antici-pation, since he knew for a fact she loathed makeup. She too was dressed much as he, save that she wore her pants above sandals, and her tunic was stark white, longer of tail, and shorter of "sleeve."

"Lookin' good," Kevin told her.

"You too."

Ramirez, who'd begun to fidget, edged toward the door, then froze. "Who's driving?" he asked. "I'm on my bike."

"I can," Carolyn volunteered instantly.

"You cannot!" Hasegawa shot back. "I absolutely forbid it—besides, it's a half-klik hike."

"And only a two-seater," Rudy noted. "Dr. Hase-gawa?"

"Mine's still charging. I didn't expect to have to—"

"Fine," Kevin interrupted. "We can take my rental car." He steered them toward the sleek gold Ford Auriga sedan he'd chosen at the airport.

"Nice," Rudy observed appreciatively, as he stepped toward the back door.

"Glad you like it," Kevin replied. "In fact—*you* drive. Cary and me'll take her car—assuming you don't mind if I drive it," he added, looking as much at Hasegawa as at his sister. "That way we can get a little time alone. You can drop us off there, Rudy. We'll follow."

"I give up," Hasegawa muttered. "Sure."

Carolyn shot him a sharp glance but nodded as well. "If it's gonna be like old times—I guess it really *should* be like old times. What's mine is yours and vice versa."

"Except for opinions," Kevin murmured, as he showed her into the back of the Auriga. "But I promise not to get into that unless I have to."

"That's a hell of a view," Kevin observed ten minutes later, nodding to the right as he urged the MX-Z up to speed on the Aztlan beltway.

"I've always thought so," Carolyn agreed. "That big gold pile's the OAS pyramid—it's an exact copy of the Pyramid of the Sun at Teotihuacán, except that it's faced entirely with mirror-glass. And those lower green and silver ones on this side are the Canadian and US complexes—*they're* clones of the Pyramid of the Moon. Oh, and the blood red job just coming into view behind OAS is Mexico's, and beyond *it*, Brazil's and Peru's."

"I'm impressed," Kevin said—and was.

"I thought you would be," Carolyn chuckled, "given your fondness for monumental architecture."

Kevin shot her a good-natured glare.

"So what's the deal?" she continued seriously. They had just passed the solar-powered desalinization/hydrogen cracking facility to the left, and were closing hard on the Ministry of Trade.

"I was just going to ask you the same question,"

he chuckled—to mask a sudden case of nerves. Was now the time? he wondered. Would there be time to even get started on *his* stuff?

"It . . . strains credibility," Carolyn sighed, settling back in her seat.

"So does mine."

"Why am I not surprised?"

"When did yours begin?"

"Yesterday morning, our time."

Kevin thought for a moment. "Which would have been yesterday afternoon my time. Which means mine's been going on longer, which means it'll probably take longer to set out right."

"Which means I go first," Carolyn concluded. "Though be warned, this is just the short form."

And for the next fifteen minutes, she talked. They were nearing the Sinsynsen exit when she finished.

"So what do you think?" she prompted.

Kevin exhaled slowly. "I don't know *what* to think. I'm not up on the nuances of science—or medicine, given that I've spent exactly one night in the hospital in my life. What do *you* think?"

Carolyn looked at him squarely. "Stress," she said flatly. "Stress of worrying about the dolphin mutilations, coupled with the stress of the attack equals mondo will to live. That's what makes most sense to me. People have been known to perform extraordinary feats when sufficiently frightened or angry. I've even got secondary symptoms: stress rash, and all that."

Silence.

"Your turn."

"How long do we have?"

"Five minutes?"

"No time, then. And there really is no short form."

"Hint?"

Kevin took a very deep breath. "Magic," he whispered at last. "What do you think of magic?"

Carolyn shifted her gaze to stare out the window. "You're not being silly, are you?"

"No."

A long pause. Then: "I believe that there exist phenomena that, by the standards of our present knowledge, it is convenient to ascribe to what in the past has been termed magic. But I also believe that the universe is ultimately explicable. That if magic exists, it's explainable by natural law—undiscovered law, perhaps, but natural law."

Silence.

"What do *you* think?" she asked eventually.

Intent on following Ramirez through a particularly intricate tangle of traffic, he did not respond immediately. Only when he had locked in behind the Auriga in the exit lane did he reply.

"I don't know, either," he admitted. "I believe there's a need for wonder and the unexplained in the universe. Which I guess means that I'd *like* to believe in magic. But—"

"You don't need *magic* for that," Carolyn broke in. "For everything science explains, it reveals another mystery. Like this project I'm working on— the dolphin mutilations. Just when we thought we knew everything about cetacean behavior—or at least that there were no new phenomena to observe—bang—out of the blue comes this spate of mutilations that are completely unprecedented, so far as we can tell, in history."

"So are seasonal hurricanes in Eire," Kevin countered, as he took the exit Ramirez had signaled, and swung the car in a tight loop—which the Auriga appeared to handle as easily as the smaller car.

"We've a small sample to base that assumption

on," Carolyn replied. "We don't know what the weather was like there ten thousand years ago, not specifically enough to preclude the existence of seasonal hurricanes."

"We don't know that orcas didn't bite the foreheads out of dolphins, either!"

"We have precedent."

"We also have okapis and mountain gorillas, neither of which were known to white men until early last century. Or sasquatches, for that matter, early in *this*."

"And we have now arrived," Carolyn observed, with relief. "I guess your big stuff'll have to wait until later."

"I guess it will," Kevin grumbled, as he swung the car into a parking lot beside a sloping sandcrete wall, atop which a steep-roofed building closely resembled a larger version of some reconstructed Iron Age houses he'd seen back in Eire—save that these sported Hopi panels.

"Later, then," he sighed. "I promise. And I know what promises mean to you."

"Magic," Carolyn mused aloud. "I wonder what *that* was leading up to."

And with that she took his hand, and followed the rest of the party inside.

Chapter XVII:
Something Fishy This Way Comes

(Kituwah Embassy—Aztlan,
Aztlan Free Zone—Mexico)
(Friday, September 2—early evening)

. . . drifting . . .

. . . or floating: he does not know *what* means it is by which he moves along. The single certainty is that it is languorously pleasant, like swimming without breath or dread of drowning, like flying without wings or fearing to fall . . .

That which he traverses is too thin for water, too thick for air. It contains no color save that of smoke spread upon high thin breezes, of warm rain misting from a cloudless sky. He breathes deeply of it, savoring it. Perfect peace, perfect comfort, perfect joy.

I dream, he tells himself. *I am Thunderbird Devlin O'Connor, and I dream.*

He stares down at himself, wondering if he even *has* a body. He is naked, and an unsourced light gleams across his skin, casting him from flesh to copper bronze.

I am aware of this dream, he adds. *I do not often know that I dream when I dream.*

It is not often worth *knowing,* a rough-edged voice answers—in his ears or mind alone, he is not certain.

Here! Behind you, it chuckles.

He whirls about—and dampness seeps beneath his feet, where he stands on sloped stone shoals beside a quick-flowing stream. Trees stand beyond, dark boughs gauzed in foggy gray. The nearer show the ghosts of color. *Cedar,* he observes. *Holly— spruce—pine: the trees of vigilance.*

Movement by the nearer bank draws his gaze. A raccoon looks up at him, eyes sparkling like midwinter stars within the mask that binds them.

Did you speak? he inquires politely. And does not think it odd to thus address a beast. After all, though himself of wolf clan, he has come to think of the raccoon as his totem, his spirit guide—his *nahual;* though the Ani-Yunwiya—the Cherokee—do not concern themselves with such notions.

I spoke, the raccoon affirms, pausing to flip a handsome crawfish farther up the shelf. *Did you know that Red Crawfish made the world?*

I have heard that speculated, 'Bird replies carefully.

What do you *think?* the raccoon wonders.

I think that which makes most sense to me, 'Bird tells it after a pause. *I think that all the matter in the universe was compressed into a ball ten billion years ago, and that it then exploded.*

The Big Bang?

You have heard of it?

Not only heard of it. *I heard it. But that ball from which everything was made was only the ball of mud Red Crawfish brought up from the Deep. And the bang itself, merely his claws clicking together when he let it fall.*

'Bird considers this. *Who are you?* he inquires at last.

I am the Ancient of Raccoons, the Raccoon answers. *I have been asked to assure that you witness certain things.*

What things?

The Raccoon waves its right paw downstream. *That way. When you see a man, watch him closely.*

'Bird starts that way, then hesitates and turns. *Who said to tell me this?*

You will know soon enough, the Raccoon mumbles, intent upon its meal.

Another pause. Then: *Thank you for your gracious counsel, most excellent Ancient One. Wado.*

You can thank me by doing what I asked, the Raccoon growls, and deftly rips off a claw.

'Bird hears crunchings a fair while longer. Loud as thunder they sound, but that does not trouble him as he trots beside the brook. It enters a wood, and he paces it. It crosses a meadow, and he jogs beside. Another wood gives way to a glade, edging a rocky bank. 'Bird realizes he is weary. He slumps against a cedar, then sprawls among its roots, panting while he watches the dancing water, while the tune it plays upon the rocks lulls him into lethargy.

Movement!

It wakes his eyes, but he does not shift from where he lazes. A white man walks from the woods, perhaps ten long-strides distant. He is middle-sized and red-haired, slim but not truly skinny. A pair of baggy checked trousers hang from narrow hips: his only garment. He squats by the stream, studies it a spell, then rocks back on his haunches, and from a waist pouch removes a finely knotted net. This he attaches to an arm-long stick with a shoulder-wide hoop at the end. That accomplished, he scoots to the brink of the bank and waits, eyes focused on the water.

'Bird leans forward, fascinated.

Movement!

With one smooth graceful sweep, the man whips the net through the brook and back to shore. Something weights it now, something wet and gleaming, like water magicked into metal and forged into fish's form. A heavy body flops against hard granite—yet it is not the sound of flesh on rock, but of a fist upon a gong. It echoes, too, rising through 'Bird's feet and legs and buttocks to stir his heart and—eventually—his innermost soul.

The man scrambles up beside the fish and frees it. It is a salmon, which perplexes 'Bird, for surely salmon only inhabit northern climes, and this place mirrors his native North Carolina, though the man's garb is utterly wrong.

Abruptly, he has a chill. He has remembered something that troubled him not long ago, and has never truly ceased to haunt him.

Not a day past he has likewise dreamed of a fisherman and a miraculous catch. That fish skinned he who hooked it. 'Bird fears to see such like again. He rises all in one swift rush. Almost he whoops out a warning.

Yet something about *that* salmon gives him pause. *I have met the Ancient of Raccoons,* he reminds himself. *Perhaps* that *is the Ancient of Salmon.*

How do I know that? another aspect demands.

I know, he counters himself. *Here, in this place, I know!*

The man has freed the salmon now, but has made no move to dress or cook it. Rather, he slides it into a shallow depression in the stone, then removes a second bag from his waist, upends it, and squeezes.

Ruddy liquid sprays into the fish's gasping mouth. A sharp, tart scent invades the air.

Wine, 'Bird realizes. *He feeds the salmon wine!*

The salmon swallows, then opens its mouth again—and speaks, though 'Bird cannot make out the words at such remove. Nor can the man it seems; for he bends close to hear. Eventually he nods and begins to sing. The salmon joins in, their voices in harmony like mountain waters merging, the man's tones low, the salmon's high and clear.

'Bird is enchanted. He eases closer. . . .

He slips behind the man, and surely so near he could hear the words distinctly.

Yet he cannot. They are not English, these words. And then, without change, they are! But 'Bird still cannot understand them. He knows them when they enter his ear; his brain supplies images; yet when he would grasp the whole, they vanish: are waiting, yes, but not to be assembled into sense at his command.

And yet the song continues. It is beautiful, and 'Bird wants desperately to join in, yet dares not.

Yet he must!

Still silently, still fearing to disturb this wonder lest it shatter like unseen glass, 'Bird slips back to the forest, to where he has glimpsed the trunk of a fallen tree, with a broken limb beside it. He kneels beside one and lifts the other. The singing never ceases, indeed, is louder: a joy to 'Bird's ears.

And, reverently and with caution, he taps the trunk with his stick. Softly at first, then louder. Softly, too, he begins to hum.

The sun is high when he kneels there. When it slips from the sky the song still has not ended, yet never has 'Bird failed to match it with the drum. *If only I knew the words,* he sighs, *then I would truly be in bliss.*

A crisp scrambling sound to his right shifts his attention, though he never drops a beat. It is the Raccoon. It blinks at him. He nods back and grins: full of unsourced joy.

The Raccoon regards him for a long solemn moment, then waddles forward. Impulsively, he extends his free hand to scratch its forehead. It suffers this—then, with a sudden flash of teeth, savages his fingers. Blood sparks across the drum-trunk like liquid flame.

Damn you! 'Bird shrieks, jerking a crimson thumb to his lips. And with that the drumbeat falters . . .

. . . and 'Bird awakened.

Sensation ebbed away like fire tossed into water—then flooded back so intensely that he gasped.

He was sprawled facedown and naked across the heirloom patchwork quilt atop his futon. The lights were out, but illumination filtered in from the slitted door to the living room. Music likewise floated in from there: an ancient piece by Jethro Tull. "Broadsword," it was called. Characterized by heavy—

Drumming.

There'd been drumming! Wonderful drumming!

'Bird rolled over, to stare wide-eyed at the ceiling. Drumming!

Impulsively, he slapped his hand on the futon: again and again, chanting in senseless monosyllables such as he used when learning a melody for his own personal Drum.

Yeah, that was it. That was precisely the rhythm.

God, it sounded good!

God, but it *felt* good, too.

And, God, but did *he* feel good!

Not just merely *good*: he felt marvelous! As though

an unsuspected weight had been lifted from both his body and his soul.

A glance at the clock on the floor by the futon told him it was nearly eight. Which meant he had slept five hours in the current round—which, along with the thirteen he'd had after the sweat, basically put him even.

It also meant he could still make the 'Wheel in time for his set.

And the way he felt right now, it was bound to be the best ever!

He practically erupted from the futon and pranced into the bath. "Christ Almighty, I feel good," he informed his smirking reflection as he turned the tap. "Jesus H. Christ Almighty!"

"Yeeessss?" came a deliberately deep voice from the open door.

Energized or no, 'Bird jumped half out of his skin. He whirled around angrily, dark eyes flashing fire. "Stormy, you asshole, are you *still* here?"

Stormy shrugged noncommittally, folded his arms, and flopped against the doorjamb. He was wearing loose tan pants with corporate creases; soft, calf-high black boots; and a serape of midnight blue hopsack, bordered with official-looking gold. "No, I'm going out of my mind with boredom over in Din-eh-Land," he drawled, with heavy sarcasm. "Day shift, of all damned things."

'Bird flipped water at him from the sink. He dodged it neatly.

"Actually," Stormy continued, "I'm not still here. That is, I've left and returned. You may surmise from the requisite uniform that obscures my obscenely handsome bod that I've dropped by on my way from work. I only stopped by to raid a beer, check on the toli game—and incidentally to see how you were do-ing after the big mojambo Z-fest."

"Excellent, just excellent," 'Bird shot back, in something between a giggle and a growl. "I haven't felt this good in ages!"

Stormy eyed him dubiously, his face all serious-ness and concern. "Any particular reason?"

'Bird grinned mischievously and pushed past him to reenter the bedroom. "Morning," he told the light switch in passing, which promptly woke pink-gold light within the room. Then: "I had a dream, oh Storming One."

"You mean like a . . . medicine dream?"

'Bird sorted through the drawers built into the left-hand wall. "Suppose so. Whatever you want to call 'em."

Stormy's eyes narrowed farther. "I thought you didn't like those things."

"I . . . " 'Bird froze. "I *don't,* do I?" He thumped down on the futon, shoulders sagging, eyes wide and wild. "I . . . Jesus Christ, man; what's *happenin'* here? I had this dream, and in it I was doin' all this really great drummin', and some singin', only I don't know the words, or even the language, only the ca-dence of the tune. But it was so neat, Stormy! And I just had to carry it with me into . . . into bein' awake. And that—I have to call it elation—obviously carried over too."

"And now it's gone?"

'Bird nodded numbly. "It's like as soon as you said what you did—made me *think* for a second—it was gone. It was like you reached into my soul and turned out a light."

"Sorry."

'Bird grimaced resignedly. "You couldn't have known—nor could I. And in any event, if not you, then somebody else. Someone at the 'Wheel, or whatever."

"The 'Wheel? You're not going—"

"Of *course* I'm goin'! I feel fine. I'm just not . . . high like I was a minute ago."

Stormy studied him carefully, from where he was propping up a wall. "This means something."

'Bird shrugged, rose, and began to dress: off-white jeans, sneaks, and gold tunic. "All I know is that prior to yesterday I'd had three medicine dreams in my life, the most recent three years ago. Now, if you count what happened out at Lox's, I've had two in two days."

"Which means . . . ?"

"Which I suppose means that since *I'm* not tryin' to evoke them, at least not consciously, that . . . something *else* wants something out of me!"

"In other words, magic's forcing itself upon you."

"Yeah—and I don't like it!"

"Doesn't matter," Stormy told him flatly. "It's what the magic likes that matters."

'Bird rolled his eyes and squeezed around him into the living room. He turned off the stereo, but paused by the TV.

"Na Hollos won again, if that's what you're wondering about," Stormy supplied, coming up behind him. "Bogue Homma's out. Looks like it's gonna be them and Conehatta."

"Which I guess means they won't be at the 'Wheel tonight," 'Bird grumbled, as he opened the door. "You comin', or . . . ?"

Stormy shook his head. "I need to crash. I'm 'bout half a day low myself, lest you forget."

"You're welcome to stay here," 'Bird offered. "My TV's bigger than yours, and I've still got beer."

A sigh. "We'll see."

'Bird stepped into the hallway, then paused, turned. "Stormy?"

"Yeah?"

"Thanks."

"It's cool."

"Thanks anyway."

"Break a leg, 'Bird. Knock 'em dead."

'Bird grinned and walked away.

A check of his watch—he loathed those earstud things that broadcast straight into your brain and told you the time when you thought about it—showed it now shortly past eight. Which still gave him time to make it to the 'Wheel and change by eight-forty-five.

If—appalling notion—he sold out and took AFZoRTA or a cab.

To his great surprise, one of the latter was sitting at the curb when he strode past the compound guards (Seminoles, today), toward the street.

"You *Señor* O'Connor?" the driver—apparently a for real Mexican, for a change—called through the intercom.

"You got it."

"Young *señor* phoned and said you'd be here *ahora.* Said you needed a fast trip to the Medicine Wheel."

"You got it," Bird repeated with a chuckle, as he climbed into the back of the Mercedes minivan. He settled into the cream leather seat, latched his belt, and felt the electric vehicle whir up to speed as the driver swung down Shield Jaguar Drive toward the beltway. But as he did, something crept into his psyche and lodged there, like a spark escaped from a flame, too dim to burn, too bright to wink out utterly. It was an odd sensation, too, and not at all pleasant. A feeling of foreboding, he concluded: a fire that could burn out painlessly—or flame too high and consume him.

Without knowing why, he glanced backward, but saw nothing beyond the ordinary. Had he known where to look, however, especially at a certain new, but nondescript, Dodge Argon sedan, he might have noticed he was being tailed.

As it was, his mind was already dancing, dancing to the beat of a dream-born drum.

Fingers in the car half a block behind danced on obsidian.

Chapter XVIII:
Wheels within Wheels

*(The Medicine Wheel, Sinsynsen—
Aztlan Free Zone—Mexico)*
(Friday, September 2—mid-evening)

"Okay, then," Dr. Mary Hasegawa sighed, "we've got a deal." She extended a blunt white hand across the cluttered table to Carolyn, who sat opposite. The folds of the older woman's tunic swished dangerously close to both the trelliswork of trout bones on her earthenware plate and the matching mug that contained her wine. (It was her second refill, Carolyn noted, which perhaps explained Hassie's less than aggressive bargaining.)

Carolyn, who, in spite of having had four glasses, had inherited an excellent head for alcohol from her mother, reached to intercept, being careful not to foul her own sleeve in the mixture of residual grease and buffalo blood that salved her platter. They shook heartily.

"Recite the terms, please, Rudy," Hasegawa commanded, while their hands were still entwined. "That's what 'neutral observers' are for."

Rudy blinked up from his last bite of venison tenderloin, then cleared his throat. "Uh . . . you, Dr. Mary Hasegawa, are to—to grant Carolyn Mauney-

Griffith one-point-five days of unimpeded work pursuant to her normal duties for every point-five days spent as subject *to* investigation, said point-five days to commence upon the aforesaid Carolyn Mauney-Griffith's presentation of herself at the office of the Pan-European Oceanic Research Center, Inc., Infirmary, and to terminate at twelve hundred hours, regardless of inception time."

"Very good, Rudy," Hasegawa said, deadpan. "So let it be."

"So let it be," Carolyn echoed, and released her boss's hand. "You should've been a lawyer," she informed Rudy with a grin that, while not quite rivaling his better efforts (*those* he reserved for wooing women, she'd long ago concluded), came close. "Or a writer, perhaps," she added to Kevin, who, though putting up a valiant front, was picking at his food like someone who had a lot more on his mind than recreational bargaining.

Which he obviously did. No way he'd have abandoned that nice little castle of his to hop a jet in the middle of a hurricane, elsewise. And damned sure no way he'd have overleapt the Schism just like that, without preamble, explanation, or apology.

Which meant that the ice had been broken on that topic—and the first obstacle toward reconciliation, the onus of weakening first, overcome.

Except that didn't explain what was nuking him now. He'd blithered a bit about magic in the car. But surely he hadn't put himself through the trauma their scattered conversation suggested solely to discuss unscientific bullshit. Yeah, it was definitely going to be an interesting evening—assuming she invited him home, which she hadn't yet determined.

At the moment, Kev looked desperately frustrated, which was generally a preamble to his being desperately unhappy, and she very much feared that the resolution of that condition could only come from her.

Or perhaps he simply didn't like iguana.

"Kev?" she prompted. "What do you think? Could Rudy be a writer?"

"If he can write like he talks," Kevin replied seriously. From which she assumed he'd used up his day's allotment of witty repartee and scintillating small talk.

"I do songs," Rudy volunteered brightly.

"What kind?"

"Ballads mostly. I don't have the best memory in Christendom, so I tend to put important things in songs. Cary's adventure'd make a *great* one."

"Except it's not finished," Carolyn pointed out. "We still don't know *if* I really died. And if I did, we don't know what caused my 'spontaneous recovery' *or* if there're going to be long-term effects."

"Oh, hey!" Rudy enthused. "I've got it. I do one about how they biopsy bits off you until nothing's left!"

"Do it," Carolyn cried, toasting him with her mug.

"Hear! Hear!" the rest of them chimed in.

"Do the dolphin mutilations count as part of that song or as a separate item?" Kevin wondered abruptly.

Carolyn kicked him—or somebody—beneath the table. From the look on his face she'd aimed true. "I don't need to be reminded of that—not when I can't do anything about it!"

"Relaxing allows your mind to flow into different, but still potentially constructive, channels," Hasegawa inserted smoothly. "Therefore, you *are* doing something about it."

"Zen," Rudy chuckled, nodding sagely.

"Tao," Hasegawa corrected.

"I think," Kevin said, "I've had enough lizard, interesting though it was. And I'm sorry I punctuated Rudy's fine idea so poorly. So can I redeem myself by treating everyone to some Baileys? Rudy, of course, gets a double."

"How 'bout Irish coffee after dessert," Carolyn countered sweetly.

"Dessert," Hasegawa broke in. "Now *that's* a fine idea—oh, don't fret, Rudy, I'll buy—you knew I would, anyway."

"Fine," Carolyn agreed, trying to catch their buckskin-clad waiter's eye. While she waited for him to finish serving a middle-aged woman what she supposed was either fried squirrel or rabbit, she appropriated the last bit of corn bread from the basket on the table and sopped absently at the liquid residue on her plate.

"Acquired a taste for blood, have we?" Kevin chuckled nervously. "I remember when you were a strict vegan. And—well, it's a long way from that to almost-mooing meat."

Carolyn shrugged. "It's what I wanted."

Which it was. Though come to it, she'd never ordered rare steak before, beef or buffalo, either. What had led her to do so tonight was a mystery—except that it was simply what she wanted. Probably just her tastes reacting to some biochemical deficiency. Shoot, given the amount of blood they'd piped out of her lately, she wouldn't look *that* disparagingly on chugging O-Pos by the liter.

And now she had the waiter's eye! She gestured to him.

As he made his way around their level of the several that made an amphitheater above an earth-floored arena-cum-stage, she conducted another survey of the environs.

Rudy had chosen well. The food had been great, especially the Native American dishes. (Kev had probably blown it with the iguana, which he had rationalized by claiming it was the duty of a writer to try new things.) The wine (or beer, in Kev and Rudy's case) had been as good as could be expected for something not designed to mate with Native cuisine.

And the decor was well-nigh perfect, what with the hard-packed adobe floors and what looked like authentic wattle-and-daub walls beneath a steeply pitched ceiling supported by imposing logs at four points, which, however, did not block the view of the arena, which butted against one wall. The entertainment didn't start until late, Rudy had told them; for now there was simply disced music: wooden flute on a very good system.

But if the entertainment *was* as good . . .

Tables got cleared; mugs got refilled, dessert orders were taken, and coffee was set to brew. (They called it Almost-Black Drink here, though they also served the real thing.) Hasegawa relaxed back into her inscrutable persona (though she was giggling more than usual, which was to say some, as opposed to none). Rudy had scooted his chair around so as better to observe the arena, which incidentally brought him closer to Carolyn, which she didn't mind.

And Kevin had evidently given up on actually *having* a good time and had settled on looking alert and inquisitive—which meant his eyes were wide open, his brows raised quizzically, and his mouth set in a crooked smirk that hinted at a midlevel buzz.

And then the show began. The lights darkened slowly, starting at the top of the amphitheater, to be replaced by real torches set around the walls. The arena faded into obscurity: a pit of gloom in which she could dimly discern moving figures. They settled quickly, and a subtle drumming commenced, so softly as to be almost subliminal. As the audience gradually quieted, the beat increased in volume, though the area behind the arena remained dark. Eventually, a man began to sing, a slow tune, simple and rhythmic, in a language Rudy whispered was Lakota. A prayer followed in that same tongue, then in English.

Still no lights.

More drumming, while a shape moved to strike a tiny fire in the center of the arena. In the sudden glimmer of ruddy light, Carolyn saw six men sitting in a semicircle behind knee-high drums. All had long black hair and wore jeans and checked shirts of the old-fashioned style that was still current in less cosmopolitan climes.

The drumming intensified, but the light remained dim.

The audience (many of whom Carolyn suspected of being regulars) held their breath, anticipating . . .

Abruptly, a figure sprang from a recess to the right of the arena and leapt to centerstage. Firelight gleamed off dark-tanned flesh and black hair as the youth (to judge by the supple fluidity with which he moved) swirled about. Arm-long sticks flashed in his hands—sticks which, with one smooth, efficient swoop, he thrust into the flame. They blazed up instantly, revealing a young, intense, and clearly Indian face. A stomp of a bare foot extinguished the floor fire.

And then he began to dance. Slowly at first, then more rapidly: stomping, twirling, stooping low, or leaping high. And as he danced, he accented his movements with the flaming sticks. Sometimes he flung them up and caught them, sometimes he swished them about so swiftly they became circles of fire. Most often, however, he passed them over, under, or around various parts of his nearly naked body. Carolyn imagined that if he'd ever had any body hair, it had long since crisped away. She wondered how he kept the shoulder-long mane that flew around his face from being singed back to a crew cut.

"Xavier Perez," a voice proclaimed after more than ten minutes of frenzied fire-weaving. "Xavier has been performing a reconstructed Aztec fire dance, based on carvings discovered last year near Mexico City."

Whereupon Xavier threw the torches nearly to the ceiling, where they pinwheeled briefly while gravity caught up with them—to be snared again instants before they smacked earth. He snuffed them with his fists. The audience gasped, tittered at itself, then applauded.

Xavier bowed. And left.

"Not bad," Carolyn sighed approvingly.

"It gets better."

It did—though not, evidently, as Rudy had anticipated.

Most of the dancers, as it turned out, were male. The majority were young, all were good-looking, and many wore no more than loincloths. And Carolyn liked looking at attractive nearly naked men—including Rudy, when he was in his skimpy swimming togs. But the big surprise was Hasegawa, whom she'd always assumed to be the very essence of reserve—which she still was—except for what could only be described as a shit-eating grin splitting her face.

Carolyn especially liked the current performer. Someone named Thunderbird O'Connor, dancing traditional-style, so the announcer had said. Which evidently meant that his elaborate costume was entirely handmade from natural materials, as opposed to the acid aniline colors, plastic gauds, and LED baubles that characterized what were termed fancy dancers. This guy was good: He had style, he wore his body like he enjoyed it, and his movements really did evoke the *gestalt* of the eagle Rudy had told her his particular dance was supposed to reverence. There was something vaguely familiar about him, too; but in a city built by Indians in a country inhabited by Indians, with a substantial Indian population itself, that wasn't surprising. Shoot, she bet even Rudy could pass for one if he let his hair grow, changed the way he dressed, and didn't grin so much.

Kevin couldn't.

Not in a million years. Not reed-thin and pale as he was. And not with that absurd orange-and-blue hair. Nor would a dye job help. Black hair and a tan would simply make him look odd—and probably even more miserable.

He was really starting to ravel around the edges, too; had barely picked at the apple fritters he'd chosen for dessert, and only sipped at his Irish coffee. But he'd calligraphed names and scribbled sketches on the paper place mat until it was nearly black, and was now intent on spearing leftovers from their various plates and burning them to cinders in the candle that guttered in an earthenware pot in the center of the table. He was also gnawing his lip a lot, and sighing with increasing degrees of both audibility and theatricality. Even Hasegawa's occasional glares did not faze him. *Trying to be good, and failing,* she told herself. *I wonder when I became his* older *sister.*

And before she realized it, had dragged her gaze away from young Mr. O'Connor (odd name for an Indian), who looked to be nearing the end of his set anyway, and grabbed Kevin's hand as he prepared to incinerate an orange rind that had garnished her wild fruit and honey. He flinched, looking startled, and not unlike someone who had just awakened—but allowed her to subdue his hand, which she placed on the table with a pat.

"So why are you *really* here?" she murmured.

He blinked at her, still—apparently—half-dazed. Or drunker than she'd thought.

"I have to give you a message."

She looked him in the eye, trying to shift her expression from vague surprise (at herself, not the least) into calm neutrality. "So . . . I'm waiting."

He fidgeted like a little boy caught doing something he shouldn't. "I can't give it here," he mumbled. He sounded utterly wretched, utterly unlike the quick-tongued wit of their hospital reunion. Or perhaps she'd only been seeing what she wanted to see then. This was more like the *real* Kevin.

"Okay," she sighed. "So let's go somewhere you can."

Green eyes widened hopefully. "Your place?"

A shrug, followed by a nod toward a semi-enclosed area to one side of the arena. "The bar's empty, and we can still see from there—sort of."

Rudy glanced sideways at her, obviously puzzled, and perhaps a trifle pissed. Hasegawa was oblivious.

Scowling, Carolyn rose and resnared Kevin's hand, to tug him up as well. "We'll be back," she told her companions. "If we're not, I'm sure Kev'll let you take his car."

"Cary, I—" Kevin protested, as he found his feet and let himself be dragged along. "Cary, I appreciate what you're tryin' to do here, but it's—it's just too complex to relay on the fly in a friggin' *diverto*!"

She paused in midflight, close by the rear edge of the arena, and swung around to face him. "If it was *that* important," she flared, "you'd have told me already, without all that bullshit about magic."

Which was a hurtful way of saying it, and which she would *not* have put that way without the influence of alcohol.

Or perhaps that was an excuse.

Kevin stared at her. "I've had a hard day. You've had a hard day—"

The rest of his reply was drowned by a crescendo of drumming, followed by a storm of applause. She whirled around instinctively. The dancer had finished and was bowing to his appreciative fans. She clapped too. So did Kevin, halfheartedly.

"*Damas y caballeros*: Thunderbird O'Connor," the emcee intoned in his carefully western drawl. "Men's traditional eagle dance. And let's give a hand for the Drum. Ladies and Gentlemen, the Maza-Kute Drum, from Santee, Nebraska."

The applause swelled again. Carolyn scowled. Kevin fidgeted.

The dancer bowed one final time, then turned and pranced out of the spotlight. To Carolyn's delight, his retreat brought him close by where they stood. She couldn't resist one final long appraising glance. Not at someone who looked that good. And maybe she'd figure out why he was so damned familiar.

He was grinning like a happy boy, his gaze sweeping the crowd like the eagle he'd so nicely striven to emulate. "Way to go, 'Bird" someone called, from behind her. He glanced that way—which sent his gaze past her—then jerked back and locked.

He froze, mouth open, fingers stretched wide. Only the glitter in his eyes, bright within the matte black makeup around them, and the slow rise and fall of his sweat-sheened chest preserved the illusion of life.

She stared back. Met his eyes with proud perplexity.

And then, abruptly, spoken with that guileless spontaneity only absolute surprise can engender: "You're the one the dolphins worship!"

It took an instant for those words to register, and then a longer moment for them to make sense—for that pronouncement in this place where she had never been, that was a far remove from her day-to-day reality, to find the proper linkage to the rest of her life.

To that dream she'd had right before she'd awakened and met Kevin!

"*You are the one the dolphins worship!*" The seal had said that in her dream. This dancer had said it again, not five seconds ago.

No way that could happen—

Or be accidental.

The dancer seemed surprised too, seemed as lost for words as she. But his face was twitching. In an instant he'd speak again, and if *that* happened—

"Come on!" she snapped at Kevin, grabbing his hand once more and yanking him toward the exit.

"But Cary, I—"

"*Now*, Kev. Absolutely right now!"

Kevin opened his mouth to reply, but evidently thought better of it, and allowed himself to be steered up the stairs that flanked the dining terraces on that side.

"But your friends . . . " he gasped helplessly, when they passed their particular level without turning in. He sounded completely confused.

"They can take care of themselves," Carolyn hissed. "You want to talk? We'll talk. But I'm getting out of here *now*!"

Chapter XIX:
Night Moves

(Sinsynsen, Aztlan Free Zone—Mexico)
(Friday, September 2—late evening)

"So, what was that all about?" Kevin gasped, as his sister stomped past the startled hostess and thrust through the carved cedar panel that comprised the Medicine Wheel's front door.

Silence.

"Cary . . . "

Warm, humid air slapped at him, as he found himself towed outside. A startled black woman glared indignation at him from where they'd narrowly missed knocking her on her ample butt. The man with her spat something unintelligible in Spanish.

"Cary!"

"What?"

"Who was that guy?"

"Some Indian!" she snapped. And neither slowed nor released his hand until they were on the sidewalk, with the high sandcrete wall that framed the Medicine Wheel radiating the day's heat against their backs.

Only when she'd glanced up and down the street did she relax her grip. To Kevin's surprise, given this was Friday night on the fringe of a major city with scads of tweenage inhabitants, the walk was nearly empty—perhaps due to the *diverto*'s proximity to that five-klik strip of no-tech Rudy had explained during dinner was called *El País Verde*. The amount of traffic whirring in from the north to turn down the street in front of them bore that out, as did the white noise rumble of voices southward, where a parked tourist bus temporarily blocked any view of actual warm bodies. More *divertos* loomed across the street, moderately populated, with, beyond them, the gold-glass-and-bronze step pyramid of the Sinsynsen Ramada Inn.

Carolyn slumped against the beveled wall, perhaps to catch her breath, perhaps to compose herself. Her eyes were wild, her body so tense she looked set to fly apart if anyone touched her. Kevin didn't know what to think, so intent had he been on puzzling out the best way to broach his own concern; and then, out of the clear blue, this! Lightning had evidently struck Cary twice that day, and each bolt had brought with it one of the gods of Chaos. He'd been close, too, dammit! The bar in the Medicine Wheel wouldn't have been the best option, but it certainly beat standing here in front of God and everybody—not that the everybody aspect seemed likely to care.

As for God—well, it suddenly looked suspiciously like his game.

Carolyn swallowed hard. "Okay," she managed finally, "what's this about, that you've been so hot to tell me? What's this goddamn message?"

Kevin's heart sank. What did it take to get through to her that it *wasn't* a simple matter? That it was not the sort of thing you discussed calmly over drinks while your friends hung around ogling dancing boys. That it was absolutely not the sort of thing you dived into without preamble—not and have it make sense.

And here Cary wanted him to blurt it out on a street corner!

He took a deep breath, steeled himself. Tried to fight through the veils of muddle too much alcohol had snared his patience with, and too much anger-born adrenaline was rapidly unweaving. "Okay now, Cary, *listen* to me—which you've seemed disinclined to do."

She glared at him, and he could sense the Schism reawakening.

"Well?"

"It's *not* the kind of thing that I can talk about here, okay? *It absolutely is not!* It'll take a while to relate properly—which I've already *told* you about half a dozen times. It's complicated, at least in implication. It strains credibility even without that—and I'd rather not be interrupted, either by repressed Orientals, charming expatriate Spaniards, or half-naked Cherokee spouting minimalist poetry, or whatever that was!"

Silence.

"*Okay?*"

Silence, while she gnawed her lip.

"*Okay, Cary?*"

"My place," she muttered finally. "You drive. I have to think."

"Me too," he yawned, already fishing in his pocket for the ignition card. "I guess I'll call Rudy from your car and tell him to hang on to mine until tomorrow."

More silence. Then, from Carolyn, as they stepped into the parking lot: "Don't even *start* until we get there, okay? If you're gonna have it your way, then by God, you're gonna have it your way!"

*   *   *

Coffee and adrenaline, Kevin decided, in that part of him that sat back and observed, while the rest of him played the *shanachie* and blithered on aloud. *Coffee and adrenaline were all that were keeping him functional. All that were keeping him sane.*

All that were keeping weariness sufficiently at bay to preclude his simply throwing up his hands, yelling "Fuck it! It's all crazy anyhow!" and running out the door.

That, and Cary's eyes, as she stared calmly at him from her armchair, sipped her tea, and—very likely—wished he would, in fact, do precisely the latter. Or perhaps simply go off somewhere and drop dead, in lieu of sprawling across her beige linen sofa like so much rumpled baggage.

He paused in mid-rant, to run a hand through his hair in exasperation, then braced himself with a sip of coffee before blundering on.

It was going *very* badly.

Not that Cary wasn't letting him have his say, in whatever excruciating detail he seemed inclined to undertake. Not that she was interrupting him, though she sometimes did, to clarify a point. Not that her face betrayed the merest hint of either anger, skepticism, or belief.

Any one of those would have been better, because it would have helped determine how to skew his story for the target market, as it were.

Stoicism didn't. Nonreaction didn't. Cold, emotionless silence didn't either.

He'd counted on everything—except dead, icy calm.

And he was but halfway through the tale—just to the part where he and Fir had been forced to take back roads to Leenane.

Dead, emotionless calm.

And then something struck him so hard he broke off in mid-sentence.

Dead!

Cary had been dead! Or that's what a number of presumably competent professionals had determined.

"Your sister is in danger," the selkie had said.

And what could be more dangerous than death?

She'd been attacked by dolphins, she'd told him. Dolphins lived in the sea. So did selkies—

"Something wrong?" Again that coldness. That goddamned condescending cold.

Kevin shook his head, briefly unable to separate ongoing verbal narrative from silent voice-over commentary and analysis of same. "I'll tell you when I finish," he sighed. "Something just occurred to me. Some connection between things that it didn't occur to me could *be* connected."

Carolyn's eyes went briefly blank, as people's did when they asked their watches for the time. "I have to go to work tomorrow morning," she reminded him. "It's late now, and I have absolutely *got* to make some headway on those mutilations. Rudy's supposed to have chased down a shitload of medical data. And I need to get back to Kat and Bo, in case something's wrong with them that might have prompted aberrant behavior like they manifested back on Thursday—assuming it *was* them that yanked out my gill hose, which I'm inclined to doubt."

Kevin rolled his eyes. "I'll try to be quick."

It still took fifteen minutes, however, to lay out the rest of the tale even minimally. Carolyn lapsed back into her shell, but Kevin plodded grimly on.

When he had finished, she continued staring at him.

"I don't believe you."

He gaped at her incredulously. *"Cary!"*

She shook her head, as if to clear it, and rose, only to plop down on a barstool. "I don't believe you, Kev. I *can't* believe you. If I believe you, I have to rethink everything I've ever thought in my life. On the other hand, you're not—forgive me—the most stable person in the world, and stress—"

"It wasn't stress. I don't—"

"Hurricanes don't cause stress?" she flared. "Deadlines don't cause stress? Living in what's to you a foreign country doesn't cause stress? Christ, driving that aircraft carrier of yours *alone* would send *me* off the deep end!"

Kevin tried to force himself to be calm. "It won't make you hallucinate, though," he gritted, his voice trembling. "And even if it did, it bloody well wouldn't last two days!"

"Something in the fish soup could have!" Carolyn countered, "—made you hallucinate, I mean. And that's not even considering more permanent psychological conditions."

"You think I'm crazy!"

She gnawed her lip—she'd picked it up from him, he supposed. "I think you very well could be—and ought to get some counseling pronto, preferably before you leave Aztlan. But if it'll make you feel any better, I will admit that I've not been so certain that everything's laser-straight in my head either. Not lately."

"You mean like whatever that was with that Indian?"

A pause. "That's part of it, yes."

"You still haven't told me about that."

"Nor will I—at least not tonight."

"Why?"

"I don't want to talk about it."

"Why, Cary?" he persisted. "Dammit, I know you don't believe me, but I swear to God that I've been absolutely as straight with you as I can be—even when it hurt my cause. Even when I could tell you thought I was crazy as a fucking bedbug!"

"Yeah, well, how would *you* have taken it, Kev?" she shot back furiously. "How would you react if I barged in on you in the middle of *your* personal chaos and started spouting bullshit about magic? You don't believe in the stuff, not really; and I sure as hell don't—not in the sense you mean! You'd have to be *stupid* not to assume that I was either crazy, or had a hidden agenda."

Silence.

"You'll believe *anything*, Kev!" she went on, in what was now a full-fledged warp-spasm which, un- fortunately, was directed toward him. "You'll believe goddamned anything!"

"Yeah, well I believed Dad when he first said he wasn't your father! And I was right about *that*!"

"I'll pretend you didn't say that, Kevin," she whis- pered icily. "I don't have a guest room, so you can sleep on the sofa," she added more calmly. "Bed- ding's in the linen closet, take what you need and make yourself at home. You're welcome to stay as long as you like, so long as you don't interfere with my job—or my peace of mind, which discussions such as we've just concluded will most certainly do."

"But we *haven't* concluded it! Don't you see, Cary? The selkie said you were in danger—and you were! You fucking well *died*!"

"Coincidence."

"Bullshit!"

"We're brother and sister. There's some evidence

for believing that *can* produce a psychic link. I'll grant you that much esoterica."

"*I* didn't say it, though! The selkie—"

She looked him straight in the eye. "There is no selkie, Kevin. I honestly think that you, here today, right now, think there was. I also think that you're less likely to think that tomorrow, and unlikely to think it at all five years from now. And while I wait for then, I'm going to bed. Shall I wake you for breakfast or let you sleep?"

"Whichever," Kevin sighed dully, rising to retrieve the duffel bag that contained all his worldly possessions—New Worldly, anyway. If he stayed—which he would do until he got to the bottom of whatever was going on, or at minimum, proved to his satisfaction that Cary was safe—he'd have to buy a whole new wardrobe.

Which was a damned stupid thing to be fretting over now.

Which in turn reminded him that he needed to check up on good old Hurricane Buckley—and, more to the point, try to get hold of someone who could tell him how Clononey had fared.

"Good night," Carolyn called from the entrance to the short hall that led past the bath to her bedroom. "Sleep well—which you undoubtedly will—but I honestly really do mean it."

"Good night."

She turned slowly, then paused and twisted back around.

"Kev?"

"Yeah?"

"It's good to see you, lad. Whatever else is going on, it's good to see you again."

"You too."

" 'Night."

" 'Night."

And with that she told the hall light, "Off," and padded away into gloom.

For his part, Kevin swallowed three Benadryl (good for stress, his doctor had told him), and washed them down with a Guinness he found in his sister's 'fridge. He chased that one with another.

And while he sought vainly for sense in an increasingly impossible situation, sleep found him instead, and showed him how simple it was to be unconscious.

Chapter XX:
Bird in the Hand

*(The Medicine Wheel—Sinsynsen,
Aztlan Free Zone—Mexico)
(Friday, September 2—late evening)*

'Bird gaped incredulously at the tiny woman he
had just accosted; at her shocked expression; at the
dazed stare of utter confusion on the narrow face of
the odd-haired man beside her.

And absolutely *could not move*.

His dreams had caught up with him and clamped
him, for a timeless instant, between all the cryptic wildness they had planted inside his head and
the hard real world of conventional reality. And with
his senses shouting one thing, and his subconscious screaming another while striving to connect
the two through the medium of his mouth—well,
something had to give, and what got left groping in
the dark was further articulation: both verbal and
physical.

"You are the one the dolphins worship."

Yeah sure!

Already the woman's expression had shifted from
shock through irritation to alarm. And before 'Bird
could compose himself for either explanation or
apology, she scowled at him, spun on her heels, and

224

stalked up the stairs toward the exit, with Mr. Two-
tone in tow.

"You are the one the dolphins worship."

And she was! 'Bird had no idea how he knew; but
it came to him that that woman—that petite dull-
haired sharp-tongued proto-bitch about whom he
knew exactly nothing except her taste in cars,
clothes, companions, and *divertos*—was the key to
whatever weirdness was shooting medicine dreams
into his subconscious every time his eyes closed for
more than twenty seconds.

And there was no way to find out *how* she connected with any of that without connecting with her.

That set him moving.

"Miss!" he yelled, leaping across the low stone rail
that separated the sand-floored arena from the
adobe-paved dining area.

"Oh, miss . . . !"

But she obviously couldn't hear him over the din
of applause that was only now fading after the fan-
fare it had given the Drum. Certainly not through
the rising tide of conversation that flowed in to fill
the ensuing silence.

"Señorita!"

Abruptly, he was running.

Trying to.

Unfortunately, he was in tight quarters in a cumbersome costume. It was therefore no surprise when
his shoulder clipped a buckskin-clad busboy, tumbling him into a breechclouted waiter clutching a
tray of drinks. Both fell: one into a table, one into a
passing patron. 'Bird likewise lost his balance and
staggered forward, which put him at the edge of the
first terrace. He promptly tripped on it and sprawled
into the nearest chair. The inhabitant yipped, then
grabbed at him, which made it impossible to break

his fall. He hit hard enough to wind himself, had a grand view of two dozen sets of ankles and twice that number of chair legs, and eventually realized his left shin was hurting like hell.

Hands were on him by then, and he had little choice but to let himself be hauled up.

"What the f—?" someone hissed. Marquez, the owner. " 'Bird, are you okay?"

"Don't know," he grunted, shaking off his assistants, to survey the exit on tiptoe like a meercat. "Dammit!" he added aloud. "She's gone!"

"Who's gone?" From Marquez.

But it was too late. He'd lost the initiative, and now the stairs were plugged with patrons intent on completing bar runs or pit stops during the intermission. Shoot, even if he made it outside, she'd surely have been swallowed up by the sidewalk shufflers by this time.

Except . . . That woman had been sitting with some other folks, he recalled—not because he had seen *her*, not closely enough to recognize through footlights with her face firelit and in profile. But no way even glaring spots could obscure the blue-blazed hair the guy with her had sported. And the Oriental woman had been distinctive too . . .

And there she was! One terrace up and a third of the way over. He threaded through the press of patrons as quickly as he could, striving, in the process, to regain a modicum of composure.

The woman saw him coming and frowned, rising as he approached. The younger Hispanic with her— a fellow roughly his own age, 'Bird concluded vaguely—swung around as well, clean-cut features dark as thunder.

"That woman," 'Bird gasped, still winded, "that woman who was with you . . . "

"What about her?" From the guy.

'Bird swallowed, braced himself on the back of the Dolphin Queen's abandoned chair. "I . . . need to get in touch with her—need to talk to her."

"What about?" the Hispanic challenged suspiciously.

"Easy, Rudy," the Oriental woman broke in. "What seems to be your problem, Mr. . . . O'Connor, was it?"

"It's too screwy to go into here," 'Bird panted. "But I— Well, I just need to talk to her."

"She stepped out for a second," the Hispanic— Rudy—muttered. "She should be back eventually."

"No," the woman corrected. "She left. This young man said something to her; she looked alarmed— and left, very precipitously indeed. She took Kevin with her."

"I need—"

The woman shook her head, and 'Bird sensed iron will being brought to bear. "Not tonight you don't! You may think you've got an emergency, Mr. O'Connor; but I will tell you right now, and you will listen and obey, that Carolyn has just gone through two very traumatic days, and may be about to have a matching night, and right now she needs to be left in peace!"

"But . . . "

"I enjoyed your performance," the woman continued with a taut smile, as she eased down in her seat again. "But you would be wise to leave."

'Bird, however, had no intention of moving until he had something more to go by. "Her name—"

"Is her business."

"Fine!" 'Bird snapped. "But I just want you to know that she may be the solution to a very major mystery, and if it doesn't get solved, it's on *your* head."

"She's already solving a mystery," Rudy shot back. "Now you heard the lady—"

"I'm gone," 'Bird growled, and turned away.

He did not add that he already had a good idea who this Carolyn person was and a line on where she lived. For while he'd been fishing for information, his gaze had been snared by the scribbles Mr. Two-Tone had made on his place mat. And prominent among them had been an intricately illuminated name: Carolyn Mauney-Griffith.

Whose number, even if unlisted, Stormy could certainly tech out.

Besides, was it actually *that* urgent? Just to catch up with someone and talk? Even someone that pretty. The medicine had waited twenty-seven years. It could certainly wait another night.

"Sorry," 'Bird grunted over his shoulder to the people he'd accosted. And hurried backstage.

Fifteen minutes later, he had showered and changed into civies. His regalia had suffered, he reflected, as had his person: a dozen broken eagle feathers on the bustle, and one nicely barked shin for him.

Which was the price one paid for acting on impulse, his father would have noted.

"He who hesitates jacks off a lot," Stormy would have countered. But 'Bird was concerned with solutions, not sex. At least not yet . . .

On the other hand . . .

A scan of the electronic directory by the pay phone between the rest rooms confirmed that there *was* a Carolyn Mauney-Griffith, revealed that her number was listed, and provided both it and a street

address. A call to Public Reference Access got him a
city directory, which turned the street address into
an apartment building and number, as well as providing the interesting tidbits that she lived alone (no
one else being listed at her code) and was an em-
ployee of that oceanographic complex on the point
to the north.

All of which jibed with what he already knew.

And tomorrow when he got off work, he'd give her
a call. Set up an appointment. Shoot, he already had
the perfect opening: an apology for accosting her at
the *diverto*. If his luck held, she'd either request an
explanation of his odd remark, or apologize for her
equally unexpected response. And he'd be home
free.

And in the meantime, he'd manage a good night's
sleep and a good day's work—finally.

Five minutes later, he was standing on the sidewalk that fronted the 'Wheel, debating whether or
not to take AFZoRTA home. Not so much from
choice as because both Stormy and Red Wounds
would raise holy hell if he didn't; and he wouldn't
put it past the *former* to access the relevant data-
bases just so he could bug him about that very point.

"Be careful," Red Wounds had warned. "Watch
your ass."

So he'd *be* careful. He'd just do it while jogging up
by *El País Verde*. After all, they'd *caught* the guy
who'd skinned that fellow. And though he'd obviously not acted alone (else why would there have
been multiple flayings with distinct culprits?—there
couldn't be *that* many copycat psychos around), it
was damned unlikely anyone would be stalking that
same stretch of beach three nights in a row.

Nor was 'Bird in the least surprised when the five-
klik trek produced nothing more than a light sweat,

a catch in his side, and—eventually—a slight limp born of the thwack he'd given his shin, which was showing every sign of being a bone bruise.

He slowed as he neared the beltway. He'd been aware of the lights for some time, of course; it was lit up bright as day. But the curve of the beach plus a screen of trees masked it until he was nearly there.

Decision time. The straight route home sent him angling left: away from the beach, and through the fringe of trees, then along the crest of the slope above the perimeter pavement until he hit the Tlaloc Street overpass, after which it was three kliks north, then half that west to home.

But certain aspects of his odd evening were still bugging him, and he wasn't certain thirty minutes of crowded streets and city lights would resolve them as effectively as prolonging his progress along the shore might. Which skewed him toward the more stimulating, if marginally less safe, option of the long way home.

And it wasn't even *that* dangerous, save in relation to the rest of Aztlan, which wasn't really dangerous at all.

It was with that firmly in mind that he continued east, skirting the arc of the bay, while the beltway curved north away from it.

So it was, too, that his route took him through the one part of all Aztlan that was not one hundred percent squeaky clean. Specifically, it took him through the Dead Marina.

'Bird's lips quirked in an ironic smirk as they regarded that ominously titled strip of once-prime waterfront looming just ahead. It had been intended to showcase a series of elaborate docks at which the diplomats and high rollers Aztlan was designed to impress could park their expensive yachts. There'd been an AFZoRTA terminal in the center, and a two-klik stretch of shops, hotels, and luxury apartments ranked along a network of canals that extended from the shore back to the beltway. The idea had been to emulate Venice, Italy.

But in this one aspect Aztlan had failed.

More specifically, the rock beneath the foundations had failed—subsided, as geologists would say, .05 to 1.3 meters, to be exact—in one of those earthquakes that plagued the region. Which was one of the reasons most buildings in Aztlan were low and sprawling, not tall and thin.

The upshot was that ninety-three percent of the structures in what had quickly been termed the Dead Marina had been declared unstable and scheduled for demolition. Unfortunately, the backers had gone bankrupt; and the rest of the OAS, who'd had the construction of monuments, museums, and ministries to oversee, had been more concerned with building than destruction, especially as they'd wanted to get their shiny New World capital up and running in time to host the '20 Olympics. Since then—well, it was simpler to seal off a beltway exit, put up hurricane fences, and post NO TRESPASSING signs than to deal with the situation.

Nor was the area actually off-limits, at least not to foot traffic and boats. It was just that there was nothing to *see* or *do* there; and even the underculture such sites would normally have attracted could do better elsewhere. For even the homeless and criminal liked level floors, straight walls, and dry feet. At least they did in Aztlan.

So it was, then, that 'Bird scrambled up a low bank, vaulted a tarnished hurricane fence, and touched down on the cracked (but only slightly tilted) concrete sweep of Dead Marina Promenade.

A klik of same, keeping an eye out for suspicious shadows, and steering wide of canalside alleyways, and he'd head west until he hit the beltway, follow it up to Sequoya, and—again—be home.

As he strode into the third block, marked by a jumble of sandcrete slabs and marble-plast Quetzal-coatls that had once been the facade of a never-completed Hilton, it occurred to him that one of his lesser perplexities had clarified. He'd wondered why that woman—Carolyn, he amended—hadn't recognized him as easily as he'd recognized her (once he'd got a good look at her). But that was simple: he'd worn makeup—and he challenged anyone to recognize someone they'd seen but once when painted eagle eyes distorted that person's features.

On the other hand . . .

He slowed and angled right, toward the stainless-steel rail that fringed the Promenade. Puffing his cheeks, he leaned against the cool metal, watching the breakers pick and pry at the ruins of a ten-million-dollar dock to his left. A breeze swept by and danced through his hair, bringing the salt scent of seashore, and, less clearly, some sort of chemical stench that might be ethanol, coupled with a sharper musk. Whitecaps slapped at the pilings that supported the pavement, while something made a creaking sound farther down the canal that probed toward the beltway a quarter block to the north.

Now where was he? Oh yeah: why that woman had reacted as she had—

More creaking, more smacks of water against piles.

And something else—

'Bird spun around, instantly on guard, hands already balling into fists.

—Too late.

They were on him: two of them, bulky men in cloaklike overcoat/serape/raincoat things with hoods Both overtopped him by a head. And they were *inhisfaceNOW*!

He managed to slam the right-hand one in the jaw with a fist, but the kick he aimed at the other caught cloth instead of crotch; and the critical instant it took 'Bird to realize that no, the guy was *not* going down, proved his undoing.

Rather than grab for his groin, the man snatched at 'Bird, flinging himself forward in the process. Already off-balance, 'Bird stumbled on a section of uneven pavement as he backpedaled and lost his equilibrium entirely. His skull grazed the railing as he flailed out to keep from going down, further fuzzing out senses that were already becoming unclear—at which point he really did fall—hard, winding himself for the second time in an hour. And before he could do more than scramble up on his elbows, one assailant had seized him by the shoulders and neatly flipped him over. 'Bird tried to snare him by the legs as they came in range, but his desperately clawing fingers could find no purchase on what seemed less like calves than pillars of adamant, both in solidity and weight. And then his chin hit the pavement tooth-grating hard, conjuring stars to complement the encroaching blackness, so that he was but distantly aware of a knee in the small of his back holding him down until another set of hands could seize his biceps and heave him up once more, arms twisted painfully behind him.

He blinked dizzily, saw the waves shimmering—and felt a sudden urge to vomit—which he did, all down his tunic front. Someone laughed; the other someone cuffed his ears, at which point a hand snapped across his mouth, stifling the scream he'd been contemplating—whereupon they spun around, and 'Bird felt himself being hauled toward the nearest alley. He struggled frantically—mostly jerks, and kicks—but the hands clamped around his biceps merely tightened a fair way past pain, as arms that seemed stronger than earth dragged him on. The one kick that actually connected produced exactly nothing; and one final attempt at shifting his weight so as to overbalance the guy he'd clobbered might as well have been aimed at the OAS Pyramid, so little did it affect that cyclopean form.

God, but these sons of bitches were strong! Strong and heavy!

Make that strong, heavy, and invisible; for excluding an impression of size and clothing, 'Bird had not so much as glimpsed a face. Stormy would not be pleased. Stormy said to always try to get at least *some* piece of physical description, preferably something that couldn't be easily altered.

In the process of sidestepping a gaping hole in the pavement, the man whose hand blocked 'Bird's mouth shifted his grip. 'Bird promptly bit him—and earned another cuff to the temple for his trouble.

Comets joined stars, and then the background blackness took over.

Somewhere in that fifty-meter jaunt he evidently passed out, because one moment they were in the middle of the Promenade, and the next, they were entering that alley. Which, now 'Bird got a bleary-eyed look at it, was floored with boards like a dock and bisected by a narrow canal.

The air stank of rotten fish and something else vaguely organic. He promptly gagged again—which only filled his mouth with foul-tasting crud and made him choke.

The hand over his mouth relaxed barely enough

for him to spit the mess onto the decking, and they were moving again, down the alley, down into a physical darkness almost as deep as that now passing in waves through 'Bird's consciousness.

Where, 'Bird wondered dimly, was the moon?

Abruptly they halted. The hand slipped off 'Bird's mouth, and he found air and a clear esophagus briefly more desirable than yelling for help—assuming anyone would have heard. And then Arm-Pinner grabbed his face from behind and pinched his cheeks, forcing his mouth open wide—across which the other promptly whipped a piece of fabric, forming a gag.

A sound hissed in his ear, but it took 'Bird a moment to realize that Arm-Pinner was speaking.

"You will stop struggling," that one said. "No one can hear you now."

Yeah, tell me more! 'Bird thought grimly, as the vises on his biceps slowly forced him first to his knees, then to an awkward sprawl, and finally onto his back. A deft flurry of motion followed by a thump and numbing pressure on his elbows told him that one was kneeling on his arms, pinning them against the boards with so much force 'Bird could already feel his fingers going numb. At which point the other eased around and made to step over his lower body.

'Bird bucked desperately, twisting sideways as best he could, but the man never faltered. A pair of kicks directly into the looming figure's crotch again had no effect; and before 'Bird could puzzle out another strategy, the man had pressed one leg to the boards with a huge foot, and was straddling him with the other. He sat down gracelessly: an iron mountain across 'Bird's thighs, and 'Bird got a sense of being compressed by at least one-twenty kilos. Once settled, the man leaned forward, bracing himself with his left hand, while he fumbled inside his voluminous clothing with the other. Unfortunately, the hood of his overgarment still obscured his face.

"We do not like to hurt things," Arm-Pinner murmured from above him, his voice oddly flat and awkward, like someone whose birth tongue was other than English, or—more aptly—like deaf people often sounded; as if he knew the words and patterns but not the nuances of inflection. "No, we certainly do not like to hurt things," he repeated, as though he'd liked the sound of that phrase, "yet sometimes it is necessary. Pain is not to be wished for, but it happens. Nor is death to be desired, yet it occurs every day to a million-million-million living things. Most have no awareness; most are so tiny one may kill them and not even know. But in the eyes of the universe, you are tiny too—*Thunderbird O'Connor*. And so, if we happen to kill you, it is unlikely that the *universe* will care."

'Bird struggled, but to no avail. He very much feared he was going to vomit again.

"Yes . . . killing . . . death by another name. Not to be desired, but sometimes necessary—*especially to those who see what they should not!*"

The pressure on his elbows increased alarmingly, as did the weight immobilizing his thighs. Arm-Pinner fell silent, but as 'Bird watched, horrified, Leg-Straddler finally found whatever he'd been rifling his clothing for and drew it out.

Something as long as his hand, that shimmered like broken glass in the light of the moon that had just cleared the roof of the defunct Hilton, there at the east end of the alley.

Glass! Not metal, *glass*! But not *window* glass or *bottle* glass—

Obsidian.

The man held an obsidian knife!

And that man on the beach: the one who'd been flayed! The guy who'd done that had *used* an obsidian knife. Shoot, 'Bird had *picked up* the damned thing after the assailant had flung it at him!

Which meant . . .

He put everything he had into bucking at least one of the men away. But a slap across his face from Arm-Pinner well-nigh brought unconsciousness. And while part of him would have welcomed that, another aspect knew that if he succumbed, he would never see daylight again, that as long as he was even numbly aware, there was hope, whereas if he gave up now, he was done for.

"Alive?" Leg-Straddler wondered softly, sounding marginally more sure of inflection than the other. "Or dead?"

"Dead does no good," Arm-Pinner replied, as Leg-Straddler ran a stubby finger along the edge of the obsidian knife as though it were some toy he had discovered. "Of course he *will* be dead when you finish, or shortly thereafter. And then we must eliminate the woman he seems to have alerted."

In reply, Leg-Straddler simply reached toward 'Bird's throat, inserted two fingers into the collar slit of his tunic—and pulled down. It was not a sharp movement; but it held the inexorability of ice caps—which was sufficient. 'Bird felt fabric press hard into the back of his neck, felt friction burn his flesh; and then, with a soft ripping sound, the hopsack parted. Cool air floated across 'Bird's bare chest and belly. A random breeze tickled his ribs. He could feel the boards pulse softly, a counterpoint to the slap of the waves.

Leg-Straddler grunted and shifted down. A huge hand fumbled at 'Bird's waistband. He heard the buzz-rip of Velcro letting go. A jerk, and his jeans were open to the base of his penis. He wished he had on underwear.

Meanwhile, Arm-Pinner's finger had found the silver tattoo of his body phone in the shadow of his clavicle. "Begin here," he hissed.

Leg-Straddler nodded, and 'Bird caught the merest flash of a gap-toothed grin before he saw a far more ominous flash as the man bent forward and inserted the glistening tip of the obsidian knife into the heart of the only remaining hope he had. A twist, marked by a sharp flare of pain, an electronic shriek in his ear, and a glitter of blood, and it was over.

But the knife's work wasn't.

'Bird held his breath as Leg-Straddler slowly drew the very point of the blade delicately across his right pec until it was centered exactly where the softness of his throat gave way to the hardness of his sternum. And then, oh so slowly, he eased that point inward and down.

'Bird barely felt it at first, so sharp was that edge, so fine and clear the pain that took fire in his chest. There was little blood—yet. That would come later, he imagined.

So why didn't they get it over with? Why prolong the agony? Why not stab him now and have done, if all they wanted was revenge against someone who had identified their fellow?

But exactly as the knife reached the lower arc of his rib cage and slid into the softer flesh of his belly, he knew.

He was being skinned!

Skinned alive like that poor guy on the beach.

And now, with that knife edge gliding a delicate quarter sim deep through his flesh, he dared not so much as flinch lest he die!

A slow death or a quick one? Well, it didn't hurt much—yet. Therefore, he didn't wish for death— yet. But he wished, very badly, he'd followed his grandfather's advice and composed a death song.

Lower, possibly deeper; and 'Bird wondered how far in that blade would have to delve before his guts started spilling out. Whether it would go left or right of his navel; how much longer he would get to be a man. He had a hard flat stomach, smoothly muscled; but down the center . . .

He gasped as the pain increased, and it took all the will he had not to flinch. Reality began to tunnel.

Pain, pain, pain, he told himself. *It is only pain.*

Only electricity and chemicals bitching at each other.

More pain now, and he ground his teeth into the gag. Sweat sprang out on his body, though he was cold. The tunnel narrowed. Shock hovered near.

He closed his eyes. When he opened them again, he saw red.

Not blood, however, but a sim-sized spot of ruby light sliding quickly up Leg-Straddler's right side before being masked by the mass of his shoulder.

A sharp crack.

A louder splat, like a water balloon exploding.

And an eruption of too-hot blood mixed with something gritty that was probably bone.

And the echo—like lightning striking in a drum.

Reality wavered, then stabilized.

Leg-Straddler vented a high-pitched wail and toppled to his left, clutching at his shoulder as he fell. 'Bird felt more blood spray across his belly and prayed it wasn't his. The clatter of the blade slipping to the boards seemed promising. The tunnel widened minutely, became the end of the alley at which showed a dark man shape, the moon, and midway up the man's body, a fallen star of crimson light.

The pressure on 'Bird's arms shifted, but did not relent—not enough for him to twist free, though he was already heaving the shrieking Leg-Straddler off his thighs. The man was sobbing.

Footsteps slapped against the boards, then stopped abruptly, to be followed by another *crack*— and a second liquid explosion.

Whereupon Arm-Pinner likewise tumbled away from him.

Blood whipped across 'Bird's face, well-nigh blinding him, but with the weight of his assailants gone, he put all his energy into rolling as far from them as he could. A foot caught him on one shoulder as he went—probably Arm-Pinner thrashing about.

More footsteps, as Arm-Pinner struggled to his feet. Another crack—two more—a muffled cry, and the world narrowed to the sound of thumpings and scufflings and echoing gunshot blasts, over all of which floated a cloud of pain.

" 'Bird! You all right?"

'Bird finally ceased rolling long enough to wipe the blood from his eyes with one hand while he undid the gag with the other. "S-stormy?" he ventured hesitantly, to the slim silhouette he could dimly see striding toward him.

"Just call me Mario," Stormy chuckled grimly, as he sauntered cockily to where 'Bird lay. A nickel-plated pistol gleamed in his hand, probably one of the 9 mm. Heckler & Koches his embassy used. A laser targeter lurked below the barrel. He looked exceedingly smug. "You okay?" he repeated, his face going suddenly hard as his gaze swept over 'Bird's bloody face and torso.

"Just a flesh wound, really," 'Bird gasped weakly, and would have laughed from pure hysterical relief had it not hurt so much. "Most of this isn't mine, so I'll . . . live, I reckon. What about the boogers?"

"Winged 'em, I hope. One in the right shoulder, the other in the left as he looked up—which took a little doing, since I didn't want to get you! I had to kneecap 'em too, but I tried to do *that* gently."

'Bird's gaze wavered from his friend to the spot a few meters away where both assailants lay moaning. Reality tunneled again.

"Hold still."

'Bird had no trouble complying as Stormy whipped off his serape and used it to dab at the blood that salved 'Bird's torso. "Yeah, you *may* live. I've got some Spraskin in the Jeep—'course it's half a klik south of here . . . "

"Like we said, I'll live," 'Bird managed, though he had no urge yet to rise.

"You wanta call the Mounties or shall I?"

"You'll have to," 'Bird mumbled distantly, as pain and shock mounted a sneak attack. "They . . . got my phone. Cut that sucker clean out."

"You never liked it anyway," Stormy snorted, reaching for the hollow of his clavicle.

"Just a sec."

"What?"

"How'd you—?"

"When you left your place, I remembered that I wanted to lend you a piece. But by the time I got past your fucking guards, you were gone. Fortunately, I saw those guys tailing you—saw the flash of that knife. I tried to call you but your phone was off, and the shitheads at the taxi place gave me a bunch of runaround about confidentiality, and I knew the Mounties would either think I was crazy or go ballistic. So I left a message at the 'Wheel for you to call me—"

"—which I never got—"

"—Obviously. So I figured maybe I oughta go down there myself, but on the way I caught up with the Dodge boys again—I thought. Trouble is, there are a lot of white Dodge Argons in this town, and I'd managed to miss the plate—so when they headed north instead of south I knew I had the wrong one. I called the 'Wheel again but they said you were in the middle of your set, so I headed south—just in time to hit the toli traffic. By the time I got through *that* you'd left. I tracked you—literally, but lost you in the Marina. And then I heard—"

Stormy's words broke off, his face went white. "Holy Mother of all the Gods!"

'Bird froze in the act of sitting up, to follow his buddy's gaze.

And saw two things, one he did not *want* to believe, one he *could* not believe.

Leg-Straddler had scooted up against a wall and lay there moaning softly, one hand gripping his shattered shoulder, the other splayed across his knee, while steady streams of blood oozed through both sets of fingers. But what put the wind up 'Bird was the fact that far from the cold-blooded vivisectionist he had been earlier, he was now sobbing helplessly like a little child.

"*Duele,*" he blubbered over and over. "*Duele. Duele. Duele.*" Hurt. Hurt. Hurt. On and on, as pinkish drool spilled from his mouth and onto his impressive chest. His face was utterly devoid of intelligence—and had obviously *never* held any.

But the other . . . the one 'Bird had assumed had simply been writhing in the understandable pain of two bullet wounds . . . what he saw *there* . . .

"Jesus Christ, *shit!*" he gulped, as Stormy squatted beside him to brace him with an arm around his shoulders. "Oh Jesus!"

For somehow, in the few moments since Stormy had shot him, Arm-Pinner had worked his way out of most of his clothing—had stripped off his over-cloak and tunic, and rucked down both pairs of pants. It was hard to get a sense of his body in the gloom, however, save that he was over two meters tall and powerfully built, and that his skin was un-cannily white where it was not patterned with the blood that made starbursts on his left shoulder and right knee.

Nor was he moaning, at least not like his drooling accomplice.

"Oh . . . shit!" from Stormy. "I ain't believin' this! No way!"

For even as he and 'Bird gaped incredulously, Arm-Pinner raised his hand to his chest, and with exquisite precision slit himself from neck to penis with one long fingernail. But instead of blood, in-stead of viscera, instead of . . . who knew what, his skin peeled away like paper, revealing something dark and pale and vaguely tubular. A leech or mag-got, 'Bird thought at first, and felt his gorge rise. Be-side him he heard Stormy swallowing.

But then the upper part slipped free and 'Bird saw that it was no such disgusting shape. Rather, it looked a very great deal like a whale—a *killer* whale, to be specific, though he'd never seen one that small.

The flukes came last, flipping out of the abdominal cavity to leave the legs flat as empty stockings.

With one final awkward roll, it flopped over the side of the boards and into the canal. 'Bird heard the heavy splash, punctuated by the ongoing, *"Duele, duele, duele . . ."*

"I fuckin' ain't believing that!" he whispered.

"Like I am?" Stormy swallowed shakily. "Jesus, man, I sure as hell hope you believe in magic now— 'cause to repeat what I said before: it sure as hell looks like magic believes in you!"

"Magic," 'Bird echoed numbly. "Magic . . . "

"The wolves of the sea: my mother's people's demons."

"Huh?"

"Were-orcas: the Makah believe in were-orcas."

"If that's what that was . . . "

"The wolves of the sea," Stormy repeated softly. "And unfortunately wolves hunt in packs."

'Bird could not reply.

Stormy's face was still pale as he patted 'Bird on the shoulder and eased past him toward the scene of carnage. "Magic or not, I'd better check out this other guy—in case there's something about him that might make it . . . unwise to call an ambulance. And if not—well, first aid would make a damned fine reality check right now."

'Bird could only sit and stare and try to reassemble his world in some way that made even half-assed sense.

He hurt so many places he might as well not hurt, though the pain between his pecs was subsiding. He glanced down fearfully, probing along his sternum. Nothing major—thank God. That must have been a preliminary incision. A light one before the clincher. Only the bottom two inches were bleeding significantly, and that more a trickle than a stream. He took off the rags of his tunic and pressed it there.

Stormy, meanwhile, was fully involved with Leg-Straddler's wounds. Which left 'Bird the dubious task of investigating the impossible. Steeling himself, he crawled toward the crumpled mass of clothing

and . . . whatever it was that seconds before had
been Arm-Pinner.

Closer, and he nudged one empty shoe with a finger. It rattled on the boards. The wad beyond was
pants, underwear, and socks, empty save for a pink/
white *something* that lay crumpled for at least two
meters farther on.

'Bird knew what it was but did not at first acknowledge that knowing.

It was skin. *Human* skin. But not the flayed skin
of one single body. By the difference in color, hair
distribution, and texture, what lay glistening wetly
there in the ghostly moonlight of the Dead Marina,
were the crudely joined skins of at least five separate
persons, one of them a woman.

"Stormy—" 'Bird began, as darkness hovered
near. "I think you'd better have a look at this."

"Soon as I tighten this tourniquet," Stormy called
back. "But 'Bird—this one's your call."

Chapter XXI:
Open Door Policy

(Aztlan, Aztlan Free Zone—Mexico)
(Saturday, September 3—
shortly past midnight)

Carolyn couldn't sleep.

For the last forty minutes she'd lain flat on her back in the precise center of her futon, arms flung loosely at her sides, legs slightly apart, head properly pillowed to remove all stress from her neck. Her breathing was regular, her clothing—an oversized Cousteau Society T-shirt—loose. None of her muscles or joints were in tension; her stomach, kidneys, and bowels had all been tended to. No knots, lumps, or ridges disturbed the bedding beneath her, and the temperature was exactly right. She'd even put an extended electronic cover of Maurice Roberts's *Tara* on the stereo.

Nothing helped. Her eyes felt big as saucers—absolutely would not stay closed. Rather, like flies, they flicked first to the ceiling, then to the sliding glass doors, then to the tall slanting windows between them, that showed her half the sky. Her bedroom faced due east, and she could see the gibbous moon from where she lay: nearing the zenith above

the head-high wall that screened her patio from
DeSoto Street.

A breeze was blowing, betrayed by the swaying of
the agave spears by the gate. She considered joining
them for a while, fixing herself a toddy, perhaps, and
lying on her lounger beneath the Caribbean stars.

Except that she'd spent too much effort getting
situated. And except that to prepare a posset required revisiting the kitchen and risking a potential
encounter with Kevin (who, to judge by the lack of
noise from the living room, had finally found Dreamland himself).

She wondered if she'd been wise to let him camp
here, given that the Schism still existed and was at
present being ignored, not dealt with, and that any
hope of further de-escalation depended, from her
point of view, *on* dealing with it—though what *that*
nebulous concept entailed, she had no idea. They
both knew the truth: Mom had indulged in at least
one fruitful fling; Dad had calmly drawn a discreet,
but very clear line in the sand; and they'd all staked
out their respective territories. But Mom was beyond
easy reach by phone just now, Dad was giving no one
grief, and nothing constructive was to be gained by
continued hostilities.

Except that somebody had to bend first.

Really bend.

God, it was a mess.

And it wasn't like she didn't have *other* crises to
contend with! Lord, but a lot had happened during
the last two days—so much, in truth, that she'd
barely begun to sort it out, never mind that she'd
spent half that time asleep, unconscious, sedated,
anesthetized—or dead.

Dead.

There was a certain dull finality to that word; a heavy permanence.

But had she *been* dead? She could remember nothing about that time—though of course no one had told her that she was about to die, so she'd hardly been primed to take notes. The facts were that she'd been flatlined: no breathing, no heartbeat, no brain activity. And though it was possible to resuscitate people after the first two had gone AWOL, the third . . . Well, she really ought to be hobnobbing with potatoes right now, instead of assailing the mysteries of her existence as viciously as ever.

So perhaps she hadn't been dead at all.

There'd been no out-of-body experiences, that much was certain. No bright light, no tunnel, no feeling of peace, no sense of welcome or love, no shadowy figures of deceased loved ones.

But what had happened? Nesheim wasn't the sort to obsess over nothing, and he'd certainly obsessed over whatever had happened to her. And while the man had driven her crazy during the past few days, she imagined that in his situation, she'd do the same. She was an anomaly. Some of science's major breakthroughs had been born of anomalies.

Shoot, until she'd died, she'd been obsessing on an anomaly herself!

What was up with the dolphins, anyway? Or the orcas, more properly? What could possibly have caused an orca (or several—perhaps an entire small pod) not only to attack a large population of dolphins (though attacks themselves were not unknown), but to mutilate them in a creepily consistent manner yet not devour their kills? It didn't make sense, not by the accepted conventions of cetacean behavior. Much against her will, she was reminded of some of her mom's gorier tales, about people who'd had their tongues cut out or been blinded or otherwise maimed, as punishment for speaking too freely or seeing what they oughtn't.

Of course, Kev had *liked* those stories—and look what it had done to him.

Well, it had put him in a castle in Eireland, for one thing, and given him enough money to do pretty much as he pleased.

But it—or something—had also got to him in a big way, had, she feared, pushed him beyond the brink, with his talk of selkies, and such.

Except that he'd looked so sincere. And there was also the not insignificant fact that he was *here*, had apparently gone through a great deal of grief to *get* here, and had then risked major ridicule to pass on his preposterous notion.

So perhaps she should cut him some slack.

After all, she'd told him something quite preposterous too. Like, how many folks dropped in on their long-lost kin only to be informed, very bluntly, that they'd been dead for nigh on an hour but were recovering nicely, and accepted it with the grace Kevin had granted her?

Besides, there was a common thread in their separate weirdnesses. Kev had talked about selkies, which, as he'd needlessly explained, were a sort of were-seal native to Eireland and Scotland (according to the folklore, at least). They were supposed to shift shape by the expedient of putting on or removing sealskins. To catch a selkie, you hid its skin—which also incurred its wrath, but, unlike leprechaun gold, earned you no three wishes.

But that odd dream—the one with her mom and the lad with whom she'd made love: that lad had turned into a . . . a seal. Well, not precisely. She'd bedded down with him in human shape, and there'd been a seal in his place when she'd awakened.

A seal that had spoken directly to Carolyn.

That had told her she was the one the dolphins worshiped.

Which was what that Indian had blurted out back at the *diverto*.

Which was impossible.

Which, she amended, conventional science and her personal belief system *said* was impossible.

And the link . . .

She swallowed and closed her eyes, as something dawned on her that would probably have occurred far sooner had she not been embroiled in a chaos of activities and emotions during the last twelve hours.

There was common ground there too.

First she'd dreamed of what might have been a selkie—and out of the clear blue, Kev had come up with that bizarre tale about the very same mythical beings.

And then the one in her dream had uttered that troublesome line—which a total stranger had repeated word for word at a Sinsynsen *diverto*!

And since she'd told no one about that . . .

It made no sense—in a rational world—but there *had* to be a connection. And if there was, then how large a leap was it to believing in Kevin's selkie?

"Oh Jesus," she whispered. "Jesus, God, and Mary!"

So what did she do now?

Lie awake all night and fret and worry?

Wake up Kev and try to puzzle it out with him?

Call Rudy or Hassie—or Mom, if she could be reached . . . or even Dad?

But there were good arguments against all those.

No, what she needed to do was sleep, simply turn

herself off for a while and reassess everything in the clear light of day.

But there was always a chance she would dream.

Which was not an attractive notion.

Fine!

But she *had* to sleep sometime. And if she was going to be functional tomorrow, she had to get in some downtime between now and then. That was a fact. That she might dream was merely a possibility.

Besides, she was *hot*—nigh onto sweating, in fact, as though she'd acquired a slight fever. Indeed, sweat was beading on her breasts, arms, and forehead even as she noticed them. She was thirsty too. And now she'd became aware of her body, she was also itching virulently, especially along her spine and at the base of her neck.

More stress reaction?

Well, she'd certainly been pondering stressful subjects. And if she *did* have a touch of something— that was one *more* good reason to catch some Zs. Therefore . . .

She'd get up, take a long hot bath, so as to direct both her blood supply and the focus of her senses away from her brain. She'd swallow *one* sleeping pill and wash it down with some OJ from the kitchen. And perhaps she'd snare a Guinness, if Kev hadn't scarfed it all.

Oh, and she'd set the alarm on LOUD.

Sighing, she rose from the futon. But the instant her feet touched the carpet, she caught a flicker of movement beyond the mirror glass doors that let onto the patio. Scowling, she padded that way, wrapping her arms around herself as she progressed. Probably a cat, skulking along the high wall there. Or an iguana, searching for bugs among the aloes.

Or a tarantula—they liked to skitter along the ledge.

And now there were two—

But not spiders, though they were roughly that size and shape.

Hands!

And a head! A dark-haired head.

And as she gaped as if ensorcelled, the hands tensed, the head withdrew—and with one awkward flurry of motion, someone scrambled over the wall.

Male, she assumed automatically, wishing she could wear a body phone, in which case she'd already be calling the Mounties.

Only . . . there was something familiar about this midsized lad, as if she'd seen him before, and recently.

And something wrong too!

For the fellow had landed badly, had lurched forward onto his hands and knees into the cactus bed by the left hand wall, and was now having trouble getting up; indeed, he was fumbling his way up the stucco as if he'd been injured—or had injured himself in his fall. And then she realized two things.

First, the lad *was* injured. His silver-gray skinshirt showed a line of seeping stains down the front that looked an awful lot like blood, while a larger splatter of the probable-same angled across both thighs of his scruffy jeans. The pale fabric was patterned with grime, too: dirt, oil—who knew what. And a fair bit seemed to have savaged his face as well—and his hands. She wasn't so sure he didn't have a black eye.

He was also someone she had seen before. In fact, he was that lad she'd nearly flattened two days ago! The handsome, if sleepy-eyed, Indian who'd blundered out in front of her while she was racing to investigate Anomalous Beaching, Number IV!

But what had happened to him?

More to the point, what was he doing *here*?

And what was so familiar about him besides his face?

And then it came to her, as sudden as Irish rain.

It was him!

Not merely the lad she'd almost splattered. He was also the dancer from the *diverto*. The one who'd struck her dumb with his ill-timed oracle.

Who'd told her she was the one the dolphins worshiped.

Who could perhaps unravel one of her mysteries.

He was staring at her now, eyes wide, mouth half-open. Dazed, he looked, or in shock. Grim. Troubled. In pain.

But he was making no move to assail the doors, merely standing there by the prickly pear as if he had reached some crucial decision point hours too soon and was unable to choose between options. Shoot, the way he looked, he was probably trying to decide whether to live or die.

Ignoring long-ingrained instincts that told her she was a pea-brained loon to unlock her door for a strange man in the middle of the night, she told the latch "Clear" and slid the heavy glass panel aside.

Night air swept in, warm and humid—to slow uneasily when it struck the air-conditioned chill of the room beyond. Heat and cold wove invisible patterns around her. She shivered, then wiped the sweat from her brow with the back of her hand. And scratched her side, where the skin was burning.

The man—what was that name they'd announced him by? Thunderbird something? O'Connor! Yeah, that was it; she'd been surprised it was Eirish—

smiled crookedly, and ventured a slow step forward, hands outstretched as though to convey his harmlessness. An eyebrow lifted inquiringly and he pointed to the open door.

She nodded mutely—whereupon good sense got the better of her, and she spun around, intent on waking Kev.

"No!" the man gasped behind her. "No—I won't—"

She froze, then slowly turned. The man—O'Connor—hadn't moved. But his eyes were huge with desperation and fear.

Carolyn held her ground for a long moment; then, without taking her eyes off her unlikely guest, slowly reached to a rack atop her chest of drawers and retrieved the antique katana Hasegawa had given her for Christmas last year. Still not speaking, she slid out the arm-long blade—and motioned O'Connor inside.

"What do you want?" she whispered harshly. "You've got one minute to explain what's happened to you and what you want with me, and then I—"

"You . . . don't have a body phone," O'Connor panted, from where he slumped against the wall a meter inside the room, "and your house one seems to be unplugged, otherwise I probably wouldn't *be* here. Now please, we've gotta talk."

"About what?"

A weary grimace. "You *have* to know."

"But—"

"Not here."

"Why not? What right have you—?"

"You're not the type to believe without proof, are you?" O'Connor sighed, his face a mask of resigned frustration.

Carolyn tightened her grip. "What's that supposed to mean?"

O'Connor opened his mouth as if to answer, then paused, scowled irritably—and leapt forward, blindingly fast, for someone who'd barely made it over a chest-high wall seconds earlier. Carolyn was so surprised, she forgot the katana until it was too late. And by then O'Connor had seized the wrist that controlled it with one hand and clamped the other over her mouth, while using the weight of his body to force her against the wall. Her first instinct was to knee him in the groin, but he anticipated that with a twist of his hips. Her second response was to use her free left hand to beat at his face, but another deft move shifted him around behind her, with her right arm in such painful tension she had no choice but to drop the sword. She heard him grunt, heard his breath catch, and gathered that his effort had brought him well-nigh to exhaustion, never mind what it was costing *her* in simple pain. He *had* to be running on pure adrenaline. She wondered how close he was to empty.

And then, slowly but inexorably, he pushed her toward the glass door and through. He paused on the patio side and murmured in her ear. "Use your free hand to close it."

She had no choice but to comply.

"The gate has a voice lock, which you will activate," O'Connor continued hoarsely. "And please, Miss—Carolyn—understand that in spite of how this must look, I absolutely do *not* have any bad intentions toward you. But I'm tired and I hurt and my gut's held together with Spraskin, and I'm just flat sick of talkin' my head off about craziness when one demonstration can explain everything. But I *absolutely* do not have time to argue, beg, or cajole. Now, if I move my hand, do you promise not to scream? Nod if you agree."

She relaxed a trifle at that, only then realizing how tense she'd been. Perhaps the lad really was sincere. Crazy, but sincere. Like Kevin.

Kevin . . . Her ace in the hole, now—maybe. If only she hadn't turned off the phone so he could give his spiel uninterrupted.

She nodded.

Carefully, tentatively, O'Connor removed his hand. She thought of screaming anyway, but who would hear? Two sandcrete walls and one of glass lay between her and Kev; her apartment was on the end, which meant no help from that quarter; and the folks in 102 were out of town. This wasn't the sort of neighborhood to encourage sidewalk traffic. And folks in cars wouldn't hear.

They had reached the gate by then, and O'Connor seemed to be using the minimum amount of pressure possible to steer her forward. "Open," she whispered to it.

It did, and an instant later they stumbled onto the sidewalk. The gate clicked shut behind them: two meters of solid redwood. A pearlescent orange-gold Jeep Juneau sat at the curb: one of those cute little jobs that looked like a clump of soap bubbles on wheels—newish, but covered with dust, as though it had recently been in the country or on the beach. O'Connor opened the glassy nearside door with his free hand. "Please . . . "

She hesitated. "I'm not dressed—"

"There's stuff you can wear in the Jeep—if you don't mind raidin' my best friend's laundry." He tried to laugh, but she heard his breath catch, and once again wondered what had happened to him for even that effort to cost him pain.

Still she held back.

"I can probably still run faster than you," he

rasped. "I'm also suffering from blood loss and flirting with shock, and if I have to subdue a struggling woman, I could be in very bad shape indeed, and you won't know any more than you do. Now: do you want that on your conscience? Or do you want to talk about your . . . dreams."

She glared at him. "How do you know about them?"

O'Connor's mouth dropped open. "I *didn't*! I— that just popped into my head!"

She regarded him seriously for a long hesitant moment, then grimaced, set her jaw, evicted a can of Spraskin—and climbed into the right-hand bucket. The interior smelled of blood.

He joined her, in the driver's seat, fumbling with an ignition card. "Not my car," he explained vaguely, as he inserted the plastic square into the dash.

"So, what do you want?" Carolyn gritted, when the vehicle had whirred to life.

O'Connor turned left at the corner, heading east along Hudson Boulevard. "Well, we evidently need to talk about dreams. But first—"

"—*First* . . . who *are* you? How do you know my name? How do you know . . . what you told me back at the *diverto*?"

A deep breath, then: "Thunderbird Devlin O'Connor, deputy cultural attaché to the Kituwah Embassy, Aztlan—that's Cherokee arts officer, to you. At your service," he added with a tired grin, looking marginally more at ease—or less pained. Certainly less frantic.

"But—"

"One of your friends referred to you as Carolyn when I tried to catch up with you back at the 'Wheel, and that guy with the interesting hair had scribbled Carolyn Mauney-Griffith all over his place mat—

which is in both the phone base and the city directory, along with your complete address and occu-
pation."

"And the rest?"

A grunt, followed by a right turn—the guy was
driving very fast indeed, as though he were fighting
a deadline. She hoped he had reflexes to match. *He*
might have a death wish, but she didn't.

"Yeah, well, as to the rest . . . that's a good question."

Silence. Then, from O'Connor. "Okay, Ms. Mauney-Griffith—there's no way to ask this but to ask
it . . ."

"What."

"What do you think about magic?"

Carolyn felt as though the breath had been
knocked out of her for the zillionth time that evening. "You're the second person to ask me that since
sunset," she replied carefully.

"What did you say then?"

"That I didn't believe in it."

"What would you say now?"

"I'm not sure."

He eyed her askance. "You're not sure about
magic? Or you're not sure what you'd say?"

Carolyn looked flustered. "Both—neither."

A longer silence, then a deep ragged breath. "What
if I can *prove* there's magic?"

"I'm a scientist," Carolyn sighed finally. "Science
subsists on proof."

O'Connor flashed her a desperate grin. "Good—
'cause that's exactly what I'm fixin' to give you."

Chapter XXII:
Rude Awakening

(Aztlan, Aztlan Free Zone—Mexico)
(Saturday, September 3—
shortly past midnight)

Kevin was asleep.

And then he simply wasn't.

Where was he?

That was his first concern, as he fumbled through a shroud of earth-toned sheeting in search of orientation—right, left, up, down—*anything* that hinted at location. Not in bed—*that* was certain—not with something soft/firm against his shoulders he dimly recognized as the back of a sofa. And not *his* sofa, because the soft-lit space beyond was too small, too clean-lined, and far too white-walled to be Clononey. It was a modern space—a modern room.

Carolyn's.

He was at Cary's.

Good, now he could go back to Dreamland.

Unfortunately, his bladder, which was what had awakened him in the first place, had more pressing priorities.

"Dammit!" he grunted, as he blinked to groggy awareness, feeling sleep tug at him like a vast soggy blanket that sought to drag him back down to slumber, where he wanted to go—and couldn't. His lids felt heavy as lead, his eyes as though someone had built bonfires there and extinguished them with sand. His head hurt like a forge, either from having slept wrong, or courtesy of the two Guinness he'd chugged after that all-too-brief and far-too-fruitless bull session. And he was sore in places he had no idea he'd traumatized—that last probable legacy of snoozing on a bench in the Shannon lobby one night, napping awkwardly on the plane most of yesterday, and being tense as a wire both days as well. What he needed was a good hot bath (which he'd never quite found time for), a nice long massage, and then a filling meal of something besides overspiced lizard. Or maybe the meal first, then—

Okay, okay, he told his bladder. *Okay, already!*

And with that, he untangled his feet from the sheet and slid them to the floor. His head swung the opposite way—too fast, given the artillery assailing the inside of his skull.

"Gaaaa!"

He yawned hugely, groaned, and finally levered himself to his feet. Now where was the loo? Oh, right: off the hall, of course. *Fool!* Yawning again, he rose and stumbled stiffly down the corridor, aiming for the single cracked door, beyond which pink light glimmered.

Bull's eye!—though the plethora of shiny tile and chrome fixtures were a marked contrast to the whitewashed stone and antique porcelain back home. Two items *were* familiar, however, which he hadn't noticed earlier—the reading material was identical. The dirty clothes hamper showed the exact edition of John Devlin's *Where Youth and Laughter Go* that graced its equivalent in Clononey. And beneath it lay the same issue of *Eireland of the Wel-*

comes. It was even facedown to the same article—
the one on him—which made him feel a lot better
about Cary's attitude toward him.

One more memo for the agenda, he supposed.

Whereupon he pushed down Cameron McMillan-
the-Younger's metallic gold bikini briefs and let fly.

It was a long whiz, and in the way of such things,
relaxing in its own right, so that he found himself
drowsing off in the midst of wondering if he ought to
really play the rebel and add a blue blaze to his pubic
hair to match that on his head, or simply abandon
the old one, which seemed badly out of place in
these more laid-back climes.

Yet more grist for tomorrow's mill.

Eventually he dripped dry, and flushed the john,
closing the lid as an afterthought, lest he disturb
Cary—though he doubted it made much difference,
given the synthesized harp music still wafting from
her room.

Pausing for one final yawn, and to scratch his butt
(both cheeks—perhaps he was allergic to metallic
gold dye), he sighed, and padded back up the hall.

As soon as he stepped into the living room someone clamped a hand over his mouth and nose full of
something fabricky that smelled suspiciously like
chloroform, while another someone efficiently
snared both flailing wrists and yanked them behind
him. He fought back instinctively, jerking and wig-
gling—to no avail. His assailants evidently possessed
infinite strength, so that resisting only strained his
own neglected muscles. His last effort—a herculean
bucking begun when he realized they intended to
bind his hands—was equally fruitless, but at least
earned him a glimpse of his captors.

Two men. Two *big* men: bulky but not fat, and
dressed in shapeless dull-colored clothing that went

well-nigh invisible in the gloom. He couldn't see their faces clearly, but there was an odd sort of blandness about them, a vaguely unfinished quality, as though someone had worked them up out of clay on a sculptor's stand but hadn't got around to refining the features. Tough to get a description there.

And then it didn't matter, for just as the man behind him finished tying his wrists together, the fumes he'd been valiantly resisting took him away from it all. His final impression was of his knees going rubbery, and of trying to twist as he slumped downward, so as not to hit his head on anything before all of him hit the floor.

. . . darkness . . .

. . . reality trickled back. He was sprawled on his left side across the hooked shag rug in front of Cary's sofa. The glass-and-chrome coffee table impeded most of his bleary-eyed view, but he had a clear line on his own bare knees and belly, and beyond them, of two big men methodically searching the apartment: every door, drawer, and curio container. Fair enough, if this was a robbery, which seemed reasonable. Except that these guys weren't removing anything and were careful to put the drawers back in place. Sometimes they'd pick up something, or stare at the most ordinary objects as though they didn't know what to make of them. Once or twice they held a utensil dead wrong; and there was also something strange about the way they moved—in large, smooth gestures, he decided. There was no fidgety nervousness about them. No small motions, save that their hands swung back and forth constantly.

Cary! Kevin remembered suddenly, and cold fingers pinched his heart. *What about Cary?*

He cursed the hangover that had made him stupid

and self-centered, and the anesthetic that seemed likely to keep him that way.

But then he noticed the third accomplice. Kevin had almost overlooked him, so still did that figure stand just to the right of the hall archway, as though to intercept anyone who should enter from either direction. Except he wasn't moving. His face—which, unlike the others, *did* look finished, down to an ugly scar across his right cheek—was utterly slack. And though he was also a big man, his muscles sagged. The effect was of a huge, well-made automaton that had been turned off. Or like one poor old fellow Kevin had seen in a Dublin hospital who'd been lobotomized. There was life, but no intelligence, no volition . . .

Kevin shuddered and closed his eyes.

A mechanical rattle made him slit them open again, to the sight of a fourth figure emerging from the bedroom—empty-handed.

Cary!

Where was *Cary?*

Or—what had they done to her?

And what could *he* do about it?

And then two dreadful thoughts struck Kevin in a row and kept him on the floor, though his every instinct had him on his feet and fighting. This wasn't his apartment; therefore, whatever these guys wanted probably had nothing to do with him, especially as no one but Cary and her two friends knew for certain he was here, and that only because she'd called Rudy right after they'd fled the *diverto* to tell him to hang on to the rental car—which meant it wasn't parked outside. Which in turn suggested that this was either random violence, or Cary had been the intended victim all along.

On the other hand, they *had* lain in wait for him.

Then again, his pissing had sounded like Niagara Falls, which surely would have alerted anyone in earshot to his presence itself, and his probable sex.

So where was his sister?

Evidently not in her bedroom. Or else . . .

The person who'd been in the bedroom had joined the others by then, and Kevin got a better look at . . . him? Not a good look, however, as they never turned on the lights. Still, he was not surprised to see the same generic-bland features as the first two men, though a fraction, perhaps, more feminine.

"She's not here," that one said, his—her—voice oddly emotionless, for all that he/she was modulating tones and stresses all over the place. Kevin only barely recognized it as English.

But at least Cary was safe.

Or was she? If she wasn't here, where was she? Even worse—

At which point the man who'd been rifling the kitchen stumped back into the living room and pointed to Kevin with a butcher knife. "What do we do with him?"

The person from the back shrugged. "What we always do." He/she turned half around and nodded toward the blank-faced man holding up the wall. "You can kill him."

"Wait!" the third broke in, his voice going almost supersonically high in what Kevin supposed was a weird sort of excitement.

"Why?" The voice dead flat, utterly without emotion, or even sex.

"Perhaps *he* knows where the woman is," the other responded, reaching down absently to grasp Kevin's leg and give him a ruthless tug that hauled him out from between the sofa and coffee table. "Besides," that one added, "haven't you noticed what a very fine *skin* he has?"

"Smooth as a female's," the third agreed. "His face is not very bristly either. Though there might be a problem with his hair—"

"Perhaps," the searcher replied tonelessly. "But not here. His kind see too much and ask too many questions."

"Especially as he is awake."

"I can resolve that right now," the one with the knife replied. Whereupon he raised the weapon and brought it down on Kevin's head.

Kevin had only time to wince and feel the tiniest twinge of relief that it was the hilt flashing toward his skull and not the blade, when that same slab of blackened wood struck just above his ear and sent him to matching darkness.

It did not require much effort.

Chapter XXIII:
Two in the Bush

(Near Sinsynsen, Aztlan Free Zone—Mexico)
(Saturday, September 3—after midnight)

'Bird had to give Carolyn Mauney-Griffith credit for one thing: she sure could keep her cool. No woman *he* knew would have reacted to what amounted to being kidnapped as rationally as she had: defiantly, but practically, knowing when to push and when to let be. She was in effect a model prisoner—though she was hardly a true captive, given that she could have jumped ship (Jeep, rather) at any one of the numerous traffic lights that had snared them as 'Bird hustled Stormy's brand-new Juneau 4-T along Aztlan's six-lane boulevards—east, first, along Abla Avenue, then south through a webwork of office parks until he hit the beltway just past the Viker Theater. It had been an irksome drive too, there being no straight route between her apartment and his intended destination. Fortunately, this late, traffic was light. He'd just turned off the beltway again, heading south toward Sinsynsen.

The only trouble (besides obvious things like abandoned buddies, a banged-up body, possible pursuit by impossible beings, and a belly that was still seeping blood along its midline in spite of a lavish application of Spraskin) was that he didn't trust her. After he'd had his say—after he'd shown her what he needed to—*then* he'd count on luck (and probably Stormy's glib tongue) to set his ass in the clear. But in the meantime, he was stalling—not to enhance the effect when they arrived, but because one had to be careful how one introduced someone as skeptical as Carolyn obviously was to the unbelievable. God knew he'd barely begun to sort it out himself when Stormy had tossed him the card to the Juneau and said, "Go! If you think these fish-faced assholes may hijack somebody else, phone 'em from the Jeep—and if that doesn't work, just take my wheels and *fly!*"

He had. And fortunately he'd remembered Carolyn's address. But he'd been too intent on trying to make even vaguely rational sense out of what he'd seen back at the Dead Marina to spare any time for puzzling out how he might relay that same information to an almost-certain skeptic. And by the time he realized that, he was tumbling over Carolyn's patio wall (that was where the light had been), and it was too late. At that point, he'd basically consigned himself to the gods of his people and relied on luck and blind instinct to BS his way through.

It had worked—barely. He'd evidently pushed precisely the right buttons with Carolyn for curiosity to override fear. Either that, or she'd found fear of the unknown a fair tonic for fear of the up close and personal.

And if whatever haunted her was worse than careening around in an RV with a sliced-up, traumed-out Cherokee in the middle of the night, it was damned disturbing indeed!

To his careful inquiries about her dreams, she'd conceded little and volunteered less. He'd countered

by relating as much about himself as time allowed—
excluding his dreams, hoping to gain her trust by
giving her more than enough rope to hang him. He'd
have his say tonight. Tomorrow would be her turn—
possibly to the Mounties. *That* was why he didn't
trust her.

As to what he'd learned about her—besides that
she was stoic, patient, and had the balls of a man
twice her size—his primary discoveries were that
she was only a couple of years older than he; that
she'd been born in Eire to an Eirish mother and an
American father, both of whom had been academi-
cian/scientists who had maintained a transoceanic
marriage, with the kids growing up in both countries;
that she had a brother who was a novelist, whom she
seemed disinclined to discuss. And that by her
mother's example (there'd been no pressure), she'd
chosen a career in marine biology, with an under-
graduate degree at Trinity College, Dublin, and graduate studies (not quite yet a PhD) at the marine
institute in Monaco, where she'd met the Oriental
woman before whom he'd disgraced himself at the
'Wheel. Her mom was semi-incommunicado on a
boat somewhere in the wet part of the third world.
Her dad was in US, Georgia, but they weren't speaking.

And though she claimed she didn't believe in
magic, his mention of it had obviously drawn blood.
Someone had asked her about it before, she'd admitted, and recently. But had not told him who,
when, or where.

Oh well, perhaps she'd open up once she had
proof.

What happened then? Who knew? Nobody in the
world was equipped to deal with skin-stealing,
shape-changing killer whales.

But she *was* a marine biologist, with a specialization in cetaceans—which connected her, yet again, with dolphins. Though when she'd told him that, and he'd casually asked, "you mean like, killer whales?" she'd merely countered that the correct term was "orca"—and fallen silent.

Which silence had persisted ever since they'd left the beltway. 'Bird was thinking like crazy. Trouble was, Carolyn clearly was too.

Oh please just keep your cool five more minutes, he prayed, as he braked the Jeep preparatory to turning into the parking lot immediately past where the Aztlan highway kinked right to form the main drag of Sinsynsen.

"Second time here tonight," Carolyn grumbled beside him.

"Let's hope there won't be a third, unless it's for fun," he replied. "Now—brace yourself and hang on."

She shot him a startled glare, but complied, as he aimed the Jeep at the hub-high curb that separated the ten-acre pavement from the beach proper, and punched the button on the steering wheel that engaged all-wheel-drive.

The Jeep hit—harder than 'Bird would have liked in someone else's vehicle—and balked for an instant while traction shifted. Then, with a whir of stressed mechanicals, it lurched across, putting them on sand.

The moon was just past the zenith by then (tomorrow would be full) and 'Bird switched off the lights in deference to whatever authorities might have noted his indiscretion. Then, keeping the car in high gear so as to lower revs—and noise—he pointed it north along the strand. Fortunately the tide was out, which minimized the likelihood of

getting stuck in sand that was either too wet or too
dry; and equally fortuitously, the moon compen-
sated for the lack of lights. Nor did it take long to
reach Destination One: the lesser of two evils, but
only by degree of personal involvement.

The neojungle of *El País Verde* swept close to the
water's edge where he stopped. Carolyn stared at
him nervously. "We're here," he said as cheerfully
as circumstances allowed. "Here Number One,
anyway."

Her eyes narrowed. "There's *more* than one?"

A sheepish nod. " 'Fraid so."

"Quicker done, quicker over," Carolyn muttered,
and climbed out.

'Bird started around to help her, only to be caught
up short by the twin pain demons of bruised shin
and lacerated torso. He froze abruptly, gasping
weakly, leaning against the side of the Jeep. Carolyn
found him there and surprised him by actually looking concerned. He gritted his teeth and straightened,
noting with a start that she was still barefoot and
dressed in a thigh-length T-shirt. "Stormy's got his
laundry in the back," he managed, "so there oughta
be at least a serape. Or—"

"Later," she broke in tersely. "Let's get this over
with."

'Bird shrugged. "Fine." And limped up the strand.

"This is it," he panted less than a minute later,
pointing to a depression in the beach, the eastern
part of which showed the touch of tide in a smooth,
unbroken surface like the lining of a china bowl. But
the west— The sand there was torn and scuffed by
footprints: heavy boots of the sort the Mounties
used. A flutter of Day-Glo yellow a meter back
showed where a police cordon had been abandoned.

The heart of the depression had not been touched,

however, save for a few indentions where someone had evidently taken samples. And *that* sand still bore dark stains, visible even in the moonlight.

Carolyn peered at the hollow perplexedly, then blinked up at 'Bird. An eyebrow lifted in delicate inquiry that was thick with resigned sarcasm.

"Do you see that dark stuff?" 'Bird asked.

"Yes."

"Do you know what that is?"

Carolyn scowled, then squatted by the nearest patch. Carefully she reached out and touched it, then withdrew a small handful and sniffed it. "Blood?"

'Bird nodded. "Very good."

"I'm familiar with blood, Mr. O'Connor," she gritted. "I've seen a lot of it. Recently. On beaches just like this."

'Bird's brows shot up. "Oh?"

An uneasy shrug.

"What—?"

A ghost of a smile played over her lips. "To use your phrase, I'll tell you later. This is *your* show, remember?"

'Bird rolled his eyes, but shrugged in turn. "Fine. Okay, then, do you know what happened here?"

Silence.

"A man died here," 'Bird said deliberately. "He was flayed alive."

"Christ!" Carolyn cried, clearly appalled. "You're, uh, kidding, right?" Which was the first real sign of emotion 'Bird had witnessed from his . . . guest since the kidnapping.

" 'Fraid not," he replied, relaxing now that he wasn't playing head games.

"But how—? Why—?" Then, more angrily, "And what does this have to do with me?"

"It's a prelude to something else," 'Bird admitted. "But I wanted to set the stage."

"You've been here before?" Carolyn gasped. "You—"

"I found him," 'Bird finished. "Found *them*, rather. I came by fifteen minutes too late to prevent it. Fortunately I got a look at the guy who did it."

"And . . . ?"

'Bird smiled wryly. "Well, to use the famous line, I'll tell you a little later."

"Looks like it's gonna be a long night," Carolyn sighed. "I suppose you'd best lend me that serape."

'Bird all but grinned as he opened the Jeep's glass hatch and rummaged inside the overstuffed basket there. He extracted a rust red serape, a set of beach sandals and a pair of cutoff jeans. "These oughta fit," he yawned, handing the bundle to her. "You're small, and Stormy's got a skinny butt and little feet."

"Thanks," Carolyn grunted tonelessly, and 'Bird found himself wondering how all this was affecting her. Most women, and certainly most white women in the West, were removed from the immediacy of death. Shoot, most *people* never saw a dead body that wasn't in a coffin, or more blood than a cut or phial. Carolyn, on the other hand, obviously had a working acquaintance with the stuff. Certainly she wasn't squeamish. He found himself respecting her more for that.

"So how does this tie in with magic?" she asked pointedly, when she'd slipped on the shorts and stuck her head through the serape, the sandals still loose in her hand.

"How 'bout if I told you that the guy who died here was at least partly killed by what I would have to call magic?"

Carolyn stared back at the torn, stained sand,

then looked at 'Bird. Her face was grim. "Why do I believe you?"

'Bird did not reply, but motioned her back inside the Jeep. He cranked it but left the lights off. And continued north.

'Bird didn't have time to tell Carolyn as much as he would have liked, not in the few minutes required to reach Destination Two. And though the woman maintained a thoughtful, considerate silence, it was all he could manage to sketch out the bare minimum of his tale—basically that he'd surprised someone in the act of skinning someone else, that the assailant had escaped, but that he'd gotten a good description—and had spent the rest of the night rehearsing it with the cops. Her only comment had been a careful "Oh, okay . . . " when he'd explained that he was just coming off several hours of interrogation when she'd almost run him down.

And by the time he'd worked through *that*, they'd reached the hurricane fence that marked the southern boundary of the Dead Marina.

'Bird parked the Jeep, but did not get out. Rather, he turned toward his companion. "I guess you're wonderin' how all this ties into that stuff about magic, and dreams, and all."

"I've been wondering *that* for some time."

"Well," 'Bird began, "I can't tell you much 'cause I've got to get this Jeep back to my friend Stormy— who's waitin' for us at Destination Two—I hope. But the short version is that Stormy's a security guard at the Dineh Embassy—that's Navajo to you—and his people have very specific ideas about what folks who are exposed to violent death should do. Basically, one needs to be purified, which I sort of was. And it was during that purification rite—it was just Thursday, I guess, though it seems like a thousand years ago—that I had a dream—vision, whatever it was—in which I saw . . . Uh, well, it was like this . . . "

Whereupon he described the sweat-induced vision that had culminated with the Botticelliesque image of Carolyn standing atop waves while dolphins paid obeisance to her.

She gnawed her lip at that, only to add, "You realize, of course, that under pressure like you experienced it would be reasonable to combine that skinned fellow and someone who nearly runs over you into an hallucination, or whatever it was."

A scowl. "Yeah, but it doesn't explain how I knew you'd dreamed the same thing too."

"I *didn't* dream the same thing."

"It was close, though, wasn't it?"

She shook her head, looking confused and flustered, and very, very tired. "I was . . . sick for a while," she admitted. "It was the afternoon after I nearly hit you. And today while I was under I had a . . . dream in which someone said, and I quote, 'You are the one the dolphins worship.' "

'Bird's eyes were huge. "There *has* to be a connection."

"So it would seem," Carolyn agreed wearily. "But I'm not sure I want to know what it is."

"I'm not sure I do either," 'Bird sighed. "But I don't think we've got any choice."

"What do you mean?"

"I think there are other . . . hands in this."

"By which you mean . . . "

"Magic," 'Bird said flatly. "Stormy says it's magic. And I'm afraid I'm startin' to believe him."

"You said there was another dream . . . ?"

"I did, and there was . . . but it's time we were travelin' ."

Two minutes later, they had crossed the hurricane fence and were making their way up the Promenade. Carolyn walked confidently, if warily, which 'Bird was relieved to see. For himself, he strove to maintain that pace as well, but kept starting at every shadow, pausing at each phantom footfall, never mind that he was also wheezing like an old man and limping—a lot. Only the Smith & Wesson automatic he'd found Velcroed beneath the driver's seat of Stormy's Jeep gave him comfort. He clutched it now, secretly, in the spacious pocket of his baggy jeans. And wondered if it would be sufficient.

"Your friend," Carolyn prompted. "We're meeting him here, right?"

"Yeah."

"Why were you here in the first place?"

'Bird chuckled grimly. "I was takin' a shortcut."

"A shortcut?"

"I wanted to think."

"About what?"

"About the dreams. About you. About where you fit into things."

"And your friend . . . ?"

"I got into trouble—and he showed up just in time. Someone got hurt, and he stayed with him."

"Why didn't you?"

"I needed to see about you."

"But . . ."

"I'll show you in one more minute. We're almost there."

Silence, as they trekked along. Carolyn, to 'Bird's surprise, still went barefoot. The moon was high, its light in a clear sky showing the Dead Marina almost as bright as day. The slow rippling of the Gulf to the right was as soothing as the tumbled structures to the left were disconcerting.

Then: "It's down here—down this alley."

Carolyn froze in place. "You want me to go down a dark alley with you?"

"I'd appreciate it if you would."

"I don't think so."

"You'll be safer with me than if you stay here alone. And what I have to show you's down there."

"I don't *need* to see more blood."

"It's not blood."

Silence.

'Bird grimaced sourly and eased his hand from his pocket. The pistol glittered in it, moonlight enhancing the pattern of the carbon-ceramic of which all but the barrel was made. Carolyn's eyes went huge, her mouth rounding as she gasped. But before she could turn to flee, 'Bird grabbed her and stuffed the weapon into her hand. "It's your call now," he growled. "Now . . . I'm goin' down that alley, 'cause I left my best friend down there, who should've heard us by now and checked in; only he hasn't, which has me worried. And *you* can follow and maybe learn something that *might* grant you one tiny bit of peace of mind—though I'll warn you, it'll cost you some too—or you can stay here and be ignorant the rest of your possibly very short life."

"What do you mean by *that*?"

'Bird smiled at her, but there was no warmth in the curve of his lips. "You'll just have to follow me to find out, won't you?"

"Or I could shoot you."

"You won't."

"How do you know?"

"You're too curious."

"How do you know?"

"You're a scientist . . . and you're a woman."

"And you're an asshole!"

"Maybe," 'Bird replied, and limped into the darkness. He did not look back, but he heard a resigned sigh, then the sound of soft footsteps pattering up behind.

"Stormy?" he hissed, when he had reached the halfway point, and still found no sign of his friend. "Stormcloud? You here?"

Silence.

"Stormy?"

Still no word. A chill raced over him. He slowed, swallowed nervously. Carolyn joined him. "Where—?"

"Not here," 'Bird groaned, pointing to a stretch of boards ahead, on which a dark dampness shimmered. "But I don't need him for what I want to show you, only to corroborate a few things."

"Like what?"

"Like how all that blood got there—some of it bein' mine."

"I'm waiting."

In reply 'Bird crossed the few remaining meters to the place he'd left Stormy tending the attacker who'd turned idiot. The blood remained, but his buddy was nowhere in sight. There *was* a note, however, pinned to the boards by a chunk of broken mortar. 'Bird picked it up, squinting at it in the uncertain light. Carolyn peered over his shoulder.

"Bird," [it read] "our friend started bleeding so much I had to have help. I'm lugging him to that closed AFZoRTA station near here. It's 00:36 now. I've phoned an anonymous 911 and will watch from the shadows till the good guys show, since he's unlikely to tell what went on or what happened to him. Call me from the phone in the Jeep—I can't call *you* 'cause they might be backtracing—should've called you first, I guess. If I'm not up to my ass in explanations, I'll talk to you soon as I can. If I am . . . see you in jail. I'd prefer the cake with the file be chocolate."

S. Cloud

PS: Wasn't sure what to do with the evidence, so I hid it in the next archway down.

"Great," 'Bird groaned bitterly, passing the letter to Carolyn. "Just *great!*"

She read it.

"So who was this guy? The one who was hurt?"

"Someone Stormy shot before he could kill me. Someone . . . who wanted my hide as an overcoat."

"You're kidding!"

"Wanta bet?" He eased a half dozen meters farther, to where the black arch of a doorway gaped to the left. It was dark as a dungeon in there, but it required scant seconds to locate what he sought— though he jerked his hand back reflexively when he touched it. "This is gonna be gross," he warned, as he set his jaw and snaked it out, to hold it up before him.

"God*damn!*" Carolyn cried, hopping back in alarm. "That's not what I think it is, is it?"

'Bird nodded solemnly and let the bloody bundle slide from his fingers. He wiped them on his jeans. " 'Fraid so. What we've got here are the sewn-together skins of at least five or six people, which roughly an hour ago was *one* person."

"Huh?"

"It was one person, and it was pinnin' my arms

down while the guy Stormy took off with was tryin'
to skin me alive. Stormy shot 'em both—to maim
'em—which saved my ass. One promptly turned
from a raving vivisectionist to a mindless idiot. The
other . . . well, basically, he slid out of that skin,
turned into a killer whale—and flopped into the canal."

Carolyn stared at him incredulously. "That's a . . .
lot to expect someone to believe, I suppose you know
that."

"I'd have said the same thing—until I saw it."

"But you've no proof."

'Bird glared at her, then yanked his skin-shirt over
his head, displaying through the transparent glaze of
Spraskin the gash beneath his clavicle and the
longer wound that bisected his torso. It still oozed
blood at the top of his belly where exertion had
ripped the substance loose. "This proves their intentions toward *me*!" he spat. "That . . . *mess* on the
boards proves their intentions toward other people."

"But—"

"They knew about me," 'Bird gritted. "They said
as much. And they also seem to have something
against someone I presumed to be you. I think the
phrase was 'eliminate the one I alerted.' "

Carolyn gaped blankly. "But why . . . ? I didn't
know you until tonight, and I didn't know about *any*
of this until you showed me, and—" Whereupon her
face twisted with realization. "*Oh my God.*"

"What?"

She braced against the wall, the pistol limp in her
hand. "There—Christ, there *is* a connection! You
said he turned into an . . . orca, right?"

A nod.

"Well, I've been having trouble with orcas too. I
can't think how the two could connect, but . . . " And

then her eyes grew very round indeed. *"Kevin,"* she wailed. "Oh, shit! I just realized what you said!"

"Who's Kevin?"

"My brother—my ace in the hole. I didn't tell you about him, because I was afraid you might get him too. But—"

"—If whoever went after me goes after you—"

"—They'll find *him*! Oh, Christ—we've gotta get back there!" Already she was running.

"Yeah," 'Bird gasped, as he limped along behind. "I'm with you."

He had almost caught up with her as they neared the end of the alley. But with roughly a dozen meters remaining, four well-shrouded shapes slipped in from the right to block their passage.

'Bird had no hope that they were human.

Chapter XXIV:
Into the Fire

*(The Dead Marina—Aztlan,
Aztlan Free Zone—Mexico)*
(Saturday, September 3—after midnight)

Moonlight shone on four hooded figures, on the uneven boards of the alley's flooring—and on the muzzle of Carolyn's Smith & Wesson .38, as she took careful aim at the second figure from the left. Him, so that if the pistol 'Bird had foisted on her kicked, there was at least a *chance* of hitting someone. And chaos, more than murder, was what she intended. Bullshit and bluff in lieu of blazing barrels.

Slowly she let her thumb slip back on the safety, felt the trigger ease beneath a forefinger that was suddenly far too sweaty. Time seemed to stop as she waited, while her heart pounded a thousand beats per minute in her breast.

A chill shook her, but she stood firm. For in spite of the fact that the figures blocking the end of the alley perhaps a dozen meters down were the size and shape of bulky human males, she could tell even at that distance that there was nothing human about them.

Nothing.

Perhaps it was the way they stood, with that same

awkward slouch bears wear when rearing on their hind legs. Maybe it was the way certain of their movements were exaggerated, as though they had not yet learned how much effort a given action required. Or possibly it was the way their forearms moved constantly, in a slow, fore-and-aft stirring, as though they'd been conditioned to swim. Whatever it was—and it could not be their faces, because those were obscured by hoods—she was absolutely convinced that they were *wrong*.

She did not move, nor did 'Bird beside her; but neither did the . . . men. Behind them stretched the shattered pavement of the Promenade, bleached gold/white by the moon, and beyond it lay the glittering silver of the sea. To the left, below a low wooden railing that was intact here, though it had fallen away back where 'Bird had shown her the blood and that awful . . . *thing*, she could hear the flop-splash of water in the canal.

Abruptly, her hearing shifted; as though she stood near a high-tension power line, or something that put forth ultrasonics. It was part hum, part buzz, merged with almost-voices, and seemed to bypass her eardrums and stab straight through her skull to her brain.

As though a circuit had been thrown, something clicked in her. *What was she doing?* Acting on impulse and instinct, instead of intellect? Those looming shapes could as well be friend as foe. They *could* be Mounties come to investigate 'Bird's friend's story, for certainly they had that same careful guardedness policemen often evinced. They could—

"Shoot!" 'Bird hissed in her ear. "Not to kill, if you can help it, but shoot!"

"But they're—" she whispered back, doubt having displaced certainty, all in a second's time.

"They're *not* human," 'Bird gritted. "Do it now—or die!"

The circuit flipped again. Carolyn blinked, shook her head, took a deep breath—and pulled the trigger.

Click.

"Chamber it," 'Bird growled.

She did—and once more twitched the trigger.

If she'd aimed true, she never knew, for all four men were rushing them. She had a brief impression of heavy feet thudding across loose boards; of enormous bodies expanding to fill the world as garments billowed wide and arms and legs went pumping; of a single face glimpsed when a hood flew back to reveal male features, but impossibly pale and smooth and bland. And then she spun around and was running.

She glimpsed 'Bird's startled gawk as she whirled—an expression that flickered past confusion on the way to honest terror. *"Shoot!"* he bellowed, even as he joined her in flight. "Goddam it, *shoot!*" He snatched for her hand even as he ran. "It's a goddamned automatic!"

As his words made no sense. The thunder of that one shot echoing around the alley, the flash of fire, the smell of gunpowder, had shattered her self-possession. She had shot at someone! Had fired a pistol at a thinking being! And by that one act of weakness, that one explicit willingness to take a sentient life, she knew she'd abandoned all claim to mercy.

"Here," she snapped, thrusting the gun at 'Bird without breaking stride.

"Wha—? Huh—?" As his fingers slid past hers to close around the barrel.

But she'd misjudged—or he had. He'd not had a firm grip, not left-handed!

"Shit," he spat, as she heard the gun strike wood, even as momentum hurled her onward. She risked a glance over her shoulder, saw the weapon gleaming on the boards and four figures charging, while 'Bird stood frozen midway between her and the gun.

" *'Bird!*"

That decided him, and he took off again, but she could hear him panting heavily, his gait halting and uncertain, and only then recalled that he'd been injured before any of this began, had a cut down the center of his chest and well into his belly, and God knew what besides. Never mind the assorted abuses he'd endured to orchestrate their meeting.

Not that she was much better. For in spite of having been "dead" for something like an hour, and having been on and off most of the day and a half after, she hadn't had eight solid hours of shut-eye in who-knew-when. Plus there'd been the wearying hike down the cliff to examine the mutilated dolphins, the hours they'd spent there, much of which had meant tugging on heavy corpses, the exertion of the swim, the tension that had lingered all through her hospital stay . . .

None of which she actually catalogued as she ran. She only knew that she was suddenly bone tired.

"Where does this end?" she gasped, as she reached to help 'Bird along.

"I dunno," he panted. "I've never been all the way down. I—Oh *shit!*"

For he had just seen the same thing she had: the alley blocked by a blank glassbrick wall at least four stories high, utterly smooth, utterly unbroken. There was clearly no way through. A glance to the left showed a series of arcaded doorways, all plugged with heavy steel. *Service entrances,* she assumed, and in spite of their abandoned status, obviously locked tight.

A check behind showed more bad news. The men were still approaching, perhaps forty meters back—they had slowed, however, as though less constrained by time. One seemed to be limping too, while another stopped, bent over, then put forth a burst of speed and joined his allies. Something hard and shiny gleamed in his hand, and a flash of white beneath his hood might have been an attempted grin. Her heart flip-flopped, and a cold dread made her shiver again. "He's got the gun," she murmured to 'Bird, who wheezed beside her, eyes wild, brow beaded with sweat—and with one hand clutching his belly.

"His buddy's got something worse," he managed between ragged breaths. *"He's* got a knife."

Carolyn stared stupidly, too dazed to determine what made a blade worse than a bullet.

"They *skin* folks with knives like that," 'Bird added. "Trust me."

The men had advanced another ten meters, but had become very wary indeed. Carolyn backpedaled reflexively, tugging 'Bird along until her shoulders smacked hard against the glass.

Twenty meters.

Twenty meters *more*—basically twenty steps—and it would all be over. She'd been dead once and revived. She doubted she'd be as lucky two days running.

Silence, save for 'Bird's labored panting, her own more throaty breaths—and the slow, measured thump of heavy feet on wood.

And the slap of waves in the canal not two meters to 'Bird's left!

"Can you swim?" she hissed through her teeth,

sparing a glance away from the advancing . . . men.

'Bird's eyes went wide and crafty, even as his mouth grew thin and grim. "Well enough," he muttered.

"Go!" she yelled as loud as possible, out of desperate hope it might startle their adversaries—and with that same cry, she pushed him.

He stumbled but righted himself, to pause for a fractioned instant on the ledge above the canal where the railing had collapsed. Then, with the air of one resigning himself to doom, he swung his arms above his head and fell forward.

She caught the awkward splash, but by then she had flung off her serape and was likewise poised on the brink.

An instant only it required, in which to hear the not-men thundering toward her, their shouts high and dull and strange, as though but part of some words registered. A moment more to stare down at a finger of glass black water two meters below her toes and thrice that many wide. And then she drank deep of the air—and dived.

She hit cleanly (God knew she'd had years in which to perfect that art), and knew she'd made barely a splash as she entered—unlike 'Bird, who'd sounded like the winner of a belly flopper match. Her next thought was that it was colder than she'd expected, and the *next* that her fingers had grazed the bottom perhaps four meters down, whereupon she arched upward and twisted to the right, seeking what she hoped was the way past the not-men and toward the open sea.

Something swished through the water ahead of her, and she caught a distant, dull report. A gunshot! Steeling herself, she pushed deeper, to brush along the bottom, praying 'Bird had sense enough to do the same—though what she expected to accomplish in the long run, she had no idea. The only truth was that they could not confront those four not-men; that with all directions blocked but this, it was their only choice; and that if they were truly fortunate, they *might* win past pursuit and reach—if not the sea, at least some place that offered options. Where they could, if necessary, split up and double their likelihood of survival. She *had* to live, dammit! Not only for herself, but for this Indian lad she'd by a long and winding route enmired in this mess, and for poor Kev, who would wake up worried as hell—if something hadn't happened to him already.

But for now, all she could do was swim as deep as possible, as long as possible, and hope 'Bird would risk as much.

And that the opposition wasn't lucky.

Or had no other gun. She wondered how many bullets had been in the lost one.

At least she wasn't running out of air as quickly as expected—or perhaps fear was stretching her endurance. Certainly she was surprised when her hand struck movement ahead, which she deduced was 'Bird's foot, still, reasonably enough, in its sneaker.

It flinched away, and she sensed him angling toward the surface. Well, the lad *had* to breathe; as, come to it—finally—did she.

Steeling herself, she kicked off the canal's stone bottom—and heaved a sigh of relief when she broke water and saw 'Bird pawing hair out of his eyes a meter closer to the looming darkness that marked another walk along the canal's northern side. They'd emerged in shadow, too, and had made it nearly halfway up the canal—which was damned good progress for both of them.

"Get under the walk," he whisper-gasped, drawing

her toward him. "There're arches under the Promenade. If we can make it there—"

"Go," she urged. "Don't worry about me! I'll follow!"

'Bird gulped air in anticipation of yet another dive; but a hand to his bare shoulder (he'd never replaced his skin-shirt after displaying his injury) reined him back. His head tilted. He'd evidently heard it too.

Not more footsteps on wood, however, nor more running; certainly not more gunfire. But a far more threatening and insidious sound: the raspy swish of clothing being shucked, followed by a low moan that accompanied a long, slow ripping. A thick, moist flopping ensued, like a big fish makes when landed. And as yet more chills raced over her, she glimpsed 'Bird's anguished scowl—and dived.

Groping blindly in the dark—for she had to rely solely on instinct and dead reckoning—she threaded past the pilings that braced the boardwalk to either side of the canal, and swam beneath, to feel along the submerged foundation wall of the building that bordered it to the north. With her fingers brushing concrete, she flanked it—and almost spat out her air when that fell away, pierced by a narrow opening that a quick exploration showed began slightly lower down and extended less than half a meter left and right—though how high it rose she couldn't determine. A disruption of the water ahead, and an accidental collision of hands revealed that 'Bird had found it too—and was breaching.

So did she, locating him already several meters farther on, and made her way toward him, swimming strongly but quietly.

"What's the best way out of here?" she gasped.

"Under the Promenade, and then . . . who knows? It's maybe half a klik to civilization if we go north, less than that back to the Jeep; but either way, we can't stay in the water—we're sitting ducks. If we can make it to land, I think we can outrun 'em. If nothing else, we can find somewhere to hide among the ruins."

"And then?"

"We retrieve your bro and try to catch up with Stormy."

"And *then*?"

"We—Jesus! What was that?"

Carolyn swallowed hard. "They—that is, I think one of them dived in."

'Bird's eyes went round. "And he wasn't human, was he?"

Carolyn blinked at him, still having trouble connecting all these preposterous notions that were suddenly becoming less so by the second.

"They *aren't* human, Carolyn!" 'Bird insisted thickly. "They—they're killer whales usin' magic to put on human skin so they can pass among us!"

"But why?"

"I don't *know*! But if one's shifted, it's in its element and we're not. Our only choice is to go somewhere it can't."

"Then we may be lucky."

"Why?"

"Because there's a hole in the wall back there. If we could slip through *that* . . . "

"Good point," 'Bird agreed. "It oughta give into a basement that, by the level here, shouldn't be completely drowned."

"Do it!" Carolyn snapped. "I just heard a splash."

To her surprise, 'Bird reached out and ruffled her hair—which was plastered to her head like a black plastic helmet. "Good thing this is short! Mine's in my ears and I can't hear squat."

Though his eyes belied his frivolity, she scowled—and floated back to where the opening showed its top few sims above water. She promptly sank, eased through into half-light, and resurfaced inside. It was more of a squeeze for 'Bird, due to his chest and shoulders, but he passed through as well. Less than two seconds later, a hard thud echoed through the gloom, and something blunt, slick, black-and-white, and toothy thrust through the opening, narrowly missing 'Bird's feet as it thrashed left and right.

But the gap was *just* too narrow, and after several tries the orca vanished.

—Leaving them treading water in a dimly lit enclosure, with less than an arm's reach between their heads and the rough-finished vaults of a cast concrete ceiling. The only light came from a swath of moonlight to the north, reflecting off oily water. A check showed the floor farther down than she'd expected, which made her wonder what sort of structure this was.

"Stairs?" she wondered, when she once again broke water.

"Oughta be," 'Bird panted shakily. "We can check—but let me catch my breath."

Carolyn led as they scouted the perimeter of what proved to be a thirty-meter square—possibly a large storeroom. But though they found three steel doors, locked or rusted closed, they saw no sign of stairs, trapdoors, or elevators.

But in the northeast corner they found something far more interesting.

The wall had fractured there, with part of it tumbling toward the Promenade. The glimmer of light they'd glimpsed earlier came from that, and when they approached indicated that not only was the wall broken, but that the pavement beyond had collapsed as well (and recently, 'Bird informed her—he'd crossed that section on his last trip through, two weeks prior), leaving a stretch of water several meters wide and easily a quarter-klik long between two impressive docks, but open to the sea. And the best thing was what floated a short way inside the basement.

A brand new windboard! Basically a glorified surfboard—with a broken mast that once had held a sail, and, at its narrow stern, a tiny outboard motor.

"Somebody's *gotta* be watchin' out for us," 'Bird sighed. "Did you order that, or did I?"

"It's probably stormwrack," Carolyn mused, drifting up beside it to tread water with one hand on its bow. "There was that blow last week, remember? All that stuff on TV about how stupid all those windsurfers were to go out in it. And about how a bunch of them were dumb enough to try to sue the city for not putting up breakwaters when they lost their boards."

"For which we may be grateful," 'Bird chuckled weakly. "That is, if you're thinkin' . . . "

"I'm thinking that those were-orca things didn't all shift shape, in which case some of them will be out there waiting if we make a break, and though they can't watch every direction, there's no guessing which they *will* choose. And I'm thinking that if a couple of them *did* shift shape—which that lad back at the opening seems to indicate—then the only thing keeping them off our butts now is the fact that the straightest way in here may be blocked by that hunk of Promenade that fell in right out there."

"Good point," 'Bird acknowledged. "So what—?"

Carolyn peered through the breach in the wall. "I don't see anywhere to climb out that'd do us any good. The left side of the Promenade's too high to reach; and the part that came down to the right's basically a vertical wall of concrete—at the top of which our friends could easily be hiding."

'Bird's grin showed he was thinking the same thing she was. "But if we climb on a certain wind-board . . ."

"And can get the motor running . . . "

His face fell instantly. "And if we can't?"

She masked her uncertainty with a grin of her own. "We'll worry about that *after* we've made the effort. Now . . . you ever ridden one of these things?"

'Bird shook his head.

"That makes two of us."

"I can crank a chainsaw, though," 'Bird cried—and heaved himself across the stern.

Carolyn followed his example amidships, and it was hard to say who was more awkward getting aboard and situated. Carolyn found herself astride but backward, just ahead of the broken mast, with 'Bird two meters aft. "That appears to be the rudder," she observed, pointing to a sturdy lever attached to the motor at the rear of the narrow fiberglass hull.

"And *this* seems to be the starter," 'Bird echoed. Whereupon he grabbed a trailing cord—and gave a mighty tug.

It was the sweetest sound Carolyn had ever heard, and the most welcome: a brief, hesitant sputter that made her heart skip a beat before it settled into a high-pitched staccato buzz. 'Bird twisted around to grin at her, then did something she couldn't see—and they were moving.

Too fast!

The board rose steeply beneath her, and she would surely have toppled off had the stump of mast not restrained her. She clutched it frantically. 'Bird's shoulders bunched and rippled as he grabbed the rudder with both hands and pulled. And then the gap was looming up *very* fast indeed, and 'Bird was trying to steer; and then they were on it—*through* it—and past, angling toward the solid slab of fallen Promenade. "Left!" Carolyn shrieked, not caring if she telegraphed their location. "I mean *right!*"

'Bird swore unintelligibly and yanked one way, then the other. The board bucked, banked, and threatened to tip over, but somehow he got it righted and steered toward the center of the channel. Already they were halfway down its length, halfway down the water-road to safety—though she'd heard 'Bird yip painfully as they narrowly missed the nearest section of broken paving that made a wall to the south, and guessed he'd taken a scrape on the foot, so close did they veer on that side. Which was all the poor lad needed.

"North," she yelled, straining to be heard above the din of the tiny motor. Then: "Oh, Christ, there one is!"

She would have pointed had she dared, but 'Bird glanced up anyway, which was stupid for someone facing backward on a speeding board. The tensing of his shoulders showed he saw it too: one of the hood-cloaked figures crouching right at the edge of the dock not twenty meters distant, with something small and shiny in his hand.

"North!" she screamed again, still more frantically, and felt the board lurch beneath her as 'Bird gave it all the rudder he dared and executed what was close to a right-angle turn—that then had to be corrected by one the other way, so quickly did they find themselves racing toward the pylons on the opposite side.

A crack, a flash of light, and a splash, all in the

same breath proved a shot had been fired and gone wide.

Another followed instantly, so close splinters of fiberglass splattered against her thigh from where a bullet entered the board a handsbreadth from her knee.

'Bird countered by zigzagging.

And then the end of the dock slid past, and they were in open sea. Behind them, one small figure stood on the broken point, aiming something at them. But by the way he flung the object into the waves a moment later, it was empty.

"Stormy will be *so* pissed," 'Bird snorted.

"I'll buy him another," Carolyn promised. They were safe now—or at least were no longer being actively pursued—not by anything they couldn't, in the short term, outrun. Though if 'Bird didn't slow this thing down . . .

"Where to now?" he sighed, having that moment figured out how to throttle down the little outboard, so that they now moved at a more reasonable clip.

Carolyn scanned the horizon, seeing nothing but the vacant facades and derelict docks of the Dead Marina for another quarter klik up the coast. Farther on were luxury hotels, then the desalinization plant. But it wasn't that far to—

She pointed to the finger of land that prodded the Gulf to the northeast, a couple of kliks away. "The breakers look too rough by the hotels—they fixed the bottom to make them that way—which means it'd be dangerous for us to try to get in there, what with the tide like it is. But the bottom's smoother up by 'Why?'—which is closer than where we left the Jeep. Plus they ought to have someone on twenty-four-hour lookout, plus they've got sensors."

"Fine," 'Bird agreed, though something about his

expression told her he wasn't that keen on her suggestion, but was too far gone to argue. Instead, he gunned the motor.

They had not gone ten meters before the board leapt from the water, heeling to the right as it did. Carolyn had to grab the mast stump to keep from flying off, and only 'Bird's legs wrapped around the board like his life depended on it saved him. Miraculously, the craft righted itself upon landing, but the comforting buzz of the motor sputtered to a stop.

"Shit fire!" 'Bird spat—whereupon they struck something else.

Or something else struck them!

Something moving invisibly beneath the ink black water.

Moving, while they were not.

They were dead in the water—which phrase Carolyn suddenly loathed.

For even as she drew her legs up to balance on the board and saw 'Bird scrambling frantically to do the same, an arm-long fin lifted above the waves.

The dorsal fin of an orca!

And as 'Bird swore fluently in English and Cherokee, she counted at least four more.

Part Three

Chapter XXV:
A Grumbly Guest

(Aztlan, Aztlan Free Zone—Mexico)
(Saturday, September 3—after midnight)

Fireworks were among Kevin's favorite entertainments—but he preferred them exploding *outside* his skull.

As it was, there were sparklers spraying glitter behind his eyeballs, pinwheels fizz-hissing like pissed-off dragons in his ears, and skyrockets pounding his brainpan like third world artillery, each salvo accompanied by a tiny explosion of light with matching pulse of pain that persisted long enough after to merge with the next assault in a crescendo of agony that would have done the Marquis de Sade proud.

His head, in short, hurt like a son of a bitch.

But at least he was *aware* of it now. Before (who knew how long ago, because his ear-watch was missing) he'd been out of it entirely. All he recalled, when memory once more became an option, was a bunch of weird guys ransacking Cary's place. They'd intercepted him on his way back from the loo, dropped a few comments he *really* didn't want to contemplate, most of them involving his skin—and had promptly knocked him on the noggin, thus precipitating the present intracranial pyrotechnics.

If he strained really hard, however, he could remember a trip in a dirty white car that involved another well-placed thwack when he threatened to
come to.

And speaking of coming to, it appeared to have
happened again. Or he was now subject to external
stimuli as well as the light show within, at any rate.
Mostly he hurt, and not just his head from multiple
encounters with blunt objects moved quickly with
force. No, his back was also sore; and certain parts
of his arms, legs, and forehead throbbed alarmingly.
Which, as more consciousness oozed back, seemed
to be directly connected to an assortment of *very*
tight restraints lashed over the offended portions to
secure him to something hard, flat, smooth, and
clammy. By the chill goose-bumping large portions
of his anatomy, he concluded he wore no more than
the gold bikini briefs he'd been stumbling around in
prior to the mugging—which made him feel even
more vulnerable, as well as profoundly foolish.

Eventually his eyes slitted open, and he was able
to raise his head far enough within whatever con-
fined it to confirm that one fear was justified. Every
articulating segment of his body larger than a finger
had been secured to what felt suspiciously like an
operating table by leather straps as wide as his hand,
most of them pulled tight enough to raise ridges of
flesh on either side, as well as restrict circulation.
Whoever had caught him didn't want him going anywhere, or looking good when he arrived.

As to where *here* was—the clearest view was of a
rough sandcrete ceiling, probably precast, to judge
by the parallel arches. Paint, if present, had either
faded or mildewed, the latter strongly favored by a
pervasive mustiness in the air that made Kevin's
nose prickle even as he noticed it.

By the quality of the light—adequate, but cold and dirty—he assumed that his prison had no windows, which, with the mildew, general dampness, and a low, almost infrasound *thrum* rumbling up through the walls, supported the assumption that he was near either the beach, one of those canals he'd seen from the plane, or both, possibly below sea level.

And then a whole phalanx of notions marched up to him clear as day and lined up in logical order.

His captors had come seeking Cary, not found her, and settled for him instead.

He was a prisoner, but that didn't mean they weren't still searching for his sis.

Neither situation was desirable. Ergo, he had to escape.

But how? Straining against the strapwork merely produced more pain, cramped muscles, and chafing at the juncture of tanned flesh and fresh. Which left Plan B.

Of which there was none.

At least there was no sign of his captors; and the one good thing about his ineffectual squirmings was that he'd loosened the forehead restraint a tad, so that he could now see a trifle more than heretofore.

The view was not comforting.

To the right, a frightful vinyl sofa shared space with a pair of equally unpromising chairs, all of which were lavishly layered with what looked like the leavings of a Salvation Army clothing sale—most of it heavy fabrics inappropriate to Aztlan's subtropical clime. A large part of it was dirty, and a few items showed dark brown stains that looked disturbingly like blood.

Farther back—as far as he could roll his eyes up and to the right—lurked a glass-and-metal cabinet of the sort encountered in clinics, a suspicion supported by the presence on the visible shelves of an alarming assortment of gleaming metal objects Kevin had a terrible feeling were surgical tools. Certainly he saw several scalpels—and, oddly enough, an array of obsidian-bladed knives.

Shifting back the other way, his feet framed a large aquarium more than a meter long and half that high, full of a murky, tan-pink liquid in which something dark and amorphous slowly writhed at the prompting of aeration jets.

To the left of the tank—left of his left foot—gray paint peeled off an institutional steel door, closed at present. And adjoining it on the same wall, a floor-to-ceiling rack held a mini-arsenal of high-tech weaponry, mostly the latest kevlar/carbon fiber/ceramic sniper jobs, though there was also one current series Uzi assault rifle and three exotic-looking handguns, one with a laser sight.

And to his immediate left, another prisoner lay bound to a table like his.

His companion-in-adversity was naked, male—and young, to judge by the smooth skin, well-cut muscles, small bones, and dearth of body hair. But as Kevin strained to gaze higher, and glimpsed the extravagant length and unlikely brown-green color of the impressive mane that crowned the head, he realized that his partner-in-misery was cast from the same disturbing mold as his unfortunate proto-friend, Fir.

He was, in short, a selkie.

He was also conscious, if the way his muscles tensed and strained against bonds similar to Kevin's was any indication, but seriously groggy, to judge by the unfocused stare in the leaf brown eyes that had not yet chanced to drift his way. Unlike Kevin, however, the selkie's mouth had been taped shut, the

gray-silver gleam of duct tape occluding both lips
and jaw. An empty cardboard spool next to an alarmingly pointed ear told Kevin that luck, not intent,
was all that had spared him the same indignity.

"Selkie!" Kevin rasped, dry-tongued. "Selkie, look
at me!"

The other captive froze, then strained more vehemently.

"Selkie! I'm *not* your enemy!"

The selkie relaxed minutely and, by twisting his
head to the limit his bonds allowed, was able to
achieve eye contact.

Kevin nearly turned away, so much misery
showed there, so much agony, so much despair.

The tape bunched and stretched across the selkie's mouth, but before Kevin could think of any useful comment, footsteps snapped beyond the door,
and the steel panel grated open. The first two figures
to enter Kevin recognized as the heavy-bodied
crypto-woman who'd rifled Cary's room and the guy
who'd clubbed him with the hilt of a butcher knife.
The third was unfamiliar, though his face had the
same unfinished quality as his accomplices. Perhaps
because he was taller, heavier, and marginally more
stylishly dressed, that one also bore an air of au-
thority. Certainly the others deferred to him, gazing
at him expectantly, as though waiting for him to
speak first.

The Man-in-Charge took three steps into the
room, which put him even with Kevin's ankles. He
stared Kevin up and down dispassionately, rather as
one would regard a used car one was evaluating. He
barely scanned his face, however, and Kevin hastily
lowered his lids, praying no one noticed. He hated
to do that, but any advantage was a big one now.
And with him officially still unconscious, perhaps

they'd be more inclined to speak freely—if they troubled to speak at all.

"You should not have brought him here," a toneless voice stated—and once again Kevin got a sense that much of the inflection was occurring beyond his auditory range. "Not when we scarcely have time to deal with this . . . other."

"We thought he might know where his sister is," a more familiar voice replied—doubtless one of Kevin's kidnappers. "Also, he is not from this land and is thus less likely to be recognized or . . . missed."

"You could have had him killed there," the first voice noted.

("*Had* him killed?" Kevin wondered if that careful phrasing was significant.)

"—Which would have left us with a corpse to abandon or carry," a third party broke in. "Either of which would prompt more questions than having him here alive. Besides," that one added so silkily it was like a purr, "he has a *very* fine skin."

Kevin's heart flip-flopped. Chills he hoped no one noticed danced across his torso. In spite of the risk, he slitted one eye open.

They were ignoring him. Rather, the larger man was gazing over Kevin's legs to the selkie. "It has not told you yet?" he wondered.

"Its English is inferior," the one-time knife wielder explained. "And like the others, it defies our efforts to learn its native speech."

"Soon enough, though," the larger man grunted. "Now, let us be about preparing your other find."

No one seemed inclined to reply, but Kevin managed to close his eye and relax his limbs just as their gazes swept back his way.

Please God don't let 'em look too close, he prayed. *Don't let 'em think I heard what they just said.*

Apparently they noticed nothing untoward, for the harsh slap of heavy feet stumping away ensued, followed by the hollow slam of the metal door.

Kevin sighed his relief and for a long moment lay still. His heart was racing, his breathing labored, and he was sweating like a pig. *Stress reaction*, he told himself. *Or shock*.

Either was understandable, given that he was in the deepest shit he could imagine. The only encouraging thing was that they'd apparently not found Cary, but opposing that was the way they kept discussing his skin. More to the point, the way they kept referring to it as an entity *apart* from the rest of him. Kevin had a sinking feeling he knew what darkened the tank by the door. Not *human* skin, but perhaps the hide of a seal stolen from someone like Fir. Or the lad on the adjoining slab.

He had just twisted his head around to address that one again, when a sound tore through both door and wall and lanced straight into the most primal receptors in his brain. A scream it was, and a shriek—and a shrill, and a wail, and a cry. Not human, but certainly mammalian: dolphin, it sounded like, and clearly in agony beyond enduring. On and on it went, punctuated with those clicks and growls and glottal quacks he'd heard countless times on reruns of *Flipper III*.

Only *this* Flipper was obviously being tortured.

On and on and on those cries continued, sometimes decreasing in volume, but never changing in kind.

But amid those pitiful sounds, Kevin heard another: softer and closer by.

"Fir," a voice hissed, level with his head. *"Fir—Man! It would be good for us to speak now."*

By stretching his neck to the limit, Kevin managed

to peer full in the face of his fellow. The selkie, evidently having sharper teeth than his captors supposed, had gnawed through the duct tape gag, which remained as rags of tattered silver around lips that looked as though they would far rather smile than engage in subterfuge. He had also, Kevin realized, addressed him in Erse.

"You *are* a selkie!" Kevin blurted, in English.

"Speak the Gaelic, if you have any," the selkie muttered haltingly in Kevin's own tongue. "These . . . evil-water-ones have not yet ripped it from my mind, though sure I am that they will, if I cannot find death first."

"D-death?" Kevin gulped helplessly. *"Mhor?"*

"Yes," the selkie replied, likewise in that ancient speech, in which he continued. "Perhaps both yours and mine. But list', for there is little time and much you should know, should you chance to escape from here, which I still dare hope, though I fear 'twill not be the same for me."

"Speak, then," Kevin said in halting Erse. "But go as slow as you can."

"Would that you could read my thoughts as I do yours," the selkie replied. "And would that your fear did not cloud your memories, for much time could thus be saved."

"You read thoughts?"

"Aye! And hide them—and yours, as I did when you feigned sleep just now. But that is not what you most need to know."

Kevin held his breath.

"What you *do* know," it continued, its voice scarcely a whisper, though Kevin heard it clearly, even above the screeches from the adjoining room, "is what I am. Your fear hides how you came by that—but that is a tale for a more pleasant time.

What is important *now* is that those who have captured us are neither your kin nor mine, but the evil-
water-ones—what some land-men call orcas and
others killer whales or the wolves of the sea. But how
can this be? you wonder, for sure they appear like
land-men. And to that I tell you that they have these
few years past learned to shift skin and take on land-
men's form. Alas, it is from captives of my own folk
that they have derived this dreadful art: captives
whom they have held under the most fearful curse
that can be laid upon our kind, which is that if they
do not reveal the arts of shifting skin they will lay
our ancient homeland waste, by which I mean what
you call Eireland. For we were land-men once, of
that country, and the bond we yet feel to it is beyond
imagining.

"As to *how* they intend to do this," the selkie went
on, "I know not, save that it involves the weather.
What I *do* know is that in order to walk in your world
as land-men, they require the skins of land-men.
Mostly they choose those without country or kin,
because such poor wights would least likely be
missed yet be most difficult to identify. And in response to the question you would ask: yes, orcas *are*
intelligent, and dolphins and other whales, too,
though not all of any kind, unlike land-men or sea.
Yet the wise among them are as wise as any land-
men, though land-men are slow to notice this, perhaps because whale-kin have no machines. Rather,
they use their minds, which are very powerful. Sure
it is that they have skill and strength enough to influence dreams. But more important, for your knowing, is that they also have skill to dwell for a time
within such minds as are less than perfectly formed,
and while so doing, control them, and by so doing,
avoid an ancient prohibition among all whale-kin,

that none of them is to directly injure a land-man, those who do being cast out. And—"

The selkie was forced to break off, for the cries from beyond the door had become so bloodcurdling Kevin would cheerfully have spent the rest of his life deaf in order to escape them. Only when they had subsided to a barely tolerable squeal, did the selkie resume its explanation.

"Now then," it went on, "as I have said, our enemies the orcas—and it is not *all* of them, be assured, about which I will speak more anon, should there be time—have stolen from us the art of changing skin. But alas, the skins they steal and put on to pass as land-men will not stand more than one shifting, unlike my folk who shift repeatedly without renewing our other skins. That is what they seek to learn from me, but I have not told them, for I do not know. But even worse, for your kin, is that being larger than land-men, they require many hides to construct one of sufficient size to effect the change—these skins being collected and sewn together by land-men under their control. This they have done for nigh on two years. And—"

He did not finish, because the shrieks became even louder and more agonized than heretofore, and continued endlessly, in an aching, anguished, screaming throb. "What're they *doin'* out there?" Kevin gasped shakily, when speech was once more viable.

"In order to be of use for shapechanging," the selkie sighed, "a skin must be taken from a living body—or else you would surely be dead. But now that orcas have learned to steal the forms of land-men, they would do the same with dolphins. They have lately captured one for that purpose. The rest you can imagine."

Kevin swallowed hard, sick at heart, both from fear for himself, his sister, and his companion, but also out of pity for the poor creature being flayed alive beyond the door. He *liked* dolphins, dammit! Any right-thinking person did. That someone would deliberately harm one of the happy beasts seemed the worst sort of sin, akin to shooting a smiling child. "But why?" he groaned miserably. "*Why?*"

The selkie took a deep, ragged breath; and Kevin wondered if he was injured, and if so, how much all this speaking cost him. "The hostility 'twixt dolphins and orcas is an ancient thing," the selkie murmured. "Indeed, it is well-nigh as old as your kind, but I know little save that it involves the regard dolphins hold for land-men as opposed to what orcas bear. Orcas feel they have been badly treated and count land-men responsible for many ills that trouble both them and the water-world. Dolphins are more sympathetic, for they see that while land-men are selfish and shortsighted, yet are they realizing that they are a part of nature, not apart from it. But be that as it may, I have heard that some recent occurrence has reawakened this hostility and brought the two into conflict in places. They want to steal the skin of that one outside, so that one of them may join the dolphins hereabouts as a spy."

"I met a selkie once," Kevin confessed absently. "I think he was a spy too."

To his surprise, the selkie stiffened. His eyes went wide and terrified, as though Kevin had himself declared his doom. "Tell me!" he demanded. "Quick! *Think* it!"

Kevin took a deep breath, closed his eyes, and somehow (for the shrieking made it difficult to concentrate) managed to recall the major events of his meeting and subsequent adventure with the selkie he'd only known as Fir, ending with the unfinished, cryptic message he'd been given at Leenane.

Throughout, his companion kept silent. "So you *are* the one!" he whispered when the last haunting image had faded from Kevin's conscious mind. "I suspected as much when you recognized what I am, and more when the evil-water-ones spoke of seeking your sister. Yet even if you were not, I would let no land-man die in darkness. A shame it is, too, and a double shame, that you are here—though now I see the reason."

"I wish you'd tell me, then!" Kevin grumbled, glancing apprehensively at the door, beyond which the screams were finally subsiding—by which he feared his captors had concluded their grisly work and would soon return to him and his companion.

The selkie likewise looked troubled. "To say it quickly then: dolphins can speak to our kind; our kind can speak to land-men, but do not understand your world. Your sister is the one we have . . . prepared, to be an intermediary."

"But Cary's not a selkie!" Kevin protested—far too loudly, he feared.

"Wrong!" the selkie shot back. "My father's younger brother lay with your mother. Your sister and I are kin."

But before he could say more, one final scream erupted beyond the door—and seemed to last forever, louder and louder until it filled the world with the ultimate aural essence of terminal pain. Kevin and the selkie could only exchange grim stares. And as the cry rose to a crescendo, Kevin suddenly found himself experiencing an odd floating sensation he could only describe as being torn partway out of himself.

One moment he was aware of cool and damp, the

next he knew heat and bright light and a horrible stickiness he recognized as his own blood bathing his entire body, but blood that was also on fire and burning its way into the flesh of his torso and belly and arms, while a sharper edge of it marched into his legs and manhood and fingers and likewise set them alight. His neck too, and his chin, his lips, his cheeks—his eyes. And he knew when light became too bright and could never be dimmed save by death, even as blood obscured his vision and he could not look away.

Yet he did—and was himself again, gazing across two meters of grimy floor at the selkie.

And fought not to close his eyes once more. For every muscle, every sinew, tendon, and ligament in the selkie's elegant, slender body had gone hard and tense as steel. Indeed, they knotted and twisted unceasingly, as though they fought each other, while the selkie himself battled some unseen agony that was beyond anything Kevin could imagine, even allowing what he had just experienced.

Abruptly, the selkie's eyes stretched wide, his mouth gaped soundlessly—and, with a hiss like a balloon leaking air, he relaxed all at once and went utterly still. Kevin knew, by his motionless chest, that he was dead.

One final piteous cry wrenched him from without, and this time, not caring, Kevin added his own. And as those shrieks rose to what had to be the last, a sharper sound rang out.

The distinctive bark of a large caliber automatic pistol.

Chapter XXVI:
Ne'er a Drop to Drink

(The Gulf of Mexico)
(Saturday, September 3—after midnight)

Something huge, slick, and vastly powerful slid past 'Bird's right leg—the one that trailed deeper into the black waters of the Gulf of Mexico, half a klik off the glittering jewelwork of the Aztlan coast.

He flinched reflexively and jerked it onto the shaky stability of the red-and-white windboard atop which he and Carolyn maintained their uneasy perch. A dark triangle cut the moonlit ripples a meter past the defunct motor: the top twenty sims of an orca's dorsal fin. "*Shit!*" he spat, and shuddered, less from the chill of a sudden cool breeze against the wet bare flesh of his torso, than because his ancestral demons were coming home to roost.

Or swim.

He was Cherokee, and Cherokee myth was *full* of aquatic monsters: the water cannibals who came ashore invisibly and stole unsuspecting men, leaving images in their place; the giant leech at Tlanusiyi, near Murphy, North Carolina, an hour west of where he'd been born. And worst of all, the great fish, the *dakwa*, that haunted the French Broad River and was large enough to swallow a man. But this was worse than any of those because the beasts slowly circling the scanty security of the beat-up board were real.

Or had physical presence, anyway. What else they might be—men changed into orcas, or orcas changed to men—he dared not contemplate. Nor wanted to.

He had forced himself to believe otherwise for twenty-seven years: that magic was a myth, that it had no place in the world of solar cells and biocircuits. And now it—or something very like it—was manifesting right and left, clearly enough to put him in fear of his life as nothing prior had ever done. Everything else—all the risks young men set themselves in the course of learning the limits that defined their manhood—were predictable; they depended on strength or will or knowledge that one could anticipate and access perfectly. The were-orcas were different. *Their* limits were as mysterious as the depth of the ocean hereabouts.

Caught between the devil and the deep blue sea, he thought grimly. *Or by* the dakwa *in the deep black sea . . .*

"I'm gonna die," he whispered to the breeze, as it whipped up a choppiness that made the windboard rock alarmingly. "I'm goin' to fuckin' *die!*"

And not alone. He'd lured an innocent woman into this foolishness, and she was going to die, too, and in that he was doubly damned. And the bad thing was that he hadn't the strength to care. His body ached abominably—from the gouge beneath his clavicle and the slice down his torso that once again seeped blood, and which burned like fire where salt water had been at it for fifteen long slow minutes (long enough for the Spraskin that had protected it to dissolve along the stress-torn edges); through the scraped shin acquired when he'd fallen back at the 'Wheel and the assorted bruises and abrasions the assault at the marina had wrought; to (most recently) the gouge along his left ankle where the windboard had narrowly missed that slab of fallen Promenade, and he had not. Bone showed there: white bone, and flesh that filled and drained with trickling blood as the sea lapped and sucked at it like another water fiend.

He prayed no sharks were about.

"I'm dead," he gasped again, this time with tears in his eyes.

" . . . ten—eleven—twelve . . . " Carolyn counted behind him, her voice dull and cheerless, as though she too was draining herself of feeling in anticipation of forsaking life.

" . . . thirteen!" she finished. "Not a lucky number."

"The number of a coven," 'Bird noted sourly, twisting around to squint at her. "As though they *needed* more magic."

She glared back. "We don't *know*—"

"Yes we do!"

"I didn't see anything," she protested, hard-eyed, though 'Bird suspected she was arguing rationality's side to protect her sanity. "I didn't actually *see* anything. All I have to go on is what you told me—and circumstantial evidence."

'Bird waved a hand toward the dark fins that wove a complex pattern close around their island of safety. "These guys are *circumstantial*?"

"All I *know* is that they're orcas, whatever else they might be, and that their present behavior is within the bounds of established knowledge." Her wild eyes belied her conviction.

"Bullshit!"

A half-meter fin shifted its arc and sliced close beside the windboard, only banking away at the last instant. The board tipped precariously in the wash. 'Bird had far too clear a glimpse of a torpedo-shaped body: black above white, with a mouthful of very sharp teeth large enough to encompass his head.

"God*damn!*" he yipped. "God fuckin' *damn!*"

"They're not acting right," Carolyn noted numbly.

"Fuckin' *right* they're not!" 'Bird snorted. Then, with a scowl: "But you just said—"

"Established knowledge and expected behavior are two different things, lad."

"Fuckin' semantics," 'Bird growled. "You're the one the dolphins worship: do something!"

"Like what?" Carolyn snapped. "For all we know that's a bunch of self-deluding mumbo jumbo."

"Like hell it is!" 'Bird retorted. "There's some other Power fuckin' around with us here—there has to be! And there's no way in hell it'd hit us with all this vision-dream bullshit without reason. And if it's *that* involved with us, there oughta be some way to access it now!"

Carolyn stared at him accusingly. "*You're* the one who claims to know so much about magic!"

"I don't claim to know *anything* about magic," 'Bird shot back wildly. "The stuff scares me shitless!"

"And thirteen orcas don't? Thirteen orcas that aren't acting like orcas at all!"

'Bird frowned resignedly. "Fuck it! Just *fuck* it! Forget I said anything. We'll be dead in a minute anyway."

"'Bird—"

He glared at her savagely. "Okay," he gritted. "I'll make this as clear as I can. I don't know shit about magic—not practically, not to actually do anything useful. But everything I *do* know, at least about tra-

ditional European magic, says *you're* the power
here. Water is woman's domain—in your native
myths, if not mine. You're a marine biologist and
these're marine animals. It's night, and the moon's
nearly full; and the moon, again, is traditionally female. What else do you want?"

"I want to wake up!" she cried. "I want the fuck
out of here! I— What's wrong?"

'Bird braced himself again. "You said something
about them not actin' normal. What'd you mean by
that?"

A weary grimace. "Okay," she sighed, "first,
they're all very small—no more than three to four
meters long, and a couple are even smaller. Orcas
can get up to ten meters . . . which means these are
all young: adolescents at best. Except that orcas this
young usually travel in conjunction with their moth-
ers until they're far older. There's no precedent for
having thirteen young ones together, without old fe-
males about."

"Maybe they *are* about and we just don't know."

"Perhaps. But there're other oddities too, that
don't make sense at all if we're dealing with conventional predators, even very intelligent ones."

"Such as?"

"There's blood in the water, for one thing, which
should trigger *some* aggressive instincts. Secondly,
this board's not much of a barrier. It would be very
easy for them to snatch us off it if they wanted. I've
seen them do that to seals on ice floes many times.
Even on beaches."

'Bird shuddered again. "Seals how big?"

"Seventy-eighty kilos."

"Great," 'Bird groaned, "I weigh seventy-five."

"So if they wanted to kill us, they could. But it
seems more like they just want to . . . *sink* us."

Even as she spoke, a fin broke from the circling ranks and arrowed toward them. But just as 'Bird was certain it was going to slam into them, it submerged. The windboard promptly shuddered as the orca scraped across the underside between him and the obviously terrified woman; but as it seemed on the verge of settling again, a blow to the keel lifted the board straight out of the water over a meter. 'Bird snatched frantically for the rudder handle—and caught it—barely—though one hand skidded off to scrape along the motor cowling. He saw the blood of yet another cut before he felt the pain.

At this rate I'm gonna bleed to death before I'm eaten or drown, he told himself. "I'm gonna die," he said aloud—and louder.

They hit the surface again. Bounced. Tilted. 'Bird's teeth rattled.

But before the board could settle, a shove from the opposite edge tilted it full on its left-hand side. Only its narrow keel and clever ballasting righted it. Carolyn's legs slipped into the waves. 'Bird twisted around to grab at her, but she was back on board before his fumblings reached her.

That did it! Steeling himself, he reached to his belt and pulled out the hunting knife he'd found in Stormy's Jeep and stuck there. Then, setting his jaw, he waited, balancing with one hand against the rudder, the blade secreted along his inner thigh lest Carolyn glimpse it and commence another tirade. She'd *had* her chance—and done nothing. It was therefore up to him. And if he was going to die, he was going to go down fighting.

He got his chance less than a minute later, when a series of waves sent the windboard on a collision course with one of the smaller orcas. As the dome of its head rose from the waves to the right, he stabbed down.

Hit—

But only barely, only a glancing blow, though glistening black hide parted and white blubber showed beneath, laced with delicate darkness that might have been blood stained black in the moonlit gloom. A shriek cut the night—a wavering, high-pitched wail that made 'Bird's blood run cold. It was the first sound he'd heard any of the creatures make, and it carried with it far too much not only of instinct, but of full awareness of the lethal effects of such damage.

'Bird jerked back reflexively, scarcely in time to avoid a mouthful of teeth that snapped where his hand had been. The flinch overbalanced him, however, and he slid off the board. Only his grip on the rudder saved him, but in the frantic struggle to regain the board's scanty security he dropped the knife. He heard Carolyn's anguished cry as she snatched vainly for his free arm—and could not reach it, felt salt set fire in his wounds all over again, and the slap of waves in his face that burned his mouth, nose, and eyes.

And yet he hung on, yet fought his way up, though his legs kicked helplessly in that cold dark realm full of terrible things with teeth.

Something brushed his thigh. He lurched upward in a rush of raw panic, only to slip off the board again—and feel another body slide along his other side. And then—to his horror—something nudged his leg and stayed there. He thrashed wildly, kicking out—only to feel a prickle of pain all down his calf as teeth took hold.

"I'm gone!" he screamed, as those teeth dug in. It was over now. Any second he'd feel pressure, more pain, and then *more* pain as his leg was bitten off. And then he would die.

But—

—The pressure had *vanished!*—though the pain most certainly had not. 'Bird sensed that his assailant had been knocked away. Water filled his eyes, clogging his nose and mouth as he lost his grip on the rudder and fell full into the sea. A furious scramble bought him air again, to glimpse the rudder rod above him. He grabbed it desperately and hung on, dimly aware that Carolyn had likewise fallen overboard.

—Whereupon another orca smashed into him, knocking him loose once more. When he finally surfaced, it was to the heart-stopping spectacle of three sets of wicked teeth ripping at the windboard, while two other orcas beat sections free with flukes and flippers.

Backwash promptly scattered his vision, and when he blinked his eyes clear again, the board was reduced to floating slivers of fiberglass and foam.

But where was Carolyn? He yelled her name, coughed, shouted it again, as he swam into the mass of splinters that had been their one hope of salvation.

"Carolyn!" he called once more, a thin, hopeless sound amid the churning waves and hissing wind. "Carolyn! Are you all right?"

Silence.

Then: "'Bird? Is that you?"

Whereupon he realized that what he had taken for a large hunk of foam was Carolyn's head, bobbing just above the wave tops as she trod water. Beyond, he could see flashing fins and sweeps of sleek dark bodies.

Orcas.

Circling orcas.

Circling in far too precise a pattern.

"Carolyn!" 'Bird panted again, and swam toward her. They touched hands across the wave tops: humanity seeking its like amid that which was totally other. And with that touch, 'Bird's strength went out of him, and he lay dazed and numb amid the swells. He didn't care now. Death would come, and soon. Death was a lonely thing, yet he would not die alone. Without willing it, he relaxed his limbs and let his body go, drifting down, slowly, slowly, wondering vaguely if he was finally feeling the effects of all that blood loss.

"'Bird! Fight it!" Carolyn snapped. He felt her arm go around him, buoying him up, even as he put all he had into kicking enough to keep afloat. Her breath was warm in his ear, her body slick and smooth against his. There were, he reflected, worse ways to die.

And die they would, for as best he could tell with his face barely above wave level, the orcas were closing in—and not merely circling now, but inscribing intricate figures that brought them ever nearer. One thumped against his legs. Carolyn jerked and shuddered, and he assumed one had hit her as well.

But none bit. Not since the one he had injured.

"They want us to drown," Carolyn groaned into his ear. "'Bird, they want us to *drown*."

"Won't have long to wait, then."

"Don't say that," she told him furiously. "I could swim to shore, even with you—*if* they'd let us, which they won't."

"Something *else* that's not normal, right?"

"Right. But not what I'd expect of magic either."

Meanwhile, the mass of orcas was clearly closing in. And very soon were crowding so tightly about

'Bird and Carolyn that he could feel one of their massive bodies against his own at all times. Sliding along his legs, sometimes, or pressing against his hips, or beside his torso. Or a flipper or fluke snapping perilously near his arms or shoulders or head—close, but never impacting. And all too often a knowing flash of eye, or teeth bared in what could only be described as evil grins.

It was hard to maintain his head above water, now. He had become a deadweight in Carolyn's arms, and he could tell that strong as she was, she was tiring.

Closer . . . The press was constant, and harder, tending to force them down.

Down . . .

Abruptly, 'Bird sensed a shift in that pressure, as though something had disturbed the orcas from without. A subtle agitation seemed to spread through the squeezing ranks. "Oh my God!" Carolyn gasped. *"Look!"*

'Bird did—but did not at first see what had prompted her exclamation. But then he glimpsed the flash of a sleek, fishlike body silhouetted against the star-filled sky.

"Dolphins!" Carolyn cried. "They're being attacked by dolphins!"

And it was true! For even as 'Bird used the dregs of his strength to strain upward, the huddled mass of orcas broke apart and scattered from around them.

"Jesus," Carolyn sobbed in his ear. "Jesus, God, and Mary; this can't be real!"

Yet 'Bird's eyes gave the lie to that. For as he watched, moonlight glimmered off another dolphin leaping on high, then another, from a quarter way around the loosening knot of orcas. And then, as best he could tell, battle was joined.

He couldn't see much of what occurred, for the

waves were quickly beaten into a choppy, heaving froth as slick round bodies and blunt-pointed heads smashed together, twisted, bit, and writhed, then broke apart once more. There seemed to be at least as many dolphins as orcas, and quite possibly more, though both moved so quickly, it was hard to decide for certain. They were almost as large as the orcas too, and their teeth seemed just as effective. More than once he saw dolphin jaws slash into orca fin or fluke or flesh and leave long gouges—or outright holes that quickly filled with blood.

On and on that fight continued, as Carolyn and he fought their own battle to stay afloat—aided, fortunately, by the largest fragment of the windboard, which had bobbed into Carolyn's grasp. 'Bird held on to it desperately, as though he were a tiny child and the splintered fiberglass his mother. Carolyn likewise braced against it, but was swimming strongly as she did—far more strongly than 'Bird expected of one so small.

"This isn't normal either, is it?" he managed between gulps and bouts of choking.

She shook her head, eyes wide with what could as well have been fear as awe. "Dolphins have been known to display aggressive behavior against sharks, other dolphins, and even orcas—but this is a little *too* organized, a little *too* aggressive."

"Just like that attack on us was too calculated."

She nodded grimly. "Yeah, just like that. I— *Oh no!*"

She broke off. Her face went suddenly slack with surprise, then hardened with disgust and horror. 'Bird swung around, following her line of sight, saw what Carolyn had—and found it as disturbing.

One of the orcas—the largest, he thought—had seized a dolphin by the head directly in front of its blowhole. And as he watched in sick awe, those jaws sank in. The dolphin struggled, its body arching wildly, its flukes slapping the water, other orcas, fellow dolphins, without regard, even as its comrades arrowed in to snap and gnaw and smash at its assailant.

But the beast held firm, its entire thick body a slick mass of tension as blood gushed from between those jaws.

'Bird heard the sick crunch of tooth against bone, and then the jaws ground shut. The orca jerked away—and 'Bird barely had time to see what remained of the dolphin before a wave smashed into his face and a flurry of movement swept the corpse from view.

It was a chilling sight, and a heartrending one; for like most men, 'Bird had been brought up to think highly of dolphins: not quite as intelligent, perhaps, but clearly friends to man. It therefore hurt deep in his soul to see one so mutilated: to see one—he forced himself to remember what shock was already burying in his brain—with the whole forward part of its head bitten off, as though someone had taken a spoon and scooped out a neat, bloody hole.

"So that's it," Carolyn gasped beside him. "*That's* what's been going on!"

'Bird stared at her incredulously.

"But why?" she continued. "*Why*?"

'Bird had no answer. All he could do was watch spellbound as the dolphins sent the remainder of their assailants swimming away, their attack against him and Carolyn utterly put to rout. The last of the tall dorsal fins was already ten or fifteen meters off, curved over to the side almost in a loop in what he'd heard was a gesture of unhappiness or submission.

And then the water around them resounded with

splashes as dolphin after dolphin broke the surface, arched into the air, curvetted there, then dived headfirst into the moonlit swells, only to repeat that dance again, time after time.

They were speaking too: their heads popping above the surface to nod and chuckle and click in that almost-language of theirs. 'Bird grinned, and would have laughed had his chest not hurt so much—and had he the strength for it.

"I don't suppose you speak dolphin, do you?" he asked Carolyn, where she trod water a few meters away.

She shook her head. "No, but maybe these guys'll let us make it to shore. Can you swim that far?"

"I doubt it," 'Bird replied honestly. "But I'll try."

"Float then, and I'll carry," she told him, easing toward him, her strokes strong and sure. "Kick if you can," she added, extending an arm.

But as her fingers strained toward his, a dolphin's head erupted from the water directly between them. She jerked back, startled, as it poised there, looked her in the face—and slowly and deliberately, reached down, seized her upper arm in its beak—and dragged her under.

"*No!*" 'Bird groaned hopelessly. "No!" But further cries froze in his throat as, one by one—beginning due south and working their way around—dolphin after dolphin leapt once into the air, struck the waves, and vanished, leaving him to stare at a dark and eerily empty ocean, on which fragments of fiberglass and foam drifted along gentle swells, while the distant lights of Aztlan, "Why?," and Sinsynsen beckoned—impossibly far away to someone who had no strength remaining.

Chapter XXVII:
Into the Dark/Into the Light

(The Gulf of Mexico)
(Saturday, September 3—after midnight)

Carolyn had no time to scream—no chance to cry out to poor traumed-out 'Bird—no opportunity, even, to grab more than the most cursory breath of air, before salt water closed over her.

The last thing she saw was a beakful of dolphin teeth silhouetted against a starlit sky, with beyond them 'Bird's face contorting into a horrified *"No!"* Then blackness, in which the only foci were the pressure already building in her lungs, the eager presence of water at the gates of her nose and mouth—and the sharp prickle of delicate pain on her left arm, as the dolphin that had seized her dragged her down.

She fought, of course: beat at it with her free hand; kicked it; pried in vain at its jaws, even as she fought to rise, to break free again into open air.

No good.

No way it could be. The beast was too strong, and short of cutting off her arm (or having it bitten off, which her captor blessedly seemed disinclined to do), she knew that unless it released her or brought her to the surface in short order, she was doomed.

325

Nor was it showing sign of doing either. Rather it continued to dive, and it came to her that even if she did escape, it would take every ounce of energy she possessed to regain the surface, and that it was stupid to waste her rapidly diminishing store of that and oxygen in resistance.

There was always a chance, after all, that the dolphin would tire of this odd game and let go.

But that would be too simple. More to the point, it would be logical—based on the norms of dolphin behavior. Except this one hadn't acted normal to start with. Nor, come to it, had *any* of the cetaceans she'd encountered in the last two-plus days. Not this lad; not the too-coordinated attack by its fellows that had routed the orcas; nor the orcas themselves, that had seemed determined to see her and 'Bird drowned, not eaten; and bloody well not whatever those things had been back at the Dead Marina. Were-orcas, 'Bird had said. Why—now that it was too late—did she truly believe him?

Oh well, belief was very like forgiveness, and since she was going to die anyway, she supposed forgiving someone was an appropriate final gesture. Except, of course, that it would do 'Bird no good—nor her, not *this* side of heaven.

Heaven . . .

The place people went when they died . . .

She was going to die . . .

In fact, she realized, with grim mental chuckle, she was going to die for the second time in two days—which meant she ought to be pretty good at it. Only this time would be for real. Stress and adrenaline and who knew what else *might* step in and save her once, but she no longer had high-tech hardware wired into her neck to send fail-safe messages to her brain.

Nope, she was going to die, and when she did, she would stay that way.

She wondered what that would be like.

Not that different from the present situation, she imagined, no big change from neutral-temperature dark.

Except that her lungs wouldn't hurt anymore; nothing would be poking sharp teeth into her biceps; and all this magic BS would no longer be giving her grief.

The transition was what she dreaded: not the fact itself—she had never feared that—but passing through the door.

Nor could it be far off. The pressure in her lungs had been increasing by the second, and she wanted desperately to breathe; but now other effects were amassing. Her eyes hurt, her pulse was pounding in her ears like the drums she'd heard at the Medicine Wheel some hours back. And of course there were still those damned teeth, holding her firmly, not injuring her, but absolutely not letting go.

And now the dolphin had shifted and, as best she could tell, was swimming almost straight down.

Deeper . . .

Deeper . . .

It was really dark now: ultimate stygian absence of even the ghost of filtered moonlight. Only . . . lights *were* appearing! She first thought it was the effect of pressure on her eyeballs, then noted that the patterns were far too regular and moved in a too-familiar pattern that could only be the result of bio-luminescence in some sea creature that had happened by.

But if she was seeing *those* kinds of things, she was very deep indeed.

Too deep to go without a suit.

Too deep to go without elaborate breathing gear.

How deep *was* she, anyway?

And why wasn't she dead?

Or perhaps she was, and simply hadn't noticed the alteration.

But that was preposterous! If she were dead, her lungs wouldn't hurt so . . . Only she wished she hadn't remembered that, because thinking about them only made them worse, and reminded her more than ever of how desperate for air she was.

The on-hand supply was lasting remarkably well, however, very well indeed. Like how long had it been, anyway? A minute? Two? Three? She had no idea.

She only knew she *really* wanted to breathe . . .

Deeper . . .

More pressure . . .

More pain . . .

And then she could resist no longer. *Everyone who loves me, forgive me!* she cried soundlessly— and exhaled.

At exactly that same moment, the dolphin released her arm.

Water beat at her nostrils, at her mouth—yet did not go in. Something kept it out, by which she assumed that perhaps there'd been more air in her lungs than she'd assumed.

And then everything *changed* . . .

She could not describe the sensation, save that it was as if every cell in her body suddenly . . . turned over. There was no pain, though a definite flare of warmth surged through her, flowing from deep in her brain to her spine, and thence to her heart and lungs, and eventually to all other organs, her muscles, and finally her bones and skin.

When it passed, her heart beat steadily—at a

slower, yet more persistent rate; and her lungs—
Well, deep as she was, and as long as she'd been
under, they somehow still held air. Only now they
knew how to process it more efficiently, store it
more securely, and release it at a slower rate—while
her body knew how to use it to maximum effect and
shut down irrelevant systems at need.

In fact—as an unseen grin broke out on her face,
there in the deep-sea dark—she felt *good*!

Death had once more been defeated. She would
never fear it again, not in the depths of the sea. For
the sea had taken her, and in some strange way
made her its own.

And then, from pure joy, she was swimming—diving down and rising up, swishing to the left then
swinging gracefully to the right; feeling the currents;
tasting the life thereabouts by its signature in the
water; knowing *exactly* how much to move which
limb which way to achieve the desired effect, as a
thousand years in skinsuits, scuba gear, or artificial
gills could never have accomplished.

She did not ponder the *how* of this miracle; she
dared not; did not let her scientist-self drag out the
rules and reference books and tell her such a thing
could not be: that a human could swim like a dolphin. Or—and that new heart skipped one of those
amazing beats when she realized this—a *seal*!

Perhaps Kevin had been right. Perhaps were-seals
truly existed—selkies, whatever one wanted to call
them. Perhaps, in fact, *she* was a selkie! Perhaps that
was what that dream had meant: the one with her
mother and that odd boy she had made love with,
the one who had turned into a seal. Could that truly
have happened? And if so, did that mean that she,
Carolyn Mauney-Griffith, was the child of a woman
and a were-seal?

It could well mean that very thing, came words into her brain.

She started at that, paused in mid-twirl. Yet it did not seem *that* remarkable that words should form that way. Too, she was suddenly aware of other presences nearby, presences her size and larger. *Who . . . ?* she thought at them.

You called me Katana, one replied.

You called me Bokken, came the subtly different thoughts of the other. *And we thought those names a pleasant irony, for though we were named for weapons, it is we who made a weapon out of you!*

A weapon . . . ?

Not now, the thought that was Katana broke in. *There are other things she should know first—and others who should tell them.*

True, Bokken replied. *I forget myself. And the first thing you have to know, Carolyn Mauney-Griffith, is that you had to die once so that your body could awaken and make the Change; and you had to die again for the Change to manifest.*

And now, Katana interrupted with the eagerness of an excited teenage boy, *you should take up the birthright that is yours.*

My mother . . . ?

Was a lady on the earth.

And my father . . . ?

Katana laughed in that wonderful unheard language. *As an ancient song of your people says, he was a selkie on the sea.*

I've heard that song! Carolyn cried.

And then she too felt like singing.

Chapter XXVIII:
Dead or Alive

(Aztlan Free Zone)
(Saturday, September 3—after midnight)

All Kevin heard for one long breath after that single muffled *blat* of gunfire was silence.

No screams or shrieks or agonized wailing screeches.

Nothing.

They'd finally shot that poor dolphin.

There'd be no more heartrending cries now, no more psychic backwash jerking him out of his head to share that torture vicariously. No more of whatever telepathic overload had lashed out from the room beyond the metal door to slay the selkie beside him.

No more of those impossibilities that had him straining so hard against his bonds that his wrists and ankles were rasped raw where they rubbed against the leather.

. . . leather . . .

Leather bound him!

What was leather?

Skin.

And what was it his captors so admired in him?

His skin!

Abruptly, he was thrashing like a madman.

It was too much! He had to escape, had to elude these crazies the dead selkie on the adjoining table had said were some sort of militant were-orcas bent on infiltrating human and dolphin kind via permanently purloined hides.

Hides they had worn in quest of Cary.

Cary . . .

He had to save Cary!

Blat!

A second shot made him freeze, for it had ricocheted off the door. Shouts followed: his own spontaneous cry, and some not nearly so human: those same odd-registered vocalics his captors uttered—

And the cold tinkle of glass breaking, the staccato scrape-slap of stumbling footsteps, the thump of heavy bodies flopping about and colliding with objects that clanked and rang and jangled—

Another shot. A dull, flat thud. A thin, metallic clatter.

And then, in quick succession, two more reports.

Kevin's heart leapt to his throat when he heard those last. Obviously, even flayed alive, the dolphin was proving remarkably fond of its life. Why else would the unfortunate beast require five bullets to end its misery?

And when would his begin?

He struggled harder.

Uselessly.

The straps that clamped him to what now reminded him far too much of a necropsy table would have stymied someone twice his strength; and his fine-boned sixty-eight kilos were no match for the loosest. All his frantic twists accomplished was more damage to his wrists and ankles, and straining a cramp into his left calf that made him gasp and grit his teeth to keep from yelling. He flexed his heel downward slowly, experimentally—

Whereupon the door beyond that foot flew open— to reveal the black-haired, wild-eyed, blood-besplattered figure of what looked a very great deal like a supremely pissed-off Native American bracing a large-caliber automatic pistol in hard, sinewy hands.

The man instantly flattened against the doorjamb, arms outstretched as, with one smooth arc, he covered all four walls with the weapon, lowering it only when (so Kevin presumed) he found it empty of threat and with no exits save that he blocked.

They faced each other long enough for Kevin to note that the guy was rangily built but not much taller than he—1.8 max—wore baggy black jeans beneath a long fringed serape, was reasonably handsome in a perky kind of way, and had shoulder-length hair gathered back in a tail. Kevin guessed he was twenty-six. And fully human.

"They're dead," the man panted, stuffing the pistol into his belt even as he darted forward to tug at the straps around Kevin's ankles. "But we've gotta get outta here fast."

"Do my hands, and I'll help," Kevin shot back as his left foot came free—which promptly sent prickles of pain shooting up that limb as circulation returned.

"Got it," the man acknowledged, shifting to Kevin's right arm—where he froze, eyes fixed on the motionless selkie beyond him.

Kevin followed his gaze. "Dead," he affirmed numbly, as his rescuer gave up on buckles and tongues and attacked Kevin's bonds with a bowie knife. "Died, not killed directly."

"Human?" the man wondered—and it did not immediately occur to Kevin that that was *not* a typical question. *Unless* this Indian-guy shared at least part of the secret.

"More than some folks," Kevin hedged.

"You got a name, white boy?" the Indian continued, with a hard-edged grin, as he moved to Kevin's other arm, leaving Kevin to fumble one-handed with the strap around his forehead. "I'm Stormcloud Nez—Stormy for short—and I'd as soon not spend all night saying 'Hey You.' "

"Kevin."

"We'll shake later, if you don't mind"—as Kevin's other arm came free.

"I'll take care of the rest," Kevin told him. "What the hell was goin' on out there?"

Stormy was already rummaging through the piles of clothing on the sofa. "Nothing pretty," he grunted absently. "You prob'ly heard it in here; it looked even worse than it sounded."

"It sounded like . . . the worst thing in the world," Kevin replied. He jerked the last strap free and slid his legs off the table.

—And crumpled onto all fours, the right knee unable to support him. "Leg's asleep," he chuckled edgily, massaging the limb as Stormy spun around to scowl at him. "Sorry."

"We need to get outta here quick as we can," Stormy urged. "Uh—you *are* okay, aren't you? No lasting damage?"

"Nothin' a week at a spa wouldn't cure," Kevin managed between breaths, dragging himself up by bracing against the table. An instant later he could stand shakily on his own feet. Stormy thrust him a wad of fabric, dark and stained. Kevin untangled a pair of jeans from the muddle and tugged them on, along with a ragged serape. The rest he discarded, as he staggered toward the exit.

Stormy, who had paused to ransack the rack of firearms to the left of the door, reined him back with a hand on his biceps. "It really is *not* pretty in there—just thought I oughta warn you!"

Kevin set his jaw, as Stormy—with pockets bulged by ammo and exotic hardware, and an Uzi assault rifle slung across his shoulders to complement the automatic he'd been lugging—stuffed a small, expensive-looking pistol into Kevin's hand, eased in front of him, and slipped into the outer room.

But even with Stormy's warning, Kevin was not prepared for what met him when he entered that place.

His first impression was blood *everywhere*: splattering the dingy walls like abstract paintings, pooling on the concrete floor from where an honest-to-God bucket of the stuff had been spilled, specked and dribbled over the sparse furniture, even dripping from the ceiling.

And the bodies . . .

His captors sprawled upon the floor: all three he had seen here. One with a hole in his/her head exactly between the eyes (which wound had expanded past fist-size where the bullet had exited); one—the leader—with the same ornamentation on his temples, away from which flesh was splitting as something thrust against it from beneath. And the third—the one who had brained Kevin in the first place—with an oval opening in his left carotid just aft of his jaw, from which rich red liquid pulsed and gurgled over skin that was likewise sloughing loose to reveal something much darker. By the angle of his leg, it was he who had upset the bucket of blood.

—The blood that had obviously been salvaged

from what still twitched weakly on a necropsy table in the center of the room.

Kevin gagged when he saw it. And though his imagination—and ears—had prepared him in somewise for what lay there, *nothing* could truly set the stage for such horror.

Blessedly, most of what registered was simply a torpedo-shaped mass of red that resembled an accident at a slaughterhouse, all two-odd meters awash with oozing redness that obscured detail. The poor beast lay on its belly, one eye miraculously free of gore, but dilated like mad and wildly staring. A pitiful hiss-gurgle came from the dark pit of its blowhole, sounding more labored by the instant.

Yet it still lived! It had survived blood loss, lingering lung collapse, and shock; and Kevin could only marvel at the constitution that could sustain life so long under such conditions.

And then that unlidded eye swiveled around to gaze accusingly up at him, and he had to whirl away, gorge rising.

Unfortunately, when he spun, he came face-to-face with the room's final horror.

It was a tank like the one in his prison, filled with what he supposed was salt water—save that the liquid was reddening rapidly, and within it clumped a gray-white-pink mass that could only be the dolphin's hide.

"Gross!" Kevin gulped—and vomited copiously onto the reeking mess on the floor. When his stomach showed no sign of aftertremors, he turned weakly to face his grim-eyed savior. "Kill it," he choked. "Kill the poor ruined thing."

Stormy's jaw hardened in disgust. "I thought I had!" Whereupon he pressed the pistol to the dolphin's head just above the eye and pulled the trigger twice.

The eye dimmed. Kevin looked away. Saw bodies again. In that brief time, more skin had split away from the wounds. Kevin stared at the gun in his hand—and dropped it. It clattered on the tiles. "People . . . you killed . . . "

"They're not human!" Stormy spat. "You got that? *Not* human!"

"But . . . "

"You *know* what they are, man; you *have* to! I *had* to kill 'em or they'd change into something neither of us could deal with!"

"I . . . "

"Let's get the fuck outta here, *okay*?" Stormy gritted, as he made his way toward what Kevin assumed by its more ornate texture and finish, and by the quality of the darkness visible through a man-wide crack beyond, was an outside door.

But just as the Indian touched the handle, the tinkling crunch of glass being crushed made Kevin glance around, once more on guard.

It was the selkie—the lately *dead* selkie—somehow free of its bonds and risen, to lean shakily against the doorjamb between the rooms. Red weals, some of them leaking blood, disfigured his wrists and ankles, forehead, neck, and thighs: evidence of straps that had not been unlatched, but snapped by force of limb.

"Take the skin," the selkie gasped hoarsely, his voice scarcely more than a whisper. "The dolphin told me to tell you to take its skin—to give it to The-One-Who-Is-The-Way. It called me back from death to tell you this. I—"

But he spoke no more; simply folded his arms around himself and crumpled to the floor.

"What the—?" Stormy growled, his gaze shifting from the dead selkie, past Kevin, to the bloody mass in the tank.

Kevin was likewise staring, aware on one level that he was on the verge of shock. Yet from somewhere he found sufficient presence of mind—and will-power to sustain it—to reach into the tank and, after one false start when his fingers brushed a too-warm stickiness and recoiled, drag out the heavy sprawl of dolphin skin.

He stared at it dumbly, where it slumped across his arms like a vast sodden gray-red blanket, uncertain even now whether he could stand prolonged contact without losing his gorge again. His senses spun, darkness hovered near. He felt perilously light-headed.

And then a rough grip around his arm dragged him back to minimal awareness of ongoing reality. "We've gotta split," Stormy hissed—and with that he thrust Kevin from the scene of all that preposterous carnage and into what proved to be a hallway outside. His companion promptly produced a pocket flashlight, and by that long clear beam, Kevin determined that they stood in what looked like a service corridor in a hotel—possibly, given the damp and the sound of the sea nearby, one of those derelict jobs along the southern coast Carolyn had pointed out to him on the drive down to Sinsynsen: the place called the Dead Marina.

A line of bloody footprints in two sizes led right, toward a flight of stairs twenty meters distant. "Stormy . . . ?" he prompted uncertainly, inclining his head that way.

"Two other folks: the ones doing the actual cutting. When I shot those . . . *things* in there, these others just turned off, just went blank, like those were-orca dudes had been controlling 'em and let go when they died. One started crying like a kid. The other was a—what's the word?—microcephalic woman. She just stood staring 'til that other guy got hold of her. I told 'em to wait, but . . . "

"We'll look for 'em," Kevin concluded, then paused, worried. "What about—?"

Stormy flashed him a dead-eyed grin. "I don't think anybody needs to find that stuff in there, do you? Hang on to yourself," he added. "This could be a big 'un!"

Whereupon he took aim at a range of red metal cans ranked along the wall inside the door—and fired. Kevin had barely time to realize that they were the sort of containers used to store methanol, which fueled most vehicles nowadays—before the cylinders, the wall, and both rooms beyond erupted into flame.

Heat smashed into Kevin like a solid thing, drying him in an instant and crisping away his eyebrows. "There's a boat outside," Stormy explained, as he backed away, his face a devil mask of reflected fire. "I think they used that stuff to fuel it. That's probably how they brought the dolphin here."

Kevin could only stand stupidly and watch the door become the gates of a white hot hell—until Stormy grabbed him by the shoulders and propelled him toward the stairs. "I have no idea how far that'll spread," he panted, as they made their way to the upper landing, two treads at a time. "But I intend to be as far away as possible."

"Murder," Kevin muttered numbly, as he climbed. "Murder has been done."

Stormy stumbled to a stop and spun around to face him. "*Not* murder," he snapped. "Get that through your head, okay? Those things back there

absolutely were *not* human. They're—I dunno—
some kind of magical shape-changing monsters."

Kevin simply gaped dully. Chills danced reels on
his torso.

"And even if they *were* men," Stormy added savagely, "anybody that'd skin a fellow being alive *de-
serves* to die."

Kevin started to counter with something about
that being a damned cold-blooded remark, then
caught the edge of hysteria in his companion's voice,
the tremble in his shoulders, the glitter of scarce-
suppressed tears in his dark brown eyes.

And then Stormy pushed Kevin through a door at
the top of the stairs and into what was indeed, by
the cobwebbed signs, the lobby of a defunct Hilton.

The line of bloody footprints they'd been following
had faded to tracery now, but could still barely be
discerned, angling toward a break in the wall beside
the boarded-up main entrance. Kevin and Stormy
paced them.

An instant later, they were pelting down the
moonlit Promenade. There was no sign of the were-
orcas' human accomplices, though Kevin thought he
saw a few spots of blood continuing north into the
maze of canals and derelict buildings. They were
safe, then; those poor folks were. And so was he!

Suddenly he could not get enough of warm fresh
air, nor of open spaces, nor the near-full moon, nor
the spangled stars of tropical skies. But he had to
keep up with his companion, so for the next few
minutes he focused on running, on keeping pace
with the fleet-footed Stormcloud Nez, as they
threaded a network of alleys that tended south and
west.

Not until they had reached a hurricane fence at
the western border of the Dead Marina did Stormy

slow again—and then only to duck around an un-obtrusive kink in the barrier, where it paralleled the base of a steep grassy bank. Kevin followed, and, en-cumbered as he was with the sloppy mass of the dol-phin skin, had to use hands as well as feet to scramble up the slope.

He gasped out his relief when he found himself on the edge of a mostly empty parking lot, erratically lit. Beyond it, a thread of freeway shimmered, and beyond *that* lay the faceted topaz jewel of the Min-istry of Transportation. Behind sprawled a dark jum-ble of shattered buildings threaded by waterways, with past them, the sea. He scanned the area warily, alert for signs of fire.

He saw none, and then Stormy slapped him on the back and pointed toward a low-slung electric Chrys-ler sedan, on the side of which, when Kevin stag-gered close enough to decipher it, was emblazoned some sort of Native American symbol.

"Mine's . . . occupied," Stormy explained, as he popped the deck lid and indicated that Kevin should store the skin there. "I appropriated this one."

Kevin regarded him dubiously, but unloaded his gruesome burden into the compact trunk.

Stormy frowned back, inserted a card into the door, and climbed into the driver's seat. "Let's see"—as Kevin slid in the other side—"that'd be breaking and entering, grand theft auto, entrance to a restricted zone, curfew violation, possession of an unauthorized weapon, possession of a weapon off duty, arson, and either cruelty to animals, hunting without a license, or murder-one." He sounded un-nervingly giddy.

Kevin rolled his eyes.

"You better be worth it, son!"

"But . . . how'd you find me?" Kevin stammered,

as the car whirred to life and Stormy swished it out of the parking lot. "And . . . where're we going anyway?"

"To look for your sister—or whoever that was you're staying with—I hope," Stormy replied in response to the latter. He sounded marginally more in control, though he seemed to be having to work at it. Kevin didn't blame him. "As for the other," Stormy went on, "basically, it started when I saw these two guys shadowing my friend 'Bird . . . "

And for the next several minutes Stormy gave Kevin a brief account of 'Bird's discovery of the flaying-in-progress, and particularly of what he and 'Bird had witnessed at the Dead Marina earlier that evening, adding that 'Bird had decided someone named Carolyn was in danger and had gone to warn her—and that hopefully (upon Kevin's informing him that Carolyn *was* his sister and had not been home when the were-orcas ransacked her place), 'Bird had managed to get her to safety.

"As for me," he continued, "basically I saw that the guy I'd shot—the one that hadn't shifted shape and escaped—was just bleeding too bad for me to handle. But I didn't want anybody asking what a security type like me was doing in a restricted zone, so when it became obvious that the poor guy didn't know shit when he wasn't being controlled by those orca-things, I just lugged him down to the closed AFZoRTA station back in the Marina, called in an anonymous ambulance tip, and hid out till the white coats showed.

"And as soon as *they* left," he concluded, "I tried to get hold of 'Bird—who's got my Jeep. Well, naturally I couldn't reach him—and he couldn't call *me* 'cause I had to turn my phone off in case the cops were backtracking the AFZoRTA tip. And while I thought he *might* come back here, and had left a note just in case, I didn't want to sit on a run-down boardwalk all night—not with those were-orca things lurking around. So I hopped on good old AFZoRTA and rode back to his place—which was empty—then on to mine, where I happened on this little item from the Dineh Motor Pool. And since 'Bird had gone looking for your sis and had told me her address, I figured I better check there, it being his last stated destination. And guess who I found instead? More to the point, guess who I found being hustled into a car by some suspicious types? I followed, of course—as far as I could. Trouble was, those suckers took a turn that I missed, and by the time I doubled back, they were all gone but their taillights. Lucky for you, I'm hell on wheels at tracking, so I trailed 'em, and—"

"But what *took* you so long?" Kevin broke in, as Stormy eased the car onto Schele Avenue.

"Mostly finding exactly where they had you," Stormy replied. "That, and finding a safe way in and out. And then . . . Well, even after I found 'em and saw what they were doing—spying through the vent grille, as it happens—it took a while to sort out who the good guys were. Obviously the little woman didn't have the chips to skin a live dolphin without someone else's programming, nor did the guy with her; and fortunately our were-orca friends have a certain look to 'em that's easy to spot when you've seen a few—their hands move all the time, for one thing. But even so, it took a while to psyche myself up to commit what a little bit of me *does* think might've been cold-blooded murder. Thank God for diplomatic immunity . . . I hope!"

Kevin shifted in his seat. "So, where to now?"

A shrug. "Well, first we oughta call 'Bird's place. I

mean, that's where I'd take your sister if I was him, since he probably thought everything was level with me. 'Course he wasn't there *earlier* . . . "

"But you think Cary's with him?"

Stormy crossed his fingers on the steering wheel. "I hope so for both their sakes. In fact, we could also call *her*. She got a body phone?"

Kevin shook his head. "Can't wear 'em 'cause of her job. What about your bud?"

"His was, shall we say, forcibly disconnected. Which means I call 'Bird's place first; if no answer, then I call my car; and if that fails, we go by 'Bird's place again. And if *that* doesn't work, we cruise his haunts—and hope the son of a bitch gets hold of me!"

Chapter XXIX:
Shore Leave

(The Gulf of Mexico)
(Saturday, September 3—well after midnight)

'Bird's lungs were bursting—and still he dived. Still forced himself deeper into womb-warm darkness in which he could see *nothing*; hear *nothing* save the dull labored thud of his heart, the rushing roar of blood in his ears that grew louder the longer he held his breath; taste naught but salt and fishiness; and smell what could only be called the scent of the sea.

But he *touched* nothing—not so much as a flick of a fish's fin or the trailing edge of a dolphin's fluke like those which had saved Carolyn and him scant moments before.

Saved them but to damn them again, he amended grimly, as false lights born of pressure awoke in his eyes. Saved them to drag Carolyn down and not relinquish her. Saved them to abandon him to despair, in which flickered but the weakest flame of desperate hope.

And then—though he had touched no more than the instinctive soul-numbing terror of warm dark wetness full of hidden, awesome life—'Bird could go no farther. His lungs felt like burning bellows, his heart like an anvil hammered too long and desperately; his head throbbed abominably with the after-pulse of that same frantic rhythm. Never mind the cuts and bruises, strains and abrasions that marked every part of him with the signs of the careless fool. And so he turned, and for the third time in as many minutes, rose.

It took a very long time—almost too long. And at the end, with only hope left to sustain him—that, and blind trust that whoever—whatever—had been calling the shots lately would not let him die in vain—he kicked one final time—

—and exploded into crisp, clear air.

He drank it down like wine.

Light stroked his shoulders and arms: the moon—gold, an invisible fraction less than full, and barely past the zenith of a sky whose stars it had, all but the brightest, drowned. The waves glittered; the pylons along the beltway shone with shattered diamonds hoarding sunset's long-vanished light; while the low faceted shapes beyond were gemstones: metallic mirrors by day, transfigured now into frozen flames of topaz and tourmaline, zircon, sapphire, and emerald. The desalinization plant was a sprawling wonderland of self-lit golden pearls. And "Why?" up the coast beyond it, a softly gleaming sweep of artfully paralleled lines in ultraviolet.

Only the Dead Marina darkened that long glittering coast.

The Dead Marina . . .

Dead . . .

Carolyn Mauney-Griffith, whom he had worked so hard to rescue that his efforts had cost her life, was dead.

While he, Thunderbird Devlin O'Connor, who had proclaimed his own doom countless times while he and Carolyn squatted precariously atop an aban-

doned windboard in the middle of the Gulf of Mexico, with orcas taking pot-bites at them—he,
Thunderbird, still lived.

Not *well*, he admitted, nor likely to remain that
way long enough to make landfall—not in waters
that had lately thronged with hostile hyperintelli-
gent adolescent orcas—but alive.

He wondered how he'd explain all this if he *did*
manage to make it ashore. More to the point, he
wondered how on earth he'd set the record straight
with Carolyn's brother.

Maybe he *should* just let go and drown. Yeah, that'd
certainly save a shitload of trouble. Then someone
else could worry about shape-shifting orcas, dolphins
that knew how to dance, dreams of fish that skinned
men (though that made sense now, he realized
numbly), and a dozen other improbable mysteries.

Unfortunately, that someone would surely be
Stormy. And 'Bird could not weight his best friend
with so much grief.

Besides, knowing Mr. Cloud, he'd be the first mor-
tal to haunt the dead!

Abruptly, something bumped 'Bird's shoulder
where he bobbed along barely treading water, there
in the vast black ocean. He flinched, yipped into the
wave-dampened silence, even as he spun around,
wishing he hadn't lost the knife and wondering when,
amidst all the recent chaos, it had gone AWOL.

But it was only a fragment of fiberglass foam: the
meter-long remnant of the shattered windboard he'd
clutched earlier. He snared it anyway, having discovered somewhere in the dark pit of despair that
did duty for a soul that he simply didn't have it in
him to dare another dive.

Besides, they'd find Carolyn eventually—find her
body, anyway. Didn't that place she worked have

both north and south bays under remote surveillance? And hadn't she said something about sonar? Yeah, they'd find her soon enough. *If*—he shuddered reflexively—there was anything left *to* find.

"I'm still gonna die," he informed a floating mass of seaweed, as a wave of fatigue washed over him like one of those shimmering around him. Already lethargy made his limbs seem heavy as lead, his lungs like weary balloons leaking away the last of their air.

I'm absolutely *gonna die!* he continued to himself. *I'm strainin' blood into the water like a sieve. If the orcas don't come back, sharks will. And I can't count on dolphins to save me twice, 'cause they worship* you, *Carolyn, not me.*

He had just sense enough to squirm out of the sneakers and jeans that had already encumbered him far too long, before he flung one arm across the slab of foam, closed his eyes, and resigned himself to drifting.

Drifting . . .

Asleep, or unconscious, he neither knew nor cared. The single certainty was that a warm, heavy lethargy had claimed him, blurring the edge of his thoughts, softening his instincts, soothing the pains that plagued him into distant throbs.

Drifting . . .

Water blood-warm around him. Breeze skin-cool about his face, as the top of his head slowly dried, and salt wove crystals in his hair.

Drifting . . .

Drifting . . .

Gone . . .

—Something scraped his toes. He snapped back to groggy awareness, as reflex jerked his legs upward. Fatigue slid them down again.

They brushed a second time, but now he had sense enough to drag open salt-crusted lids and note that he was not that far offshore.

Which shore, he had no idea—though a darkness loomed to the right, which some part of him identified with north. And a contrasting brightness spangled the southern horizon, some of it sky glow, but much of it true electric light.

And then he was once more in free water—by which he concluded he'd just floated across a submerged sandbar. Yet that simple fact gave him hope enough, strength enough, *will* enough, to set him kicking, thereby hastening his progress toward land. And this time when his feet touched bottom, he shifted his weight and, with considerable effort, found himself walking.

Wading, rather, through waves that were mostly gentle, though now and again one set him staggering sideways or curled above his head, as if striving one last time to claim him. He ignored them, though the effort required to resist the undertow sapped his strength relentlessly.

Still, every step freed more from the sea's dominion—shoulders first, then chest, then the lower arch of his ribs . . .

I'm gonna live! he told himself dully. *I'm gonna goddamn live!*

And you're gonna have some explainin' to do too, another aspect added. *No rest for the weary yet, boy-o; not by a bloody long shot!*

His belly was clear now . . . his manhood, his thighs . . . his knees . . .

And then Thunderbird Devlin O'Connor staggered out of the Gulf of Mexico, across four meters of hard wet sand, and fell into the warm white powder of salvation.

Darkness hovered near. The susurration of the waves was a soothing lullaby.

He dozed.

Maybe he dozed. Certainly an amount of time passed. Perhaps it was a wave sliding high up the beach that awoke him some time later.

He blinked, shook his head, rubbed grit from his eyes with equally abrasive fists, then thought better of it. He made to slap them clean on his jeans—and discovered that he was naked, only then recalling how he had traded modesty for a few crucial kilos of buoyancy.

Which hardly mattered—not here on what he had tentatively identified as *El País Verde* between Sinsynsen and Aztlan, south of the Dead Marina.

Which meant . . .

A slow scan of the premises showed no more than the expected jungle, so he set off up the strand, using the dregs of his scant new store of energy to force each step along.

Eventually he saw it: the glistening glassy egg-on-oversized-wheels that was Stormy's Jeep. That heartened him, though he had no strength left to cross that last few hundred meters at more than the same numb limp he'd been maintaining—until, without truly being aware he had drawn so close, his hand slid along the smooth bubble of the right rear fender. He leaned into the vehicle for support and sprawled there a long moment, panting. Then, mustering his last bit of energy, he told the passenger door to unlock; and, when he heard the resulting click, opened it and reached inside.

It required mere seconds to locate what he sought: a can of nameless soda in the cooler built into the back of the console; and, when he had chugged it all, the voice-activated phone in the dash.

"Phone: on," he mumbled. "Thunderbird O'Connor to Stormcloud Nez."

The phone clicked, then buzzed, then crackled. And finally, blessedly, unbelievably, he heard a familiar voice.

" 'Bird? *'Bird!* Is that *you*?"

Stormy's voice had that hollow flatness that indicated he was responding from his body phone. " 'Bird," he repeated, more loudly. "Where the fuck *are* you?"

"*País Verde*, just south of the Dead Marina," 'Bird managed, as fatigue—or blood loss—mounted a sneak attack and made him reel.

"How—?"

'Bird cleared his throat, as blackness hovered near.

" 'Bird? Shit, man; are you *okay*?"

"No," 'Bird croaked. "I'm . . . dead."

And with that, he pushed back from the Jeep and slumped heavily to the sand. And this time he did not awaken.

He dreamed again: a simple dream in which he sat naked on a nameless shore and pounded a beat from a leather-skinned drum. On and on he pounded, a certain rhythm he had heard before, that had come to him first in John Lox's sweat lodge, and again in a more mundane dream about which he remembered nothing except a raccoon.

Or perhaps it was simply the rhythm of his heart . . .

. . . *dum*-dum-*dum*-dum;*dum*-dum-*dum*-dum . . .

" *'Bird?*"

Silence.

" *'Bird?*"

"Go 'way, man; I'm dreamin'..."

" 'Bird! Goddamn it, 'Bird, wake up!"

And then something cold as ten thousand north pole deaths splashed onto his face, and the drumming dissipated . . .

'Bird blinked angry eyes up at the weary ones of Stormcloud Nez.

"Welcome back to the land of the living, bro," Stormy said, his grin sincere, though his face was grim with ill-concealed concern.

"Where am I?"

"Where you were."

'Bird tried to sit up and discovered he'd been lying on his back in dry sand. His fingers dug into it as he heaved himself upright, concluding before Stormy's disapproving scowl confirmed it that standing would be a mistake. Instead, he sat where he was, and in that position noted that Stormy's Jeep was two meters to his right, the jungle beyond it, and that it was still, to judge by the location of the moon, not that long after he'd conked out.

Stormy squatted beside him and held out a bottle of what proved to be orange juice. 'Bird drank it greedily. It hit him like cold fire, and he felt life pouring back into his limbs. Even his brain began to loosen. Shoot, he could almost think again.

"He gonna live?" came another voice from farther off. He twisted around, to see, strolling from behind the Jeep where he'd evidently been fooling with the phone, a skinny, haggard man in a ragged gray serape and dirty jeans that, even stylishly baggy as they were, were clearly too big for him.

A man with a narrow, haunted face beneath a matted shock of blue-blazed orange hair.

A man he'd seen before, both in person and—he realized for the first time—in the dream he'd had before going to the 'Wheel: the dream about the raccoon and the drum and the Salmon-catcher. "Been fishin' lately?" 'Bird giggled giddily—as unconsciousness once more swooped near. Stormy grabbed him as he wavered and urged more juice on him.

When 'Bird had drained the bottle and regained some grip on himself, it was to see that same man squatting opposite him, his face hard with something between raw anger and naked hate. "You're Kevin," 'Bird said flatly. Because it was true.

The man's face darkened, and in spite of his obvious youth, looked suddenly centuries old. "What have you done to my sister?" he growled. "What have you done with Cary?"

"Drowned . . ." 'Bird said numbly, before he could stop himself.

Whereupon the man lunged forward, arms outstretched, fingers curved to curl around 'Bird's throat.

'Bird flung up an arm ineffectually—which unbalanced him. He flailed—and fell on his side.

And by then Stormy had one arm around the man's chest, another around his neck, and was hauling him back, hissing, "Cool it, Kevin!" under his breath.

"I tried to save her," 'Bird gasped desperately, even as the fire in Kevin's eyes flashed brighter and he struggled weakly in Stormy's grasp. "I tried to save her," he repeated. "But I guess I'm not a very good hero."

"Or maybe you are!" Stormy countered, nodding toward the ocean. "Look there—both of you—and tell me what you see!"

'Bird did—and came well-nigh to shouting.

Chapter XXX:
Word, Way, and Singer

(The Gulf of Mexico)
(Saturday, September 3—well after midnight)

'Bird!

And with that name ringing in her conscience like a gong, Carolyn's brief playtime was over.

How could she have been so selfish? How could she have become such a goddamn self-centered fool? It was one thing to enjoy herself—and frolicking with dolphins in the depths of the Gulf was certainly entertaining, never mind the enlightenment their revelations had wrought, which brought joy of another kind. But it was something else entirely to indulge herself so profligately while a friend—someone who had saved her life—struggled to stay afloat in the dark waters far above.

If he wasn't dead already: drowned, bled dry, or eaten by orcas—or, more likely, sharks. He'd looked like bloody hell when Katana had dragged her down—and who knew how long ago that had been? 'Bird could well be dying even now.

But she had to know.

And so she twisted around in a tighter, cleaner arc than she could ever have managed . . . *before*, courtesy of joints that were suddenly far more supple, and commenced the long ascent toward what she now thought of as the lower sky: the one that marked the juncture of sea and air.

A bulbous dolphin nose prodded her inquisitively. Another slid so close beside her she recognized it by the texture of its skin.

No! she thought at them, with that wonderful gift she had possessed so briefly; that already seemed so natural, so much a part of her, she could not imagine having lived without it. *No! I have to see to my friend.*

You are our friend too!

I will have time with you again. 'Bird needs me now.

He lives, Bokken chimed in. *He is conscious. More than that I cannot tell unless I go there. It is only his slow thoughts I can hear, and now his fast thoughts shout above them.*

Fear? From Carolyn.

Not any longer. Not of the sea.

Still, I must see to him.

Whereupon Carolyn redoubled her efforts, swimming strongly in a steady upward spiral. She had to breach for air anyway. Even this strange altered body could not hold its breath forever.

And she had played too long.

Already the water was brightening in a way she would not have noted earlier, and was now less black than a luminous silver-gray, which grew lighter and brighter still until—abruptly—she burst through the dome of the lower sky and gazed at the stars in the upper.

Carefully—*guiltily*—she exhaled the last of her slow, secret horde of air, then sucked fresh new breezes into her lungs. And closed her eyes, for once again she felt that odd sensation of every cell in her body flipping over, the process marked by a warmth that awoke in her nostrils and lungs and flowed outward like low-level electric shocks. She gasped and for an instant was stricken deaf, dumb, and blind.

And then her senses realigned, and she heaved a long sigh of relief. Reflex had already told her what her brain had not yet found time to process and relay.

She was no more than forty meters from rolling offshore breakers. And beyond them, perhaps another twenty, three men struggled clumsily on the sand, two of whom she recognized by their distinctive hair as Thunderbird O'Connor and her brother. The third was unfamiliar: black-haired, rangy, and perhaps a few sims taller than the others. Behind them crouched two vehicles: the orange-gold Jeep Juneau 'Bird had driven earlier, all glass and bulbous curves; and a midsized, sand-colored sedan with a gaudy emblem on the door.

"*Kev*—" she began as she made her way to land—still swimming, for she had not yet found the bottom. Unfortunately, an ill-timed swell slapped her and washed her voice away. She coughed and tried again, only to have that effort swamped by another.

But her toes brushed sand now, and a moment later she was wading through the breakers.

Intent as they were on their altercation, the men had not noticed her—nor heard her, evidently. But then the unknown one chanced to glance up from where he held Kevin in a restraining stranglehold. He froze instantly. "Look!" he yelled, though Carolyn wasn't sure if it was his actual voice or the joyful expression that blazed across his face that relayed his words.

'Bird jerked his head her way; Kevin stopped resisting; the stranger relaxed his hold. And then they were scrambling to their feet ('Bird a bit uncertainly, though with no less enthusiasm), and she was moving too, and suddenly they were all running toward each other, and calling out, and slogging through the waves; and then she was standing in knee-deep water with Kevin's arms locked around her, and 'Bird hovering close by, looking by turns happy, confused, and more than a trifle traumed-out. As for the new lad—the only one who actually fit his clothes—he was hanging back discreetly, and it came to Carolyn that this was probably that friend 'Bird had referred to so often—the one whose borrowed shorts she wore beneath a soaked T-shirt.

Which beat that baggy mud-colored mess Kev sported, or 'Bird's attire, which at the moment consisted solely of a towel.

"Cary!" Kevin sobbed in her ear, clutching her close. "My God, you're alive!"

"Jesus, lady, what happened!" From 'Bird, who had splashed closer. "I mean, *Christ*—I saw you . . . I saw you go under!"

"I'm fine," she assured them, as her eyes streamed with tears, and her cheeks curved with incipient laughter she had feared never to know again. "In fact, I'm *better* than fine—and would be finer still if I had dry clothes and something to eat and drink— on dry land!"

Kevin pulled away from her and stared her in the eye, an odd expression on his face. "Something's . . . happened to you, hasn't it?"

"You could say that," she nodded seriously, as she wrapped an arm around his waist and let him lead her ashore. "How could you tell?"

A shrug. "Your body temp. You're warm—*too* warm, like you've got a fever."

"Not a fever," she laughed back. "This feels as good as those do awful."

At which point she felt hard sand beneath her feet, and a few meters farther, dry powder.

Stormy, who had jogged ahead, was already building a fire in the angle formed by two sections of driftwood palm trunks, using dried fronds as tinder. He rose as they approached, took one look at her and slipped back to the Jeep, where he flipped up the glass hatch and proceeded to rummage inside. He returned with a bundle of fabric. "Good thing I hadn't got 'round to unloading my laundry," he told Carolyn with a grin. "Got towels, got jeans, got T's and skins and skivvies. Sorry, no skirts or serapes. Oh, but here—" He ducked out of his serape and passed it to her.

"Cary—what?" Kevin began, but she set a finger to his lips to shush him. "Nothing's happened that won't wait five minutes," she told him, with that strange, calm confidence that still pervaded her— the afterglow of that incredible joy she'd felt so lately, that had not yet faded enough for the repercussions to show through. While Kevin retreated to the fire, she sorted quickly through the clothing Stormy had produced and ducked behind the beige sedan. As she stripped off her sodden togs, toweled down, and changed into dry shorts and a worn Loch Locklin T-shirt, she noted over her shoulder that Kevin had taken charge of the fire, that 'Bird was swapping his towel for a pair of cutoff jeans, and that Stormy was waiting patiently a discreet distance away from the Chrysler, ignition card in hand.

"Drinks in the trunk," he explained, when she'd finished and emerged from behind it. "You check in with your chums. I'll do dinner."

She studied him thoughtfully. "But 'Bird looks like he could use a doctor."

Stormy gnawed his lip, then shook his head. "He'll

be okay. For now . . . there're some stories that need telling, and somehow this seems a better place than inside walls. 'Sides," he added, nodding toward Kevin, "I suspect your bro's been cooped up enough tonight." Whereupon he unlocked the Chrysler's trunk.

Carolyn nearly gagged—for an odor had reached her she would never have noticed before. But now, though she did not consciously acknowledge as much, some unsuspected part of her recognized the stench of blood and pain and dead dolphin. Stormy caught her reaction and puffed his cheeks, then shrugged perplexedly. In reply, she held her breath until she had reached the fire, then inhaled again. And caught smoke, the scent of the jungle behind her, and the sea.

Kevin was still stuffing the stems of palm fronds into the small blaze, with 'Bird helping, though he moved stiffly, and that nice slim body of his was torn and abraded in far too many places, while still more—notably his left ankle and clavicle, and a long line bisecting his chest and belly—showed the telltale glassy shine of freshly applied Spraskin. At least he wasn't bleeding. He smiled weakly as she eased in beside him and leaned back with her shoulders against the log. "Glad to see you," she murmured. "Thanks."

"Sorry," 'Bird grunted wearily. "I'm just sorry I got you into this."

"You may have saved her butt, though," Stormy broke in, as he lugged a shiny orange-gold cooler down the beach and deposited it behind the nearer log. A paper grocery bag bulged atop it. "But for now . . . I got OJ, I got water, I got milk; I got bread, cheese, chips, peanut butter, cold roast beef, cold ham, oranges, apples, beer—'cept that 'Bird can't have any of that."

'Bird rolled his eyes. "I *can't*?"

"Not good for replacing blood, kid," Stormy replied, passing 'Bird a liter of Minute Maid. "Sorry."

"Good Boy Scout, you are," Carolyn observed. "You obviously came prepared."

Stormy responded with a crooked grin. "Actually, Kev and I snared most of the wet stuff while we were cruising around trying to get hold of 'Bird. The rest . . . is some stuff I picked up for tomorrow's toli game and stuffed in the Jeep's built-in cooler."

"Once again I fuck things up," 'Bird sighed contritely. "I guess you'll just have to kill me."

"Not until I find out what's been going on with you three," Stormy shot back. "We got food, we got fire, we got first aid and dry clothes, all courtesy Stormcloud's Catering Service. Now Stormcloud gets some answers—and maybe, just possibly, we can get this craziness we seem to be up to our asses in sorted out in a way that makes sense."

'Bird lifted a brow expectantly.

"Don't look at *me*, man!" Stormy protested, wide-eyed. "I just work here. Oh, sometimes I show up in the nick of time, with guns blazing, but that's only 'cause you—by whom I mean you and Kev—keep gettin' your butts in trouble!" He fell silent, and grinned encouragement at the others.

Carolyn looked first at Kevin, then at 'Bird. "I don't know how it started, not with me," she said flatly. "Kev, *you* were the first to encounter anything strange—at least that has any direct bearing on what's been going on, so perhaps you'd best begin."

Kevin grimaced resignedly in the midst of constructing a roast beef–and–swiss on rye. "Nobody laugh, okay?"

"Nobody will," 'Bird assured him. "Go for it."

"Well, to use a *very* worn cliché," Kevin began. "It was a dark and stormy night . . ."

And for the next fifteen minutes he related a much-practiced account of the hurricane in Eireland, the selkie's visit, the cross-country chase by the Citroën, and finally the cryptic message the poor creature had so frustratingly failed to complete.

"And you're *sure* that was the phrase?" Stormy asked, when he had finished. Carolyn was glad 'Bird's friend had taken charge, given the condition the rest of them were in. Certainly he seemed the most alert.

Kevin nodded and helped himself to a swallow of Perrier. "I'll never forget those words—or the way the poor guy looked with half his face destroyed and him still trying to talk. 'You are the Word, she is the Way; I don't know who is the Singer.' And then he died."

Carolyn, having heard the tale before, had no comment.

"And that's all he told you?" From 'Bird.

Again Kevin nodded. "All *he* told me. 'Course I've learned a hell of a lot *since* then. But if you or Cary think you oughta get your part in . . ."

'Bird shook his head. "Go ahead."

So Kevin continued his tale—and this time Carolyn listened attentively, for she knew nothing of what had chanced since 'Bird had spirited her away from her apartment—barely in time, as it now appeared. It all made sense, too, given what the selkie had confided about the plot by a faction of rebellious young orcas to infiltrate human and dolphin kind. But so intent was she on puzzling out the ramifications of that fact, that she blanked part of Kevin's narrative, only to be brought up short by a remark-in-process.

" . . . so the selkie was standing there in the doorway—"

"I thought you said he died from . . . psychic backwash, or something," Carolyn interrupted, startled.

Kevin shifted uneasily and found another frond to unravel. "Yeah, well, he did and he didn't. See, just after Stormy shot the flayed dolphin, he . . . revived—sort of. And he said the dolphin had told him to tell me to take its skin to you—to The-One-Who-Is-The-Way. He evidently thought you'd know what to do with it."

"Well I don't!" Carolyn cried, still trying to come to terms with Kevin's first intriguing revelations, never mind this troubling second batch. "And where did he *come* from?" she went on desperately. "How did he know about me being . . . special."

Kevin shrugged helplessly. "Well, we didn't exactly have time to trade life histories, but he spoke Gaelic and referred to Eireland as their ancient home, from which I presume he was from there; Fir was, and he said they were kin—'course there're supposed to be selkies in Scotland too: Sule Skerry and all that. But the point is, he was a captive, just like I was. They were trying to get him to explain how to turn into humans without having to skin a zillion people each time."

"I know *I'd* appreciate it," 'Bird snorted.

"He was also really freaked when he found out Fir hadn't been able to deliver his message. I guess if he had, we wouldn't all be here."

"And you think those lads in the Citroën were also shape-shifted orcas?" Carolyn wondered.

"That's what makes the most sense. I never saw 'em up close; but from the way they suicided at the end—it was kind of spontaneous, like one of 'em had suddenly realized it might not be cool if they died and someone *human* found their bodies—from that, and what they were shooting, and that arsenal back at the Dead Marina—"

"—They knew that Fir knew something," Stormy finished.

"But what?" From Carolyn.

"That Kevin was the Word, that you were the Way. I assume it had something to do with the Singer."

"Like they didn't want the three gettin' together?" 'Bird suggested.

"And what happens if we do?" Kevin asked nervously. "I mean, I feel like a goddamn *pawn* here—and I don't even know what the fucking game is, much less who's playing."

"Dolphins, probably," Carolyn said. "And if Kev's finished, I think it's time you heard my story." She paused, looked at Kevin—"Or 'Bird could tell his . . .?"

"I've already told *you*," 'Bird replied. "And Stormy was there for the hard-to-believe part. But Kevin—"

"I told him about the weirdness at the Marina while we were on our way down here," Stormy supplied. "Most of what we need now is how you and Carolyn wound up in the Gulf in the middle of the night!"

"Okay," Carolyn sighed. "I won't be able to tell this as well as Kev—he's the clan storyteller—but to begin at the beginning . . ."

She commenced with the phone call informing her of the latest dolphin mutilations, and continued through her investigation of the site to the impulsive underwater exploration that had ended with her presumed death. She paused for a drink when she finished the part about awakening in the hospital.

In conclusion, she related the dream she'd had about the selkie and her mother, that had finished with the seal's saying, "You are the one the dolphins worship."

"Dolphins again!" Kevin spat. "More bloody dolphins!"

"Dolphin *magicians*," Stormy appended suddenly. "But more on that later. You go on, Carolyn."

She did, though she tried to keep her account as concise as possible. Indeed, when she came to the part where Katana dragged her underwater after the battle between the orcas and dolphins, which had resulted in her second death, she found it oddly difficult to be specific. She knew everything that had happened, but it was impossible to describe the . . . *change*, never mind the way she suddenly felt as comfortable in the water as on dry land. The way she simply *knew* things—the way so many of her fundamental beliefs had been forcibly altered.

"Well," Stormy mused finally, "I guess if anybody doubted Kevin, we've got confirmation now: dolphins *are* intelligent."

"And orcas," Kevin added.

"Orcas *are* dolphins," Carolyn corrected. "And to that we probably need to add all whales. I suppose I'll find out for sure when I go back."

Kevin's face paled with alarm. "You're goin' *back*?"

"Of course I am!" Carolyn cried. "Oh, not *now*, not until we figure out what's going on here, but I'm definitely going back. It's . . . it's like being underwater and needing air; only I'm in the air, and I need to get back underwater. There's so much to know, so much to discover—"

"Magic," 'Bird broke in. "Much as I hate to admit it, it all goes back to magic."

"Undiscovered science," Carolyn insisted. "But you haven't had your say yet . . . "

"I don't have much to add," 'Bird said. "You guys know as much as I do. Except about my dreams, I guess—visions, whatever they were. Carolyn, you've had 'em too—but I think I've had more than any of you."

Whereupon he recounted them.

"So where did they come from?" Kevin wondered.

'Bird regarded him seriously. "You already know the answer to that: they *have* to come from dolphins. It's like that selkie-guy told Kevin: they can only touch our minds when we're unconscious—when we're asleep or in an altered state of awareness, like I was in back at the sweat lodge."

"Or . . . aren't all there," Kevin inserted. "At least orcas can fool around with folks like that. As best I can tell, they use 'em as surrogate arms and legs and hands until they can assemble enough skins to make their own way on land. And to keep from killing humans directly, I suppose," he added. "If what the selkie said about that prohibition's true."

Carolyn studied 'Bird frankly. "I think you're right. The dreams must've been sent by dolphins."

"But why?"

"Because they can't—or couldn't—communicate with us directly. And when their chosen emissary— that poor Fir-lad—got killed, they had to come up with another way to get the message to us."

"Which message we still haven't discovered," 'Bird observed.

"Yeah," Kevin echoed. "What's all this *really* mean about the Word and the Way and the Singer?"

No one answered. Carolyn, at least, had no idea— none that made sense, anyhow.

Stormy stared straight at her, then beyond into the glitter of the nighted Gulf. "I bet *I* know," he whispered. Then grinned with the joy of discovery and pounded his thigh with his fist. "I bet I goddamn *know*!"

"We're listenin'," 'Bird growled pointedly.

"It's simple!" Stormy cried, his joy as clear as a child's. "Oh yes, guys, it's so simple! See—well, Cary, your brother here's a writer. Not only that, he writes books of great power; otherwise, they wouldn't have sold so well and everybody wouldn't be hot to make 'em into movies, and all. He has a magic for words, a magic that's not been seen in a long time! Shoot, *I've* even read the damned things, and I *never* read fantasy. But if what the dolphins told you about your birth's true, *and* what the selkie said about you guys being kin, *and* what your dream all but blurted out . . . well then maybe there's more to old Kev's birth too. Maybe he's not entirely human either."

Kevin shook his head. "No way, man. Dad had the tests done. I'm his kid—and Mom's."

"Yeah," Stormy countered. "But were both of *them* full human?"

"You mean somebody fooled around with a selkie before?"

"It doesn't have to have been a selkie," Stormy shot back. "Once you accept that *they* exist, it opens up an enormous Pandora's box."

"Fir mentioned the *sidhe*," Kevin noted quietly. "He spoke of the . . . king of the fairies as though he were real."

"Fine," Stormy went on excitedly. "But that doesn't really matter anyway. What matters is that from somewhere you've got a power for words—a *magical* power for words. And my people say that words—and a belief in what they are and say—can change material reality. I mean, we sing songs to bring rain, and sometimes it rains. We—"

"It's not just your folks that believe that," 'Bird broke in. "My folks believe that too. In fact, I think we all do."

"Even in Eireland," Kevin admitted. "Kings once feared satires more than spears."

"So Kev's the Word?" Carolyn mused. "Then what about the Way and the Singer?"

Stormy stared at 'Bird. "My guess is that you're the Singer, 'Bird. Or the musical component, anyway. I mean, think about it, man: you dance, you drum, sometimes you sing. The songs have words, but the song goes beyond the words, and the drum has no words, yet it sings too. And put the two together, and—wow!—you've got something special, something that hits you right in your soul and draws out stuff you had no idea was in there. Sometimes it goes right on down to your instinct, right on down to your lizard brain, to that part down below consciousness that runs on pure instinct and the desire to keep you alive!"

Kevin scowled. "Huh?"

"What's joy, Kevin?" Stormy went on excitedly. "What's love? What's sadness? They're not things you turn on or off; they're basic instinct; they just *are*. When you—'Bird—shoot, *anybody*—sings or drums, or dances to a song or a drum, it's instinct that's working. It makes you feel joy or sorrow or fear because of itself! It's its own kind of magic."

"Which . . . means?" 'Bird asked hesitantly.

"Which . . . means . . . that whatever it is that Kev's supposed to do, you're supposed to sing it—maybe drum too. Yeah, that's it: you drum and you sing!"

"Which still leaves me as the Way," Carolyn said. "But what does that mean? Way to *what*?"

Stormy gnawed his lip. "I haven't figured that out yet. But as best I can tell, based on what the selkie told Kevin—the *second* selkie—about how dolphins can talk to selkies—or half bloods like you, I guess—and selkies can talk to us, that you're the only person who knows shit about the workings of mainstream human civilization who can also shape-shift into a form your finny friends can access easily. Seems to me you were part of some kind of long-range plan that's only now coming to fruition. Shoot, I bet you were literally conceived with this event in mind—probably not *executed* like this, I'll grant you, but . . . Well, I think the time has come for you to fulfill your destiny—since you're apparently the only being presently alive who can access all three worlds—"

"Selkies can access 'em too!" Kevin corrected.

"But they don't know our world, not really," Carolyn gave back. "From what Kevin said, I don't think they want to be anything but what they are. Whereas I'm a child of this world, by conditioning, if not by . . . genetics."

"Yeah," 'Bird chimed in. "But nobody in *our* world can talk to dolphins directly—not without somebody havin' to die."

Carolyn sighed wearily. "Which still leaves one question: What *is* this message? What is it I'm supposed to actually *do*?"

"Magic, evidently," Stormy replied. "What I've told you is as much as I've been able to put together so far. I—"

"I think *I* know how to find out," Kevin interrupted, looking Carolyn straight in the eye. "But I don't think *you're* gonna like it."

Chapter XXXI:
The Tide Turns

(El País Verde)
(Saturday, September 3—the wee hours)

" . . . I don't think you're gonna like it."

Kevin felt the flare of anger that fueled Carolyn's reaction like a tangible blow as soon as he pronounced those words. She flinched, then froze, then slowly looked up from her last bite of sandwich and stared at him solemnly from across the fire. The flames transfigured her: made her look wild and queenly and . . . pagan. That in spite of her faddishly short hair and mismatched male clothing.

"What is it, Kev?" she asked mildly, but with a sharp edge of command to her voice that would not be denied—and that he had not heard before. He swallowed, and instead of meeting her gaze began dismembering another strip of palm frond. He heard 'Bird and Stormy inhale sharply, as though they likewise sensed the sudden tension and perhaps expected the fire to blaze up in sympathy.

"You wanta know how to talk to dolphins? How to talk to 'em one-on-one?" Kevin sighed at last.

"I can already do that," Carolyn replied uneasily. "It's telepathy."

"—In which case they should've *already* told you

what they want out of you," 'Bird pointed out.

Carolyn finished the sandwich and folded her arms across her stomach, brow suddenly furrowed with uncertainty: the pagan queen become a nervous Girl Scout at a campfire. "I . . . think it's hard for them," she admitted. "I get the sense that they have to work at it."

Stormy gnawed his lip thoughtfully. "But you've only talked to the ones you know, right? And they're young, if I remember."

A nod. "In dolphin years."

"So—"

"So could it be that they don't quite have the grasp of the . . . situation the older ones have?" Kevin broke in eagerly, glancing at Stormy for agreement. "But since you *know* them, and you were in a stressful situation, *they* were sent to greet you 'cause they'd be less threatening?"

Carolyn shrugged. "I suppose so. But what are you getting at?"

Kevin took a deep breath, wondering if what he'd lately survived was sufficient fortification for what he was about to blunder into. "Well basically," he began, "the selkie told me dolphins could talk to them—telepathically, I guess—and they could talk to us. But though you've got selkie blood, you're obviously not a true selkie—so one of the reasons you may have had trouble 'talking' to the dolphins may be that your brain's simply too different. It isn't made to receive telepathic communication. Selkie brains obviously are; but you've presumably got only part of a selkie brain—and whatever it is that makes that aspect different is evidently so subtle as to be undetectable by that roomful of technotrash your doctor plugged into you. Either that, or your brain hadn't changed yet, which I suppose is also a possibility—which is another thing you could find out by talking to the dolphins. Which brings us back to the point we keep getting sidetracked from—or you keep evading. *What are you gonna do with the dolphin skin?*"

'Bird regarded her levelly, looking marginally more alert. "And more to the point, *are* you gonna do it?"

Carolyn rounded on him, eyes flashing brighter than the fire. Kevin didn't envy the poor guy. "*Am I going to do it?*" she raged, her body gone taut as thin-stretched wire. "What the fuck do you *think* I'm going to do? Of *course* I'm not going to do it! First of all, it might not work—I mean, neither me nor that skin comes with an instruction manual. And second, I can achieve the same ends without it. I mean, I'm apparently telepathic either way, and I'm *dying* to get back underwater—in my own skin. The only difference I can see, is that since communication *might* be quicker if I had a dolphin brain, it could take longer if I stay . . . human."

"To which I feel compelled to wonder, can we *afford* longer?" Stormy observed.

Carolyn shrugged helplessly. "I don't know! I don't know *anything*, dammit! I don't even know if I'm *supposed* to know anything. We're grasping at straws here, people."

Silence.

"Besides, it'd be like . . . like blasphemy! It's the sickest thing I've ever heard of!"

Silence.

For some reason she focused her anger on 'Bird. "Yeah, and *you*, Mr. O'Connor; I figured *you'd* at least understand, seeing what people have been doing to your ancestors for three hundred years! Digging them up whenever they feel like it, putting their bones on display in museums—"

"*I,* however, am not the apparent focus of a multispecies conspiracy!" 'Bird countered sweetly.

"Hear! Hear!" Stormy cried. Then, more seriously, to Carolyn: "I see your point, though; I really do. And I'll admit it doesn't sound like a real pleasant proposition. But remember, that selkie knew more about shape-shifting than you do. And if it thought you could use that skin, then you can. Besides," he added, glancing at Kevin, "the dolphin—the now *dead* dolphin—essentially called that selkie back from death to tell it to have Kevin take the skin to you! That smacks of some pretty heavy-hitting commitments, lady. So what I say is . . . try the skin on. If it works, then we proceed to the next stage—whatever that is. And if it doesn't— Well, we'll have put you through something really gross and unpleasant, and we'll all apologize profoundly, and dispose of the skin in whatever way you see fit, including . . . Oh fuck, I don't know: making whips out of it and walking stark naked into an OAS meeting flagellating each other, or something!"

Kevin gazed at his sister seriously. "So, what do you say? We learn, or we don't. But one other thing to consider is that for that skin to be any good, it has to be fresh. I don't know *how* fresh—maybe a couple of days, even; that's how long Fir was without his. But we don't have forever, not if we're gonna use *that* skin. And," he went on, "wouldn't you feel *really* bad if that poor dolphin had to undergo that torture in vain? I mean, I *heard* its cries, sis. And I hope I never hear anything like that again, 'cause it's like what you hear in those nightmares that wake you up with your bed soaked with sweat and your heart racing ninety kliks an hour!"

Carolyn stared at him dully, her face bleak with resignation. "I was afraid you'd come up with something like that."

"Yeah, and this time tomorrow you should know the rest," 'Bird inserted. "Assumin' you put on that blessed skin!"

But still Carolyn looked uncertain. "I don't know guys, I just don't know! I mean you're asking a *lot*— a lot more than you even know."

"We're asking you to be the emissary of humankind to a whole new world, Cary," Kevin told her softly. "It's like first contact. Think of all those movies we saw as kids about people from space arriving on earth. Only this time *we're* the space people, and the earth folks have sent the ship to us!"

" *'Gort: Klaatu barada nikto,'* " Stormy quoted, with a wary chuckle. "Or however you say it."

Kevin glared at him, then shifted his gaze back to his sister. She looked wretched: absolutely miserable. He knew she hated making decisions like this: when head said one thing and heart another. "Something else is botherin' you, isn't it?" he ventured at last.

She nodded bleakly. "I'm . . . afraid, Kev," she replied in a small voice. "I'm really, *really* afraid. Not of shifting shape, or anything like that, not really. Nor am I scared to meet the dolphins or to find out what it is they want me to know. It's just that . . . Well, basically, I'm afraid of the orcas."

Kevin cocked his head. "You think they're still out there?"

"No reason to assume otherwise."

"But what about those sensors over at that place you work at?" 'Bird asked suddenly. "Couldn't you use them to find out if the coast was clear?"

"Not without prompting about a zillion questions,"

Carolyn shot back instantly. "Of which I've had quite enough lately, thank you very much! Never mind what would happen if Nesheim found out I could shape-shift! Plus I don't want to drag Rudy and Hassie into this, which I wouldn't be able to prevent if they knew. But seriously, 'Bird . . . I've only got a hunch about this, and it's a brand-new idea so there may be holes in it as big as some of those that've lately been punched in you. But . . . well, I *think* our cetacean friends—or enemies, one—have been fooling with the electronic records over at 'Why?'. I think they've sabotaged cameras—probably the orcas did that so they could bite the melons out of dolphins undetected. But I think they've played head games with people too, and made 'em go to sleep, or fool with records, or—"

"—And you don't want to go up against anything that could do that," Stormy finished for her.

"You got it."

"And you've only got maybe an even chance of it being friend or foe," Stormy added. "I mean, if I'm gonna play devil's advocate . . . "

"Right. I . . . Well, basically, I don't want to have half my head bitten off by a whacked-out killer whale!"

Kevin could only grunt agreement. "It's your call, sis," he said finally. "We've all had our say, but at the bottom, it's your call."

Stormy started suddenly, then leapt to his feet and peered intently at the ocean. "Yeah," he echoed, his eyes narrowing as he strained his vision. "But I think you might want to check with those guys, too!"

Kevin turned to follow his line of sight—and was not surprised to see, immediately beyond the breakers, where the sea floor fell away more steeply, the shapes of half a dozen dolphins dancing and cavorting in the waves. "I'd say you don't need to worry about the orcas," he cried cheerfully. "I think you'll have an escort all the way."

'Bird likewise stood, his face hopeful, but grim. "Give me your card, Stormy," he sighed. "I'll go get the skin. Cary, I'll hold it up behind you. You won't have to even look, just do it by feel, just . . . put it on."

Carolyn gnawed her lip—so hard Kevin feared to see blood there. Her gaze darted first to the dolphins, then to the expectant faces looming above her. Kevin knew she was confronting the hardest decision of her life and was having to make it tired, hungry, among impatient strangers, and without adequate time to consider all the ramifications. She was, in short, being asked to act on instinct. And that was a situation she loathed.

Abruptly, she stood. "I'll do it," she announced flatly, not looking at them, but continuing to gaze at the sea. " 'Bird, you hold it, like you said. I won't look at the skin. And I'd appreciate it if none of you looked at me. First, because I guess I have to do this naked; but second, because—well, it just seems like a very private thing. On second thought, 'Bird, get the skin, but give it to Kev. He's actually watched shifting done—and he's already seen me bare."

Kevin nodded solemnly, but couldn't resist a triumphant half smirk when he saw the disappointment that flickered briefly across the other men's faces. *Boys will be boys*, he chuckled to himself. *Men will be men; selkies will be selkies, I guess . . . and my sister's gonna be a dolphin*!

Carolyn had doffed all her clothing save Stormy's serape, and had waded knee-deep into the ocean when 'Bird returned with the skin. He held it reverently, as though it were a priceless fur—which, given what had been paid for it, it most certainly was. Kevin took it from him, holding it by the flesh just above the pectoral fins. The upper parts flopped forward like a hood, obscuring the less pleasant details of blowhole and eye slits. The flukes trailed in the water between his legs. Blood swirled there, even after all this time.

Walking slowly, as though he were carrying the host at church, which he had done many years ago, Kevin made his way into the water until he stood directly behind his sister, subtly seeking to impose his body between her and the other men as he did. He thought they had too much class to leer at so serious a moment, but one never knew.

"Ready when you are," he whispered so softly only Carolyn could hear. She stiffened. Beyond her, silver shapes continued to leap and play in the moonlit night.

"Ready," she called to the waves, as though she addressed not only Kevin, but her incipient escort as well.

And with that, she tugged the serape over her head, hesitated an instant, then dropped it into the lazily sliding water at her feet—and reached blindly back for the skin.

Kevin took a half step forward and thrust it upon her, rather as though he were helping a woman into an exceedingly large and ill-fitting coat.

It slipped from his fingers—or tugged away, almost as though it had a will of its own. He gasped, made to grab for it, but then he saw what was happening. Even from *behind* he saw, though he looked away quickly, out of respect for Cary, and—he admitted it at last—the presence of magic. But even so, he glimpsed enough: saw that skin mold to the shape of his sister's back and shoulders, then saw a shift and flow of the muscle and bone beneath as they likewise realigned to fill out the dead dolphin's hide. He thought he heard her cry out—a startled, "Oh!"—and closed his eyes, unable to watch any longer.

Not until he heard a heavy splash, as of some large object hurling itself into water, did he dare open his eyes again.

—To see a sleek gray dolphin leaping through the breakers, while a dozen more arched through the waves toward it, chirping out a joyous greeting.

Kevin stood silently for a moment, watching, then scooped the sodden serape out of the foam and slowly trudged toward shore, where his other two . . . friends, he supposed they were now, were already stoking the fire.

Chapter XXXII: Vigil

(El País Verde)
(Saturday, September 3—the wee hours)

" 'Bird?"

"Wha—? Huh?"

Something warm pressed against 'Bird's forehead. He batted it away reflexively, utterly without thinking. It took him an instant to realize it had been heavy—like a hand.

A friend's hand.

Only a friend would have touched him so.

" 'Bird? You okay?"

He blinked his eyes open, only then aware they'd drifted closed. He saw fire: a knee-high blaze on a beach of white sand between a V of palm logs facing the ocean. A man sat opposite: skinny and wild-haired, in baggy clothes—nervous-looking. *Kevin,* his groggy brain supplied. Another knelt beside him, shirtless and in jeans. He appeared concerned—angry too, at having had his goodwill rejected. *Storm-cloud.*

Buddy.

Best friend.

"Must've dozed off," 'Bird yawned, twisting his neck to loosen it. It popped obligingly. Something

378

hard prodded his shoulders, where he sprawled half on one of the trunks, half upon the sand. He shifted up on his elbows. Blinked again.

"Dozed off—or passed out?" Stormy snorted, peering at him though eyes narrow with suspicion. "Results're the same; cause is different. You've got a fever, man—I just wanted you to know that."

"Like you can tell, with me facin' a bloody fire!" 'Bird growled back, levering himself full upright. "Jesus, I hurt," he added more softly. God knew Stormy had saved his ass twice in the last six hours. He therefore owed the guy something approximating politeness.

Shoot, he'd *give* the guy a lot *more* than that—if he'd leave him alone long enough to get some shut-eye. "What time is it?" he mumbled. "I seem to have lost my watch."

"She's been gone fifteen minutes, if that's what you're wondering," Kevin supplied tersely. 'Bird stared at him and tried to see any resemblance between him and his sister. Half sister, he corrected; so he'd divined. There wasn't much: pointed noses, delicate builds—probably their mom wasn't a big lady. Though come to it, he thought Kevin had said something about selkies being lightly built: sleek and lithe like gymnasts or swimmers. As if it made any difference.

"Waiting's a bitch," Stormy acknowledged, padding around to kneel behind him, from which position he began to massage 'Bird's bare shoulders unasked. It felt good: a comfort as much to the mind as the body, a token of closeness between them.

" 'The hardest part,' as the old song says," 'Bird agreed, and hunched over so Stormy could work lower.

"Standing vigil's even worse," Kevin opined, rising

and beginning to pace. "I wish we'd thought to set a 'panic-by-when' limit—we don't know how long we'll need to stay here, or if she'll even return—never mind return *here*."

"She will," Stormy assured him. "Her new chums'll see to that."

Kevin stopped in place and turned to face 'Bird, hands in pockets, face fire-gilded, hair like an orange flame, burning blue down the center. "I'm sorry I jumped you earlier," he muttered. "I was . . . not a happy camper."

" 'S cool," 'Bird sighed, closing his eyes blissfully as Stormy shifted his attention to his temples. "You keep on doin' that, Mr. Cloud, you'll have me snorin' again."

"Not a bad thing," Stormy murmured. "I wish we had time to get you to a doc."

"Nothing's broken, ruptured, or dislocated," 'Bird replied. "The rest is designed to heal."

"Yeah, but hurting's not a lot of fun, as I recall."

"Dyin's not either, and Cary's done it twice in the last two days."

"Don't get any ideas!"

"Ha!"

"Besides," Stormy went on, "you don't get that slice down your middle seen to, you're gonna have some scarring."

"Just one more thing to brag about to the ladies."

"You brag about *this*, you're nuts!"

'Bird could think of no reply that wasn't obvious, stupid, or inappropriate to the gravity of the occasion. Instead, he simply sat silently for a good fifteen minutes, while Stormy worked over his neck, back, shoulders, upper arms, and head with his strong and supple fingers. It felt good—sooo good. Eventually 'Bird loosened his waistband and let his friend have a go at the big tenderloin muscles in his lower back, down past the top of his buttocks. He sighed luxuriously.

"I don't do this for just anybody," Stormy informed him, shifting back to his shoulders.

"I'm glad," 'Bird yawned. He really was starting to fade now. The massage, the comfort of the fire, the steady rhythm of Kevin's pacing, the susurration of waves getting fractious as the tide began to turn.

"So what do you think about magic now?" Stormy asked sometime later.

'Bird shrugged—and was pleasantly surprised at how much looser his shoulders felt.

"Eloquent but imprecise," Stormy informed him. "Try words."

But 'Bird couldn't answer—not in a way he could articulate in his present half-fevered half-lethargic state. *Something* had changed, though. Where before he had resisted magic because he couldn't decide how it could function in the same world as holograms, now he wasn't so certain it was *that* incompatible. Certainly the events of the last day had shown him that the world wasn't as cut-and-dried as sixty hours of college-level science had led him to believe. And it occurred to him then that one reason he'd resisted magic was simply fear of ridicule. For in spite of free college for all Native Americans, courtesy Hopi Solar, Inc., Limited, few of the young men and women he'd grown up with back at Qualla had elected to avail themselves of that opportunity. And the ones who had—mostly the folks who staffed Past-Blast Corporation, which was the flashy commercial extinct-and-endangered species preservation-and-resurrection arm of the genetic engineering combine that (with a little Hopi cash on the side), kept his people solvent and therefore independent—were all first-rate (to use a slightly archaic term) nerds.

Which in the real world meant that though he'd been brought up to believe in what most of the world called magic, it wasn't a subject he mentioned in his peer group circles for fear of being thought unsophisticated. And as to discussing it around all but a very few white boys—no way.

Only Stormy had broken through the armor of his misgivings, and that but recently.

Now, though, it looked as if magic *was* real—or that something that could easily be described as magic was—and that in order to come to grips with how it fitted into his life he had no choice but to throw in with Carolyn and Kevin—and Stormy—if he was to keep himself sane.

Yeah, magic might not be so bad—long as you had other folks around who believed in it too, to provide reality checks now and then.

Which still didn't tell him what to do now: not what it meant to be what some were-seal off in the wilds of Eireland had proclaimed was a Singer. Make that *the* Singer.

Of course, he *was* a singer—as his people meant it. He drummed and he danced and sometimes he sang songs while other folks danced and drummed. But Singer was a far more formal title to Stormy. Shoot, John Lox had been a *Dineh* Singer, and to them it meant someone who guarded the rituals by which Navajo life was properly defined, sanctified, and—sometimes—protected.

But what did it mean to selkies—or dolphins?

"What I need right now," he announced—too late to recall it before he was committed—"is a good medicine dream."

"*That's* an odd answer to a question I asked ten

minutes ago," Stormy muttered, giving 'Bird's shoulders the rapid-fire pounding that signaled he was done. "Besides," he continued, "aren't you the one who said you despised those things?"

"I hated what I feared," 'Bird replied. "I don't fear 'em any longer. Or maybe there's so much more I'm afraid of now, that I have no choice but to consider 'em part of the solution 'stead of the problem."

"An excellent attitude," Stormy observed, giving his back a final friendly slap—which left a pleasant aftertingle. "Now then, you wanta know something *really* embarrassing?"

'Bird shot him a sideways grin. "You mean besides how you got that scar on your pecker?"

"I've never had a medicine dream in my life. I talk about 'em all the time as though they were familiar things—but I've never had one."

"I think," 'Bird countered, "yours simply come to you as part of day-to-day reality."

"Perhaps."

"*You* wanta know something really embarrassin'?"

"You mean besides how you ain't *got* no pecker? Shoot."

"I think I've waited too long to take a leak."

Stormy rolled his eyes. "Just stay away from the tires on my Jeep."

'Bird bared his teeth at him as he staggered stiffly to his feet. "I may be a while," he cautioned. "I need to be by myself for a spell. But don't worry, I'll leave a clear trail. And honk three times if Cary gets back 'fore I do."

"You got it," Stormy nodded. "Now . . . piss off."

Five minutes later, a hundred meters back in the jungle, and with basic biological functions having

been attended to, 'Bird found what he sought. A huge
tree stood there, of a species he didn't recognize, but
that had wide-based roots like flying buttresses.
Moss grew between, comprising a springy cushion
for the serape he spread atop it, mostly to minimize
contact with bugs. Not that he found the natural
world repulsive; far from it. But he liked his contact
with anything sporting more than four legs to be in
seafood restaurants.

So it was, with his butt on four square meters of
loose-woven wool and his back against fifty meters
of very tall tree, that Thunderbird Devlin O'Connor
closed his eyes and, for the first time in his life, *tried*
to summon magic.

He wasn't sure how he did it, and part of him acknowledged that perhaps it was in large part due to
the hot-and-cold flashes he was having (Shock?
Chill? Fatigue? Nameless Malady? Exotic Tropical
Disease? Grossly Unpleasant Local Parasite? Allergy
to the Utterly Unbelievable? Who knew?)—but
whatever its origin, 'Bird found himself starting to
drift in no time. His main conscious contribution
was the seldom-practiced meditation exercise his
TM teacher in college had called centering. Which
basically meant that he focused on his breathing—
inhaling deeply through his nose, and exhaling
slowly through his mouth—while trying to make the
rest of his body relax. Over and over, and thank God
for Stormy's massage, which had him half-puddled
already.

Before he knew it, his eyes had rolled back in his
head, his consciousness was collapsing toward some
unseen center—and he was floating.

. . . floating . . .

. . . darkness first, and then that darkness acquired tiny sparkles above and a wider sweep of

shimmers below that slowly resolved into a moonlit
sky above a choppy ocean. A line of duller darkness
to one side might have been cliffs, but it was hard to
tell, for by then he had become aware of a third type
of glitter, these in long, straight slashes. *Meteors,* he
told himself in delight, then realized there were too
many, that they were tangibly cold, and that the sky
which seconds before had been clear was now wild
with flying, tearing cumuli. *Rain,* he corrected himself. *Storm's brewing.*

As soon as he noticed that, all hell broke loose.
Clouds gathered like black flames on spilled gasoline. Thunder rumbled. Lightning flashed. The rain
stabbed the sea—and the nonbody that was 'Bird
that hovered above it—like silver darts of ice. It was
worse than any hurricane.

'Bird retreated from it. But even so, he felt himself
beaten to—not earth, for the earth was too far off—
but to the sea. Waves flashed close below him, flipping foam at him, while more and colder rain slashed
him from above.

It was then that he heard the song. Not one with
words, however; it transcended that—if transcend
was the appropriate term for something that by its
very tone, rhythm, and cadence filled his soul with
dread. It was like Bach's Toccata and Fugue in D
Minor—the old *Phantom of the Opera* music—only
a million times eerier, darker, and more strange.
And no organ, not one with ten thousand pipes,
could have conjured the subtle menace of that half-
heard melody. Dark music that was: darker than
night, full of subsonics and infrasound, as though the
continental plates themselves were sounding boards
for what was too deep for human lungs.

It was horrible—and wonderful—as death and violence and wild winds in the sky are wonderful in

their own way; but intolerable by implication because the whole theme of that song was defeat and destruction and utter resignation to despair.

'Bird shuddered and tried to move away, but the music had trapped him, had hooked onto the hidden dark depths of his soul and would not let go.

Down and down it dragged him, pouring his *self* ever fuller of a nameless, hopeless dread.

Deeper . . .

Another few seconds, and he would give up and will himself to die.

And then, beyond hope, a second song intruded. It commenced as a counter to the dark melody that had enthralled him, and some part of him told him that it was almost a mirror image: its highs as high as the dark tune's lows were low, the two melodies barely interfacing at their highest and lowest notes respectively.

He found hope with that, and rose with it, and gazed at the sky again, in lieu of the inky depths of what must be a bottomless, empty ocean.

The sky was clearing, and the song of light grew stronger, and with it the clouds were swept away, and stars showed, and a moon, and the song grew even louder, even brighter: brass replacing bassoon.

But the dark roared back: a thunderous shout that split the heavens like the organ chord that opened the final movement of Saint-Saëns's *Organ Symphony*. And so they fought there: light and dark. And each time the song of light overpowered the other and filled the world free and clear, the clouds fled the sky and peace reigned over the ocean. But every time the dark hymn countered, the clouds came flapping back like carrion birds, and waves rose like a vast army rattling foamy spears.

'Bird did not know how long that battle lasted—
for it was a battle as sure as day followed night, as
sunlight followed storm.

Yet still there was no obvious victor, though 'Bird
got a sense of vast weariness on both sides. Never
once did he see the singers—nor get any notion,
even, of what sort of beings they might be, to use the
very elements as weapons in their wars. But there
was one aspect of the sunlight song he latched onto
as though it were a rope thrown to a drowning man,
and that was the beat that rode under it and wove
through it, and strengthened it and gave it drive,
where the song of the dark was mostly atonal and
formless, without focus or rhythm.

'Bird had heard that beat before, too—if only he
could remember . . .

He did!

He'd heard it first during the vision in John Lox's
sweat lodge. It was the rhythm of the song the dolphins sang as they worshiped Carolyn Mauney-
Griffith.

It was also the beat the Salmon-fisher had
pounded out not a day later, while 'Bird slumbered
heavily on his own bed.

And finally, it was the beat of his heart in this
latest medicine dream.

And this time he would remember.

When his eyes slitted open, it was to see a flicker
of ruddy light straight ahead: the fire on the beach
miraculously making its way through a hundred meters of tree trunks and foliage to comfort him here.

But more importantly, it was to hear his nails tapping out a blessedly familiar beat on the taut wooden
buttress of the nameless tree that had sheltered him
while he dreamed.

He continued tapping, tapped for at least five minutes, and along with it he wove the syllables of a wordless song, to better fix it in his memory—until he *knew* it was locked away, a hoard of power beyond price, there in the vaults of his mind.

Chapter XXXIII:
Deep Trouble

(The Gulf of Mexico)
(Saturday, September 3—the wee hours)

This is so *neat!* Carolyn all but crowed to herself, as a flick of her flukes sent her flying through the latest phalanx of wave crests faster than she could have imagined. She loved water anyway—always had. And she'd instinctively been a first-class swimmer, indeed could recall no time when she could not hold her breath (both quirks due to her latent selkie blood, she now concluded). And *whatever* had happened to her during her second "death," when her whole body had simply *reversed*, had, in its own way, been wonderful too.

But *this* . . . ! Flashing along the currents at what seemed the speed of thought surpassed everything she'd ever dreamed. Up, down, right, left—it mattered not which motion she chose; she could achieve it instantly, without the irritation of augmenting apparati, however unobtrusive.

And best of all, she finally had someone to share it with, where before, even among her closest comrades, she'd been unable to let go those last few degrees that truly defined her limits—mostly because she'd already been better at anything involving water than anyone at either Trinity, Monaco, or even "Why?".

Here, however, she had peers, challengers—competitors, even: a bloody *lot* of those. Of which nearly two dozen were scything through the water with her now, poised for the nonce, as was she, in that clear/ gray zone barely beneath the wave tops where moonlight still worked its glittering way. Kat and Bo were two of that company: the two who swished closest beside her, that poked her and prodded her most vehemently, and bade her play tag with them with the greatest enthusiasm. But others swam with her as well: a score of steely shadow-shapes, that had met her past the breakers and now escorted her who-knew-where.

As if it mattered! Well, yes it did, but the going seemed as important as arrival.

And then there was the song. In some ways, that was the best thing, simply because it was so utterly unexpected. Oh, whales sang—humpbacks in particular—and dolphins could be as chatty as old women in Dublin pubs. But the song she was reveling in was that *unheard* symphony that drifted through her consciousness like countless radio stations all playing different tunes, but all set to the same beat, and with harmonizing melodies. There were even words—of course. Though a more apt description might have been image sequences—except that didn't work either because there were strong shades of emotion, like (in the primary world) lonesome blues or stirring overtures or joyful marches. But even that wasn't precisely accurate, because there was also a shading of subtle intricacy—a game, almost, of fitting exactly the right image with the ideal "sound" with the proper emotion, with the correct . . . Well, *word* was far too narrow a concept, but nothing else suited. It was like trying to "read a Celtic interlace," or write poetry to fit a fugue.

Never mind the . . . *color*. That was the only way Carolyn could describe the ever-shifting differences in intensity and urgency that seemed vaguely analogous to a synthesis of accent, body language, and age/sex/experience.

And on top of all that, a disconcertingly large number of the images were not of dolphins at all, nor of anything else in the undersea universe. Rather, they were sight bites of humans and affairs on land. And not merely today's world. Already she'd caught a flash of snowfields and soldiers in heavy fur caps and thought Imperial Russia. She'd noted Roman soldiers and Irish warriors, and glimpsed three distinct naval battles involving those huge floating palaces that had sailed the Spanish Main. She'd even seen a sequence involving a vast stone pyramid atop which a man in gaudy feathered regalia flourished a human heart on high. Never mind countless humbler moments in human affairs. It was like being in an electronics store: the ones with wall-wide banks of television sets, all turned to competing channels.

If only it weren't so darned confusing! For marvelous as it was, sometimes the visual snippets came close to fast-forward chaos, the singing to cacophony.

But suppose she tried to attend just *one*. One . . . color, maybe, the simplest melody, perhaps.

Yeah, that was working. It was like tuning a radio—*and* a TV, both at the same time. But she managed it: focusing first on one theme—a sprightly piece, like a psychic jig. She almost had it now, and the more intently she tried to key in to that song alone, the easier it became.

And then suddenly she had it, bright and clear.

Only it wasn't a song anymore, it was . . . words. *Real* words, but without the underlying sense of effort—or reserve—that had tempered them when she'd still been overtly human. And with a far greater, yet more subtle, richness added.

Welcome, a dolphin "said." *You have been a long time in coming. A long time learning to listen.*

Katana?

Not my name, but if it pleases you, I will answer to that.

And Bo? Is she here?

Listen a little loud *of me, a little faster, and a little* blue.

Carolyn would have scowled had she had the muscles for it, but attempted what Katana suggested, one "quality" after another, and found success.

Welcome, Carolyn, came Bokken's "voice," then: eager and joyful and amazed. *And what . . . Katana has forgotten to tell you is that while you were indeed a long time in coming, we had hoped* never *to need you at all—and yet it has come to this.*

Come to what?

Let me *explain*, a third voice inserted—like a soft yellow reel.

We defer to you, Mother-Queen-Sister, Bo replied instantly.

And I! From Katana.

Welcome . . . land-daughter, seal-daughter, and now, dolphin-daughter too, the new presence told Carolyn, and somehow she knew that speech was for her alone.

Greetings . . . Mother-Queen-Sister? *It is an honor to speak with you.*

It is an honor to speak at all! the Mother-Queen-Sister replied. *Would that our shadow-kin the orcas remembered that more often than they do.*

They do seem to have been . . . forgetting *themselves a lot lately,* Carolyn agreed cautiously.

Rather say that they are remembering—but remembering the wrong things. But come, I should tell you my name.

Carolyn listened, but the complex knot of combined sound, image, and rhythm that came into her mind had no human analog. Yet she knew she would recognize it again, no matter when she heard it, the same way she could identify someone's face and yet have no way to describe him or her.

And you already know mine, apparently, Carolyn noted when she had finished.

And much more—which I am certain you also would like to know.

And will be glad to hear when we get . . . wherever it is we are going.

Ah, but in that you are thinking like a human, which is to say you are thinking that thinking *and* doing *are two separate acts, that one cannot* think well *while* doing.

I see . . .

We are going nowhere, in particular, for there is nowhere to go, but also everywhere; therefore, it is always time to talk—except of course when it is time to sing.

Ah, yes . . . and very fine singing it is too.

No better, though more complex, than some of your people's own.

Thank you.

You are welcome—and welcome again, for though we could converse like this for a thousand sunrises, yet it would put neither your mind to rest nor ours.

Ah!

*You are too polite to hurry me, yet curiosity
shades your voice toward orange.*

Carolyn would have laughed, had she been able.

*Let us drink air, and then I will tell you the krill
of what you need to know.*

And with that, her companion flicked her flukes
and flew upward—to launch herself into the sky.
Carolyn followed, and felt, for a moment, as though
she too were a moonbeam: a creature of liquid light
suspended between sea and heaven.

—Then impact, like sliding into silver, and she
was swimming again, while the Mother-Queen-Sister
resumed her image-song.

*Bokken has told you that we have long hoped for
you to join us, yet we feared that too; for though we
had prepared for you, we hoped never to have need
of you—for we had hoped this time would never
come.*

What time?

*That dolphin magicians would need the aid of
human magicians to strengthen our ancient song.*

Song . . . ?

Listen, then, child of earth, and know . . . !

The first things the Mother-Queen-Sister of the
Aztlan Dolphins told Carolyn were mostly items she
already either knew or suspected, the majority of
them via her brother.

Dolphins were intelligent; that was a given. Indeed, though they seemed to have come to sentience
later than humans in the long scale of time, they
were at least as intelligent in terms of raw *thinking*
power, learning capacity, and such. The differences
lay in the obvious fact that, lacking physical means
to measure, assess, and manipulate the material
world, they—as was inevitable with thinking beings
cognizant of the passage of time and their own mor-

tality—had found no choice but to fall back on their mental skills to achieve those same ends—and sometimes in lieu of them. The upshot was that most were telepathic, the same way most men could speak. But not *merely* telepathic, for that art took several forms with them.

Mind-to-mind communication was the most common, and the one most easily experienced and understood by humans. Oral "speech" among them served much the same function that gestures, hand signals, or body language did among humans: to add subtlety or spin to emotions or facts. But not only did they speak mind-to-mind among themselves, they were also able to communicate that way with many other sea mammals, including selkies, whom, however, they imperfectly understood, perhaps because of their dual natures.

More interesting, however, was the fact that dolphins could also hitchhike in human minds, the more skilled among them to the point of sharing all human senses simultaneously with the unwary host. In the case of subnormal host minds—the mentally deficient, the profoundly unconscious, and such—it was often possible for the cowalker (that was the way Carolyn thought of it, though the term from Scots folklore actually meant something slightly different) physically to manipulate the human host. Unfortunately, orcas tended to be better at cowalking (co-riding rather) than other delphinidae—the results of which Kev and 'Bird had only too graphically witnessed. Carolyn wanted to press that subject, but the Mother-Queen-Sister suggested that other things were more rightly to be explained next, so she fell contritely silent.

And just as well, for the next bit of information truly floored her.

As I have told you, we often coride, the Mother-Queen-Sister began. *But what I have not explained is that while coriding, our kind have witnessed the entire scope of your kind's history—and shared it amongst ourselves. And of even more importance, to your kind, is the fact that it is typical for one of our folk to coride with only one particular human throughout his or her life. We find that it provides a richer experience, for our emotions begin to resonate with the host's, and vice versa.*

Very interesting indeed, Carolyn acknowledged.

Ah yes, but even more *interesting is the fact that, unlike your kind, who bind up your learning in external things, while the vast seas of your mind go unused, our kind never forget save when we will it!*

A useful talent.

More useful than you imagine, to the scholars among your kind. For not only do we not forget, but information acquired by coriding is often passed from generation to generation entire; as your kind pass down stories, novels, cinema, and so on!

So you're saying that we—humans—our entire species—is . . . a library or . . . or video store for dolphins?

There is more to it than that by far, but the analogy is accurate.

Carolyn froze in mid-stroke. *How . . . long have you been doing this?* she asked carefully.

As long as your kind have dwelt near enough the sea for us to coride. Distance does make a difference. If the host ventures too far inland, coriding becomes dangerous—though that has not stopped some of us.

And you remember perfectly? *And pass these memories down?*

Yes.

But that means . . . that you—that you might
know *what history only speculates about—assuming you coride with the proper people! Oh my God!
You . . . must have a store of human history surpassing our own.*

*We do! Which is another reason you should aid
us.*

But the Mother-Queen-Sister's remark slipped
right over Carolyn's head, so intent was she on pondering the ramifications of what she had just been
told. *Jesus Christ,* she cried suddenly. *He lived near
the sea . . . And London's not that far, so the princes
in the tower . . . ! And Saint Brandon's voyage . . . !
And the* Marine Sulfur Queen! *And . . .*

*The mysteries of the ages—your ages—all laid
bare, when speech between our two kinds becomes
facile. But if that is ever to be a reality, you must
aid us.*

*Oh . . . right. You keep referring to needing my
help. Sorry . . . but—Well, you just gave me a lot to
swallow!*

I thought you would be pleased. . . .

So . . . what can I do for you?

First of all, the Mother-Queen-Sister replied, *you
should know that some of our intentions are totally
selfish. Humans are the only other beings on this
planet as interesting to us as we are to ourselves;
and since your world is one we can never access
easily, whereas you sometimes venture into ours,
we would hate for anything to happen to our primary source of wonder and entertainment—and
scientific knowledge, of course.*

I sense a but *impending.*

*Indeed there is! For you are surely aware that
your kind have been less than . . . discreet about
how you have threatened the treasures of the nat-*

*ural world. I certainly do not need to tell you what
you have done to the sea!*

But we're improving! Carolyn protested. *It's
taken us a while, but . . .*

You are, the Mother-Queen-Sister agreed, *but perhaps not fast enough. And here I should tell you
something else your historians may find of interest.
For not only can we control those who are mentally
deficient, we can also unite, by singing, to control
conventional minds. We do not like to do this for
ethical reasons, and it is seldom done, but it does
happen. Too, we can sing dreams—ideas—and
such like into the minds of those to whom they
might be useful . . . like you, or your friend Thunderbird O'Connor.*

*So basically what you're saying is that through-
out history you guys have sometimes united to sing
us to a higher understanding of ourselves and our
world?*

*Yes. You, who have so many external things to
tempt you, sometimes do not spend enough time in
your own minds. Ethics, logic, philosophy—in
these our kind surpass you.*

But . . .

*The Renaissance was not wholly spontaneous,
Carolyn,* the Mother-Queen-Sister confided, with
humorous sly pride, like a parent producing a long-
awaited present for a child. *Nor were the ethical crises of the mid-years of the last century, nor the
political upheavals and peace movements that followed. Surely you have heard it said that it was
almost . . . magical the way the repressive govern-
ments in eastern Europe collapsed one after the
other!*

You guys did that?

We . . . assisted.

But why?

To preserve our source of entertainment, to draw your attention from fear and sadness to more profitable concerns. And, incidentally, to protect ourselves.

From what?

Let me tell you something else, as a means to that.

Everything you've told me incites me to wonder, so tell me whatever you want!

There is a problem. With the orcas, there is a problem.

I've seen some of that, I think, but I didn't know why.

Why is because many of them, especially the young and impatient, do not see your affairs as quite so benign as we. Their view is that humans are far too dangerous to play with as we do. Therefore, they have lately adopted two tacks to thwart our effort to bring our kinds together. The first is that they have taken to attacking your kind by the only means they have: by singing up "natural" disasters, such as the hurricanes that have plagued your mother's land these last few years—which act has also carried with it the subsidiary intent of forcing selkies to cooperate with them, to protect that land that was their ancient home.

And they do this through singing?

By singing together, those among them—or us—who have strong minds can use those minds to affect those forces your kind have not yet discovered—those energies you would call magic. For is not magic the manipulation of the forces of the world by intangible means? Certainly that has been said. But it has also been said, in response to chaos theory (I told you we were philosophers) that a butterfly flaps its wings in Peking and a hurri-

cane hits Miami. And . . . a butterfly is a very easy thing to manipulate . . .

I see.

Which brings us to our second problem with our orca kin, the Mother-Queen-Sister went on. *I have told you that we—and they—can unite and sing and so, among other things, affect the weather. This is not an activity we have often practiced in the past, for your world is your world, and not for us to meddle with in a way that does damage. But with some orcas determined to destroy your kind by contriving natural disasters, we have no choice but to oppose them.*

Unfortunately, the Mother-Queen-Sister concluded, *they have begun to oppose our opposition— by reducing the number of our singers—our magicians—who can challenge them. You have yourself seen the results of their efforts to this end. The last was in a bay not far from here.*

The dolphin mutilations!

We would say magician assassinations, but yes.

If I can help prevent that! Just ask!

That is exactly what I am doing. Orcas sing up literal storms, we sing up figurative calm seas; it is as simple as that. The balance between the two has been wavering in their favor lately. And in the last few years they have learned to walk among men themselves. Who knows what mischief they may wreak now?

Well, Carolyn said after a pause. *You've just told me so much . . . it's going to take a while for me to assimilate it all.*

Which time we may not have. For the orcas—and it is not all orcas, be assured—have been training magicians faster than we, and destroying ours as well. Now the balance is upset, and we fear that while we wait to rebuild our strength, they will sing more disasters—so many they could spell an end to everything.

So what can I do? Carolyn asked simply. *I've been told my brother is the Word and my friend 'Bird we think is the Singer, but I'm supposed to be the Way—and I don't know what that is. Which is why I actually came here!*

Carolyn sensed an emotion that was the telepathic equivalent of a smile. *What can you do?* the Mother-Queen-Sister echoed. *Why, your role is simple: humans have a magic of their own, though they do not often use it. Sometimes, however, it surfaces—for example, in your brother's books, the power of whose words can actually influence belief, which is a crucial component in magic. He thinks he is composing stories, but in reality he is contriving mighty spells—for as your friend Stormcloud speculated earlier this evening (one of us corides with him quite often), to name a thing and describe a thing is to gain power over that thing; and to then sing about it, is to imbue it with yet more power, so that to change the song can sometimes change the thing itself!*

I'm not sure I understand.

Think about it . . . think about those very words, and you will come to understanding.

So you're saying . . .

That should your brother write the proper song, and have it empowered by a singer such as Thunderbird O'Connor, you, who can speak to our kind, can translate it into a form we can use to defeat the troublesome orcas hereabout.

Oh! Carolyn replied in surprise. *Actually that doesn't sound all that difficult.*

It is far more difficult than you imagine! And

*there is one final complication, which is that what-
ever is done must be done quickly. Dawn is nearly
upon us; the next sunset will bring the full moon,
which is when those forces the orcas draw on to
produce their weather magic are strongest. We
have learned that when night comes again they will
try to sing up a mighty storm—the strongest ever
known. They will do their singing near here, for it
is from here that the seeds of mighty storms arise.
And you, Carolyn Mauney-Griffith, must help us
stop it!*

Chapter XXXIV:
Shanachie

(John Lox's compound)
(Saturday, September 3—midafternoon)

"I'm a wizard," Kevin informed Hosteen John Lox's black-and-white tomcat, as he sat drinking ferociously strong coffee in the dubious shade of a juniper tree. "The queen of the local dolphins says I'm a goddamn bloody *sorcerer!*"

The cat cocked its head ambiguously and blinked yellow eyes at him. He winked back and risked another sip of what tasted like overbrewed Antigua. "Wanta be my familiar, kitty?"

Evidently not, for with a flick of its elegant tail, the cat turned and flounced away.

Kevin watched it go, saw it ooze from blue-green shadows into the blazing golden light of the stone shelf on which he was ensconced a hundred meters uphill from Lox's hogan. Small shadows now, he noted; but tonight *all* would be shadows. Shoot, with the moon full, even shadows would have shadows.

He hoped they'd all be ready.

More to the point, he hoped he would be.

The Song, the Singer, and the Way, huh? Well, he had confidence in one of the three—and not necessarily himself or Cary. On the other hand, anyone

403

who could undergo what Thunderbird O'Connor had
during the last few days and still be functional was
probably up to an all-night caterwauling. Drumming
too, if one got picky, since 'Bird was convinced that
the rhythm he'd acquired in his most recent medicine dream had been the one to use. Certainly he'd
spent half an hour rehearsing it as soon as he'd
yawned his way out of Stormy's bathroom far too
close to sunrise that morning, and another thirty
minutes putting it on diskette so Kevin could fix the
rhythm of the song he was supposed to write.

Yeah, old 'Bird had it made. He'd been unani-
mously designated first recipient of a shower and
shave at Casa Cloudy (Stormy's apartment at the
Dineh Embassy), where they'd all spent what little
remained of the night after Cary had returned full of
wild tales about orca conspiracies. She'd worn her
own skin then; the local dolphins evidently having
quite particular plans for the other—about which
Kevin didn't like to think. And since then—since
they'd made their assorted catch-up calls (Cary's to
Mary Hasegawa by far the longest; though 'Bird's to
someone named Red Wounds, in which the word
'tickets' oddly enough figured prominently, hadn't
been short either), and abandoned civilized comfort
to trundle into this godforsaken dust bowl around
two that afternoon—'Bird had been taking it very
easy indeed.

Of course, he'd had it hardest—had, Kevin gathered, been running on air and imagination long before his adventures of the previous evening had seen
him first unseamed from nave (a hand's width lower
than nave, rather) to chaps, then terrorized by orcas, and finally four-fifths drowned in the Gulf. Not
much time in there for food, sleep, or healing. Which
explained why 'Bird had found the coolest place in

Lox's compound—a grassy bank near the stream behind the hogan—and was watching dead channels behind his lids. If Kevin sat up straighter, he could just see him past a screen of scraggly willows—see his bare feet, more precisely, the rest being obscured by greenery.

He grinned at that; for, excluding his reasonable, if overreactive, conduct upon their first encounter— basically that he'd tried to throttle the poor, half-drowned guy on the beach—he discovered that he liked their Singer-designate as much as anyone he'd ever met.

In fact, now he considered it, they made a nice set: Singer and Songwriter. But on a more obscure level they were more like mirror images, at least where magic was concerned. 'Bird had been brought up to believe in magic (so he had confessed to Kevin on the drive up from Aztlan). And *had* believed in it, even when he didn't want to—until it had forced itself upon him in terms that could not be ignored.

While he, Kevin Alistair Mauney, author extraordinaire, had desperately wanted magic all his life, and not found it until four days ago when a certain knock had sounded on a certain door of a certain castle in County Offaly. Before then . . . Well, he lived in a country as rife with ghosts as any on earth—and had seen exactly nothing, not even one of the four said to inhabit Cameron McMillan's parents' nineteenth-century manor south of Dublin, where he'd spent more nights than one. Never mind fairy rings galore, and more significant mythological sites than one could shake a shillelagh at. But had *he* ever seen anything? Not so much as a booze-born leprechaun. *Nada.* Zilch. Nothing.

But that hadn't stopped him wanting to so badly he'd sifted his yearning into a landmark novel about ley lines and straight tracks—and something had clicked there. He had only to summon images and they appeared, full-blown down to the most obscure detail. Characters had but to open their mouths, and they were talking without supervision from him at all. As for plots . . . they wound themselves out like knotwork, intricate as carpet pages, and as dense, but with patterns clear as Waterford crystal.

If only he could achieve the same with his song.

It wasn't going well *at all*. The laptop PC by his hip contained twelve false starts, and the drum diskette had played through twice already.

So much for having faith in the Word.

The Singer he had just considered.

Which left the Way.

Cary.

Poor, poor Carolyn.

For stressful as this whole complex situation had been for him, Cary's task was orders of magnitude more arduous. Not only for what she'd endured physically—two literal deaths in three days, among other things. But also for the fact that she alone had been forced to deal with a complete realignment of her worldview. Stormy was cool about practically everything (though he *had* asked Hosteen Lox if he thought sentient nonhumans left something called *chindi* when they died). 'Bird and he had at least made room for magic in their realities—'Bird by walling it up in a corner of his head like a crazy relative, Kevin by planting a seed of solid gold in fallow ground, then watering and fertilizing it daily—to no avail.

But poor Cary had awakened one morning with almost three science degrees in her head—and had gone to bed the following night an acolyte to the Salmon of Wisdom (Dolphin of Wisdom, rather). It was a bloody long leap, too, and upstream: from Jacques Cousteau to Jack-in-the-green; from *Phocaena phocoena*—the common harbor porpoise—to *Homo sapiens . . . pinnipediae*, or whatever selkies were. (He was reasonably sure they'd simply prefer their names—except he didn't actually know any.)

Never mind that she was worn to a frazzle, and had to cope with a body that was, with no warning, no longer merely the old familiar friend she had worn through childhood, puberty, adolescence, and a fair hunk of adulthood. Or, more accurately, that her bod was everything it had been *plus* a talented doppelgänger that could swim and hold its breath like a seal—*plus* a shapechanger on top of everything else. At least three variations, there—and most folks took a lifetime coming to terms with one.

And she might have to test the bounds of all three come full moon tonight—with major damage to relations between (at minimum) two sentient races riding on her shoulders, should she not prove equal to the task.

She would, of course, always had; world without end, amen.

But he sure as hell didn't envy her.

And like 'Bird, she too was doing exactly what she ought—what Stormy, as the person most comfortable with the magic/mundane interface, had suggested was the only real preparation they could manage on the fly: undergoing ritual purification in John Lox's sweat lodge. Kevin could see the fire that heated the rocks from here, east of the low domed structure. Stormy was tending it solemnly, hair unbound, stripped to a breechclout that looked far more natural on his lean graceful body than jeans. Every now and then he'd use a forked stick to lift a few stones from the fire, which he'd then stash in the lodge, deftly undoing the door flap as he passed through.

He wondered how Cary was doing in there. More to the point, he wondered what she was thinking.

But if he didn't stop worrying about everyone else and get this bloody song composed, 'Bird and Cary would be sitting around with their fingers up their noses—and he'd be watching the world he knew go bye-bye. Well, actually, probably not, 'cause if the orcas raised the storm Cary had predicted, and they were out there trying to forestall it (for song or not, all four of them would certainly be where the Mother-Queen-Sister had ordained), there was a good chance they'd not return. In fact, without something to counter the orcas, they'd likely be first victims of their weather mojo. Four bodies found drifting in the sea come dawn. *If* dawn came, and *if* there was anyone to find them.

"Shit," Kevin growled, aloud this time, as he saw Hosteen Lox emerge from his hogan and amble toward where Stormy sat vigil outside the sweat lodge. "I've gotta write a song to save the world—and I still don't know where to begin."

Whereupon he drained the last of the coffee, turned on 'Bird's drum diskette, and once more picked up his PC.

No go.

It was exactly like before: he'd begin something, it would skip along for a couple of lines—and then fall flat as a clumsy tumbler. Part of the problem, of course, was simply pressure. So much rode on whatever he wrote, that the *fact* of import overrode the *what* of the product itself. The knowledge that this had to be absolutely the best thing he'd ever composed didn't help, either.

God, but he hated deadlines!

Write a song to turn a storm, huh? And how did one do that? Where did one begin? Did one commence with images and run from there? Did one simply describe a storm, then describe a song doing the turning? Or did one cast it into dialogue and make it a sort of rant? Who knew? *He* for certain didn't. Shoot, he'd even dragged out that old 'dark and stormy night' fossil, on the theory that what was cliché in the world of mundane letters might not be in arcane realms.

But *that* had quickly gone to doggerel.

He'd even asked Hosteen Lox for advice—the man was, after all, a certified Singer—and learned nothing. "I would help you if I could," Lox had said. "But this is not my battle. No one has sent me dreams; those who asked you for songs have not asked for mine; and all else I could do would take longer than you have. But I will think on it, and if I arrive at anything you might find useful, I will tell you."

So far he hadn't.

No, his one useful clue was something 'Bird had confided about the theory of Cherokee magic. In it, every direction had power over certain things: West was death, north was defeat and trouble, south was peace and happiness, and east was success and triumph. Each likewise was linked with a color: blue in the north, black in the west, white in the south, red in the east. And each direction maintained a set of overriding animal archetypes—a Black Dog of the West and a White Bear of the South and so on. Thus, when one began a spell—and all the world was magic to traditional Cherokee—one invoked the appropriate animal of the appropriate direction to vanquish its analog on the opposite side. Or alternately, one ascribed sentience to *everything*, so that if one wanted to turn a storm, one simply informed the storm that its wife was sleeping with someone else, and it had better stop acting the destructive fool and go deal with real trouble elsewhere. There was even a legitimate traditional formula for that last—except that 'Bird didn't know it, and hadn't even remembered its existence until it was too late to run back to the embassy where boxes of Mooney's *Myths of the Cherokee*, which contained it, lay neatly packaged for sale.

All of which would have been a lot more encouraging if Kevin were Cherokee—*Ani-Yunwiya*, rather, as 'Bird gently insisted. (*Kituwah*, as on their embassy, was evidently an ancient ceremonial name, not to be used in passing.)

But perhaps it was a place to start. After all, it *was* magic, and the Ani-Yunwiya had possessed mighty magicians. And now he thought of it, hadn't the druids of the Tuatha de Danaan back in good old Eire called down storms and rains of blood on their Fir Bolg foes? Not what he needed, obviously; the opposite, in fact. Still, it meant that there was precedent in his own ancestry for weather magic. So maybe the thing to do was begin with an image. Man as archetype, rising to greet the dawn, seeing a storm approach, and cursing it as a toady of the lingering night! And from there . . .

Yeah, *that* might work.

He turned up the volume of the diskette, resettled his PC, and began.

"You *are not a storm*," he typed. "*You are a shadow, a not-thing, a scattered smear of water on the wind. And what poor water you have found! Water so weak air can wrest it on high; water so frail it must cleave to dust or vanish; water that wends where air—which is nothing—sends it!*"

Well *that* was certainly a different beginning, as he paused to read it over. Not great—yet—it didn't scan worth a damn with 'Bird's beat. But unlike the others, it showed promise.

If he could keep it up.

"If one were to look at you, one would think your aspirations and your art were not agreeing," a voice rumbled behind him—a voice with which he had not yet grown familiar. He started, jerking his hand as he did—which scribed a line of asterisks across the screen before a final twitch sent the PC skittering.

"Shit, man, don't *do* that!" Kevin yipped at Hosteen Lox, as the Dineh Singer eased from behind the juniper tree. He sought for the laptop frantically, found it being investigated by a sunning lizard he'd not noticed until that instant.

Lox selected a seat on the stone to Kevin's right and in front of him. He looked at Kevin, but obliquely, then peered at the hogan and the sweat lodge and T-Bird-by-the-river the same way.

Kevin caught the sideways question, too, and recalled from his reading that such was typical Navajo. Well, two could play at that game. "Is it this you are asking me?" he replied, in the roundabout way of the Irish. "Is it that you think that my work does not go well?"

"It did not *look* as if it goes well. It is not wise for one man to think for another. Too often we can not even think for ourselves."

"I *was* having trouble thinking," Kevin admitted.

"The problem is not in the thinking, though," Lox chuckled. "It is in too *much* thinking. One thinks about too many things besides what one ought to think about. One thinks about why one is thinking what one thinks; and one thinks about how much one hates having to think what one thinks when one would rather be thinking something else; and one thinks about what happens if one does *not* think what one needs to think; and one thinks about what others will say if that thinking does not go well, and so on . . . you get my meaning well enough."

Kevin eyed him dubiously. "I . . . *think* I do, " he grinned.

"And what *you* are thinking, young Kevin Mauney, is that you do not want to be writing this song. You do not entirely believe in the threat it is intended to counter, yet you fear that if the threat *is* real, it will not be good enough. In effect, you fight yourself. You must think *only* about the thing and create for its *own* sake; for creating itself is the most magical thing in the world. Write it as if you were a character in one of your novels whose duty it is to vanquish a storm. Make *yourself* believe, the rest will be easy."

Kevin shrugged. "That's . . . sorta what I was tryin' to do!"

"Then do it! Belief can do more than anyone imagines. It can heal, and it can kill. *I* know that when I sing; my people know that; Thunderbird's people know that. Those who practice voodoo in the islands east of here certainly know that. Your ancestors, I have no doubt, knew that, or they wouldn't have done those satire-things I heard you talking to Stormcloud about when you got here. And they believed in curses right and left, too, didn't they?— Yeah, I've read those books. I've even read *yours*! And by God I'll say for the time I was reading 'em, I believed 'em! So what you must do, boy, is forget this is all real and pretend that turning that storm tonight is just one more climax in a book that you must make your reader believe!"

Kevin managed an uncertain grin.

Lox grinned back. "Now get to work! I'll be back

in an hour—*belagana* time—to check on you, and
if you aren't done, I'll make you drink more of my
coffee!"

"Is that a promise or a threat?"

"Your choice," Lox laughed, and rose. Kevin
watched him saunter down toward the sweat lodge.
He wondered when *that* would end; how much
longer Cary would stay in there—and what she
would be like when she emerged.

And that was a nice image right there! The warrior
queen striding from her house already shaking her
spear at an approaching storm. Maybe he could work
that into a second stanza—make it a boast, like a
Celtic queen would have done. Pretend Cary was
Boudicca cursing her unreliable Roman "allies"—
only instead of Romans, it was a whale-wrought
storm!

"You claim to be a storm," he began. *"You roll
across my lands like warriors reaping lives, and
yet I tell you that however great a host is yours, I
command a greater. You are wind and rain; I am
lightning! You are air and water, but earth drinks
you down; I am fire and air, and when I strike the
earth the very ground quakes to hear me!"*

Not bad! And in its wake came others.

When Kevin finally blinked up from filling his
fourth screen, it was to see the sun seriously westering; it was to see Thunderbird O'Connor drifting
blissfully in the stream; it was to see Hosteen John
Lox bringing a handful of twigs to where Stormcloud
Nez stood sentinel beside the now-smoking embers
before the sweat lodge. And, as he screwed up his
eyes after nearly an hour squinting at silver-gilt
glass, it was to see Carolyn emerge from her place of
purification.

A queen indeed she looked. Small, yes; and naked—which surprised him. But also sleek as an otter and suntanned as gold as the ores that had called men to this hemisphere and doomed those already present. Yet Cary's gold was far more precious than that of any Inca or Aztec.

Impulsively, he set the laptop aside, rose stiffly, and wandered down the hill. A moment later he confronted her where she stood, still gleaming with sweat, still panting into the clear air as Stormy censed her with sage, cedar—and in honor of her Irish blood, hazel—though where he had acquired the latter, Kevin had no idea.

She smiled at him crookedly. Wary, tired, but confident. Unselfconscious. Maybe a little punchy, which was not unreasonable.

He smiled back. "Feel better?" he asked carefully.

"—Different," she concluded after a pause, eyeing the stream speculatively, and then fixing an even more speculative eye on the lazily floating 'Bird. "I think this just might work."

"It might," Kevin agreed. "In fact," he added, sparing a glance at the lingering John Lox, "I *believe* it will."

"And *I* believe I'll go wash off this sweat," she sighed dreamily. "That is, if Mr. Shaman here agrees."

"Such is prescribed," Stormy assured her with a grin. "In fact, if you can stand naked men around, I just might join you."

Kevin gnawed his lip. "Three kinds of water," he mused. "Water of the sea, water that is fresh, and the water that heat calls forth from men's skin."

"A triad!" Carolyn cried. "Welsh, but still Celtic."

Stormy lifted an eyebrow wickedly. "Well, 'Bird and me *are* buddies . . . !"

"A *triad*, not a *trio*!" Carolyn growled at him, with

another grin—which convinced Kevin that stress really had made her silly. "Poetry not poking."

"But poking can be poetry too," Stormy shot back, throwing out his chest and clamping his hands on his hips—which incidentally slid his breechclout a significant handspan lower. "Or I've been told it can."

Kevin rolled his eyes at Lox.

"Different," Lox repeated neutrally. "This just might work at that."

Kevin sighed and went to revise his Song.

If other music was made, it was not his concern.

The day passed at its own speed anyway.

And, inevitably, night drew nigh.

Chapter XXXV:
Riders on the Storm

(North of Aztlan)
(Saturday, September 3—near sunset)

"For God's sake, man, will you leave that *alone!*"
'Bird froze with a finger on the CD remote built into his armrest and regarded his friend sheepishly from across the Jeep's glassy cabin. *"Sorry!"* he growled, with far more sarcasm than he intended. Forrest Jackson's "Warhammer" continued to strain the speakers unabated.

Stormy countered with a hard-jawed glare, as though he'd contrived a scathing retort but bitten it for the sake of friendship. He shifted his hands on the wheel and squinted through the steep bubble of windshield. 'Bird followed his mirror-shaded gaze to where Carolyn Mauney-Griffith's Mazda two-seater was kicking up major yellow dust on the new, but ill-paved road ahead. The landscape itself consisted of low hills splattered with scrubby gray-green vegetation. The mountains made a ragged line of purple to the left, where they swung sharply west away from the sea—which glittered blue as glass beyond the escarpments opposite. Those cliffs were growing higher, too, and the terrain more rugged, for all they

were only a few kliks up the coast from Aztlan's ritzy
northern suburbs.

"No big deal," Stormy conceded finally, having
fallen back a tad. "It just seems to me that the last
thing on your mind right now would be somebody
else's music."

"Except that it takes my mind off mine," 'Bird retorted, through a yawn. " 'Sides, little stuff's as important as big stuff when you're fixin' to be dead!"

"Optimistic little shit, aren't you?"

" 'There was a young Dineh from Aztlan/whose
dick looked just like a fry pan,' " 'Bird shot back instantly. "There, is that better?"

"More like the 'Bird I know and . . . love, anyway!"

"Watch it!"

"Metaphorically."

"You mean platonically."

"Tectonically?"

"That too."

"Speaking of which—"

'Bird held his breath, as Stormy swerved to miss
a pair of potholes Carolyn had threaded her smaller
car between. A Galapagos tortoise could have slept
off a bender in either one. "So how *do* you feel, anyway I mean, seriously?" Stormy asked, when the
road improved.

"Seriously?"

"Preferably."

"I . . . Well, physically I feel like shit: functional,
but sore everywhere I can be. Nothing hurts worse
than anything else, but I've got bruises on my
bruises, as you so tactfully pointed out to Cary back
at Lox's creek. They're all slippin' off to the Dull-Pain
Land, though. Nothin' to keep me from doin' my job,
if that's what you mean."

"And the rest?"

"What is this? The fuckin' Inquisition?"

"Fucking insurance, I'd say. You're gonna have my life in your hands in less than an hour. I'd prefer to know how reliable those hands are. And if they're gonna break, I'd as soon know where the stress points are. Forewarned is forearmed and all that."

"Fine."

"So . . . how's your headspace?"

'Bird shifted in his seat so he could watch Stormy with one eye and Carolyn's car with the other. "You want an honest answer?" A pause, a prompting sideways glare from Stormy, then: "I . . . don't think I'm solemn enough—or something. I mean, I almost feel kinda drunk and giddy. I dunno. I guess . . . Well, to tell the truth, I don't think it's really sunk in yet. I mean it's not *real* to me that we're gonna do this screwy battle. Like, I can feel it out there already, like a cloud on my future; and I can feel us all bein' sucked into it. 'Cept that it's . . . like a movie, or something. I keep thinkin' I'm gonna wake up and it'll all be a dream. I guess what I'm sayin' is that while I *know* that an hour from now we'll be in the middle of it, the whole mess is so unreal, I don't *believe* we will. And therefore I can't get properly freaked."

"Which may be a problem," Stormy observed quietly. "You gotta believe, man."

"I will—when I have to. But 'til then . . . how 'bout this? 'A pencil-dick Dineh named Stormy/got so wired that he started to bore me—' "

"A Cherokee bastard named 'Bird," Stormy countered, much louder, "had *no* dick, so far as I've heard—"

"—though in *fact*, he had eighteen inches/ and—"

"—and screwed both the lads and the wenches—"

"—and . . . and wrote lim'ricks that weren't worth a turd!"

"You're right," Stormy sighed. "You're not *nearly* solemn enough."

"Yeah, well it was good while it lasted," 'Bird sighed back, nodding through the windshield to where Carolyn was pulling the MX-Z onto a widening of the shoulder at the side of the road beside a gold Ford Auriga with Hertz plates. "Looks like we're there."

"Hassie wouldn't come," Rudy Ramirez explained roughly a minute later—as soon as he had breath again, after Carolyn's hearty hug.

"I . . . expected that," Carolyn replied slowly. "I figured she'd see through that 'personal family crisis' story."

"*I* did. One doesn't commonly request the loan of an inflatable rubber raft when trying to heal a . . . schism, or whatever you're fond of calling it." He gestured toward a canvas-wrapped bundle beside him.

"She pissed?"

"Well, she probably wasn't real happy when she had to scrape Nesheim off the ceiling when you didn't show today, but she'll live."

"I *hope*."

Rudy stared her in the eye. "You wanta tell me what this is really about?"

Carolyn glanced toward the westering sun, then at Stormy. "Five minutes," Stormy supplied. "Explanation, but no arguing."

"It's cool, man," Rudy agreed shakily. "Something really weird's going on, I can . . . *feel* it. But Cary's always been straight with me, so I've gotta trust her—which means I've gotta trust you guys as well."

"Hush," Carolyn whispered. "And listen."

"Magicians first," Stormy chuckled nervously, a short while later, as he, Carolyn, 'Bird, Kevin—and a tight-faced Rudy Ramirez—paused at the top of a thirty-meter cliff overlooking the semicircular bay south of the beach that was their destination. The beach where "Anomalous Beaching Number IV" had enflamed this whole odd affair.

'Bird shot him a resigned glare. "Don't remind me!"

"I don't *need* to," Stormy snapped back, pointing toward the eastern sky, where low streaks of dark clouds already shadowed the horizon like a pack of ravens mustering to ravish a battlefield. Their edges were stained red with the light of the sun fading over the mountains behind them. *Red as knife wounds,* 'Bird thought. *Red as this slit down my belly.*

Kevin shifted the large backpack that weighted his skimpy shoulders to a more comfortable position, and blinked at Carolyn quizzically. "Any time now, sis. It's your call."

Carolyn, in turn, slid her gaze back to Stormy, who was freeing the bodhran he'd borrowed from Carolyn from its leather-wrapped carrying case. "I just work here," she murmured, and 'Bird could tell she was trying to mask a serious case of the frights with very transparent frivolity. "Stormy's the Master of Ritual . . ."

Stormy glanced over his shoulder, past the turn-out where they'd left the cars, toward the sunset. 'Bird followed his line of sight. The sky was clear there, but in the few seconds since he'd last checked, the eastern clouds had thickened perceptibly. The wind had picked up, too, was playing teasing games with his and Stormy's long hair. It also held an ominous quality, and that same tense, electric tingle it carried before a major blow. And with every troubling gust, 'Bird felt his earlier punchiness peeled away, leaving a hard, grim core. For his part, Stormy scowled for a long thoughtful moment, then nodded resignedly. "Okay, folks, when the sun hits the mountain, we go down. That's as close as I can call it. The moon oughta be cruising up opposite at the same time—which is fairly rare, by the way."

"Which oughta be in about two minutes," 'Bird supplied. "Come on, I'll lead the way—unless Mr. Magical Shaman Stormcloud Nez has changed his mind . . : "

"Actually, I have," Stormy replied—and from a belt pouch produced a cedar-and-stuffed-hide drumstick. "I'll go first. Since I won't be singing later, I'll drum you down! Kev, you're the Word, so you follow me; then 'Bird, as the Singer; then Cary. Rudy—you come last, with the raft."

"Sounds good," 'Bird told him. "Go for it."

Squaring his shoulders, Stormy eased in front of him, gripping the strut in back of the bodhran in his left hand—and, sparing one eye at the vast red disk behind them, struck the tight-stretched leather. The rhythm was the one that had come to 'Bird in his medicine dreams; the tone deep and soft, but with a ghost of thinness in its resonance. It faded as Stormy followed the path the few meters to the rim of the cliff, paused there to give the sun time to kiss the mountains, then eased over the edge—whereupon the volume rose again as 'Bird followed Kevin onto the narrow goat trail that snaked down the escarpment to the beach.

It took them all of ten minutes to make their way to that narrow strip of sand, and during that trek, 'Bird had an uncanny sense of being caught at a stasis point between elements. Earth was at his bare feet and brushing his left hand: solid, close, and comforting; air still picked at him, blowing threat and danger from the east through the weave of his serape and baggy jeans. Water glittered to the right: the most contradictory substance in the world, solid as steel when driven with force, soft as silk when the touch brought against it was subtle—tsunamis and sea spray both. And fire—the unseen sun to the west drawing flame across the crests of all those waves and the clouds that rolled in above them, so that the sea seemed transfigured into burning blood.

And through it all 'Bird moved delicately, balanced among all those entities, as the eagle he reverenced when he danced floated between substance and space.

And always there was the drum: at once the voice of the earth—for that which comprised it was born of the earth—and likewise the voice of the wind and the voice of 'Bird's dreams. Tangible linked with intangible via the real but unseen.

Gettin' crazy, kid, he told himself. *Gotta watch it.*

Scowling, he forced himself to focus on the gritty stone beneath his feet, the steady beat of the bodhran, and the rhythm of his breath, then blend all three into one whole, while staring fixedly at the hollow below Kevin's backpack where the tan fabric bunched and stretched along the crests of his hips as the Warden of the Word worked his way along.

It succeeded too, calmed him as intended, so that when the trail flattened into the beach, 'Bird was taken so off guard he staggered a dozen steps before he could stop. Carolyn caught him as he stumbled to a halt. He shot her a nervous smile and clasped the steadying hand she laid on his shoulder.

Far too soon thereafter, Stormy had marched them to the point beyond which lay the bay from which they would depart to do battle. The tide was higher than on Carolyn's previous visit (so Rudy observed behind him), and they had no choice but to wade through calf-deep water while bracing themselves against the sharp, wet rocks. But then the cliffs kinked sharply left and they were there.

'Bird held his breath. Even two-plus days after the beaching, the place still reeked of death—though whether it was an actual odor that had soaked into the sand or something less tangible, he wasn't certain. Four of the smaller corpses had been taken away for study at "Why?," Carolyn told them; the others piled between the tide lines, sprayed with gasoline, and set alight. Scavengers and waves had done the rest. All that remained now was a dark smudge on the sand. Stormy led them to a place just above it, almost exactly in the center of the half circle defined by the cliffs and the bay—at which time his bodhran cadence grew more complicated, increased in volume—then, with a final hollow *boom*, ended.

Twisting around, he set the drum behind him, just out of reach of the waves that slid perilously close to his bare feet. The others crowded around to either side. Carolyn and, especially, Kevin gazed at him expectantly. The clouds to the *west* were darkening, now; and the wind was stronger yet. Carolyn inhaled sharply. "Now—or later?" she prompted edgily.

"Later," Stormy told her. "We still need to do a couple of things—besides the obvious. Speaking of which, 'Bird, you think you could rustle up a fire there by the cliffs? Kev, you and Rudy can get the raft up and running."

'Bird grunted assent and trotted to the base of the cliff where he stripped off his rust-toned serape and quickly located enough driftwood to fuel the small fire he lit, after too many false starts, with a bow drill—not because anyone had suggested that mechanism, but because it seemed appropriate. As he sawed the wood-and-fiber bow back and forth with one hand, while pressing the spinning drill into the cedar slab with the other, so friction would bring forth flame, he watched Kevin and Rudy inflate the raft—by about as antithetical a means as 'Bird could imagine: hooking a cylinder of compressed air to the valve at one end and turning a knob. The raft stretched and strained and made rubbery thumping noises against the sand long before 'Bird had a reliable blaze. Not until Stormy had helped the other two drag the raft out of reach of the waves, did the tinder finally catch, but the rest was easy. 'Bird stood as they approached, grateful that the concentration required to build the fire had burned away the last of his detached frivolity. Now that he was actually *doing* something he felt fine. It was *not* doing—anticipating—that mucked around with his mind.

"Okay," Stormy said, when the fire was knee-high, "I'd like to try one final purification rite, and then we get the show on the road. I doubt this has much to do with dolphin magic, but I *do* think it'll help put us in the right frame of mind. 'Sides, the dolphins thought we had magic—so maybe we do."

"Fine," Rudy muttered shakily. "So what do you want us to do?"

Stormy blushed ever so slightly. "Uh, well, first everybody take off as much as you're willing to. We're gonna be dealing with natural forces here, so we oughta be as natural as possible ourselves. Rudy, that's optional for you, I guess."

Carolyn frowned, but began tugging off the tan serape she wore above a gold slick-suit and black jeans, continuing with the jeans. Kevin too looked unhappy, but set his jaw and stripped to the skin. "What the hey?" he sighed. "Cary's seen it all before, and none of us lads have braggin' rights over the others, best I can figure."

"Same here," Stormy told 'Bird, as he likewise doffed his togs, leaving 'Bird and (after a brief hesitation) Rudy to follow suit. Though she'd been skinny-dipping with two of them a few hours earlier, Carolyn paused at the slick-suit she wore in lieu of underwear, then peeled it off as well. She had a nice body, 'Bird couldn't help but note anew: small and slim, but perfectly formed. Then again, none of them looked really dreadful.

Stormy squatted to retrieve the pouch that had hung from his belt. When he rose, he held a handful of bound herbs 'Bird recognized as sage. Setting it alight at the fire, he withdrew it hastily. It went out at once, but continued to smolder voluminously. "I don't know your traditions," he told Kevin, Carolyn, and Rudy, "and I'm not as clear as I should be on yours, 'Bird. But every one I *have* heard about attributes significance to the number four—and often identifies it with the directions. The world of my father's people, the Dineh, was traditionally bounded by four sacred mountains; and the directions had great power for 'Bird's folks. I'm not sure what you others are—or if you've even got a religion—but my guess is that since you've got Irish— or Latin—roots, you were at least exposed to Catholicism—"

"Yeah," Kevin acknowledged softly, "we were."

"—in which case you've got four Evangelists and, in a darker tradition, four Archangels as Lords of the Directions. So what I want us all to do is to cense each other with this sage, and then I'll light my pipe"—he gestured to yet another bundle 'Bird hadn't noticed before—"and blow smoke in the directions plus up and down, then pass it on. And when you get it, do the same, and ask whatever Powers are important to you—even if they're just your ego and your id, or whatever—to be with us through what we're about to embark on. That's all I can think to do. The rest . . . is the rest. Oh, except for one thing, which I'll get to in a minute."

Whereupon he took the bundle of sage and swirled the smoke around Kevin, commencing at his feet, then raising it over his head, then back around, taking care that the smoke wafted over most of his body. When he had finished, he handed the herb to Kevin and whispered, "You do 'Bird."

'Bird closed his eyes as the smoke danced around him, suppressing an urge to cough. When he sensed that Kevin was done, he accepted the bundle and repeated the ritual around Carolyn, silently asking *his* Lords of the Four Directions—Asgaya Sakani and Asgaya Tsunega and Asgaya Gunnagei and especially Asgaya Gigagei, the Red Man of the East, Lord of Victory—to aid him, adding that he knew he'd been long gone from the circles of his people's power, but if that could be overlooked, he planned to be more attentive in the future.

Stormy was gazing at him seriously when he made one final flourish and extended the sage to Carolyn. Seriously, but with approval.

Carolyn's face was impassive as she swept the smoking herb around Rudy—who then followed suit with Stormy. The round completed, Stormy retrieved it and thrust it into the fire. From another bundle behind him he retrieved an arm-long pipe, lit it, and blew smoke in the sacred directions, plus up and down. That concluded he passed it to Kevin, Kevin to 'Bird, and so on through the circle. Once it was back in his hands, he carefully placed it on a pair of rocks, squatted by his pouch again, and brought out a stick of what 'Bird recognized as red ocher. "Kev?" he called softly. "Come here." Kevin stepped forward obligingly, though he looked nervous—as, probably, did they all. "This just seems *right*," Stormy explained simply. And with that, he drew a Celtic-style tri-pointed star on Kevin's forehead, then repeated the motif on his upper chest. "By this I claim knowledge of your ancient soul; by this may the gods of your ancestors likewise know you and give you power."

That accomplished, he shifted his attention to 'Bird, repeating the same formula. 'Bird couldn't see what he sketched on his forehead, but the design centering his sternum was a familiar one: a cross-in-circle.

Stormy paused when he came to Carolyn, puffed his cheeks thoughtfully, then drew a design 'Bird hadn't seen before. Mostly it resembled a yin-yang symbol, save that the two components were fish— or dolphins. It took longer than the others, but 'Bird thought the effect was worth it. Certainly Carolyn looked pleased. That concluded, Stormy extended the stump of ocher to 'Bird. "You're the closest thing to a brother I've got," he murmured. "Would you do the honors?"

'Bird flashed the briefest of resigned half smiles and accepted the red pigment. But what did he do now? Stormy hadn't warned him about this. And he had no idea what iconography might be appropriate—his specialty was Southeastern art, not Southwest. And then he remembered something he'd seen on a flag at Stormy's apartment. Grinning, he sketched a circle, flanking it with a complexity of rays oriented in the cardinal directions.

Stormy smiled his approval, then glanced uneasily at Rudy.

"I . . . don't think I deserve one," Rudy whispered. "Not if I'm just gonna stay here and keep the home fires burning. Magic spread four ways is stronger than magic spread five."

"It's your call," Stormy told him solemnly. "But not your battle."

"I know," Rudy said quietly. "Maybe another day."

Stormy stared at him an instant longer, then lifted his head to check the sky. "Well, let's to it," he sighed. "Looks like we're gonna be just in time."

"I'll . . . meet you there," Carolyn said slowly. "If you lads don't mind."

"Go to," Kevin urged, pausing to give her a quick, firm hug. "And hey, sis: take care. I love you!"

"You too—*all* of you."

And then Carolyn was jogging toward the north point of the bay, where a series of caves carved pools of shadow in the cliffs, many of them half-full of water. 'Bird watched her wade waist-deep into one that was maybe a meter wide and taller than her head. She disappeared into it, and did not return.

But a *dolphin* did: a sleek silver shape skipping into the waves. It called to them in its chattery language, leapt once into the air, then dived.

"Good," 'Bird breathed in relief. "Cary's new buddies got the skin to the hidey-hole after all."

"*Very* good," Stormy echoed. "One little orca ambush, and we'd have been in trouble."

Kevin glanced to the east and frowned. "Quicker

begun, quicker done," he mumbled, rummaging in his well-nigh empty backpack. "Let's get our duds on and get going." He flung a pair of skimpy white swim trunks at 'Bird, who snared them from the air and put them on. He and Stormy did the same. Rudy retrieved his gym shorts.

Without a word, Stormy produced a heavy canvas-wrapped bundle the size and shape of a bucket, then motioned them to the raft. A tiny outboard motor had been strapped to the back, its propeller tilted up for the nonce. While 'Bird and Kevin donned orange life jackets, Stormy stowed their gear, including the bulky parcel—which proved to be a section of tree trunk as long as his forearm and roughly that wide, hollow along most of its length and pitched inside, with a tanned skin beside it, ready to be drawn across the open end. A water drum. *Red Wounds's* water drum: one of the most precious things he owned. They had almost no volume close in, but 'Bird knew from experience that the sound would carry for kilometers.

Stormy slipped his life jacket on and eased around to the raft's north gunwale. 'Bird took the south and Rudy the rear—when Kevin (to 'Bird's surprise) strode out decisively to grab the pull ring at the bow. Together, the four of them dragged the raft into the water. Fortunately, the bay was shallow and its floor smooth, with few breakers to disturb their footing, so that they were easily sixty meters offshore—with the water still scarcely more than waist-deep—before all but Rudy scrambled aboard. As the Spanish youth wished them luck and released his hold, Stormy claimed the stern, cranked the little motor, and steered them toward the open sea, keeping the headlands to north and south as equidistant as possible. Kevin sat in the bow looking grim and wor-

ried—and a lot younger than the day before. Really
scared, 'Bird concluded. On the other hand, he had
the most to lose: not only his own life, but that of
his sister. Impulsively, 'Bird clapped him on the
shoulder. "You're a good man, Kev. I hope you know
that."

Kevin shrugged, but managed a half smile and
squeezed the hand. Silence fell among them, then,
as Carolyn—identified by a distinctive zigzag pattern on her right fluke—slowly guided them into the
increasingly choppy water in the center of the bay.
For his part, 'Bird focused on filling the drum
clamped between his legs one-third full of water,
then dousing the brain-tanned head in the puddle
he was already sitting in, and stretching it across the
top. If anything happened to *it* . . .

And something could. For they were nearly half a
klik offshore now, and the weather was worsening
rapidly. The clouds that earlier had hung low to the
east had spread like locusts to obscure half the sky.
And where before they had looked thin and striated,
now they roiled thick and heavy as the smoke of a
thousand oil wells burning. Lightning flickered
within them, too, though 'Bird's more optimistic aspect hoped that was still the fading fire of the de-
parted sun. The moon, if any, was prisoner behind
them. What sky remained looked purple-blue and
sullen, like a bruise. The cliffs at their back were a
barrier of black—as forbidding to the humans as sky
and sea. Only the tiny spark of the fire left burning
there gave comfort. 'Bird felt like that wavering
flame: an ember of warm bright hope set against a
world rapidly going *loco* with the dark primal force
of a rising storm.

Even as he thought that, the wind picked up,
sweeping his hair in his eyes, blinding him with

spray. The waves, which had been disconcertingly smooth, became abruptly rougher. Water slapped at the rubber gunwale, dousing him from ribs down. He grabbed frantically for the drum.

Lightning flashed—far off, but clear. Thunder rumbled an eager reply. Challenge made and accepted. Threat and counterthreat.

—And as if that had been a signal, Carolyn leapt straight up into the air—higher and higher she rose, *impossibly* high, then poised aloft as if weightless before arching to begin her descent.

And the instant she entered the waves, all the world went crazy—

Lightning flashed again, closer this time, stabbing the sea so violently 'Bird expected to hear the waves hiss.

Instead, the world below—the watery world around them—suddenly dissolved into what 'Bird could only describe as an upward rain of dolphins. As one they leapt, shattering the bay's surface with their flight, so that, for a timeless instant, sky, beasts, and sea became one, with the raft suspended between.

Then, as quickly, the dolphins smashed back into the water, and the fractious waves returned. But this time the whitecaps were shattered over and over by what 'Bird suspected, from the many-score fins that dipped and dived among the wave crests, was a protective ring of dolphins, easily ten meters across on every side. How many individuals comprised that living rampart, he had no idea. Hundreds, maybe. Or thousands. *Unnaturally* many. In spite of himself, he shivered, for it reminded him far too much of the previous night, when he and Carolyn had found themselves on a barely less perilous craft surrounded by cetaceans. That these were the good guys was little cause for optimism, however; for just as 'Bird's chills subsided, he caught sight of another, though less defined, host of fins arrowing their way out of the east: larger fins, and darker.

"Orcas," Kevin breathed. "Straight ahead."

"Got it," 'Bird grunted grimly. "Stormy, cut the motor."

"Guess I'd better," Stormy sighed. And did.

The air lost one sound, but the ensuing vacuum was instantly filled with the slap of waves, the hiss of the wind, the flop of flukes and fins breaking the surface of the sea.

"They gonna actually *fight*?" Stormy wondered, motioning toward the approaching orcas.

"Cary didn't think so," Kevin answered. "This is supposed to be beyond that: magic versus magic."

"Magic," 'Bird muttered. "God, I hope we're up for this."

"We are," Stormy whispered. "Man, we've *gotta* be."

"Oh, Jesus, look!" Kevin broke in, pointing past the gunwale, east, to the open sea.

'Bird peered around him—and saw the orcas suddenly slide from chaos into rigorous formation, fins alternately close and far, as they swam in a counterclockwise spiral around the dolphins and the raft. And then, one after the other, as they reached the eastern extreme of their circuit, they dived.

He suppressed a shudder at that, for cyclones in the northern hemisphere likewise spun that way.

"Dolphins too," Stormy gasped. "See."

And indeed the dolphins were mirroring the orcas—save that they swam in the opposite direction. But like their adversaries, when they reached true east, they dived, leaving the raft alone in increasingly rough water.

" 'Bird," Stormy murmured, bending close. "I think it's time."

'Bird simply closed his eyes and tried to center himself, even as his fingers sought the head of the water drum. This was it, then. The Singer had to Sing, the Drummer had to Drum. Kevin had given them all copies of the words, laminated in plastic, though 'Bird had memorized them. The execution was up to him—and Carolyn.

But as he held his breath, striving to calm his heart and his brain and his breathing, it came to him at that point of stillness at his center, that somewhere close by there was already singing. Steeling himself, he drifted deeper. And *knew*!

They'd begun, the dolphins and orcas had: singing, singing, singing. He sensed it with his soul more than his ears, but for all that he knew it was true. Knew that somewhere beneath him a dark heavy humming had begun, thick and discordant, above and around which a bright melody darted and spiraled and interwove, like a net of gold cast around molten lead.

The wind slapped 'Bird's hair into his eyes, then; and he blinked back to himself, to see his friends' faces wild with alarm. The raft lifted, settled, lifted again, tilting as waves rose higher around it. The sky was black. The air felt thick as cotton, tense as wire. Any second it would rain.

Gritting his teeth, 'Bird tightened the drumhead one last turn, set the wooden base against the rubber in the center of the raft, wrapped his legs around it, settled his spine as much as he could into a proud, poised arch—and tapped the taut leather with his fingers.

The sound was soft, yet he heard it. But he felt it more, felt it thrum up through his bones and his blood and twine like a lover with his spirit. And the water beneath him, he prayed, likewise listened.

He sang first in Cherokee, a song from Mooney's *Myths* they had risked a few minutes to retrieve. It was the formula for turning storms:

*"Yuhahi, yuhahi, yuhahi, yuhahi, yuhahi,
Yuhahi, yuhahi, yuhahi, yuhahi, yuhahi—Yu!*

Sge! Ha-nagwa hinahunski tayi. Ha-tasti-gwu gunskaihu. Tsutalii-gwatina haluni. Kunigwatina dulaska galunnlati-gwu witukti. Wigunyasehisi. Atali tsugunnyi witetsatanunusi nunnahi tasanelagi degatsanawadisesti. Kunstu dutssuni atunnwa-   sutehahi tsutunelisesti. Sge!"

And then he sang in Lakota, a song he had learned at a powwow long ago.

"Ate wiohpeyata nawajin yelo. wamayanka yo! Ite Otateya nawajin yelo . . .

Stormy joined him then, on the choruses, adding his higher voice more strongly when 'Bird started over. It would have added a nice kind of symmetry, he thought, to insert a Navajo song next, but he didn't know any, and the only ones Stormy recalled were inappropriate. And, as his friend had noted, the last thing Navajo generally wanted to do was *banish* storms.

Oh well, they still had Kevin.

Kevin . . .

No time like the present.

So it was, then, that as the sky turned darker yet, the waves began to wash over the gunwale far too frequently, and the wind howled like one of Kevin's ancestral banshees, 'Bird shifted the beat to that which had come to him in a medicine dream and began to chant the song Kevin Alistair Mauney had written to banish this storm from sky and sea and earth.

> *"You are not a storm, besotted thing! You are a shadow, a shred of smoke, a smear of stagnant water on the wind . . . "*

Kevin joined him on the second verse, and Stormy added his voice on the third.

Louder and louder they sang, and harder and harder went 'Bird's hands on the drum.

But still the storm clouds thickened.

Chapter XXXVI:
Battlesong

(The Gulf of Mexico)
(Saturday, September 3—shortly past sunset)

It was like meeting three old friends together, and being welcomed like a long-lost sister by each one.

But of the three, the skin was Carolyn's biggest surprise. Before—the first time—she'd been so disgusted by the very concept of putting on another sentient creature's bloody hide—and so tired—and so confused by irreparable fractures in her most fundamental beliefs about the nature of reality, that she had actually paid little attention to the mechanics of the *change*. She'd simply stood in the breakers, as nuked as she'd ever been, reached back, felt something warm, wet, and sticky—and then . . . a tingling, a wash of warmth like liquid fire flooding through her, and that screwy *reversal* sensation . . . and then, quite simply, she'd been a dolphin. Oh, there'd been a moment's queasy panic when she realized the impossible was actually occurring; another fleeting thrill of doubt as the *change* washed through her heart, prompting first a pause, then a shift of beat; and a final flare of warmth and sound and light as her senses realigned. But no pain, no unpleasantness.

The second *change*, there in the half-drowned cave, had been identical, save that this time her scientist persona had been primed and taking notes—not that she expected actually to *use* them, she hastened to add. No time soon, anyway.

That assumed, after all, that she lived through the night.

Which brought her to the other two "old friends." For if putting on the skin had been one, had been like easing on a comfortable pair of jeans, slipping into the sea had been another and merging herself with the subtle harmonies of the dolphins' "song" the third.

Only for an instant was she alone in the water, before she caught the first ripples of melody/image/conversation. She recognized it immediately as Katana's "voice" and homed in on it eagerly. But before they had time for more than an exchange of greetings, others jostled in; only this time she was able to sort them out with effortless facility.

And those greetings filled her both with a wonder she had never known, and a sense of responsibility she could not have imagined. For as soon as Katana's adopted pod recognized her—and as more and more members added their acknowledgments while she sped to what she knew instinctively was the rendezvous point at the mouth of the bay—she sensed a swelling tide of welcoming that was almost overwhelming. Kat and Bo had been first, of course, and then the Mother-Queen-Sister, and then others—so many others, each with names, histories, relationships, each with some priceless fragment of humanity's heritage locked in those vast mental archives that might not survive the night. Which would be a tragedy for both species.

But was she, Carolyn Mauney-Griffith, up to protecting even a fraction of such closeness? A hundredth part of such an unimaginable store of knowledge? She didn't know. She just didn't know.

You are the One, they chorused, reassuringly. *You are the Way! You can help us vanquish the storm and the waves and the night.*

The night . . .

The very manner in which her companions thought that word filled her with unspeakable dread, and the closer to the center of the bay, the more that dark undercurrent wore through the thoughts around her, like a favorite photograph browning with age.

Yet she continued on, rising now, almost subconsciously, and arching through the water to guide Kev and 'Bird and Stormy on that suddenly very frail raft that carried them to their own private rendezvous with destiny. She was sorry for them, too: up there so alone. As she was not, for the dolphins never left her; indeed their numbers increased by the second, as first one pod, then another, then a third added their strength to the ranks, so that the nearer she drew to the open sea, the more she sensed a good-sized army being marshaled.

We are the fin-folk of Bimini, one group proclaimed, surprising her with the human place name. *We are from Veracruz,* another added. *We have come from Curaçao,* a third chimed in. More and more. Four—eight—fifteen. She lost track of them, there were so many—and felt a surge of panic as the presence of all those excited, anxious minds threatened to overwhelm her. But just as she began to yield to doubt, the thread of melody that had been drifting through all those greetings and fears and concerns strengthened and asserted itself.

She did not truly understand it—not as she understood speech when it was directed at her. But at some far more fundamental level she knew it was a song of peace and protection that an entire small pod was singing to calm the waters around Kev and 'Bird and Stormy.

She listened, briefly caught up in yet another tiny wonder. And at that moment, with her mind tuned primarily for that song, she likewise heard the other.

So low, so deep, so dark and subtle it was, that she had missed it. It was like white noise, like infrasound, like the slow grating of the plates of the earth grinding and pressing and fumbling at each other—sending out vast waves of power that no one heard.

No one human! But dolphins—and obviously more importantly, orcas—had evidently been hearing them for millennia. And not only hearing them, *studying* them, *analyzing* them, and *examining* them; and—finally—learning to duplicate them—a thousand times faster, stronger, and more violently.

And they had given the same attention to the magma pressing up through the rocks from the mantle of the earth, and the sweep of currents through the sea, and the slide of tides against the land—and the thump and glide of winds and air pressures and temperatures that gave rise to hurricanes.

All those forces—all those assaults and resistances—made their own sorts of unheard sound. And those whose minds were already tuned to reading such messages as those primal powers sent tolling through the seas had learned them and copied them and boosted them with their minds—and now, in a mighty, evil chorus, brought them to bear.

For when one sang the essence of wind a certain way, then amplified that song, the real winds had no choice but to respond. And when one hummed the fundament of cold pressing down from the sky and the counterchord of rising heat—there was no need to sing the cacophony where those two clashed and sent chaos rolling through the heavens.

And Carolyn knew that was happening: knew that the orcas had already begun that deep and terrible hymn born of sounds that were far too slow for ears, copied by minds that were far too strong and subtle—and by that complex craft conjured a hurricane.

The battle has begun, the Mother-Queen-Sister told her. *But this is still the formal stage—threat and boast, boast and threat. It is an art we learned from coriding with your folk! Now come, join me—join us all and let us rise to meet the Lower Sky and the Upper. Leap with us—lead us with your leaping—for we have no spears to flourish, nor shields to beat, and so we must make spears and swords and darts and arrows of our bodies. Now—RISE!*

And Carolyn simply flipped her flukes a certain way and swam straight up. —And kept on swimming as she broke through the dome of the lower sky and let momentum thrust her twice her length into the upper. She saw Kevin and 'Bird and Stormy down there, their faces grim, then shifting to joyous surprise—and then gravity found her and she was falling. But even as she struck the water, she felt other forms following in her wake—and as they broke through the surface of the sea and made it one with the air and the sky—she heard one bright chord of the countersong begin.

Carolyn did not join in, however; she did not know how, did not know the—*words* was too poor a concept, too limited, better say *will* or *dream* or *drive*. But that did not concern her, the Mother-Queen-Sister had told her to wait, that she would know the time. And it would be soon . . .

In the meantime, she listened.

What she "heard" was well worth listening to.

If the orcas' song had been born of infrasound and the dark forces of the earth, of press and push, grind and shatter, the song her companions used in riposte was the opposite of all those things. 'Bird had told her of his latest dream—how the orcas' music was cacophony and chaos bound by the most tenuous form, like the pedals of an immense organ randomly stomped by a child, while dolphin music was all rhythm and energy and intricacy, like a fugue played purely on the high keys. And he'd been right—only there was more to it than that, for he had only heard the melody, not truly felt its source—which *she* did. It was the tinkle of ice crystals growing, of fractals spiraling infinitely fine, of light slicing into lattices of glass and dispersing in all its separate colors, of equivalent magic wrought in the sky to stretch those tenuous bridges called rainbows.

And on a more primal level, it was the weakness of countless small things opposed to the strength of the immense-but-few. A net of complexity set to bind that which was simple—and brutal.

The orcas hummed an earth chord, and the sea floor shifted, and the force of that release thrummed through the land, through the ocean, and into the sky. And they growled another tone, and two air masses collided, and began to spin, and caught up others with their force, like feuding lovers, then drank the energy the earth had sent them and grew more violent still.

But then the dolphins whistled back, and the air drew water from the crests of whitecaps, and made friction that slowed the storm. And they chanted a complex chorus, and fragments of vapor that hid in the vast wave fronts of the rising winds slowed and spun a different way, and weakened the unity the orcas desired.

It was more than Carolyn could comprehend, and the images she conjured to help were but shadows and approximations. Yet even so, the strangeness of it staggered her. Intangibles—thoughts, ideas . . . desires, *dreams*—were manipulating concepts scarcely better understood: gravity, magnetism, even—apparently—the lesser and greater atomic forces, those things that were acknowledged to *be* but could not be measured or touched or totally defined.

Do not try to understand, the Mother-Queen-Sister warned her suddenly. *You know science— and you know that when things grow too small or too large they cease, in any realistic sense, to be— and yet they are. The physical world could well be made up of particles that have no mass; the universe as a whole is mostly empty space. Your mind is water and chemicals and electricity. Yet you know that you and the world are very much more than that. It is that more you should concern yourself with now. Not the how—but the simple desire. You must desire that we win—desire that this storm that tortures the seas and the skies—shall fade away and be gone.*

I—

You are not yet able to think large enough yet subtly enough to aid our song. But we are not able to think specific enough, and . . . emotionally enough, to sing any other, without aid. The orcas sing the earth. You must sing the soul.

And then, as if on cue (and perhaps, Carolyn thought, there had even been one that 'Bird or Stormy or Kev had sensed at some level below conscious thought), another song began.

She felt it first as a beat—the force of 'Bird's fingers striking a drumhead, then thrumming through its wood, and thence through the floor of the raft and into the water, whence it entered her ears. But the drumming did not stop there, it sifted beyond that to permeate her whole body, so that every cell resonated to that primal dream-born pulse.

And then, even more amazingly, words began to join it as well—words that rose from human lungs and were shaped by human tongues and mouths and lips; that leapt into the air the orcas were even now seeking to bring to their will, and defied it; that then struck the seas—and vanished. Except they did not; they simply shifted form. And Carolyn's ears—or something—could hear them still; and not only hear the literal sounds, but with the new strength in her mind, read the more basic emotions that drove them.

Carolyn had not heard Kevin's song, not the words and the beat as one, and had only read it twice; thus she had a sense of it, but not an intimate understanding. Not that it mattered at the moment, for 'Bird was singing something else—something from his own heritage that he hoped would lay a foundation for what would come later. And it seemed to be working—perhaps in part because 'Bird himself sensed that he was heir to an ancient tradition of power: that the mighty among his people (and he was himself mighty among them now) had once dared to defy storms and conjure their defeat.

And around her she sensed a stirring and a shifting of the dolphin song as they grasped 'Bird's melody and wove it with their own—and to her amazement found that it strengthened it, as melted wax can blend with the softest fabric and make it firm.

She tried to sing it too, but failed. Her voices—

inner and outer—seemed forced and discordant.

Another song, then, one she did not know at all—on an intellectual level. *Lakota*, she identified, only because 'Bird had told her. And yet again it spoke not to her mind but to something more intimate and instinctive, and conjured grasslands stretching for a hundred score of miles, bowing under summer rains. But not all, never all at once. And however long they were beaten down, they always rose again, sprang up stronger than before, as soon as storm winds passed.

And somehow, she sensed, the physical war—the war in the upper sky—was changing with that too. The winds were weakening, the force of their most dangerous spins unraveling, the waves lessening their perilous rise and fall.

We're winning! she cried. *And without even using Kev's song!*

Perhaps . . . someone countered. *But we dare not relax for an instant.*

Carolyn was confused, then realized what was meant. For as soon as 'Bird paused at the end of the Dineh song, the orcas' song came surging back, and she could feel the very water around her go tense as the storm roared to fury once more.

And then—blessedly—the drum spoke again, and the rhythm altered; and where before it had merely spoken to her soul, now it began to court it: to cajole and resonate with it.

Words reached her too—words she knew. Kevin's words!

She started to sing . . .

Only . . .

—She was failing. She could not make her voice match what 'Bird's voice and Kevin's words and images fed into her mind. She was supposed to translate—and could not. Something was blocking her—not something external, she hastened to add, something in her own weak human soul. She couldn't do this! Whatever shape she wore, her *mind* was human, she could not change that. Oh, she could play at the other—but she could not understand it, as a child could hear and appreciate the complexities of a Handel chorale but not imitate one, or feel wonder when gazing at a carpet page from the *Book of Kells*, yet not be able to keep inside the lines of a coloring exercise.

And even as she realized that—a wave of despair surged through the ranks around her—those ranks whose physical selves she had forgotten existed. Abruptly, she remembered her eyes—and saw chaos: dolphins shaking, shuddering, twitching oddly and without grace. Without thinking, she surfaced—had to, for whatever else she was, she wore the shape of a mammal and had, now and then, to drink air.

A flick of her flukes and she was there.

Gazing on horror.

The sky was black, save where here and there lightning bolts fought their own bright battles among the clouds.

And the ocean was wild. Huge waves rolled and dived a hundred meters to either side, their crests so shredded by a hard, cold wind that the border between sea and air was blurred. Only closer in, where the raft that held her friends tipped and turned, was the chaos marginally subdued. But even there the raft dipped and leapt alarmingly, making it doubly difficult for the grim-faced 'Bird to maintain his beat, or for Stormy in the stern or Kevin in the bow to read the words laminated between plastic sheets.

And even as she watched, the winds picked up alarmingly, the waves beyond grew higher. And the zone of calm water shrank around her.

She dived.

I can't do it, she groaned—to everyone and none.

Then we are lost, came the reply. *We are lost and you are lost and your friends are lost and maybe men's dominion over the land is lost as well; for what can be done here can be repeated a thousand times over. And there are not enough of us to counter it all.*

But . . .

We cannot tell you how. But it is in you—we sense it in you, the same way these orcas sense the stresses in the earth and call them forth with their cold dismal song.

But . . .

Think, the Mother-Queen-Sister suggested softly, *you who have done it twice already, how it would really be to die!*

What? Carolyn cried, in shock. But then had no more time for explanations, for 'Bird had finished the initial rendering of Kevin's song and was starting over. And in that moment's hesitation, she felt the latent energy of the storm double in force—and likewise felt the force of his fear, so strong it was that it reached out through whatever lay between their two minds and touched her.

Naked, primal fear. Instinct for survival. Flight or fight. The lizard brain had overridden intellect—and it was that which had spoken to her.

And then she knew what she had to do. She'd been analyzing while she sang—had still been playing scientist, had never ceased observing cause and effect—and by so doing, had damped down her gut-level power. No, what she needed to do was simply sing the *feel* of the song: the desire, the belief, the *soul*—and let the rest go. After all, wasn't that what Kev had done? Hadn't he been locked in doubt, thinking about everything besides the song he was supposed to write, even while he was composing it? And hadn't it only come together when he forgot about analysis and what logic said should be there, and gone straight to raw emotion?

And what did she want most in the world?

To end this: to be victorious and see this chaos cease.

And to do that she had to forget that this was a curious juncture of no-longer-so-New Age mumbo jumbo and theoretical physics, and simply recall that they *had* to win and that she was the one to make it happen. She had to do nothing in the world but want that one thing. The rest—Kevin had defined the wanting, had already honed an edge onto it. She had to give it drive and direction, and let it sink home.

And with that in mind, she tried to remember the *nothingness* of her deaths—and then, when she had (and it was simpler than she'd expected, and clearer as well), to fill that nothingness with a rage for victory.

Yet still she heard the song. No longer as images, however, but as something far more primal, something wrought of raw emotion and gut-level need. Something that the seat of her power, and the dolphins' power as well, could identify and use.

Kevin spoke defiance and gave defiance form. She read those forms and stripped them away, and left defiance distilled, for others to drink down—

And Carolyn Mauney-Griffith, child of sea and earth, child of science and magic, child of selkie and man, now in the shape of a dolphin, finally began to *sing*.

And the dolphins drank that defiant song, and copied it, as the orcas had copied the stresses of sky and earth—and duplicated it over and over, stronger and stronger, and with one huge voice likewise *sang*.

That was all. For a very long time: she was less an intellect than a conduit for emotion.

Yet somehow, as she reduced herself to that, another part of her—a remote part she had not known she possessed—awakened, so that she saw the combat—not literally, but in some obscure way read the shift of forces in the earth and sky and sea. And that self saw the forces of violence—the forces that fueled the storm—slowly start to waver.

Sing victory now, that shadow-self told her. *You have sung defiance, now sing victory! Sing the joy of discovery—but not the thing, the sensation! Sing the wonder of the new—but not the instigator, the intuition.*

And she did.

And the chorus around her grew stronger—became less a net or a grid than a wall—a wall that pushed outward ever farther, ever stronger.

And she was with it, part of it, a brick in it—better yet, a reinforcing beam. And she sensed minds pushing back—in concert first, but then slowly a few began to drop out, and then others, then tens and twenties, and finally the remaining multitude.

—Until, like a needle popping a balloon, the resistance opposing them collapsed, and the strength of their song rushed through to quiet the storm and quell the sea.

They had won.

Breathe now, a voice—Katana?—commanded. *You must remember to breathe.*

Carolyn did—and felt rather as though she had been in a very deep dream and was only now regaining consciousness.

But around her she heard only joy.

A body slid by her, humming happiness. Another, a third. An army, all thanking her. All urging her upward.

She surfaced.

To see an ocean in which what scant minutes before had been giant waves now coasted down to calm.

To feel winds diminishing as fast as a shout could become a whisper.

To watch clouds dissolving into a brief quick shower, through which moonlight was already streaming.

To see, best of all, the laughing faces of her brother—and 'Bird—and Stormy—all wet with rain and foam and their own lavish, joyful tears.

But what of the orcas? she asked abruptly. *What's to stop them doing the same again?*

They called up the powers of the earth to aid them, the Mother-Queen-Sister replied. *They set those powers against the wind and the waves—but surely you know that every action has an equal and opposite reaction. Those forces the orcas called from within them and sent without have returned whence they came—with all their original strength.*

And as Carolyn swam leisurely toward Rudy Ramirez's light on the shore, trying to understand what she had just been told, the first orca corpse bobbed to the surface of the Gulf of Mexico. A surface turned to gold and silver by a moon that now had a clear sky in which to shine.

Epilogue:
Unwinding

*(Aztlan Stadium—Native Southeastern
Confederacy Compound SkyBox)
(Sunday, September 4—midafternoon)*

"Dukes just scored for the Na Hollos," Ambas-
sador-Chief William Red Wounds informed Thunderbird O'Connor helpfully, as the latter blinked
back to minimal awareness in the luxurious tan
leather stadium seat from which he was nomi-
nally watching the darkhorse white boys upset
the mostly-Choctaw Red Warriors for the Toli
World Championship.

In a matching seat on his friend's other side,
Stormcloud Nez took a sip of the double-brewed Jamaican Blue Mountain coffee he'd snared from the
lavish buffet along the box's rear wall, and tried to
observe the excitement taking place one set of plate
glass windows and thirty meters lower. His eyelids,
however, had other plans. He blinked extravagantly
and forced his gaze away from the tiny figures
swarming across the sage green field, to the occupants of the seats ranged in two tiers behind the skybox's windows: 'Bird, Red Wounds—plus Carolyn
Mauney-Griffith, Kevin Mauney, Rudy Ramirez—
and a dazed-and-wary-looking Mary Hasegawa. All

but the latter were dozing. The sky, blessedly, was clear.

"What's the score?" 'Bird yawned.

Red Wounds grinned broadly. "Sixteen to thirteen, with five to go in four. Looks like I was smart to bet your hunch."

"They liked my dancing."

Red Wounds spared a glance around the rest of the suite, apparently determined that the other Cherokee occupants (including his wife and the infamously ponderous Cathy Bigwitch) were sufficiently engrossed in the game not to be eavesdropping, and that Hasegawa posed no threat—and motioned 'Bird and Stormy closer. "I hear someone *else* liked your drumming too," he muttered pointedly.

'Bird rolled his eyes, but did not immediately respond. Stormy, in turn, held his breath. His buddy wasn't exactly firing on all chips right now—none of them were. God knew *he* certainly wasn't, not with no more than a three-hour nap during the last twenty-four.

Red Wounds cleared his throat.

'Bird did likewise. "Was that my boss, my chief, or my tribe's ambassador reporting rumors just then?"

"How 'bout the *friend* who lent you a valuble antique water drum yesterday without asking questions?"

"Hmmm, well, in response to *that*," 'Bird replied—much more astutely than Stormy had feared, "one might feel inclined to wonder *why* that friend agreed to such an unlikely request so easily. *And*," he continued carefully, "one might *also* wonder—forgive my disrespect—how that friend came to ask what he did."

"My father roomed with John Lox at Yale," Red

Wounds conceded. "And as of your little encounter with the Mounties, I've had your earring and Mr. Nez's Jeep bugged. One learns interesting things that way. One might almost say *unbelievable* things."

An angry light flashed in 'Bird's eyes at that, even as Stormy suppressed a rage of his own—both of which Red Wounds noted. "Lox knows," the ambassador said. "I know. Our security head knows, as does Stormy's. The Irish Ambassador knows a very selective little. That's it. The Mounties do *not* know any more than I told you earlier—though it took a bit of sleight-of-hand on my part to swap earrings with you at the station, let me tell you."

Stormy managed to convert his anger into relief and vented a nervous chuckle. "I *wondered* what possessed you to ask such a . . . conveniently odd assortment of people to share your box." He took another sip of coffee and regarded his dozing companions. Carolyn obligingly chose that moment to awaken.

"Welcome back among the living," the ambassador drawled promptly. "And yes, I know *precisely* the implications of that statement."

Carolyn eyed him dubiously, then shot a glance at Hasegawa, who was glowering but trying not to. She reached down beside her to secure her own mug of coffee—which was probably cold. "Why do I believe you?" she sighed.

Hasegawa promptly snorted, rose, and wandered off in the direction of the restroom. "Sports bore her to tears," Carolyn confided.

Red Wounds shrugged expansively. "It was easier to invite her than argue with her about having you up here."

"And easier to talk freely with her gone," Stormy added. "Since we evidently don't need to keep on

guard around the chief here anymore," he continued, in response to the unmistakable look of alarm
spreading across Carolyn's features. "And now that
that's settled, I have to say, Ms. Mauney-Griffith,
that I definitely like you better in your *own* skin!"

Carolyn grinned back, though he only barely
caught it, and snugged the tie of her turquoise silk
dress-tunic tighter. "There're advantages either
way," she told him, still with a wary eye fixed on Red
Wounds. Her brogue had thickened with sleepiness,
he noted—or maybe he was noticing everything
about her more, now that crises seemed, for the
nonce, to have ended. Or gone into abeyance long
enough for four quasi magicians plus Rudy to fake
their way through an afternoon at the ballpark, at
any rate.

'Bird shifted his bare feet from the padded foot rest
to the thick bronze-toned carpet. "One thing I've
been meanin' to ask you," he said. "We've, uh . . .
that is, we've seen you put the skin *on* . . . but how
do you take it off? What does it feel like, and all?"

"I'll vote for that," Rudy agreed, though his eyelids
stayed closed. "Shoot, I'll vote for *anything* that'll
clarify this even a little."

Carolyn puffed her cheeks thoughtfully, then shot
a glance at her brother, who, still oblivious, lolled
behind her. "It . . . hurts, initially," she admitted.
"And you have to do it yourself—that's part of the
price, so I was informed. And it's not as easy as what
you and Stormy said you saw—which was basically
that one of *them* simply slit himself up the middle
with a fingernail. Frankly, I think that'd be a lot better. But what *we* have to do—or I had to do when I
was a dolphin, anyway—is to bite *through* my skin.
And the only easy place to do that is inside your
mouth! So you nip at yourself a while, and then

worry at it with your tongue until you get a bunch
of it free, and then you find something to push
against, and pretty soon it splits off. And after the
first part it doesn't really hurt—mostly it feels like
when you slap really sticky tape on your skin and
pull—only it doesn't yank out hair—not that dolphins have any to speak of, of course. It's easier for
selkies when they do it with sealskins, 'cause they
can get at more of their bodies with their mouths.
Dolphins aren't really designed for that."

"Very interesting," Stormy inserted, as he rummaged through a platter of Southeastern *hors
d'oeuvres* someone had just set atop the slab of Lu-
cite-encased tree trunk that comprised a sort of end
table between him and 'Bird.

"Very interesting indeed," Kevin sighed, having
perked up a bit—presumably at the smell of replen-
ished food. "But what the hell does it all mean?"

"Shape-shifting?" Carolyn wondered, reaching
past Stormy to secure an iguana roll, which she
passed back to her brother.

"Among other things."

"You mean like the battle? Or like the fact that we
several in here know that the world's not quite like
most folks think it is," 'Bird wondered. "I'm cool
about that. Shoot, if any of this *does* get out, folks'll
just think we're loonies—which most of 'em already
do anyway. Present company excepted," he
amended, for Red Wounds's benefit. "I also think
we've picked up on some tidbits that'll be definite
boons to mankind—but we've gotta be damned careful how we use 'em."

"Like contact with two other intelligent species,"
Carolyn nodded. "Or more, depending on what selkies are, exactly—and whether you count different
dolphin species and orcas together or separately.

That is, whether they're *functionally* one species or whether the differences between them genetically are equivalent to the *acquired* differences between the various races or nationalities of men."

"You mean like are there dolphin rednecks?" Rudy asked. "And dolphin fundamentalists? And dolphin . . . bushmen? And dolphin abos, and dolphin effete intellectuals?"

"Something to that effect, yes."

"But, I repeat," Kevin mumbled through a mouthful of lizard, "What does it all *mean*?"

"It means we won," 'Bird told him flatly. "Thank the God of your choice—which I have—and whose various existences we might all want to, at some point, reconsider, given that at least *one* set of myths has proved true . . . "

"It means we won *for a while*," Carolyn corrected. "Metaphysics notwithstanding, this was a skirmish, not a war. It couldn't be anything else, not with the whole world to consider—the *whole* world, mind you. Oh, Kev's song's a good one—they'll use it again and again, all over, now that they know what the emotion that drives the words is supposed to feel like—thank those aforementioned gods for those people's perfect memories. But sooner or later he'll have to write another. Sooner or later the orcas—or some other batch of dissenters—will find their own human magicians, and then it'll all be to do over."

"But for now?" Stormy asked edgily.

She grinned at him, and he liked the twinkle in her eyes, though 'Bird and Rudy probably didn't. "For now . . . I guess we all rest. Sooner or later we all go back to work and try to lead normal lives. We try to figure out who knows what about which, how to explain it, and who we can trust with that information. I mean, there's a *lot* that still can happen, a lot we have to be on guard against. But at least we know more now, at least we've got better weapons. More to the point, though, at least we all know better what *we* are."

"Na Hollos won!" Red Wounds yelled at the top of his lungs. "Now what was that you folks were sayin'? I didn't think it was polite to listen in."

"Oh, I was just saying that we're human," Carolyn told him, with a wink. "But also that we're a whole lot more."